FATAL CLIMATE

Also by David Hood

THE CHESS MEN

FATAL CLIMATE

CLIMATE

David Hood

VICTOR GOLLANCZ

LONDON

First published in Great Britain in 2000
by Victor Gollancz
An imprint of Orion Books Ltd
Orion House, 5 Upper St Martin's Lane,
London WC2H 9EA

A CIP catalogue record for this book
is available from the British Library

Typeset by SetSystems Ltd, Saffron Walden, Essex
Printed and bound in Great Britain by
Clays Ltd, St Ives plc.

For my children,
who must live in this world
when I am done with it.

'The earth was created by the assistance of the sun, and it should be left as it was . . . I never said the land was mine to do with as I chose. The one who has the right to dispose of it is the one who has created it. I claim a right to live on my land, and accord you the same privilege on yours.'

Heinmot Tooyalaket (Chief Joseph of the Nez Percés), c. 1840–1904

PROLOGUE

The waterline had moved six feet up the beach. He had been away eight years and the sea had grown to reclaim the land, the height of a man gone in its swell. His sister's child looked up from its wicker-basket, big brown eyes and trust.

What does this child expect?

Uli Masoni could not hold the smile of his nephew. It was too innocent, too trusting. Instead he wandered out as far as the new waterline. The South Pacific had risen just a few inches, its rise magnified by the gentle slope of the beach. But Uli knew, on an island forty miles by thirty, a move such as this is more than significant; it is the beginning of the end.

His father caught him gazing out to sea and put a hand on his shoulder.

'Memory is never enough,' he said, following the sad eyes, 'not for this.' He spoke in the language of Maawi, rolling island words that plunged at times of sadness.

'I'm glad you came for the ceremony,' he added, patting Uli's shoulder blade.

Masoni di Masoni, Uli's father, was still wearing the traditional dress of the South Seas, the clothes of the ceremony and of his position of authority within it. He reached up, gripped his feathered head-dress and pulled it off to the side. Now he stood bare-chested, wrapped from navel to knee in an elaborate masi cloth made from the bark of the paper mulberry tree, and his arms encircled by green leaves bound together with twine.

Uli turned to him and smiled. 'I'm not sure I belong here any more,' he said. 'Why did you ever send me away?'

His father gripped him, pulled him closer with both hands, as if pulling him back, reclaiming the prodigal.

'Even kings cannot turn back the tide, Uli. Remember Canute. Hasn't your American education taught you anything?'

'It was English,' he protested, 'Cambridge . . .'

'But paid for in dollars.' Masoni di Masoni pointed over the water in the direction of Arasodden. 'Dollars and coral,' he said.

It was miles off, beyond the reef of this island, and had long since sunk into the Pacific. Even so, Uli knew what his father meant.

Arasodden once belonged to their family, a small uninhabited part of his grandfather's lands. He had rented it to the Americans in the fifties for the sum of 200,000 dollars. They exploded a nuclear device that cracked the coral base.

Twenty years later, his father, by then the crowned chief, withdrew the money from the Swiss bank account that had never been touched and gave it to Uli.

'Get an education,' his father said.

So Uli went for eight years.

Standing together now, Uli saw his father's eyes narrow in the glare of the sun as he looked out towards his lost island. Beneath his faltering gaze, the sea was blue and blue and blue and blue, shades of sea more in number than there are names to call them by.

They drank from its beauty, father and son, not speaking. Then, at last, his father asked, 'What do you think of the baby?'

'Beautiful,' Uli said. 'A warrior.'

'Ah, the tradition. The tradition of fathers and grandfathers. Tribal ways. I used to think these things were important . . . Our life here.'

'These things are important.'

Masoni di Masoni smiled. His eyes counted each and every one of the unnamed shades. Then he turned and glanced up at the sky, clear and unblemished.

'Cancer,' he said. 'Heat in the sea and poison from the sky – invisible. Twelve already this year . . . too many on an island of a few thousand. My councillors say they want a republic. They say I should let in foreign money. Tourism . . . Every other island is doing it. We've got their poison, why shouldn't we have their money?'

He looked at Uli. 'Will you come back to rule after me?'

Uli found himself unable to speak.

Eventually, Masoni di Masoni turned back from whence he came, back towards his grandson's ceremony.

'He deserves a full life,' he said. 'He will not get one here.'

*

The man addressing the President of the United States was a short fat Californian hippie, a throwback to the sixties. His hair had no style, merely elongated tangles, and his unweeded beard looked like it had been grown in the wild.

This man, Professor P. J. Pfister, stood confidently in the Oval Office, bringing his presentation to a close.

'And you are quite sure of this?' the President asked from his seat behind the big desk. His gentle mid-American accent seemed to caress the words, squashing any implied distrust.

'Yeah,' Pfister replied.

They both looked to the President's right, where two 'suits' – a man and a woman – sat with ramrod straight backs in seats along the wall, listening to every word.

'We've checked his numbers, Mr President,' the male 'suit' said.

The President nodded. 'We've seen a dozen guys come and tell us that the world is heating by tenths of a degree a year, making predictions for the lifetimes of our grandchildren. They disagree on the number of tenths, but I have to tell you, Professor, they don't disagree on much else.'

'Maybe they don't understand,' Pfister said. He lifted both hands up in front of his face as if cupping the globe between them. 'It's crazy the way the science business works. Have you ever seen a pressure group commission an independent study and the result not come up exactly the way it wanted? Independent? When was the last time anyone did something independent? When was the last time you saw anyone come up with something definitive?'

'You're saying everybody's been faking results?'

'Hell, I can't think of a branch of science where half the results in the last twenty years haven't been faked. Trouble is, as a serious scientist, knowing which half to believe.'

'But we should believe you? You and your definitive result?'

'You got two choices.'

The President stroked his chin thoughtfully. He stood up and walked back and forth across the room. 'What would you say was at stake here?' he asked.

Pfister seemed surprised by the question. 'Just about everything,' he said, as if he thought the answer was obvious.

The President shook his head. 'Now, you see, you think too much about weather. I'd say what's at stake is the way we live.' His emphasis on the word 'we' made his intention clear. 'That's what's always at stake in politics,' he added. 'Protect. Keep the peace. It's not about a disaster that's happening somewhere else.'

'But don't we have a moral duty . . .' Pfister began.

'Some would say that, Professor, it's true. But in government, there is no such thing as morality. There is only that which will keep the peace and that which will not. Elected governments have no power to act with morality. They have a mandate. And the mandate is to protect and keep the peace. That's what's at stake here.'

The President turned back to his rigid assistants. 'We need to take advice on how to handle this. This could create some severe fall out . . . the economic and political kind.'

The woman stood up. 'Shall I start the normal procedures?'

'No, I wasn't thinking of that. Get Mike. I think we need to mark this one "Top Top Secret." '

' "Office of the President Only"?'

'Right. I guess we better mark it that way. I think there might be some other parties – governments, perhaps business interests – that would be all too eager for this kind of stuff. I wouldn't want any of their Washington moles getting their hands on it.' The President turned again to Pfister. 'What I need to know . . . what I really need to understand . . . is exactly how the United States is affected by all this.'

That was three years ago.

PART ONE

I

Watson Thomas looked up at the hail clattering on the top of the cockpit bubble. Whatever strengths and qualities he may have otherwise possessed, Watson had a problem with helicopters. They hung in the air by magic. Two whirling blades fighting the rage of gravity. In his head, he counted their many risks. Birds, overhead wires, other aircraft. Not to mention engine failures, rotor-blade failures, pilot errors. The list was endless, a multiple choice of catastrophes.

He considered getting out, making a run for it. But this was irrational, a phobia. He knew he needed to control it.

'Are you OK?' the pilot shouted, looking across at his ashen passenger.

Watson forced a smile, but he couldn't raise his voice loud enough to be heard. He put his thumb up and tried to nod enthusiastically.

Closing his eyes because he thought it might help, he considered why he was imperilling his life in this way. The two words became an almost religious mantra, a habit he had learnt from Patty, his estranged wife, who always repeated her objectives under her breath like a drum rhythm . . .

Chas Buemann. Chas Buemann. Rat-tat-tat. Rat-tat-tat.

Chas Buemann Junior, to be precise, was the second-generation son of a Texas oil billionaire. Yesterday afternoon his PA had called Watson out of the blue and invited him to a golf game. When he'd said yes on pure instinct, Watson hadn't realized it would be St Andrews rather than the local municipal. It came as a shock when the PA started talking about private aircraft and exorbitant green fees.

As he sat waiting for the helicopter to crash, Watson picked at the reasons for that instinctive yes. It was a throwback to the early days, his buccaneering penny-scraping pre-millionaire days, all seat of the pants and networking. A knowledge of the 'Royal and Ancient' had been necessary to the way he did business back then.

'Everyone goes to everyone else's golf match.' Almost the first advice his friend Monty had ever given him. 'It's how you meet the movers and shakers.'

True enough, but Chas Buemann? You hardly expect to meet Chas Buemann at the first tee. This was a mover and shaker who registered off the Richter scale.

Somewhere over Cumbria the hail stopped and the sun broke through as if they had crossed a geographical border in the sky. Suddenly they were chopping through cloudless skies with a hot sun diffracting through the bubble overhead, clearing the last of the water.

Watson told himself he was going to be OK. He tried to find something else to worry about . . . something like the state of the rusty clubs he'd dug out of a back cupboard and which were now clenched between his knees in a torn PVC golf bag. He thought these betrayed all too obviously the size and state of his handicap: twenty-four and unaltered in the last three years. Not exactly St Andrews material.

Still, this was Chas Buemann. Chas Buemann. Rat-tat-tat. How could he have declined the invitation? Too late now anyway.

'Thought it might be waterlogged,' Watson told the great man as they finally met on the helipad. He was trying to sound as though he wasn't surprised to be alive and wasn't embarrassed at carrying clubs bought from Argos.

It took him several seconds before he looked into Buemann's face.

Pictures of Buemann were famously rare and his host was not what Watson expected. The man's head sat not quite square to the shoulders and a giant scar ran from left temple back across the right side of his cranium. The leavings of other minor and long-healed lesions meandered across scar-tissued cheeks. Buemann was forty, fifty maybe – the ruined face made it hard to tell.

'I usually wear a baseball cap outdoors,' Buemann said, gesturing to the cap in his hand. It had evidently blown off in the helicopter's backdraft. 'They say the scars aren't good for the company image. Call me Cash, everyone does. It's an anagram of Chas. My father's pet name for me.'

'Cash,' Watson repeated dutifully, eyes refusing to come unstuck from the Texan's face.

'Car wreck,' Cash explained, 'it's a long story. I wanted to win Le Mans, and of course I had the money. Just not the skill. I would have been all right if I hadn't tried to drive like it on public roads. Showing off. I was younger then . . . you know, foolish.' He paused. 'I got you

8

one helluva caddy. Best in Scotland, they tell me.' He took Watson by the arm and started towards the first tee.

A statuesque black woman of Amazonian proportions was waiting for them. She towered over Watson as she put her arms out to take his golf bag. This – apparently – was the caddy.

Watson looked at her in amazement. She was dressed in Pringle trousers and shirt, both immaculately ironed. Her hair was short and slicked back neatly.

'She once worked for Nicklaus,' Cash assured him, 'the year he won the Open . . . one of the years anyway.'

Watson nodded vaguely, but the caddy didn't speak. It didn't seem right to have her carry his unworthy bag. He gazed down the fairway, wondering about the supply of balls he had brought. He had figured one extra box would suffice to get around a championship course, but that assumed his usual slice withstood the pressure. Looking over the terrain, maybe that was optimistic.

Three of his first six drives pinged trees, but only two of the balls were lost. He was four down by the time they reached the turn and the 'friendly' side bet he had made with Cash was beginning to look expensive. Although she had still said nothing, he got the impression his Amazonian caddy was laughing quietly up her Pringle sleeve every time he addressed the ball.

Meanwhile, Cash talked incessantly, spraying out anecdotes about golf and the oil industry – mainly apocryphal tales of his family's early drilling exploits – whilst hitting the ball poker-straight with a series of boron-shafted clubs.

Cash's own caddy, a wiry red-haired Scot in tartan plus-fours, walked up behind each shot, examined its position carefully and pronounced on the next requirement as if he were the MC at a royal function. 'Five,' or 'Wedge,' or – just once – 'Niblick,' in a broad Highland accent.

Each time, he waited dutifully for Cash to nod, which he always did, then produced the named weapon from the bag.

'I take it you've not played recently?' Cash said, after Watson's shot to the tenth disappeared into some particularly deep gorse.

'No . . . No, I haven't.'

'I suppose you're wondering why I asked you here.'

Watson nodded.

'You know a company called BBS?'

'Everyone knows BBS,' Watson said. 'It's one of *the* modelling software companies in the world. You own it. Or rather, yours is the second "B".'

'Buckley Buemann . . . yep. You're right, I'm the second "B". Buemann Oil has a thirty per cent holding and I'm non-executive chairman. Up to now, I've been extremely non-executive. Ray handled it all. I hooked up with Raymond Buckley twenty-odd years ago. We were at Harvard together. He was there because he won some overseas scholarship or other. I was there 'cos my daddy said so.'

Cash paused to loft his golf ball on to the tenth green. It spun to a stop six feet from the pin.

'It cost me a hundred thousand bucks in therapy to be able to admit that,' he added.

'Putter,' his caddy interjected.

'Don't get me wrong, BBS's been a great investment. Ray always brought in the bacon. You know, they started out doing state-of-the-art geology modelling. Run it through their model before you sink millions of dollars actually drilling. If they said go for it, you hit oil or gas seven times out of ten.'

'That's why you bought in?' Watson asked.

'Kind of,' Cash agreed. 'I'll give you a hand looking for that ball. Went in deep, I reckon. No, let me tell you, back then we were all thinking the Oil Age was going to be over real quick. Most oil companies were looking for new things. Mountains of dough, nothing to do with it. Computers seemed sexy and Ray was mustard on them. Geology was only the start of it, the tip of the iceberg. BBS has modelled everything from weather forecasts to variations in women's bust measurements. Ray saw the dawn of the personal computer as well as anyone, shifted his resources that way . . . dumped mainframes. Real smart.'

They took a detour into the gorse where Watson's ball had disappeared. Watson started sorting through the undergrowth using his club as a probe. 'I once lost a fortune on the personal computer,' he said. 'I sold out of hardware at the right time, but when I got into software, I backed Apple against IBM and Microsoft.'

'They tell me you made and lost fortunes a couple of times before you were thirty. That's going some,' Cash said. 'They tell me you're a rich boy now, though. WT Gaming had the number two and number five best-selling computer games in the high street. Sold out *big* a few months ago.'

Watson nodded, surprised that Cash should have heard of the deal.

'There's got to be something about a guy who falls over and keeps getting back up.'

'Bloody-minded? Stupid?' Watson offered.

10

Cash smiled. 'They also told me you're a deceptive character.'

'They did?'

'Yeah, they warned me you'd come across neurotic and paranoid.'

'Nice of them.'

'They said, underneath you're a mixture of Svengali and Machiavelli. No one to touch you in software.'

Watson smiled. 'Bill Gates might have something to say about that . . .'

'When's he ever had to dig a company out of the shit? I reckon your ball's lost for good,' Cash said, tramping down several clumps of gorse. 'Here's the deal. BBS is in the proverbial deep and smelly. I guess that's old news by now. Have you seen the papers?'

Watson shook his head. He considered telling Cash that he never looked at such things any more, but thought better of it.

'Well,' said the big Texan, stretching the word out, 'day before yesterday, one of the summer students found Ray Buckley sprawled across his desk. A twelve bore was lying next to him. Son-of-a-bitch looked like a party popper that'd popped . . . Seems he stuck the shotgun under his chin, and . . . you can imagine.' Cash took a moment, looked at the ground, then back at Watson. Watson realized Ray Buckley probably meant more to Cash than his bravado suggested.

'That's only half the story,' Cash continued. 'Ray, or somebody, seems to have dropped a pretty effective timebomb into the BBS computer network.'

'A virus?'

'Yeah, a good one. We've got scrambled egg for an operating system. We could start again, but we'd lose just about every programme they've been developing.'

'Back-up tapes?' Watson asked.

'The virus seems to be on a fair few of those too.' Cash hesitated for a moment. 'Listen, there's more . . . Ray was not performing. He hadn't been for a while. The trading figures are bad to the bone. Have you heard of a guy named Uli Masoni, head of some environmental group trying to save the Earth? He wanted to know if global warming was really happening, if it was really man-made, you know? Anyway, it was only a small contract, but Ray seems to have got himself hooked, spent millions in people and equipment on the model.'

Watson nodded sagely. He'd never met Ray Buckley in person, but the man was a legend in the industry, brilliant but flawed.

'I come over here for a goddam holiday,' Cash mused, 'and day one, I've got media ringing me up . . . The stock price crashed thirty points.'

Cash's eyes scraped the ground again. 'I don't mean that . . . Ray was a friend. I don't understand it. He never seemed like the type, you know. But I suppose there isn't a "type". There's just desperate men, and that's all there is to it . . . Truth is, I need to put a new MD in there quick.' He took a last despairing look at the unforgiving gorse. 'Why don't you just drop another ball and play?'

'I might as well concede the hole,' Watson offered.

'Nah, have a free drop on me. Take a swing at it. Who knows?'

Watson gestured to his Amazonian caddy. She reached into the bag and handed him the last new ball from his extra box.

'Seven iron, please,' he said.

He took two practice swings, stepped up to address the ball and swung through it in a manner completely unrelated to his practice attempts. The ball set off in a low curve from right to left. Going way too fast, it caught the apron of the green, popped up twenty feet in the air, then rolled slowly into the hole.

The caddy was impressed.

'Nice shot,' she said, taking back the seven iron as if it were a hallowed object.

'I reckon you've been hustling me,' Cash said.

'Don't read too much into my reputation,' Watson told him. 'That was pure luck.'

'I guess I better go pick up my ball. One to you. Back to three up.'

'Are you saying you want me as MD?' Watson asked abruptly.

'What I'm saying is, I want you to take a team – two, three if you need it – and sort the damn thing out. Christ, we got a body here, Watson, and fuck knows what else going on. Shareholder value – that's what I gotta think about now. The market's a mean thing. You're hot right now. The market trusts you. We put you into play, the stock price stops sliding, at least in the short term. You've already had more than enough success in turnarounds.'

Somehow the comment triggered a plunge in Watson's mood. 'More than enough,' he repeated in monotone. Cash couldn't possibly have imagined how pertinent that turn of phrase might be. You know what 'more than enough success' does? Patty – his wife – had gone, or rather, he had gone from Patty. 'More than enough success' is a drug. You get dependent on the highs. You become impossible to live with in the lows. He was supposed to be taking a holiday to recover from the break-up, not plunging straight back into the deep end.

'You want time to think it over?' Cash said. 'You can have until we get to the eighteenth. I'm a generous man, Watson, but I gotta have your answer. Today's Friday. I need a press release out. And I need you in place Monday morning.'

Watson looked at his caddy. Tremors had started in his hands. 'What do you think?' he asked her.

The Amazonian was cleaning dirt off the ball with a towel, staring up the eleventh fairway. 'All things considered,' she said, 'go with the seven iron. Stick with what works for you.'

E-mail to: PPP
From: Weather Station Antarctica
Hi there, Prof, from the cold, cold south. When we met in Tokyo (great choice of restaurant, by the way, I didn't know you were such a karaoke star), you said you were interested in what was going on down here, so I've been looking out for anomalies for you.

To tell you the truth, it hasn't been so exciting this year. The carbon dioxide levels are up again, but it's following the trend. Our latest samples show another 1.5 parts per million compared to last year. If you keep shoving twenty billion tons of the stuff into the atmosphere on an annual basis, what do you expect? I reckon Mother Nature's keeping a pretty good lid on it – at least so far.

We've had some scattered reports of elevated sea levels in the eastern Pacific, but no pattern to the results. We should have the latest ozone figures in a couple of weeks, so I'll pass them on when they come in.

Keep up the singing.
Yours,
Weatherjunkie

I I

As the lift doors opened, Patty Drake Thomas entered the air-conditioned sanctuary of the European Environmental Projects Agency. So far, her Saturday morning had encompassed the littered battleground of Heathrow at 6 a.m., the cramped cabin of a 737 with its recycled air full of club-class bacon and egg, and the oppressive heat of Paris in company with a garlic-chewing taxi-driver who hadn't shaved or washed for a week.

Concentrate now, she urged herself. Work was here. And today she needed to be professional. She needed to be oh-so professional. The next few minutes were going to be difficult.

Slowly, her inner voice repeated the positive truths in simple, assertive language, just as the tapes advised. She was a tallish, stylish brunette with talent. She was a PhD, wasn't she? And she had a fine-boned face – a little quirky perhaps – and the lingering fitness of a one-time sportswoman turned business professional. OK, so she only did the occasional exercise class now, but it was good enough for maintenance purposes. She looked good for thirty-two.

Professionally, she had been lucky to get the job at the agency – Scientific Advisor, Climatology – but everyone deserves a break. And anyway, she had held on to it for two years, performed admirably. She wanted to hold on to it now through all the personal turmoil, through the mess. And my God, it was a mess.

After a pit stop in the powder room, she went wandering along the fourth-floor corridors. The décor was so archetypically French it could be nowhere else in the world: the waste of space for the sake of art, the strange lines of glass tables and elegantly uncomfortable seating, the horribly dark coffee from designer vending machines. It often seemed worth the trip just to gawk at this furniture.

She found André Pielot in the conference room, preparing for the morning's meeting. He was juggling papers, arranging and then rearranging the six seats around the central desk. Pielot was a craggily handsome Frenchman in his forties, decked out in a casual suit that must have cost a month's salary.

Patty stopped at the door, adrenaline sloshing in her system. This was the moment she was dreading, the point where the various threads of the mess came together, the professional job she loved crashing into the personal.

'Patty! Good flight?' Pielot asked in perfect English. 'I'm sorry to have to call you over at the weekend, but this is important. I have news, but . . . oh, no, later. It must wait a while. We are late and not ready.' He reined himself back and looked at her more closely, taking her in from top to toe. He said, 'You look good.'

The sentence produced a smile and she felt a little weak-kneed. Here was the crux: what do you say when your last meeting ended with such an unfortunate kind of interruption?

'You expected me to look wrecked?' she asked. It was as good as anything she could think of.

'On the telephone, it seemed a possibility.'

'It was two months ago,' she said brusquely.

He shrugged, still smiling.

She had to think for a moment before proceeding. She wondered if she had the courage to just come out and say it. Would that make it worse or better? It was hard to tell. She backed her way to the door and closed it. The one thing she did know, she didn't want anyone else hearing this. Her lips quivered uncertainly as she turned to Pielot. Here goes.

She said, 'I'm not going to sleep with you. Not again.' Then she put her hand to her mouth as if to stop it saying any more.

'I understand,' he said casually.

'No . . . no, I don't think you do.'

He opened his arms as if to show that it made no difference. He wasn't going to blame her one way or the other, but neither was he going to accept blame himself. Sex just happens, that's what the gesture said.

She wanted more. She felt a stab of anger. 'Easy come, easy go. Is that the way it is?'

'It's the way I am, Patty. That's why you chose me, no? It's of no consequence.'

No consequence? It had only completely fucked up her marriage, that's all. Sure, it was a hellish marriage, but that had put the tin lid on it.

15

'It was a mistake,' he added. 'I am still your friend, still your boss. It changes nothing.'

She caught the lingering look in the corner of his eye and knew, all of a sudden, that he was right. How well he could read her. She *had* chosen him. Not because of any feeling that existed, but because there wasn't any feeling. He had just been there, a necessary tool to finish off her marriage. He had been used, and he didn't even bear a grudge.

'We work now, talk later, OK?' he said cheerfully.

'OK,' she agreed, not sure quite what she was agreeing to.

'Let's get ready. I can't decide . . . blinds open or blinds shut. What do you think?' He gestured to the enormous window overlooking the Paris skyline. It had a dangling set of thin-bladed venetian blinds, colour matched to the light grey scheme of the room. He twisted the Perspex control rod backwards and forwards, opening and closing the blinds to show her the effect.

Patty's mind reeled for a moment, rewinding the last few minutes, trying to find something else to say. But it was clear Pielot was moving on. The state of blinds was more important now, important for the meeting. He was waiting for her answer.

She walked to the window and glanced down as casually as she could manage. You could throw a stone through the glass pyramid of the Louvre from here, she thought.

'Closed,' she said decisively, her mind filled with a strange premonition of ruined art.

He laughed and closed the blinds and somehow that seemed to finally close the subject.

It had not been as bad as she'd expected, she told herself. She was glad she had 'dealt' with it.

'Who exactly are we meeting?' she asked, changing tack.

'Paul Radleigh, the US senator,' Pielot told her. 'And some junior British minister. You handle him. Brit on Brit, you understand what I mean?'

She tried to smile. 'This is an informal meeting, then?'

'As informal as we can make it,' Pielot confirmed. He was leaning over the table, fussing about the position of the agency's complimentary notepads and pencils.

'Why exactly are they here?' Patty asked.

'They've come to tell us to back off.'

'Back off on what?'

'We keep saying global warming might be worse than everyone thinks. They don't like that. They say we're spreading panic.'

16

She raised her eyebrows quizzically.

'I agree,' he said, 'I don't see anyone running around screaming hysterically either. In fact, I don't think I see anyone doing anything much. Politicians are like boiled frogs. You drop a frog in hot water, it jumps out. But if you put him in a pan of cool water and slowly raise the temperature, he sits there, smiling at you until he is boiled. If the world only rises one or two degrees before the next election day, what does it matter? It's a problem for our grandchildren and, right now, they're too young to vote.'

Patty smiled. This was typical Pielot, the maverick with the student-protestor background, anti-establishment to the core.

At that moment Pielot's secretary pushed open the door. She was followed by Paul Radleigh and the junior British minister, a man she introduced as Monsieur Smith.

Patty and Pielot offered the usual pleasantries and their guests accepted coffee, explaining who they were, lying casually about their personal agendas. All that took the best part of twenty minutes.

Patty tuned in and out of the conversation. As the meeting dragged, her mind drifted back to a bedroom, to the moment her crumbling marriage collapsed, the crick-crack of car tyres on the drive, *coitus interruptus*.

Now that Pielot was sorted, she found herself thinking about the driver. Seeing the whole thing not from the bedroom, but from the car below. What had he thought? What was there to think? Watson had thought he could save their marriage by selling WT Gaming. He hadn't seen that it was already too late. Perhaps she hadn't seen it either, not until she heard the stones on the drive.

The surrounding conversation began to hot up, snapping her back into the present. Elected officials like US senators and British ministers tended to think of Pielot as a civil servant, simply because he was paid from the EU finance budget. They thought he ought to take orders. But his view was that money had nothing to do with it. He was paid to be an independent watchdog. If he gave up that independence, he might as well take his packet of Gauloise and head for the beach. Pielot put this point with Gallic ferocity.

US Senator Radleigh listened, then countered. He knew how to draw battlelines. He was a crusty-looking southern states career politician: red cheeks from too much complementary booze, the familiarity of a 'man-of-the-people,' grey-white whiskers as though he had fallen out of another century. When he spoke, his deliberately patronizing tone raised the hairs on Patty's neck.

'The point is, Pielot,' he said, 'we understand you're giving the keynote speech at the United Nations summit next month. It's not that we're objecting to. We just want to make sure, with so many international guests, you don't say anything too "radical." '

Smith, the wiry Brit in a bland suit, nodded supportively.

'Radical?' Pielot repeated the word with an overblown French accent.

'We've heard you recently saying things about the global-warming situation that we consider unfortunate. You said, for example, that there was no evidence that the slow rise in global temperature wouldn't at some point lead to "sudden and catastrophic environmental changes". I believe those were the exact words. Rather shabby tabloid sensationalism, isn't it?'

Pielot glanced at Patty, winking as he did so. She understood him well enough. She was the agency's consultant climatologist, employed to play the environmental Rottweiler in this situation.

'I'm sure you are not unaware of the ice-age threat to Britain resulting from global warming,' Patty began. She was aiming at Smith, something with a distinctly British flavour, hoping to execute a kind of 'divide and conquer' strategy.

'I'm sorry, but what's that supposed to mean?' Smith enquired. This was his first real contribution to the meeting.

'Everyone assumes that Britain will slowly become a tropical paradise, a tourist's dream. I guess the UK government is even welcoming the prospect. But I'm talking about thermohaline flow. If Britain loses the Gulf Stream around its coastline . . . well, remember that Hudson Bay's due west of Britain. We're just as close to the Arctic Circle. If it weren't for that warm water, we could have polar bears running through Trafalgar Square.'

The look on Smith's face told her he had absolutely no idea what she was talking about. Here was her chance. She could feel the knots of tension melting away from between her shoulders. A rising excitement, the release of all that adrenaline, exploded through her body. She stood up and walked to the head of the room. She picked up the dry-marker pen and started drawing on the white board.

'The sun, the composition of the atmosphere, the existence of carbon-dioxide-absorbing mechanisms like trees and sea-dwelling phytoplankton, these are major factors in determining our climate, gentlemen. These are all pretty stable. At least, if we don't start throwing atom bombs at one another and blocking out the sun altogether. Good news! However . . .' She wrote the next words on the board in big letters. 'Thermohaline flow.'

'What is it?' Radleigh asked, voicing the question that Smith clearly had on his lips.

'It's the flow of heat around the world caused by the sea. Water is a bad conductor of heat. Blocks of ocean that get hot or cold pretty much stay that way; they just move en masse. The direction they move in depends on whether they are at the top of the ocean or the bottom. At the top they move with the prevailing wind, and at the bottom they move in the opposite direction. Of course,' Patty said, ready to explain something she thought should be obvious but probably wasn't to these scientific beginners, 'the hot blocks of sea would normally be at the top, but the thing gets screwed up by differences in salinity. Hot salty water sinks in cold pure water.'

'Come on, what the hell has this got to do with anything?' Radleigh was getting frustrated.

Patty could tell Radleigh was a 'bottom-line' kind of guy. He liked you to get to the point. She smiled in Smith's direction.

'The world has a great but invisible conveyor belt of heat pumping around it, a warm part of which – the Gulf Stream – keeps the UK weather temperate. However, if carbon dioxide levels in the air keep inching up the global temperature, there comes a point when the poles start to melt. That's what we're talking about. Lots of cold pure water dumped at the poles. When I say lots, I mean more than you could possibly imagine. The likely effect is . . . well, we don't know, frankly. But it seems likely that the conveyor belt gets cut.'

'So what you're saying,' Radleigh interrupted, 'is you don't know what the hell happens. Isn't that right?'

Patty's growing euphoria took a sudden hit. Of course the man was right, but it felt like a cheap shot.

'We do know that you may get a runaway situation once the poles start to melt,' she protested. 'A few degrees' change in global temperature could trigger it, send it over the edge. Warm waters are no longer blown away from the poles; the very cold pure water from the melted ice is on top and stops that happening.'

'And you know this for certain?'

'It's too difficult to model.'

'So you don't know it.'

'Well, I . . .' Patty stopped.

Radleigh turned to Smith. 'Scare-mongering, just like I told you,' he said in triumph.

Patty's mouth opened, but nothing came out. She should have told them about the recorded rise in iceberg numbers. There *was* a melting at the poles. How else were these floating icebergs breaking away from the great monolithic ice-shelves? And just because you couldn't prove that this would have a catastrophic effect on the global climate didn't mean . . .

'Don't you realize we're looking at a fatal climate here!' The words blurted out of her mouth. And as soon as she said them, she regretted it. She had lost her audience a long time ago. They were now taking little or no notice of anything she said.

Look at them, she told herself, choking on her own disgust.

The witless Smith sat musing about the opportunities global warming presented. Sure, the UK would lose a little coastline in the inch by inch rise in the sea that everyone predicted, but the benefits of a warmer climate were there for everyone to see, weren't they?

Pathetic . . .

And then there was Radleigh, leaning back in his chair, contentedly rubbing his moustache and beard. He represented a nation that polluted the world more than any other, and so far had resisted more strongly than any other the proposed international agreements that might curb its inalienable right to screw up the atmosphere.

If the world was in danger – and Patty fervently believed it was – then its destroyer was represented by that white-whiskered messenger of satanic smugness seated not ten feet from her.

But all she could do was fume! She wanted to cry. And if she hadn't been so damned professional, if she hadn't so wanted to show that she had her life together, she would have done it right there in front of them.

'Mr Radleigh,' André Pielot asked suddenly, 'who pays your bills when you stand for election?'

'What's that got to do with it?' Radleigh said testily.

'Isn't it Chas Buemann? Don't you come from the heart of the American oil interest?'

Radleigh jumped to his feet, his red face turning purple. 'You people need to understand something,' he said, 'you need to understand what you're dealing with. The environment is becoming the last battleground between nations. The miracle of modern economics is the way trade has brought the major nations together. Mutual interest. We've had the bomb over fifty years and we haven't blown ourselves up.'

'You think that's an achievement?' Pielot cut in.

Radleigh glared at him, but just as it seemed he might explode, he pulled himself back. 'I'm just warning you. Baseless propaganda about the environment does the peace no good. We can't stand for that. The

US has already been made to look like the shits in this . . . apologies for the language, ma'am.' He nodded patronizingly towards Patty.

'Is that you or Chas Buemann speaking? Are you the oil lobby here?' Pielot jibed.

'Boy, this is the fucking American government speaking. It has nothing to do with Cash Buemann.'

Pielot tipped his head and clutched his hair with one hand. 'Boiled frogs,' he muttered.

'Oh, God, I made it worse, didn't I?' Patty moaned after they had gone.

Pielot smiled and shrugged, the same easy-come-easy-go shrug he had used to dismiss their brief affair.

'I know I did,' she continued, 'they were practically threatening you at the end.'

Her concern seemed to surprise him. He came over and sat down next to her. He looked into her troubled face and brushed the hair off her forehead with his thumb.

'Patty, I've been living with this for years now. Threats? I've had them before. I get followed. It means nothing. People are threatened by what we do here. It's natural . . .'

She suddenly felt a wave of panic. Her mind skipped back. Was he coming on to her? No, surely not. This was a serious situation. God, she was a mess.

'Come,' he said. He stood up and beckoned her forward with a crooked finger. 'I want to show you something.'

He led her out of the conference room and down the corridor towards his office.

'What is this?' she asked.

He didn't answer.

Pielot's office was small and windowless, in stark contrast to his profligate use of space and light elsewhere. A rickety bookcase leant tiredly against one wall, its shelves bowed by journals and tomes of reference with heavily environmental themes. On his desk were an in-tray and a telephone. To the right of it stood a large antique globe of the world in a cast iron frame on castors. The globe itself was two feet in diameter and, within its mounting, the North Pole came up just below chest height.

Slowly, Pielot reached down into a side drawer and pulled out a folded piece of fax paper. He placed it on the desk. 'This came to me last night,' he said.

His voice told her this was the moment he had been leading up to.

21

'THE EARTH GODDESS COLLAPSES,' the fax announced in a banner headline.

Below that, half the paper was a graph. The years going forward along the horizontal axis from now to ten years hence. Vertically, there was a scale of temperature. The graph had two lines plotted. One, marked 15° North, went flat across the graph, showing constant temperature. The other, marked 15° South, also ran flat to begin with, then turned up suddenly. Within five years, it reached a new plateau 12° centigrade hotter than its starting point. An arrow marked the knee of the curve: 'Natural climatic event triggers shift.'

'What is this?' she said. 'What does it mean?'

'It's the latest,' he told her, 'the latest and the last. It came to me from the head of the SSEO. You may have heard of him, Ulysses Masoni? Read the note. According to Uli, this is the last communication he got from Ray Buckley.'

III

A Saturday full of rain. Watson Thomas, managing director elect, arrived at BBS two days early and unannounced. In his straining briefcase he had a newly-annotated copy of the company accounts, the last three-monthly management reports for each of the departments, and Xeroxes of every file in the company's personnel records.

BBS's headquarters stood on an island in an artificial lake, locally known as 'Buckley's Island'. The only way across was a limestone bridge which the company had saved from demolition in Yorkshire and transported piece by piece to its current location, six miles outside Stratford.

The building itself was a strange combination of old and new – thick stone walls and lots of glass; in particular, an odd glass dome that bulged from the top storey like an eye.

Watson stopped his Jaguar XK8 Convertible a hundred yards away to view the scene. He got out and stood on the soft grass, lingering for a minute or so, admiring. Then he got back into his car, feeling slightly soggy from the water running down his neck, but feeling also a begrudging respect for Buckley.

He started the engine and put the car into gear and crossed the bridge. Inside, he was churning with excitement, that new-kid-on-the-block feeling, the surge of adrenaline that made his life worthwhile . . . worthwhile after all he'd been through.

There was no one in the gatehouse and no one at the reception desk when he reached the main building. He made a mental note.

Reception itself was a great open hall full of modern sculptures and acutely angled leather chairs. There was a security door for controlling entry into the main office block. A black plate was mounted on the wall for presentation of the requisite magnetic pass. Watson didn't have one, but this was not an insurmountable problem. Someone had wedged the door open with the folded remains of a Domino's Pizza box. He stooped down to look at the arrangement and laughed. Pepperoni flavouring was oozing out between the folds.

Watson strode up and down half-dark corridors inside the main block for several minutes, gripped by an elevated awareness, noticing everything about his new empire.

There were unattended computers in every office. The screens were off, but the 'mains' lights glimmered on the base units. This seemed very odd. As he turned into the next corridor, Watson heard the familiar click click click of a keyboard.

In a corner office a young woman was sitting in the glow of a VDU. Surrounding her was the detritus of a long work session: three plastic coffee cups and a plate of pizza crusts.

He coughed and she turned, looking momentarily startled.

She had blue eyes – that was the first thing Watson noticed. She was not much more than twenty, he guessed. Her leather biker jacket gaped over a baggy army jumper which, in turn, billowed over her ski-pants like a pregnancy.

'You scared me,' she said, closing her eyes as if winded. He noticed her accent even when her voice was strained. A tad too much education, he thought.

'I'm sorry.'

'Who might you be?'

'Watson Thomas.'

'Oh . . .' Although the word was short, it had an enormous weight in the way she delivered it.

She swung around, back to her work. A plot appeared from behind the screen saver. She started circling her mouse on its plastic mat. The simulated 3–D surface within the axes heaved up and down in slow waves like a blanket shaken out on wash day, while figures in the top right of the screen counted off years.

'The new MD,' Watson said, trying to reattract her attention.

'I know who you are. I read the press release.' She didn't even turn around.

'What are you doing?'

She shrugged. 'Watching the world fall apart . . .' she said. 'This is the global warming sim. An early version of it. Seems it's all that's left. We've still got an irremovable virus on the network. Until they get it off – ' She hesitated. 'We can't even begin trying to recover the corrupted data files. The technical director has had everyone working on it for the last three days.'

24

Watson made a show of looking around. 'Where is everybody, then?'

'Most of them went home around midnight.'

'But you stayed?'

She shrugged again. 'Nowhere better to go.'

'Still, they left you,' Watson mused, noting the point. There didn't seem to be much planning in the company's attempt to right itself. He pulled over a chair and sat down. He started inspecting the screen, fascinated by the way the wash-day blanket was now rising as if caught on an updraft of hot air. 'What's happening here?'

'Thermal runaway. All the early versions showed weird, impossible shit like this. You try to run the comparitors, you get garbage.'

'What are "comparitors"?'

'If you want to know how good a model of climate is at forecasting the future, you run it backwards and see what it says about the nineteenth century. This model says the Victorians lived at minus 107° centigrade . . . Garbage.' She spat the word angrily. Then she paused for a moment and stared straight at him. 'Look, don't get the impression you're welcome here, OK?'

Watson was taken aback. He was used to hostility in new companies, but this sort of naked aggression surprised him. Normally the employees don't try to get fired on the boss's first day, even if he is forty-eight hours early.

'You company surgeons always want to get the full feel of a company,' she continued, 'before you slash the life out of it.'

'Is that what I am?' he asked, trying to buy time while he got himself rebalanced.

'Listen, we all know why Cash Buemann put you in here. BBS is in trouble.' Her face hardened like cement run on fast-forward. 'You think I need to see a CV to know what kind of man Cash is going to send? For all I know, it was probably him who had my father murdered.' She swung herself away from him and put her head in her hands.

'Alexandra Buckley,' Watson said, clicking his tongue at the realization. He had noticed her name in the personnel files, Ray Buckley's daughter. What the hell was she doing at work? Shouldn't she be in mourning? At home?

Watson waited several minutes, but she made no move to emerge from behind her hands. They were clasped so tight over her face he couldn't even tell if she was crying.

'I need to find my office . . . I guess,' he said hesitantly.

Still nothing. He got up and backed towards the door. He was standing on the threshold when she raised her head.

'I'll show you where it is,' she said weakly, as her bone-dry cheeks emerged.

She got up and pushed past him. He muttered his thanks as she led the way out of the office and down a corridor he hadn't previously explored. They passed the front of a closed door. Police tape was sealed across it: 'Crime Scene – Do Not Enter.'

Watson hesitated, forming a question he didn't dare ask.

'Yes, that's where,' she said, as if she knew what was coming all too well. 'Some people thought my father was the messiah. Environmental types, you know.' She ran a hand through her hair. It was long and curly, trapped in a loose ponytail at the back. 'He and I, we weren't that close, if it's any of your business. I suppose I only came back here to get a job. No one else would have me. You know what they say about family – they have to put up with you.'

Watson shook his head. 'It must be horrible.' He thought back over the anger she had spat at him. Her accusations about Cash Buemann. Then it struck him. She had talked about murder.

Thoughts cartwheeled through his mind. Was she in some kind of denial? God knows, Watson knew something about denial. Why else would she be at work on a weekend four days after her father's death. He wondered whether he ought to suggest going home.

He followed her up a flight of stairs, sensing an unexpected perfume that trailed in her wake, flowery and quite intoxicating.

Media images he had seen of Buckley's face danced before his mind's eye. Clumsily, he started to ask. 'Are you certain? I mean, I was told . . .'

'The murder thing? Oh, yeah, I'm sure,' she said. She had reached the top and was looking down on him reproachfully. 'Cash clearly hasn't briefed you properly.'

He raised his eyebrows.

'The police thought it was suicide at the time. Now they're not so sure.'

'Not so sure?'

'A shotgun under the chin doesn't leave a lot of forensic evidence of any use.' She spoke in a hard tone, but full of cracks, as if she was doing this to prove her strength.

'So what changed their minds?' he asked.

'His fingers mainly.'

'Fingers?'

'Yes, fingers.' She came to a dead stop. 'Your office is over there,' she said.

*

What does it mean? Patty kicked herself. She was supposed to be the climatologist here. Surely she could recognize labels that were supposed to be lines of latitude. There was a globe not three feet from her on which they were marked quite clearly.

But no, it wasn't the labelling that caused the problem. It was the frightening temperature shift that confused her. Her eyes darted around the document, but her overloaded brain didn't seem to register the content. On top of everything else, today had already been too much.

'Read the text,' Pielot invited.

The sender's fax number at the bottom was US based. Its logo said 'South Seas Environmental Organization'.

'Uli Masoni is the President of this?' she asked. 'I've seen him. He's on the TV a lot now.'

'His face is everywhere,' Pielot agreed. 'I've never met him, but he's been bombarding me with data for the last year.'

'So these are Radleigh's radicals?'

'A threat to the security of the world,' Pielot said, adopting Radleigh's accent.

'*André,*' she read, '*this is the last data got out of BBS's climate model.*' She broke off and looked up. 'Ray Buckley's company?' she queried.

'The very same. Buckley Buemann Software,' Peilot confirmed, 'that's the company SSEO have been using. Apparently throwing lots of money at them. Their computer model is, or was, quite extensive. You've seen the headlines about Buckley?'

She nodded.

'*Ray was very alarmed and felt we needed to push this into the public domain urgently. For him, that's not possible now. Could you and I set up a meeting as soon as possible, either here or in France? Ulysses Masoni.*' Patty read to the end, then she looked at the graph again. 'Twelve degrees.' She mumbled the figure from the graph. She pursed her lips, suddenly feeling very tight inside. 'I don't see how . . . "the Earth Goddess collapses".'

'He is talking about Gaia, right?' Pielot said. 'The Gaia hypothesis?'

'I guess.'

'What do you think of that?'

'Of the hypothesis? It's been around a while. Put forward in the sixties by Lovelock when everything was love and peace. "Gaia" after the Greek word for "Earth Goddess", someone who watches over us.'

'A living Earth, am I right? That's what Lovelock said. He thought that the Earth had internal mechanisms that kept everything roughly in balance?'

'Sort of. But, of course, if you believe what we were telling Radleigh, you could disturb the heat flow and make it fall apart.'

'So that's what Buckley's saying? Only he's saying he has evidence?'

'Yes, but of what?' Patty said. 'I can believe certain things, but not that the southern hemisphere is spiralling out of control. Let me tell you, there's no hint of that, not in any of the current data I'm seeing from the weather stations down there.'

'But you already said it could be a sudden thing. That's what you told the good senator and his sidekick.' Pielot sat down at his desk. 'So . . . all in all, you think this is fiction?' he asked vaguely. He reached out a hand to the globe and rotated it slowly on its axis. The globe was heavy and getting it to move took some effort.

'This thing weighs a couple of hundred kilos with the frame. It belonged to an English admiral.' He pointed to a brass plaque mounted on the frame below the globe.

Patty watched the countries going round. Pielot's effort had set up a momentum and the world revolved before her as she considered what the fax might actually mean.

'There're a lot of cranks around,' she said defensively. 'He's not telling us why, or how. I'd like to *see* his evidence.'

'Whatever Buckley might have been, I don't think Uli Masoni is a crank.'

'I know.' She did know. She had seen Masoni in action on TV. He was a personality *par excellence*. And although people like Radleigh would never approve, Masoni's brand of radical was a good thing in Patty's eyes. She said, 'You should go and see him, André.'

'This kind of thing scares you, doesn't it?' he said.

'What scares me is that something bad could be around the corner and we just can't model what it is very accurately. What scares me more is that every politician in the Western world won't lift a finger without an accurate long-term forecast. It's Catch–22.'

'Catch–22,' Pielot repeated as if he had never thought of it that way.

Patty looked at the graph again. The sloping line of 15° south leapt out, and hit her. *Natural climatic event triggers shift.*

'One thing's for sure, André,' she said, 'this kind of climate change is not "boiling the frog slowly". This is dropping it into the bubbling water.'

I V

Montgomery 'Monty' Radford was already out at the course by the time Watson tracked him down. Saturday afternoon at the races: eight-race card, several top jockeys flying in for the feature event. Now that he had effectively retired at his planned age of sixty, horse racing was Monty's greatest public pleasure.

He was seated at a table by the window in the bar, whisky in hand, listening to the rattling commentary as the horses sprinted up the straight. From this position he had a view down on to the finishing line and the entire panorama of race-goers below.

As Watson approached, pushing through the crowds, Monty stood up to greet him.

The man's race-going attire was eye-catching: a dinner jacket, red and grey check, topped off with a yellow bow-tie. Even on a lesser man, this would have been a strange combination, but Monty was twenty stone, five-foot-nothing and completely bald. That moved the effect of the ensemble well into the realm of the bizarre.

'You took your time, Wat,' he complained. 'You said an hour on the phone.'

'I had trouble with the traffic,' Watson explained, 'then the bloody turnstiles. I didn't think this kind of shindig would be so popular.'

'The masses queuing up to give money to the lucky few,' Monty said sweeping his hand in front of the glass to indicate the scene below them: crowds circling around bookies with their wooden boards and hurriedly written odds, tic-tac men sending hand-signal messages from one bookie's pitch to another, and to the far right a parade ring of overpriced horse flesh.

Monty turned back to Watson. 'You look like shit,' he said, 'I thought you were going on holiday, taking your money out for a spin.'

Watson hesitated. 'Patty left me. Or rather, I left and she stayed.'

Monty's head dropped, suddenly crestfallen. He crumbled into the chair. His mouth opened but nothing came out.

'You didn't hear?'

'No.'

'It finally happened about a week after we sold. I've been staying in a hotel.' Watson swallowed hard, thinking of exactly how completely his life had fallen apart. He'd spent his first weeks of riches in a painfully bare fifty-pound-a-night hotel room, staring at a cheque for eleven and a half million pounds. He'd made sure an equal amount had been mailed to Patty.

'One's usual network is obviously not working,' Monty said slowly. '*Kaput*. I must do some work on it.'

'Eight and a half weeks now. I've got used to the idea, I suppose.'

'Are you OK?'

'What d'you think?' Watson opened his arms as if to reveal the true state of things.

'My boy, why didn't you come to me when . . .?' Monty started, but he didn't finish. He didn't seem to know how. And Watson felt embarrassed. Monty was his sage, his wise man. Something was wrong with the world when you managed to reduce him to silence.

'I see you came dressed for it,' Watson said, looking at the dinner jacket. It was the only thing he could think of to shift the conversation.

'I came dressed for anything, my boy,' Monty replied, taking the prompt. 'I'm here losing the thousands I made on your deal. The first race cost me a hundred. You said you wanted help. Wasn't that what you said? My mobile phone's not that good. You sounded like you were in Scotland or something.'

'I was there yesterday,' Watson said, 'playing golf with Cash Buemann. You know him?'

He heard the breath that Monty sucked through his teeth. 'Sure, I've heard of him. I've done business with his father . . . unfortunately . . . I had to count my fingers after I'd shaken his hand. But that was years ago.'

'Look, I want to show you something.' Watson handed over the ring-back file he had under his arm.

Monty read the company logo on the spine.

'BBS? I heard the whistling sound as the bottom dropped out of the shares. This company has skeletons in the cupboard . . . almost literally. I read about Buckley. Hell, you're not thinking of buying in?'

'No.'

'What, then?'

'Cash Buemann offered me the MD-ship.'

Monty looked at him, long and hard as if looking for signs of sanity, or perhaps for the opposite. 'You've just got out of a company because it was driving you nuts. And BBS? The Buemann family?'

'I said yes,' Watson said quietly, 'that's where I was when I called you.'

'What?'

'I get appointed on Monday.'

Monty stared back at him. This seemed to be the most stupefying thing in the world. Slowly, he leaned forward, took Watson's hand and started pushing up his sleeve.

'What the hell are you doing?' Watson said.

'Looking for the needle marks. Looking for a fresh one with BBS written next to it.'

'Very funny.'

After a moment's contemplation, Monty said, 'My friend, you must be fucking crazy.' The vowels were slightly too rounded to be offensive, but the implication was plain enough.

Watson said, 'I've got to have something. I've been going mad.'

'You had that with WT Gaming. You had me sell it for you, remember? It was going to change your life.'

'I found my wife screwing someone else.'

Monty shook his head.

'You know, I was sitting in my drive, looking up at the window,' Watson continued, trying to grasp a meaning in history that was too painful. 'I just knew.'

'Are you sure you want to tell me this?'

'Yeah. Yeah, I guess. Who else am I going to tell? I saw her peep through and I knew she'd seen me. I . . . I drove away, Monty.'

Monty reached past his whisky and the BBS binder and put his hand on Watson's. Watson smiled sardonically.

'I came back an hour later. She was sitting on the sofa in the lounge, T-shirt untucked like she'd got dressed too quickly. She was staring at the wall, holding her head in her hands. "I want you to go." That's what she said. *I want you to go.* Can you believe that? I looked in her eyes, Monty. I was expecting something . . . something. But it wasn't there any more.'

'I see . . .' His friend's voice trailed away.

'But you're not surprised, are you?' Watson asked, as if it were an accusation.

31

'Let me go to the bar for a drink,' Monty offered. 'As a big man, I'm more likely to survive the throng. What can I get you?'

When Watson didn't answer, Monty said, 'I'll get you your usual then, shall I?' And slipped off, levering his way into the group that seemed magnetized around the bar.

He returned with a gin and tonic, which he pushed across the table to Watson. 'Drink this,' he advised.

'You haven't even read the file,' Watson said sulkily.

'OK, let me look,' Monty agreed, sitting down. He shot his friend a glance that told him this was just out of sufferance. Then he took the papers and rifled through them at breakneck speed. He produced a pocket calculator and worked out a few ratios. 'You suspect fraud?' he asked. 'You ought to.'

Watson shrugged. 'The profits are down and the former MD is dead, murdered according to the conversation I had this morning.'

'That sounds like fraud,' Monty acknowledged. He buried his nose in the papers, making more calculations. His speed with the Casio grew to awesome proportions, finger-smashing computations that strained the solar cells. 'Paper never shows the depth of a company's sickness,' he said, pausing for the technology to catch up. 'We all know how to take accounting liberties. Valuing valueless stock. Failing to write off bad debts we know there's no chance of collecting. You want me to go and "due diligence" them?'

'Maybe,' Watson acknowledged with a smile. 'Cash's vision is: we come in, poke about a bit and a few people walk with slightly tatty golden handshakes. We plead differences of opinion over corporate strategy. A few tissue-thin quotes in the press which everybody laughs at. People think the smell of death on BBS has gone away.'

'And you believe it's that easy? In a Buemann company?'

'What does that mean?'

'The Buemann family are vipers. OK, so I only knew the old man, but Cash Junior has more than lived up to the family name. You don't know what shit you'll find in BBS.'

'That's not my style,' Watson said.

'I know. You're as straight as a poker. You're too straight to see someone throwing you a curve.' Monty stared at him for a moment, then relented. 'Shall we go and look at the nags?' He put down the file and downed the remains of his whisky in one hit.

They descended the steps from the bar and wandered towards the parade ring. The afternoon was hot and humid and people wearing almost nothing stared at Monty's elaborate clothing. Meanwhile the tannoy maintained an assault on the ears, all harsh sibilance and echo. There was an award ceremony going on; its garbled contents seemed to make no sense.

'Strange weather,' Monty said, restarting a conversation. 'It was raining buckets this morning.'

Watson didn't answer.

They were leaning on a rail now, watching shining horses led by stable workers. To either side other punters pointed out the good and bad points of each thoroughbred and commented on its odds.

'Which do you fancy?' Monty asked.

Watson's gaze scanned the attractions. He pointed casually.

'The rank outsider?' Monty said. 'OK.'

He disappeared into the crowd for a moment, returning with two betting slips. He handed one to Watson.

'Fifty on the nose,' he told him. 'Personally, I'm on the favourite.'

Watson didn't reply. He was staring at nothing in particular. Monty put his hand on his sleeve. 'How long were you two together? Ten years?'

'Thirteen.'

'I don't know many couples who last that long, not in this game.' Monty tried to control himself, but the next words squirmed out. 'You should take some time, Wat,' he said, looking away. 'Don't do anything hasty.'

'Hasty like joining BBS?' Watson asked. Then he added, 'She hated you.'

'Maybe. But I didn't hold that against her. Patty was good for you. Hard as nails. Pretty nails perhaps, but hard none the less. That's what you need, Wat. Someone who can stand up to you. She was bright, she was intelligent. She might not have liked me, but I couldn't help admiring her.'

Watson said, 'What would you know about it?'

'I know you.'

'Sure, but have you ever been in love? With a woman, I mean?'

Monty sighed and put both hands on the rail, gazing blankly into the ring of circulating horses. They were gradually being mounted and heading off to the start, multicoloured men on their backs like overgrown children. Eventually Monty said, 'You forget I was married once. A disaster from the beginning, I agree, but love? Oh, yes, I loved her. It was more a question of sexual orientation.'

Watson thought about it – Monty's spectacular exit from the closet that had ended his City career. He cast his eyes down and patted Monty on the back, perhaps realizing self-pity had gone too far.

'I guess I'm just going to have to get through it,' he said. 'You know, that's why I need to get back in the game. Work hard, forget about it.'

'And that's why we're talking about this BBS shit now?' Monty asked, turning from the rail.

'Can you help me?'

'I can help you. The question is: will I? I'm supposed to be retired.'

'Will you, then?'

Monty shrugged.

'You think Patty was my fault, don't you?' Watson said. 'Didn't you hear me? She was screwing someone behind my back!'

'Not to begin with, she wasn't,' Monty replied. 'You want to believe your marriage was suddenly and unexpectedly shattered by this, this and nothing else.'

'Wasn't it?'

'You could try to turn that into the entire reason, but it's never like that, Wat. Love dies of cancer, never of a heart attack. I know you. You left home a long time ago. And I don't mean when you finally took away your clothes. Do you want my advice?'

'No.'

'Well, I'll give it to you anyway. You screwed up, but you're still in love with Patty. An adolescent waiting to happen – that's you, Watson. You were when I met you and you still are.'

Monty stopped. Watson's eyes had sheened over, but he was fighting it.

When next he spoke, Watson's voice was heavier, burdened. 'You talk like you don't want to work with me any more,' he said.

'Are we talking about BBS now?'

Watson nodded.

A moment later, Monty nodded as well. 'I guess you know I won't refuse,' he said.

'Do you want to?'

'I should. But I can't . . . same as you, I guess. It's an addiction.'

E-mail to: PPP
From: Weather Station Antarctica
    Hi, there, it's me again. It's still cold. We're moving into the Antarctic winter and that's always bad news. All we've got to look forward to is darkness and month-old baseball videos. Go Yankees!

34

I got Ozzie Jack's figures on the ozone layer. You won't be surprised to know they didn't make pretty reading, but I'm appending the file for you anyway. It seems a thicker hat is now in order.

Have you seen the funny results from the Galapogos? The sea level there's up 4cm and rising. They reckon it's been going up for the last three months. You know what that could mean.

Yours,
Weatherjunkie.

V

Watson followed a common pattern when he went into a company. Although he liked to poke about on a casual basis to start with, he always met the senior managers *en masse* before doing anything official. He called a meeting for nine o'clock, suggesting the boardroom as a location before he had even visited it.

Monty Radford was waiting there when Watson arrived, already pushing the telephone aside and creating space on the table to deposit the papers they had both worked on the night before in the hotel.

'It's very early to hold a meeting like this,' Monty advised. 'You haven't even said hello to them.'

'Do you think we have time on our side?' Watson asked, idly looking around the room at its uncomfortable combination of age-old oak panelling and audio-visual aids – a whiteboard and a large video monitor. There was an arched ceiling and Picasso reprints on the walls. It wasn't his kind of décor, but it would do.

The big man was pondering Watson's question. 'No,' he agreed at last. 'Urgency may be called for. You can say I'm going soft in my old age, but it still seems a little "Et tu, Brute?" for your first day at the helm.'

'Monty, I need three things. I need a computer network that works. I need some sales and I need to get back into profit quickly. We've got to do this and we've got to do it now. We discussed this last night.'

Watson was in full swing, the mode in which he felt happiest with himself. This was Watson Thomas the business manager, the Machiavellian Svengali Cash Buemann had hired, so much more competent in a company crisis than in a personal one. He stopped for a second to ask himself why that was, then continued. 'I think you had better get them in here while I'm still up for this.'

' "Et tu, Brute?" ' Monty repeated.

Watson blinked but his eyes were as hard as stone. He was prepared now, like an actor about to deliver Macbeth. He positioned himself at the head of the board table.

Monty picked up the telephone and spoke into it. A few moments later the company's heads of department started filing in. Soon there were six anxious faces looking back at them – all that was left of Ray Buckley's old management team.

Watson introduced himself and then Monty and then asked the managers to do the same. 'Give us a brief report on where we stand in each department,' Watson instructed as he turned the floor over to the team.

They each spoke in turn. Watson listened, hearing bad news upon bad news without flinching. What he had learned from his fiery meeting with Alexandra was true. They couldn't get the virus out of the network. Until they could, BBS was crippled.

'OK,' Watson said as the last one finished his party piece. 'To business. I know the death of Ray Buckley came as a big shock.'

'You can say that again,' one of his audience contributed.

'And I guess having the police crawling all over us hasn't helped. But that doesn't change the company's position. That means money. For sure, we have to crack the virus problem – that's down to the technical department. In the meantime what I want is a revised budget by tomorrow lunchtime.'

'What?' The six seemed to mouth the word as one.

Watson knew this was pushing it, but that was part of the point. He had to find out who was with him and who was not. He put on his best hard face.

'That means sales numbers by three this afternoon. I want everyone to redo their operational expenses figuring in a 15 per cent staff cut.'

'What?' That same incredulous question again, voiced almost simultaneously by half a dozen sets of lips.

'Fifteen per cent,' Watson confirmed.

'Hell, we can't get rid of that many staff. It's not possible. Besides it's surely not the time with the network down.'

The statement created a general buzz of agreement and Watson waited for it to die down. He picked up a single piece of paper from the pile in front of him.

'This is an alphabetical list of our staff. I've crossed off every seventh name. That's 14 per cent. If you guys want to go away and come up with a better proposal, have it on my desk by seven-thirty this evening. Otherwise, we'll go with mine.'

The room was silent. Watson looked from face to face. He picked out Bob Collins, the chief accountant. 'Monty will work with you,' he said. 'If we agree the names by tonight, can you finish the budget and give me approximate redundancy costs by noon tomorrow?'

Collins nodded sheepishly.

Watson turned to the general audience. 'That's all folks. Let's get to it. Except . . . I almost forgot . . .' He focused on the technical director, the man responsible for clearing the virus from the network. 'I'm still one per cent short.'

On the way back from the boardroom to his office, Watson dropped into Alexandra Buckley's office. She was gazing at the same image as she had been on Saturday morning. She made no acknowledgement of his presence as he approached.

He leaned over her shoulder and turned off the screen. 'I want you to go home,' he said.

'Why? I'm working,' she protested.

He looked into her face. 'A week's compassionate leave,' he said. When she glared back at him, showing no intention of moving, he added, 'I can get someone to escort you . . .'

'You can't throw me out of here.'

'I don't want to,' he said, 'but I can and I will. As of this morning, this company's my responsibility.'

She seemed to stare at him for ever. Holding her eyes, he thought of Patty. He thought of Patty's anger, although that had a completely different source.

He tried to lift the compassionate voice from somewhere inside him. 'It's for the best,' he said. 'It doesn't do to try to work off grief.' The words came out hollow. He heard Monty's tone in them. Why had he – Watson – come to BBS if it wasn't to work off his grief?

Alexandra was collecting her crash helmet from the coat stand in the corner. 'OK . . . Look, see, I'm going,' she said. She hesitated as she caught his gaze. 'You really don't know what the fuck you're doing, do you?'

She took a step towards him. She put out her hand, flexing the thumb in the air. 'The top of this thumb was blown off. Didn't Cash tell you that? Let me demonstrate.'

She reached out and adjusted his position so he was standing squarely in front of her.

Watson allowed himself to be moved.

'Put your hands up,' she instructed, 'as if I've got a gun on you.' She waved palms upwards to show what she wanted.

Watson imitated scenes he'd seen in films, raising his arms, hands spread high and open above his head. Slowly, she leaned forward and brought a long-nailed index finger under his chin, pointing it up into his jaw.

'Click,' she said gently. 'That's how my father died, Mr Thomas.'

He winced.

'Now, I don't want this to be too gruesome,' she continued, though Watson was sure that was exactly what she wanted.

'No, not at all,' he said through clenched teeth.

She moved her head close to his chest and twisted her face upwards, so her eyes looked along the imaginary line extending from her shotgun finger. 'See the trajectory. It's going to take your skullcap off, but look where your thumb is, almost directly above your head. That's how he lost it.' She waited a second for the point to sink in. 'You'd have to be a contortionist to blow your own head off with one hand stretched above your head, especially using a shotgun, don't you think?'

'How do you know this?' he asked.

She smiled as if enjoying the flavour of his question. 'Maybe I slept with a policeman,' she said.

Watson was walking along the corridor in a daze when Monty found him.

'I think you better come with me,' Monty said.

Watson looked at him in confusion.

'Upstairs.' Monty pointed, then set off, leaving Watson to follow.

At the top of the BBS building was the enormous glass and steel hemisphere that looked out over the lake and land beyond in every direction. The only furniture was a cluster of armchairs and a small coffee table. According to the staff, this had been Ray Buckley's 'Thinking Sanctuary', the place he retired to when he needed quiet contemplation.

Monty led his friend past the furniture and over to the glass panel through which the limestone bridge between Buckley's Island and the mainland was clearly visible.

There, forming a chain to block the bridge, were twenty or thirty protestors and half as many media photographers. A TV crew was setting up. Many of the protestors carried placards that could not be read from the Thinking Sanctuary, but there was one large cloth banner stretched between poles by two burly men. In red block capitals it said, 'DON'T LET THE CLIMATE MODEL DIE.'

V I

International conferences are supposed to focus on the scientific facts. Is there global warming or is there not? That was what André Pielot had always thought, but it clearly wasn't Ulysses Masoni's view.

Asked to appear as a guest speaker, Masoni's language and subject matter were far more emotive than that. A large nut-brown man, six feet and more, he looked like he might handle two or three aggressors simultaneously and with some ease. He looked too as if he would do it with compassion for their folly. His eyes had a gentle captivating depth and the suit he wore was Saville Row perfect. Standing on that platform, delivering his talk to an assembled audience of 500 delegates packed into a New York conference hall, Masoni stuck up like a rock in the sea.

Normally, Pielot knew, it would have been easy to dismiss what he said. Protestors come and go; they are two a penny. But it wasn't easy with Masoni. The manner of the man was pervasive as well as persuasive.

Alongside his eloquence, there were particular glances, moments when he had the alien look of a man uncomfortable in his suit, uncomfortable with the stage he commanded so well. It was picture-plain to Pielot, and he assumed to everyone else, that Masoni was a man who had made sacrifices to talk to the world. He had come all the way from his island. He had learned the language. He had bought a suit and was standing under spotlights in a stuffy hall when he would much rather be basking in the sun of his South Sea island home.

And what was the message he brought?

'Imagine . . . Imagine a world in which the sea and the temperature rise,' Masoni urged the gathering. 'Take a city. Any city will do. Let's call it San Pedro Sula. Honduras. Population 300,000.'

Pielot found himself nodding. Honduras, yes, of course. It was the perfect place to devastate in any kind of hypothetical climate change. It's been devastated before, by other more transient weather anomalies. All of us remember 1998. We know what sort of things can happen. Delegates can see it in their mind's eye.

'The floods rise.' Uli Masoni flexed his knees and then lifted his whole body, his arms spreading upwards, palms raised, like a preacher appealing to heaven.

'Homes are wrecked. Whole families drown. They cling together, trying to protect the weak, in the flow of muddy water, four feet deep in what was yesterday a street. Children. The elders. You can see their grasping hands, desperate not to let go. You can see the fear in their eyes. They fear to lose their lives. They already know they have lost everything else.'

Masoni paused. He gazed from the platform, his own eyes tracking from the face of one delegate to the next, to the next, to the next.

'The water seeps in and raises the waste from the sewers. Now the new rivers are running, not just with mud and rocks and the debris of a broken city, but with cholera and typhoid, the diseases of disaster and poverty.

'Those who avoid drowning, those families whose grasp was strong enough to hold each other, see the faces of their loved ones turn pale. Do we know what disease *is* in the West?'

Another pause.

'Cholera is the loss of a pint of water in an hour. It is acute dehydration. And though you watch the floods carrying more and more of what was, there is no water that you dare drink. In the midst of all this – all this change of climate, this rain – you die of the very opposite . . . of thirst.'

At this point, there was a great guffawing in the audience. A representative of the British government, a woman Pielot had crossed swords with more than once, got to her feet and stammered out an accusation of sensationalism.

Masoni turned and looked at her.

'Are you saying that climatic disasters like this do not happen? How many millions of pounds has your government sent in aid to countries devastated by hurricane or by drought in the last ten years? You are always too late. You keep wanting to put a sticking plaster on the problem. The problem is climatic change. You are the problem. The industrialized countries of the northern hemisphere are the problem. They are causing it. And we have yet seen only the foretaste of what will come.'

41

He looked beyond her and appealed to the wider audience, his eyes blazing.

'What will we do when these climatic changes become permanent? When the waters rise and do not go down. What will we do when the heat and the drought comes and the ozone burns away over vast areas of the inhabited world? I'll tell you.

'We will see a migration greater even than when the Nation of Israel fled over the Red Sea. We will see the diseased rump of nations trekking north and south to those parts still inhabitable. And we will see the guilty untouched populations of those parts turning back these survivors at their borders. Let the plague-ridden die, they will say, for they are victims of the acts of God.

'Only there are no acts of God when it comes to global warming. The industrial nations cause global warming. But they do not suffer from it and do not want its after-affects turning up on their doorstep. They export it over their borders through the air . . . and close their eyes.'

Masoni stepped aside. Half the audience, mainly the delegates from third-world nations, applauded. The other half, learned scientists in the pay of Western governments, sat stonily silent.

Following Masoni, an almost impossible task in Pielot's opinion, was an American professor, P. J. Pfister. He stepped up to the podium, waiting what seemed like an age while the noise subsided.

Pielot knew Pfister's reputation. He had once been a great researcher, but not any more. Four years back, just as Pielot had started campaigning with the European Union, the government of the United States had granted $10 million to Professor Pfister and his team in order to search for the link between global warming and carbon emissions. Pfister was smart – at least, that was Pielot's cynical view. The man realized all too quickly that the only result acceptable to his sponsors was failure, so he took the second installment of his grant money and bought a beach house. He went surfing. His research team consisted of two silicone-enhanced beach babes who attended to his every whim and a Colombian dealer who supplied coke in catering packs. Through the nose is an easy way to blow away millions when you're entertaining permanent house-guests. As far as Pielot knew, the only computer model Pfister had ever constructed was small enough to run on a portable. It meant nothing.

What had capped the good professor's reputation for Pielot, and he would remember this to his dying day, was when Pfister gave his speech at the last UN environmental summit. He got up in front of two thousand people and told them that, although he had spent $10 million and many years searching, he had uncovered no link between emissions and global warming. He got applause, but in fact all he had done was not find what he hadn't looked for.

Pfister began his latest speech by referring obliquely to Masoni, calling him a pessimist. He accused him of being 'evidentially deficient'. That charge, at least, Pielot knew to be true. After the death of Buckley, all the SSEO seemed to have by way of evidence of a coming eco-disaster was a single piece of a paper with two worrying lines drawn on it. He noticed that Masoni hadn't dared to refer to it. There were some boundaries to his 'sensationalism'.

Pfister's speech went on, trashing the work of every other environmentalist on the planet. There was no evidence of a lasting danger to the ecosystem from industrialization, he concluded. No evidence – that word again. He repeated it four or five times over the course of a fifteen-minute speech. No evidence. No evidence.

Just as he was coming to a conclusion, and Pfister was expecting deafening applause from all those who had been silent previously, Uli Masoni stood up in the front row of the audience. He said nothing, didn't heckle, but the hall filled with whispers and side conversations. Pfister's speech trailed away, as did the whispers.

'What does a man do when he learns he has cancer?' Masoni asked when the silence was complete.

Pfister gazed down nervously from the podium. No one in the hall offered an answer.

'He stops smoking,' Masoni said.

'What is that supposed to mean? Jesus, who is this guy?' Pfister sneered.

'Must I bring you proof that the world has cancer?' Masoni said. 'Before it quits its pollution habit. What happens to smokers who get cancer? They die . . . even if they quit once they are diagnosed. You ask for evidence. How many smokers in the fifties and the sixties and the seventies have died, because they waited for evidence?'

Masoni sat down.

Pielot felt like he wanted to get up and applaud. Not so much because of the message, but because of the way it was executed. Masoni was brilliant. He understood what this was all about.

Thinking back to the meeting in Paris, Pielot knew the mistake they'd made, he and Patty. It wasn't about the figures and statistics they could quote. That just lost people; they weren't interested. Even Radleigh and Smith, two politicians who ought to have been rallying to the environmental cause, had tuned out as soon as he and Patty had started talking to them about the science of the situation.

No, this wasn't about science at all. He realized that now.

It was about living and dying.

It was about who was killing whom.

Watson's new office was pretty much standard-issue: one desk, one telephone, a matching chair with a computer workstation within swivelling distance, a couple more seats for visitors, two filing cabinets and a bookcase. On Saturday he had simply dumped his personal stuff and left. It was late afternoon on Monday before he had the chance to return.

The desk was littered with messages, mostly from journalists. He sorted these out of the pile, screwed them up one by one and threw them towards the wastepaper bin like basketball free-throws. Then he sat back in his chair and called the local police.

He told them he was the new MD of BBS and asked them to contact either Monty or himself for anything further they needed in their investigation. The detective inspector the switchboard put him on to confirmed exactly what Alexandra had said. Ray Buckley had been murdered.

The detective asked for a meeting and Watson agreed a time the following day. When he put the phone down, Watson felt he needed to breathe deeply for a while before he took his next action. This was a new situation even for him. He'd been in companies with crises all his working life. This one had no money, its major asset strangled by a network virus and a killer running loose in its corridors.

He swivelled indolently in his chair, turning on the computer at his workstation just to see what sort of equipment he'd inherited. Instead of the opening screen of Windows he had expected, Watson found himself staring at a strange message.

Give me a job, shithead! I can sort out the network.

The message flashed on and off, but whatever keys Watson pressed, he couldn't remove it. After a minute the message changed. A telephone number appeared.

VII

The voice on the other end of the telephone was male. Thirty minutes after Watson made the call, a jeans-clad, green braces punk with a 'Vote Ecology' T-shirt and various formations of acne was standing in Watson's office. He wore thick-lensed plastic glasses.

Watson noticed the yellowy pallor of his indoor skin, computer junky's skin, the Victorian pit-boy look. He felt a stiffening at the back of his neck. 'Connor Giles?' he inquired.

'Yeah,' replied the young man.

'Please.' Watson gestured towards the chair opposite his own.

Watson never used a desk in these circumstances. He'd shuffled his new furniture so that they could sit facing one another with no barriers between them.

Connor Giles sloped across the room towards the proffered chair, taking in the walls. 'Nice room,' he said without sincerity. 'I like the Jackson Pollock.' He pointed at a splattered masterpiece hanging in the corner that Watson hadn't even noticed.

'A diabolical way to light a painting though,' Connor added. 'Did you like my little message?'

' "Give me a job, shithead," ' Watson repeated.

'In 3D,' Connor added, 'with flashing lights. Did you have the right soundcard? I wasn't sure about that. Did it play you the *1812 Overture* as well?'

Watson shook his head.

'Shame,' said Connor.

'Impressive, even so,' Watson admitted.

'Thank you.'

'The question is why?'

'I want a job here,' Connor said simply.

'You have one, don't you? You're on the staff.'

'I'm a sandwich student,' Connor told him. 'Been here three months, that's all. I'm due to leave next week.'

'I see,' said Watson. 'The records here are not exactly well kept. I looked you up after our telephone call. This is all I could find.' From a manila folder he produced a picture postcard of London. 'As far as I can tell, this is the CV you sent to Ray Buckley.'

'Correct,' said Connor, rolling his 'r's.

'You were the one who found him, weren't you?' Watson asked, trying to tread carefully. 'You found Ray Buckley after he . . .' His voice faded and got no further.

He saw Connor shift uneasily in his chair, but the young man managed to hold his attitude when he answered. 'Yeah, I found him,' he said, but for the first time his eyes dropped a little towards the floor. 'I came in early. Ray had been on holiday for two weeks. No one even expected him to be in that day. I don't know . . . Perhaps he surprised someone.'

'He did some checking before he employed you,' Watson said, dipping into the manila file again for another piece of paper.

The young man looked surprised.

'Want to know what he found? I've got the notes right here,' said Watson.

Connor's hesitation lasted only a second. 'That I'm a megastar guitarist?' he asked. 'I keep it at work . . . my axe, just in case I need to strum. That's my real love, you know?'

Watson ignored him. 'According to Ray, your school project was something called "Blocky Bits in Software", an intriguing title.'

'My teacher didn't like it.'

'I don't suppose he understood it. You won't be surprised to know, Ray thought it was the most original concept in virtual-reality programming he'd read in years.'

Connor shrugged, fiddling with the elastication of his braces at the same time.

'Tell me what's going on in this company,' Watson said.

'Going on?' Connor slouched back in his chair. 'OK, I'll tell you. Someone dropped the best virus I've ever seen into the BBS network. Half your senior managers have been trying to fix it for days.'

'Not you?'

'They won't let me near it. I'm a student. They're too fucking scared they're going to lose everything.'

'Are they?'

'Look, I didn't put the fucker in there, if that's what you're driving at.'

'But you think you can get it out? Can you recover the data files? This climate model everyone's getting excited about?'

'For a price,' Connor said.

'What do you want?'

'I want a job, a full-time job. And a big salary.' Connor produced a postcard from his pocket – Stratford by moonlight. 'I never like to discuss money,' he said, 'so I wrote it down.'

Watson took the card, read it and laughed aloud.

'Now, you see,' Connor told him. He wagged his finger in admonishment. 'If it had really shocked you, you never would've laughed.'

'I'll offer you half,' Watson said, 'if you can remove the virus.'

Connor smiled. 'I've read up on you too,' he said. 'Adventure Updater was a great game. I'd loved to have worked for WT Gaming. Ray was really big on computer graphics, great big 3D stuff for outputs, you know, and he never believed in big supercomputers. All BBS models, including the climate model, are interlinked matrices of files. We have to recover each and every one of them to make sense of the thing.'

'Why are you telling me this?'

'To let you know that I'm offering value for money. Putting this back together will be tough. But I'll tell you what, I'll flip you for it.'

'Flip me?'

'Toss a coin.'

Watson laughed. 'You want to risk half your salary on a coin toss?'

'No, all of it. One flip. Heads – I get exactly what's on that paper. Tails – I'll fix the virus for student rates. Come on, it's a pittance to a man like you, especially in this kind of mess.'

Connor took out a fifty-pence coin and put it on the low table. Watson looked at him and then at the coin. Slowly, he leaned forward and picked it up. He turned it over and over, checking the 'head' and the 'tail, then handed it back.

'I'll tell you what,' Watson said, 'I'll take your bet on the salary level, but you get the job only if you can get the virus out of the network in the next forty-eight hours.'

'OK,' Connor replied casually and flipped the coin into the air.

Monday had dragged on late into the night. Watson sat right in the middle of the glass and steel that was the Thinking Sanctuary, looking out over the lake of Buckley's Island. On one side of the room there was now a computer station which Watson had dragged up from a lower floor.

Monty appeared through the door that led down the stairs into the main building. He was carrying three white plastic bags smelling of Chinese takeaway.

'Dinner is served,' he chimed. 'Where shall we set out our culinary delights?'

'Stick it on the floor, I guess. We'll get the authentic oriental experience.'

Monty gave a look that said it all. Me . . . on the floor?

'Come on, big man, you can hack it,' Watson said.

The floor was polished wood. Monty seemed to examine every grain of it before nodding.

They sat down cross-legged and started unloading the plastic bags. Shiny silver cartons were carefully spread out between them. Watson put down papers so the cartons wouldn't leave marks, while Monty unwrapped chopsticks as if preparing for a ritual, each pair emerging from inside its own decorated paper packet.

'Look at me now,' Watson said, 'back where I started. Eating Chinese off the floor with a fat gay in a loud suit. You want to tell me about your day?'

Monty grasped a large slice of chicken between his chopsticks and thrust it eagerly into his mouth. 'Not really.'

'But you're going to anyway.'

Monty shook his head. He took his time to answer, squirming to get his enormous bulk comfortable on the hard floor. Finally, he was forced to catch Watson's eye. 'You want some coffee to wash this down?'

'Stop changing the subject.'

'You might need it.'

'Give it to me straight. Have you found something?'

Monty swallowed. 'All right. Here goes . . . I don't think your new budgets are going to help us . . . because we're insolvent.'

Watson didn't say anything at first. He got up quickly, staggering like a gangly newborn foal as he uncrossed his legs. He puffed out his cheeks. 'That I didn't expect,' he admitted. 'Maybe I will have that coffee . . . though a couple of brandies seems more appropriate.'

There was a tray of leftovers from an earlier meeting piled on the coffee table. Watson recycled two of the cups and poured some half-hot coffee from a cafetiere. He passed a cup to Monty, handing over a sachet of UHT milk at the same time.

'BBS reported profits of half a million last year,' Monty said, taking the cup as his cue, 'down from two the year before, and four and a quarter the year before that. Bad enough, but I don't think the half million was real. I think we were already into heavy loss.'

Monty corralled and delivered another mouthful of food with his chopsticks. 'Someone deliberately misrepresented the sales at the end of last fiscal in order to make the numbers look good. If you're looking for a culprit, I'd say let's start with Bob Collins.'

'The finance guy?'

'Chief Accountant,' Monty corrected.

'Have you spoken to him?'

'Not yet. I think it's a job for the police.'

'The police?

'Wake up, Watson, there's a murder here,' Monty reminded him. 'Besides, there's more.'

'More than this? Go on.'

'I started looking closely at a string of credit notes reversing last year's sales invoices. I found a great pile of them relating to work done for SSEO. But the SSEO contract is a simple billing for work done. Whatever happens, I can't see why you'd want to reverse that and give back credit.'

Watson went limp. He leant his hand on the back of an armchair, staring at Monty disbelievingly. 'This guy Connor Giles who found the body said maybe Buckley had walked in on something he shouldn't. Do you think he caught Collins red-handed?'

Monty said, 'Do you remember Collins from the management meeting?'

'Not really.'

Monty nodded. 'Exactly, he's anonymous.'

'Not the type, I agree,' Watson said. 'Also I can't see it. If you catch someone with their hands in the till, you don't wait for them to go home and get their shotgun before you call the cops. It's not exactly the kind of concealed weapon you carry in your shoulder holster just in case.'

'Maybe Buckley was in on the fraud. Maybe this was a falling out between thieves.'

'No,' said Watson, 'I sense something more here.'

'What?'

'I don't know yet, but I don't like the way there's suddenly a crowd of protestors outside the gates.' Watson sighed and pinched the bridge of his nose, allowing his forefinger and thumb to slide forward as if he were trying to pluck out a thought jammed in the front of his brain. 'You advised me never to get into this company.'

'Not because of this,' Monty said, 'I didn't foresee this.'

'But you knew Cash Buemann was bad news.'

'Correction, I knew Cash Buemann's father was bad news. And, hey, we've found nothing that shouts "Buemann". Not yet, anyway. I've only seen this big credit-note scam once before, Wat. I'm almost certain that someone in the SSEO has been creaming money out of their funds using Collins as the inside man.'

Watson was quiet for a while. At last he nodded and started speaking in a low, flat voice. 'You know, I've run five companies in thirteen years. The first two made a profit eventually, the third one ruined me, the fourth made me a millionaire. Here I am in the fifth. I don't even own this one . . . but I have the worst kind of feeling.'

Watson was driving away from BBS. The only things that were still open were motorway services. In the little shop he went straight to the greetings cards. He spent an age checking the poetry inside various birthday offerings.

None of them seemed to fit.

He picked a jokey one instead. All it said inside was 'Happy Birthday'. He figured he'd write his own message.

He paid for the card and bought a book of stamps. Then he went back to the car, took out a pad of A4 from his briefcase and began the delicate task of composition.

What to say? And how would she read it?

Five. Ten minutes. Three drafts screwed up on the floor on the passenger side. In the end he signed his name beneath the 'Happy Birthday' and addressed the envelope and stamped it.

There was a post box outside the main building of the services. It wasn't until he had dropped the envelope in that he realized what a waste this was.

So Patty would know he'd not forgotten her birthday. So what?

He thought about reaching his hand into the post box to try to retrieve the card. There was so much more he wanted to say. But he had heard the envelope flutter down into the bottom of that iron casing.

He stared at the post box for a while. Then he leaned forward and rested his forehead against its cool red metal.

VIII

Monty and Watson had arranged a Tuesday-morning boardroom ambush for Bob Collins. At 8.58 he was given two minutes' notice of the meeting.

'I want to see him before we turn the evidence over to the police,' Watson told Monty.

'They won't be able to do anything, Wat. All we've got is circumstantial and a few wild guesses.'

'Then it's really down to us, isn't it?' Watson said.

Collins appeared one minute and fifty-nine seconds after being called. Watson gazed at him in the doorway. Monty was right – Collins was totally anonymous. You couldn't imagine him doing anything. Early fifties, medium height and twelve stone. He wore M&S suits and ties, M&S shirts, and M&S shoes and socks. Watson would have bet the underwear said St Michael as well.

'Bob, we need to talk to you,' Monty opened. 'Please sit down.' He gestured at one of the leather-upholstered chairs on the far side of the table.

Watson saw that Collins' face had whitened already. Monty's officious tone was enough to unsettle anyone, but Collins was such an unusually timid example of manhood. Watson thought of the various mysteries that existed in BBS. He thought fraud was possible, but murder? No, that was beyond a Bob Collins.

'We want to talk about last year's profits and the bonus calculation,' Monty continued.

Collins flinched but said nothing.

'You see, we think someone fiddled the sales and profit figures so the company would look good. In a listed company, this is called fraud.'

'It wasn't me. I had nothing to do with it,' Collins said. He sounded like a guilty schoolboy.

'But you knew it was happening. You signed the accounts.'

Collins looked at the floor. Monty and Watson stared at him.

Thirty seconds later, as if their stares had bored through his resistance, Collins suddenly said, 'I knew it was happening. But it was Ray Buckley. You don't understand. Ray Buckley was this company. What he wanted, you did.'

Monty lifted his great bulk forward in the soft armchair so he was perched on the edge of its seat, leaning towards Collins. 'Let me be clear, Bob,' he said. 'This was a Ray Buckley scheme?'

Collins pressed his hand to his mouth. Releasing it just enough to speak, he said, 'Yes.' Then again, 'Yes.'

'I'm going to need more than that,' Watson told him.

'Ray came down to me one day and said we had to improve on the profit projections I'd just sent him. Ray didn't usually bother with those, but someone had clearly been pushing him about the company's performance. If you want to know, Ray hadn't paid much attention to anything for far too long. That's why it was all going wrong . . . ever since he got involved in that stupid project.'

Watson pursed his lips. OK, he thought. Maybe it had been Buckley. He couldn't imagine Collins having a creative thought in his head, even a fraudulent one. 'We have also found,' he said, 'certain evidence that points to a fraud over invoices.'

Collins squirmed visibly. Watson could see immediately that this hit deeper.

'We think someone in BBS has been helping cream money out of the SSEO,' Monty continued.

'I don't know what you're talking about,' Collins said, too quickly to be believable.

'Was Ray Buckley involved in that as well?' Watson asked.

'I don't know what you're talking about,' Collins repeated.

'I am collating the data for the police,' Monty told him calmly. 'Whilst that's going on, I think it would be better if you weren't on the site.'

'Is this a sacking offence?' Collins asked suddenly.

Watson said, 'It's a going-to-jail-type offence, Bob.'

Collins started mumbling about his family commitments. Watson always hated this part. He steeled himself for the five minutes it took and did what was necessary. Collins was suspended and escorted from the building.

'What do you think?' Monty asked when Collins had left.

'Beats me,' Watson said. 'Perhaps Buckley was in on all of it. Perhaps his model was a complete hoax. Perhaps it was just a fabrication to extract money. To start with he used it to shore up the company profits. When the business started to fail, perhaps someone in SSEO helped him and Collins cream off the money a little more directly. Maybe he realized the model was about to be exposed as a fraud. What could save him? Perhaps a convenient virus.'

'So why did he end up with his head blown off?' Monty pointed out. His eyes connected with Watson's. 'You don't believe it, do you? You're starting to warm to Buckley.'

'I don't sense fraud in Ray Buckley,' Watson admitted. He drew the fingers and thumb of one hand down the side of his cheek. 'Financial incompetence, sure. But remember, the problem with the profits was how much money Buckley had poured into the project. That doesn't square with him trying to scam it off.' He hesitated, thinking for a moment of his encounter with Buckley's daughter. 'How does someone get you to put your hands in the air while they carefully manoeuvre a shotgun under your chin and blow your brains out?'

'I don't understand.'

'It just seems to me you'd need to be a pretty cold, professional kind of a killer,' Watson said. 'I don't think we're going to find the answer in a little amateur embezzlement scam.'

When Pielot set out for the SSEO's offices the next morning, he wasn't surprised to find himself tailed from the hotel by one of those grey men in grey suits. He had become somewhat used to these on previous trips. It happened to him all the time, especially in America – and it struck him now with a mixture of annoyance and amusement. They never seemed at all threatening, content just to tag along, presumably on the theory that French environmentalists loose in New York were likely to become dangerously subversive at any time and needed watching. Fair enough, Pielot thought, let them follow. They're protection from the muggers.

He got out of his taxi early and wandered aimlessly for a while, watching his grey shadow conspicuously trying to be inconspicuous. The man tried to hide in a doorway as the smiling Pielot doubled back and walked past him, waving. Then Pielot ducked into a crowd for a moment, and there was the man dodging between passers-by, knocking paper shopping bags in all directions.

At last he felt he had tortured his 'tail' long enough, so he went into a souvenir shop, bought a helium balloon proclaiming 'I Love New York' and tied it to the rear-most belt loop of his trousers. He figured even the most harassed pursuer was never likely to lose his mark with that sort of floating patriotism as a guide.

Pielot was still laughing to himself when he finally found the SSEO.

By the standards of his own agency, the SSEO offices were not impressive, a third-floor suite in an unfashionable quarter. He read the adjacent nameplates. Sharing the same floor were a dog trainer, a no-hay-no-pay solicitor and the telesales office for 'Mr Jackson's Cure-All Elixir'. 'South Seas Environmental Organization' was marked in uneven lettering on the frosted glass panel of the last of the doors.

Pielot knocked and entered. It was like falling into a time warp. The reception was pure fifties pulp fiction, complete with a peroxide blonde at a rickety desk. He expected to see a private-eye walking through at any moment.

He asked for Ulysses Masoni, but was told he had not arrived yet. Pielot checked his watch. The receptionist said, 'I know . . . He's late. Go in, why don't you? I'll go tell Miss Sharpe you're here.' Her voice was squeaky.

Probably has the brain of Einstein, Pielot thought. He nodded and followed her pointing finger.

This inner office was larger than the reception. It had chairs that didn't match, a desk with a plastic top, a coffee table with a broken corner and walls with unmatched patches of paint. There were four hanging decorations: two paintings of the beaches of Maawi, two charts showing the annual sea temperatures and the extending diameter of ozone depletion at the South Pole.

André Pielot examined these charts with interest, contrasting the gently rising trends against the enormous and sudden shift Buckley's model seemed to predict. The two charts were three feet by four, in full colour, laminated. The data came from the *Antarctic Research Study*. It stretched back to 1947, the year America liberated Maawi from the Japanese.

'A worrying trend,' Pielot remarked.

He was repeating the same in French beneath his breath when a voice cut him off.

'Especially if you come from there, I guess,' it said in pure American.

He turned to see a woman standing in the doorway, leaning lopsidedly on the frame.

Pielot recognized her immediately. Among many magazines scrabbling to use the handsome South Seas face, a few had made the shot wide enough to take in his PR guru, Caroline Sharpe.

'Uli's homeland,' she explained. 'His father's the chief. Can you believe that?'

Pielot stared at her for a moment, searching for common ground, making comparisons. Thirty-five-ish and passably good-looking, he mused. She seemed like the outdoor type. She did the power-dressing thing admirably enough, but he got the impression that something inside was trying to burst out. This was a body that wanted to wear jeans, or better still, combat fatigues.

They greeted each other politely and shook hands and she said, 'I'm sorry. I'm sure Uli will be here shortly. Journalists, you know.' She laughed with a touch of unease. 'They were all over him after yesterday.'

'Quite a speech,' Pielot said.

'Made for television.'

'Really? Admirable.' Pielot nodded. He thought his comment sounded suitably complimentary, but Caroline Sharpe didn't seem to understand. She seemed distracted. There was a short and uncomfortable silence while he tried to work her out.

Then she said, 'Nice balloon.'

Pielot's 'I love New York' fashion accessory was nestling against a light fitting on the ceiling, its string trailing limply beneath it.

'Oh . . . A private joke,' he said awkwardly. He tried to disentangle himself.

She laughed.

Still smiling, she walked across the room and perched herself on the edge of the plastic-top desk, crossing one leg over the other. 'I'm sorry about our location,' she said. 'With Uli's pulling power, you'd think we could afford better, but Uli won't hear of it. Every penny goes into research.'

'I see,' Pielot said. That answered the first part of a question he'd been forming since he saw the state of the building. 'This is the only office?' he said, moving to the second part.

'We have two others: Sydney and Tokyo.'

'Reasonable enough choices,' he agreed. 'Just how much has the SSEO been able to put into this research?'

'Uli took the presidency two and a half years back,' she said. 'Since then, more than a million dollars, but . . . of course, you know about Ray?'

'I heard. A tragedy.'

'Yes, well, Ray was a little unusual. He believed in the results . . . in the cause.'

'Did that have anything to do with his death?' Pielot asked.

Caroline Sharpe shrugged her shoulders and shuffled her bottom on the hard top of the desk. 'His company had not had a good time. Two years ago, he was being fêted as the CEO of the fifth-fastest-growing company on NASDAQ. Don't get me wrong, he was very good to us. We got a lot of *pro bono* help from Ray.'

'I'm surprised,' Pielot said, 'considering the pressure he must have been under.'

'Pressure?' she repeated. 'Do you think his results were born out of pressure?'

Pielot pursed his lips non-commitally. He took one of the plastic chairs, straightened his trousers and sat down.

'Is that a yes or a no?' she pressed.

Pielot struggled for a moment, trying to find an answer, but before he was obliged to speak, Uli Masoni strode into the office.

'André,' Masoni said, rolling the 'r' in his bass voice. He moved forward and embraced Pielot in a bear hug as he rose from his seat.

Pielot wondered whether he had missed something. Amnesia perhaps. How come Masoni was embracing him like some long-lost brother?

'I'm sorry I'm late,' Masoni said. 'Please, don't let me interrupt.'

'I was just asking André if he believed in Buckley's results,' Caroline Sharpe explained.

'And I was going to ask,' said Pielot, 'why Uli didn't mention Buckley's results yesterday.' He turned to Masoni. 'You based your argument entirely on the current theory of long-term global warming. There was no "don't you realize that the southern hemisphere is going out of control?"'

'You expected that?'

'You paid a lot of money for that research.'

'He didn't mention it,' Caroline Sharpe cut in, 'because I advised him not to.'

'And I said,' Masoni continued, 'it would be so much better if someone like André Pielot made the first announcement. Say, at the UN summit at the end of the month.'

'You . . .' Pielot didn't know where to go with his sentence. He looked from Uli Masoni to Caroline Sharpe, bemused by the fact that they were not laughing. This was not a joke to them.

At last Masoni nodded. 'I admit the evidence is thin. And you couldn't consider using it in such an academically rigorous forum. That's the point you want to make, isn't it?'

'The evidence is one fax as far as I know.'

'Oh, it's a little more than that,' Masoni said.

While Pielot watched in a kind of daze, almost as if he had been mentally winded by the words, Masoni spread an armful of papers over the desk.

'This is what Ray Buckley left us,' Masoni said. He beckoned Pielot towards him. 'We have a computer file of his results and these summary graphs. These are Ray's best- and worst-case projections of global temperature rise by latitude and year.'

Pielot felt his heart leap in his chest. He hadn't expected this. Recalling the fax, he said, 'I thought you told me the graph was the only thing you had.'

'No, I told you it was the last thing. Ray sent us monthly reports. He told us he was getting closer and closer to something valid. He started sending us selected results.' Masoni stopped and gestured to the pile of papers. After a few seconds he said, 'But we don't have the model, André. We have the results but nothing to show how it was generated. As far as the world is concerned, these could have been hand-drawn by an eccentric madman.'

'Then, I mean, what are you asking?' Pielot stepped back and almost fell into his chair.

'You, André, are giving the keynote speech at the UN conference.' Masoni repeated the point. 'That's what we need, someone to air the results in a big forum.'

'But you just said you had nothing to support the data,' Pielot protested.

'No evidence. No evidence,' Masoni chanted in a voice that aped Pfister's speech of the previous day. 'Tell me, what did you think when you heard him say that?'

'I don't know,' Pielot said, but his mind was working twenty-to-the-dozen, thinking through exactly what he had thought at the time.

'Look at this,' Masoni commanded. He unrolled another large chart drawn on A1 paper. When he laid it down, it covered most of the desk, a two-dimensional chart showing the last two thousand years along the bottom axis and temperature running vertically.

Two wriggling lines ran almost together as they crossed the page. Masoni said, 'These are average temperatures from Ray's model run backwards into history versus the best archaeological data available from various ice-core studies.'

Pielot peered at the lines, bringing his face closer to examine the minute differences.

Masoni said, 'I guess you could say that to predict the past is easy.

Hindsight is perfect.' He pointed to the chart, tracing the troughs and rises in past temperature with the dry skin of his fingertip. 'These are only a few degrees compared to what Ray is saying, but as I understand it, no one has previously shown a mechanism by which any of these changes took place. The Earth is like a ruler balanced on a pencil. Sometimes it lies this way, sometimes the other.' He held up his hand, the palm out flat, and tipped it back and forth to illustrate his point.

Pielot said, 'Yes, but now you're talking about taking away the pencil and snapping the ruler in half.' He tried to laugh, but it didn't come off. He looked at the chart again, the way a man looks at something that changes his life. 'I don't know how he did it,' Pielot said with reverence, 'but this model seems to get ten times closer to the historical data than anything I've ever seen before. And believe me, I've seen everybody's work on this.' Pielot stopped for a moment. Something occurred to him; something that had been nagging. 'But you seem to be doing fine on your own. And you have here the greatest and the worst revelation of all. Why don't you simply announce this yourself?'

'No,' Masoni said. The word fell off him like a weight. 'No, it is a question of who can best use it. How can we convince the world of this? We need action . . . you can see.' He shook his head. 'To be popular with the public is one thing. Oh, I can raise money. I got sacks full of letters after I was on *Jay Leno* and *Letterman*. A smile and a passionate concern for the environment seem to qualify you as a tabloid target, but nothing more.'

Pielot laughed politely. His insides were beginning to churn – how did you convince the world of something so unimaginable? Especially when it showed only on a computer model?

'This celebrity status doesn't make me serious,' Masoni continued. 'With a word, I can get devoted followers to stand outside BBS with placards. But that doesn't mean I can get serious with politicians and governments. I'm not the one who occupied a North Sea rig for twenty days, or threw himself in front of hunters when they came at the seals with shotguns. I have no political clout . . . no scientific credibility.'

'That was a long time ago.'

'Maybe. But neither was I the one who persuaded the EU to fund an independent, and radical, agency for the environment. Staff of twenty? Quite a success, André.'

'Let's not compare our work,' Pielot said.

Masoni smiled and opened his arms. It seemed to Pielot that the man might just be able to fly on those enormous arms of his. 'I will not press you, André. I will not ask you again. I will give you the whole results file to consider. If you want, you can take a copy away on a floppy disk. But I will not advise you. It is a matter of . . .' Masoni hesitated. He looked towards Caroline Sharpe as if looking for the word. She gazed back at him blankly, somehow lost to the conversation as if some side thought had suddenly stolen her.

'Conscience,' Pielot offered at last.

'No, it is more than that,' Masoni said, 'Suppose we all keep quiet and, in a few years, we find Ray was right.' He held out a hand, palm up as if weighing the possibility, then he held out his other hand in the same way. 'Suppose we say something and are proved wrong and indeed nothing happens. We are ridiculed.'

'You mean, I am ridiculed,' Pielot said.

'Oui, mon ami. My friend, I'm afraid that is what I mean.'

Pielot nodded as if he understood.

Masoni said, 'I come from an island where the waters are already rising. The risk of being ridiculed means nothing to me, but my word has no weight. I have told you this. I am a thing displaced. Neither man of the islands, nor citizen of the world. What am I but what my father has made me? A tool. A bridge. We all have duty.'

'And you think this is mine?'

'I cannot answer,' Masoni said.

'Cannot or will not?'

Masoni looked at him. He held Pielot in the grip of his dark, gentle eyes. 'When I first approached Ray Buckley for help, he said the money the SSEO could offer was half what BBS was worth. I pleaded. I said it meant everything to the South Seas. He thought about it for a while. "At times," he told me, "I have done work that meant something to a lot of people . . . but never everything."'

Connor felt disturbed. He had thought he must be in the building alone, but over the last few minutes the feeling of insecurity had grown.

He had worked on the virus non-stop. The clock on his wall had made two complete revolutions – a day lost – and the hands pressed on past midnight a second time.

How long did he have left? Seventeen hours if he wanted to collect the enormous salary he had set up on the flip of a coin. He should be concentrating on the task, he told himself, but he was drifting increasingly. The night-time noises unsettled him. Perhaps because there was something planted in his mind that would for ever remind him of Ray.

He stood up and, as he moved to the door, he felt the flashback coming.

Walking along the empty corridor. The office door slightly ajar. The purple-black splat against the frosted glass panel. The body lying there without a head. Bloody fragments of skull splattered. Drips down the vinyl wall-map. Ray's Hush Puppy loafers. You know it's him. Stomach heaving. Fainting. Panic . . .

Stop!

He commanded himself.

Calm down. He breathed in and out slowly, trying to focus on the present.

Connor found himself walking along that same corridor, convinced now that someone else was in the building. The noises weren't right. The silence wasn't right. Something.

Along the corridor and up the stairs. He put on the first-floor lights. Nothing. He had a good scout around the square of the building. Still nothing.

Second floor. Nothing there either.

Then he noticed that the door up to the Thinking Sanctuary was open. The light of the moon that flooded into the glass dome above was leaking down the short staircase back into the main building.

'Hello,' he shouted softly, realizing the contradiction of a soft shout. The same contradiction was churning like a lottery-tumbler inside his stomach. Did he want to find something, or did he want to find nothing?

'Hello,' he said again, allowing slightly more volume.

Suddenly he smelt it. And he realized it wasn't a sound that was or wasn't there that had been disturbing him, it was an odour, a sweet spicy odour he recognized all too well. Though how he'd smelt it two floors away was a mystery.

The prickling hairs on his neck fell back limply into their normal positions.

'Alex,' he said in a whisper.

She was sitting on the floor in the darkest part of the room, propped against one of the stanchions of the steel and glass structure. He could see her in silhouette, her head hanging forward, her long curling black hair covering her face. She was barefoot, her motor-cycle boots placed neatly to one side; she seemed to be staring at her toes. Between the first and second fingers of one hand rested a twisted cigarette, its ash long and precarious beyond the red glow.

As he moved towards her, he saw the black shadow of a tear fall off her cheek and land on her outstretched thigh. The ash followed, dislodged in a sob she had otherwise managed to stifle.

'Have the bastards gone?' she said without looking up. 'Thomas and that fat crony of his.'

'Yeah. They're gone for the day.'

'They wanted to keep me away,' she told him.

He said, 'You scared me. I didn't know . . .'

'You want a cigarette?' She stirred herself, reached into her jacket pocket and pulled out a slim silver case. When she flipped it open, he could see half a dozen roll-ups neatly laid out.

He shook his head uncertainly. He was close enough to see her properly now even in the dim-lit corner she had chosen.

'Take one,' she said, pressing the case towards him. 'Go on, have it later, if you don't want it now. I want you to. I know you do them. You have a little private store in your office.'

'That's just a few Dexys for staying awake.'

She shrugged. 'You know what we have in common, Connor, you don't belong here either. Come on, it'll make a nice cocktail.'

He reached out and took the roll-up nearest him. Running it under his nose, he said, 'My God, how much stuff have you got in this?'

'Enough,' she said. 'Well, not enough.' She wiped another tear away and stubbed out her cigarette on the wood floor. Then she raised both hands to the sides of her high cheekbones and swept back her hair, its ends now wet with tears. It stuck for a moment on the top of her head before falling forward.

'Families,' she said, 'I don't understand them.'

'I don't either,' he said, kneeling down a few feet in front of her.

'My mother died when I was born. I don't remember her. I never figured out my father.' She seemed to hit a brick wall. She sniffed loudly. 'I left home when I was sixteen, you know.'

'But you came back.'

'I came back here, not to home. He never made me feel like I belonged. Do you suppose that was to do with my mother?' She looked at him. She seemed to sense he had no idea how to answer. Instead, she asked, 'What was it like when you found him?'

'Bloody,' he said instinctively.

She laughed, a short laugh which she terminated by biting her lip. 'Bloody,' she repeated. She seemed intrigued, perhaps embarrassed, that the word should amuse her.

'I never thought so much blood could come out of one person. I tried to tell the police there must have been someone else shot in there as well. They said, no, they'd checked. All your father's bog-standard O-

61

type. I asked them if they'd done DNA testing, but I guess they thought I was crazy. I never saw anything so . . . horrible.' He used the word because he could think of nothing else.

'I freaked that Watson Thomas out,' she said, manufacturing a grin, 'described the shooting. He thought I was the daughter-from-hell. For all I know, he thinks I did it.'

She started to laugh again. This time she didn't stop. It ran away with her, so she was shaking and laughing at the same time.

Connor recognized the condition. Not the emotion of it, but the lost control, the hysterics, of the narcotic. Can't blame her for that, he thought. He knew he'd done far worse for simple recreation himself, and she had the best excuse he'd ever come across.

'You know what I'd like to do,' she said suddenly, 'I'd like to fuck. I'd like to get good and fucked.'

Connor tried his best not to be thrown by the language. He tried also not to take her too seriously. 'I don't think that would be appropriate,' he said.

'"I don't think that would be appropriate,"' she repeated, adding a large dose of scorn. 'Where are your working-class flat-cap principles in that one?'

'Who said I was working class?'

'You didn't have to. Me, I'm the daughter of the *nouveaux riches*. They always go wrong.'

'I wouldn't say you've gone wrong.'

She laughed and pulled the silver case out from her pocket a second time. She opened it. 'Sitting here smoking this, and asking for a fuck. You think I haven't "gone wrong"?'

'Look, if you're OK, I'm going to go.' He started to rise from his knees.

'No, don't,' she said. He heard the panic suddenly naked in her voice. For a moment she was quiet, selecting from the silver case. Then she said, 'I would like . . . I need you to stay a while.'

'OK.'

'OK. Connor, do you think you could answer a question for me?' She tapped her latest roll-up against her wrist and slipped it between her lips. A chunky Zippo was produced to light it. 'Who would want to kill my father?' she asked.

'I don't know. I guess it depends on what was in that work that was destroyed. I'm struggling to get the network back first.'

'You?'

'Yes . . . it's my project.' He stammered slightly, wondering if he should tell her about the deal he had made. Watson had caught the fifty pence in mid-air, cupped it on to the back of his hand and conceded defeat without even showing it to Connor. Connor hadn't thought about it at the time, but perhaps Watson was happy to lose. And hell, if Connor couldn't crack this today, he had won nothing.

'Have you ever considered that if you do get it back, perhaps you've got your hands on something dangerous?' she said suddenly.

He looked at her blankly.

She held up the cigarette like a digit. 'One man knows something that somebody . . . somebody powerful . . . doesn't want spread around. What happens?' She drew the hand with the cigarette across her throat.

'What are you suggesting?' Connor asked.

'That, if you recover this thing, you think about spreading it around as fast and as wide as you can. Call it a survival instinct. Perhaps that was my father's problem. He was very secretive about things.' She dragged on the cigarette, letting the smoke pass down and up and out through her nose. 'That feels so good,' she said, as if she knew its goodness was wicked. 'Now, are you sure about that fuck?'

A cool New York evening. Mike Plummer entered a nameless diner carrying a briefcase. He ordered a four-dollar cappuccino and took it to a booth in the back.

On the other side of the table, waiting, was a woman, blonde hair tied back, dark glasses. She had an espresso in front of her.

He placed the briefcase on the table next to his cappuccino and sat down. 'I'm ready, Margie,' he said in a low voice.

'We've got a problem . . .' Pause. 'Pielot.'

'I thought you said you'd "disappeared" all the data.'

'I killed the model, sure. But Pielot's a radical. It's like he wants to find something bad. And he wants to shout it out to the world. He got one sniff of those graphs and he was salivating.'

'Options?'

'Masoni hasn't got the credentials to endorse the Buckley results without the details of the model. He'd sound like a crackpot.'

'We could laugh him off the front pages.'

'Pielot would be a different kettle of fish.'

'Sure, politically, he's a big hitter. So, give me the options,' he pressed.

'Hell, Mike, there's only one, isn't there?'

Mike seemed slightly perturbed at being called by name. He glanced around furtively. He said. 'You want authorization? OK, you've got it.'

'How come so quick?'

'You want my authorization, you've got it,' he repeated.

'Doesn't this need . . .'

'Listen, this is not about a couple of environmentalists who've stumbled on something they shouldn't have. Don't you understand? This is about war . . . or at least, the threat of it.'

For several seconds they didn't speak. That last sentence hung in the air like a mustard gas neither wanted to breathe.

Then the woman said, 'I take it this has to look like an accident. I'll need some stuff. I need it tonight.'

'Write it down,' he demanded.

She took out and wrote in pencil on a small piece of yellow paper. When she had finished, she slid it across.

'You'll have it by midnight,' he said.

'What do you want me to do with Masoni?'

'Just hang on in there. Let's not create another martyr to the cause, not unless we have to.'

The woman raised her eyebrows.

'Pielot? OK, that's unfortunate,' he admitted, 'it has to be done. Masoni? We could create one more accident, but the last thing we want is the media sniffing a Mafia-style hit on Prince Charming. The public already believes the dirty side of big business runs the world's environmental policy. No, I think we'll stick with our current plan for Mr Masoni.'

He stood up, straightening his coat as he stretched to his full height. He walked slowly to the door and left without another word. The woman left a minute later.

A waitress came across, looking to clear their used cups. She found them full and untouched. There wasn't a tip.

I X

The card came on Wednesday morning. It fell through her door like a scream. Patty opened it. She screwed it up, then unscrewed it, then threw it away, then retrieved it and placed it on the mantelpiece in a position of honour. After half an hour of see-sawing decisions, she didn't know what she was doing, or why.

Work as therapy. Work. Work, that's what Patty told herself, the panacea.

She and Watson had split two months ago. She thought she was glad it was finally over. But in the last few weeks she had been asking herself if she'd got caught on purpose. Pielot had suggested as much. If her subconscious had planned the infidelity, it had done a damned good job of it: one outraged husband delivered to the driveway just in time to witness her indiscretion.

She took her mug of morning coffee into the study and switched on her computer. The first thing she saw was an e-mail from André Pielot:

Patty, can you look at this attached file I got from Uli Masoni while out here in New York. As far as I can see it's just graphs. No sign of the data or calculations that support them. Even so, I have come to believe that Buckley's model is – or was – the genuine article. I have decided caution is not an option. I want to make this public, just as soon as you can verify that the comparisons of the model's results with past climates check out. They appear to as far as I can see, but I've only looked at them briefly. And, anyway, you're the expert. I'll call you when I get back to Paris to discuss exactly how I should proceed.

Regards,
André

There was a PS that described Masoni's speech at the conference, how he had heckled and bested Professor Pfister. '*I know he's an old hero of yours,*' Pielot added, '*but these days he acts like a grant junky!*'

Patty read the message several times and examined the extent of the attached file from her mail menu. Her computer had downloaded a megabyte of something entitled 'Buck.xxx'.

She tried to open it using various software packages. In the end, it turned out to be a file in Microsoft Powerpoint format. This was a package that sat on her computer virtually unused, so she was surprised when she double-clicked the file and found that it was driven by some sort of internal macro.

It presented her with a slide show.

How a man thinks – that wasn't the title, but it might as well have been.

Within five minutes Patty had looked through several dozen pages of Ray Buckley's 3D doodles showing his results in physical form, moving cartoons of the world with its seas, and land, and climate.

In the first section the Earth was drawn like a flattened soccer ball, suspended like a trophy in the 15-inch cabinet of Patty's PC monitor. Green for land, blue for sea and white for the ice-caps.

Patty sipped her coffee.

'What happens when the poles melt?' said the next caption.

This, she thought, was surely the crux of it. There was historical evidence that the ice ages of Earth had come to an end rather abruptly. Sharp increases in temperature had taken place in a timescale of tens of years rather than the usual few thousand it took to do most things on the global scale. She remembered a paper she had read about the Greenland Ice Core Project in the early nineties. They had bored deep holes in the ice sheets, reading off each year's average temperature from chemical analysis of the layers that showed the ice's growth.

But no one had ever explained these abrupt temperature changes satisfactorily. Did the temperature rise cause the melting ice, or vice versa?

Right here, in front of her, in the slow-moving graphics, she saw the imagination of a dead man. She saw the mind of this ghost teacher – how it worked.

Buckley was projecting backwards, using his model to produce a worldwide image of past temperatures. As far as she could remember without looking it up, these hindsight predictions looked pretty accurate. They were also very detailed. She had seen static models that gave a single average value for the temperature of the world a million years ago, but here Buckley produced a moving picture, showing the temperature distribution through the latitudes.

The screen shimmered as Buckley took you back through the ice ages. He took you back to the time of the dinosaurs. It was beautiful.

She watched the view of history: Buckley's 3D image of the Earth, with its thermal profiles wrapped like a rainbow flag around its spheroid body.

Victoria died, reigned and was born. Then a hatful of kings before Elizabeth I. The great monarchs, the great figures of the past, went through their lives backwards, as Buckley's model back-projected the Earth's climate. Julius Caesar, Stonehenge, the pyramids of Egypt and of South America.

Ice ages came. And she was drifting out beyond the dawn of man.

And then she saw something . . .

Rewind!

Something she had not expected. Something that Pielot must have missed when he looked at the data. Perhaps he didn't go back that far.

Right there, about 7,500 years ago, after the last ice age, was the strange prediction of a wild fluctuation, an up and a down in temperature, affecting a slice of the earth centred on the equator.

She looked at the time taken for each transition. It was astonishing, maybe ten years, maybe less – she couldn't tell from the scale on the graphic. Afterwards the disturbance slowly faded back in ripples into the normality of the rest of the plot.

This fluctuation had surely never happened!

She leaned back from the screen. Stunned. Deflated. She wasn't quite sure which. Wasn't it a good thing if Buckley's model was flawed, if it had predicted earlier bogus environmental disasters? Surely you didn't want him to be right?

She thought about Pielot's note, its tone of certainty. 'I have come to believe that Buckley's model is – or was – the genuine article.'

She waited for it to sink in. Why, André? Why?

Buckley was wrong. Or at least, he had been wrong before.

Watson calculated that Connor had worked precisely thirty-seven hours without a proper break, so it wasn't surprising he had reduced the office Watson had allocated him to the state of an average pig-sty. Around the screen and keyboard was an outcrop of plastic cups and chocolate bar wrappers. Connor was holding his Fender Stratocaster across his lap. He was picking at it unplugged – the intro to 'Wonderwall', over and over. It was all he seemed to know of the song.

'Proving your value?' Watson asked, his sarcasm gentle, delivered with a smile.

Connor stopped and scanned the self-inflicted chaos around him. 'The ravages of war,' he said.

Watson laughed. Connor tried to get up, but seemed to struggle. It was then that Watson noticed his shadowy, sleep-deprived eyes, peering out myopically through the thick lenses of his glasses, the sockets hollow.

'Not doing so well?' Watson asked with as much familiarity as he could muster. He had already guessed what the gaping dilation of the pupils meant.

'Looks like you're on to a winner,' Connor said.

'Don't you believe it. I rang the SSEO in New York last night. I spoke to a very unhappy lady. They want their model back. They're the ones sending invites to our little picket party at the gates.'

'It figures.' Connor shrugged.

'They have a results file. The lady says she'll e-mail it over,' Watson told him. 'I've done some checking. When Ray put this climate model together, he had about five different programmers writing bits of the system. I've talked to them.'

'Me too. There were about a dozen main files that made this thing work.' His voice had a touch of desperation. 'If I can ever get the network up, that might be relevant.'

'I'm beginning to think we ought to start from scratch and cut our losses.'

'You'll lose man-years of programming code if you do that.'

'And you'll lose your salary hike.'

'I've still got ten hours or so, haven't I?' Connor stretched himself and leaned the guitar against the wall. He repositioned himself at the workstation.

The faint whiff of body odour reached Watson as Connor turned. He figured he probably smelt half as bad himself. It had been a long week already.

'A few days ago I was a man of leisure,' Watson said with a sigh.

'Welcome back to the real world.'

He tried not to inhale as he leaned over Connor's shoulder to get closer to the screen.

Connor looked up at him. 'I've worked on this . . . I can't puzzle it out. I've named it RAT,' he said grimly.

'RAT?'

'Rattus Norvegicus. It acts like one. Its code jumps from one computer to another in a network. But it's not like your common-or-garden virus. It doesn't replicate. That is, not unless you try to pull one of the computers out of the network. I tried that . . . tried that last night. As far as I can see, its payload means that every time you try to do anything anywhere on the network, it turns the operating system to spaghetti.'

Watching him as he spoke, Watson noticed the jerky hand gestures, barely under control. Some sort of amphetamine, he guessed. At least the boy was a user in the company's cause.

'I thought I had it cornered. I did,' Connor continued. 'I isolated it in the next-door computer. Then just turned the power off. When I turned the network back on, there it was. There must be something in it that – I dunno – detects the shutdown procedure, allows it to jump back.'

'A rat leaving the sinking ship,' Watson said.

'Exactly,' Connor slurred. 'Here, I have a present for you.' He waved a printout under Watson's nose.

'What is it?'

'It's the name and create details of the original source file for the virus. Of course, the contents are screwed like everything else.'

'Not much use, then,' Watson said.

Connor shook his head. He pointed an index finger at the date and time. 'There are not many people in BBS at six o'clock on a Sunday night. I checked the log on the security system . . .'

'How did you get to that?'

'Simple hacking,' Connor said casually. 'You want to know who was in the building? Bob Collins . . . no one else.'

'Shit!' Watson looked at the paper for a long time. He pushed his bottom lip into a thoughtful pout, his mind slowly recycling towards the main and immediate problem: a network that didn't function. 'What about the computer you switched off?' he asked suddenly. 'The one you took out of the network . . .'

'It was still infected as well. But I don't know. I never tried to remove the virus from that.'

Watson smiled knowingly then without speaking, disappeared into the next room. In a minute he was back, carrying the base unit and keyboard of a computer. 'This the one?' he asked.

'Yeah,' said Connor, his eyes growing even wider.

'I'm going to set up in here, next to you. Can you give me a hand with the monitor? You've got a spare network port in here, haven't you?'

'Do y'know how to do this?' Connor asked lifelessly.

'I started my career in hardware,' Watson said, 'I thought you'd read up on me.'

'Yeah, but my memory's fucked.'

Watson looked at him. 'I'm not surprised,' he said.

They struggled to fit the second computer on Connor's desk. The plastic cups and chocolate wrappers had to be cleared and then there was the tangle of leads dangling down the back, so many it was impossible to see what went where without a degree in knot-tying.

'Where were you up to?' Watson asked when they were ready to turn on the new machine.

'Map of the computer network,' Connor told him, pointing at the screen of his own machine. His voice had found a little energy now. 'I wrote it last night. Thought it might be useful.'

There was an array of blue boxes with cryptic labels, interconnected with green lines. A red circle was hopping from one machine to the other. 'That's our RAT. The block of code that moves,' Connor explained. 'I've managed to write a little low-level routine to track it. Trouble is, it seems to know.'

'That's just paranoia,' Watson said, underlining his own conclusion about the chemicals in Connor's bloodstream.

'No,' Connor protested, 'ever since I put this tail on it, it's been running from machine to machine much quicker.'

'A hunter and his prey?'

'Yeah, if you want to look at it like that. This took away Ray's work, Mr Thomas. You should respect that.'

Watson nodded. Whatever else Connor might be, he was loyal.

'I reckon this is more like a vapour trail of where it's been,' Connor continued, pointing at the red circle. 'Are you going to switch that machine on?'

'Sure, but first, *without* connecting it to the network.' Watson booted the machine and within half a minute he had the corporate logo up on the screen. 'Will your detection routine work on a single machine?' he asked.

'Should do.'

'Give me a floppy of it, then.'

Connor reached under his desk and pulled out a box of 3.5-inch disks. He inserted one in his own machine, copied several files on to it and handed it over. Watson had Connor's 'Detect' programme up and running on the other machine in less than a minute.

'It's there all right.'

'To get rid of it,' Connor said quickly, 'I gave you another file: RAT_Trap. It was supposed to be the disinfection routine. It didn't work in the network, but now you've got it confined . . . I mean, maybe.'

'OK. We'll run "RAT_Trap",' Watson agreed, speaking as he typed.

Connor's programme had a graphic that showed a small cartoon rodent and a large mouse trap culled from the company's picture library. As the programme executed, the trap sprang, and the rodent tried to jump out of the way. After two attempts, the screen announced, 'Computer 1 RAT 0.'

'That it?' Watson asked.

Connor laughed. 'Sorry. I needed something to keep awake . . . that's it.'

Watson stared back at him reproachfully. If only that was all he'd used to stay awake.

'Run "Detect" again,' Connor prompted, 'see if it's gone.'

Watson could feel Connor's excitement rising. He was squirming about in his chair.

Watson ran the programme and waited . . .

Nothing. RAT was stone dead.

'Yeah!' Connor shouted. He got up and strode around the room, flexing his fist and stretching his arms and legs.

Watson watched the odd spasmodic movements, the face cracked into an unworldly smile as if Connor's spirit had pounced on a dead body and was trying it for size.

Connor circled and sat back down. 'What next?' he asked. He banged the flat of his hand against his forehead. 'Think! I want this thing. I want to get it . . . Think!'

'Got it!' he shouted suddenly. 'We've got to corner it in one of the network machines, right? We know we can kill the little fucker then. Of course . . . Of course, but I've been trying to do that for the last five and a half hours. No can do.'

'Yes, but there was only you,' Watson said calmly. 'If one of us flushes it out . . .'

'Yeah. Poweee!' Connor breathed. He demonstrated the motion.

'That's what we're going to do. Find some tools and open up the machine while I reconnect it to the network.'

Connor looked at him for a moment as if assessing, a slight tick in his cheek. Then he dipped into his desk drawer and, from among a handful of 3.5-inch disks, discarded company memos and a half-eaten chocolate flapjack, managed to produce a small screwdriver. Taking it,

71

he seized the base unit of Watson's computer and wrestled it into submission on the carpet like a rodeo rider roping a steer. In less than a minute, he had the top case off and its innards exposed.

'I don't know what to do next,' he said.

Watson took the screwdriver from him and began tracing the wiring, finding the motherboard and its various connections to the units within the case. 'We get the RAT into the hard drive of one machine, then instead of shutting the machine down, we unplug the hard drive with the machine still under power. Simple.'

Connor spouted several more questions, but Watson wasn't listening. He was busy looping more wire to make the connection into the spare network port on the far wall.

'Of course,' Connor burst out suddenly, 'the machine's gonna crash, but the virus can't disappear back into the network during shutdown. Then, all you gotta do . . . all you gotta do is disconnect the machine from the network, put the hard disk back and run the disinfection programme. That works on a stand-alone, right? Christ all-fucking Mighty, you're a fucking genius.'

Watson looked up from his preparations. 'That's overstating it a little. All right, let's get on with it.'

'Brilliant,' Connor said, as if the instruction hadn't sunk in.

'Connor,' Watson said sharply.

'Yeah, oh, yeah, yeah, of course.'

They powered everything up, Watson working at a ferocious pace, remembering everything he thought he'd forgotten years ago about computer hardware.

Connor gathered himself and restored the tracking programme on to his own screen. 'It's in the office three up,' he announced.

'Can you budge it for me?'

'I've been shooing this fucking thing for hours.'

'Well, shoo it down here. Port 01H2.' Watson pointed out the appropriate blue box on the screen.

'OK,' Connor said. He moved his face closer to the screen as if that would help the work. 'Come on . . . Come on . . . You little bastard.'

Watson watched their prey as it neared the trap at 01H2. Suddenly, the screen of Connor's machine flashed as the RAT virus entered.

'Shit, wrong way,' Connor cursed and punched buttons on his keyboard furiously. 'I'll get it. I'll get it.'

'Just gently,' Watson encouraged.

Connor activated the disinfect programme, so the virus would jump for another safe haven. Almost before the red screen blob moved,

Watson thrust his hand into the exposed innards of his machine, ripping apart the connector that joined hard disk to motherboard.

They both stared as the red blob flickered briefly in box 01H2, then faded.

'Where is it?' Connor screamed. 'There's no red blob any more.' He glanced across at the screen of Watson's machine. It had crashed into a wallpaper of broken computer icons, multicoloured yet unmoving.

'We got it,' Watson said slowly. He sighed, relaxation spreading through his body.

It was over. They had the virus beaten.

But Connor hadn't finished. Rather than calming down, he suddenly plunged both hands into the open computer base, ripping the hard disk off its mounts like a pagan priest tearing out a heart. He threw it across the room, pursuing wildly, kicking at it. He grasped the Fender, the nearest object, and smashed it down on to the hard disk, rock-star style. Sharp fragments flew out like bullets. He kept smashing, smashing, sledge-hammer strokes in manic fury, again and again until the disk was entirely destroyed and his hands were covered in his own blood.

It took Watson several seconds to understand what was happening. He hadn't realized Connor was so high. A little hyper perhaps, but that was all.

He tried to reason the boy through the flailing arms, saying, 'Connor. Connor, it's all right.' When that didn't work, he grabbed him around the chest, clamping the forearms. 'Calm down, son,' he said.

'But I . . . I . . . I want to . . . I mean, Ray's work . . .'

'OK. OK. It's OK.' He had to exert considerable effort to keep all of Connor's limbs under control.

Slowly, he waltzed Connor over to a chair and deposited him. The young man slumped down and Watson backed away, taking the broken guitar as if it were a weapon from a disarmed criminal. He found himself another chair, panting as he let his full weight sink into it.

By the time he got his breath back, Connor was already stammering apologies. 'I . . . I . . . I don't know what . . .' Half-sentences tumbled out without ever finishing.

Watson looked across at him. He took a second to prepare himself. 'I think we both know,' he said. He allowed himself a political pause. 'Connor, you did a good job on this virus.' His voice was twisting into an enacted anger. 'We did a deal and you'll get your money, but if I ever find you stoned on these premises again, I'll personally insert the jagged end of this Strat up your arsehole. Do you understand?'

Connor turned and looked straight at Watson.

Watson saw something in the face change. 'Good,' he said with relief. He stood up, still clutching the Fender, its broken neck and strings dripping with torn-away tuning keys like untended metallic flowers. As he turned towards the door, feeling pleased with himself now, he saw her, standing there, watching them.

'How long have you been there, Alexandra?' Watson asked.

She was holding her hand to the side of her chin like an indulgent mother. 'Are you trying to fuck up everything and everybody connected to my father, Mr Thomas?'

He thought about this for a moment. Then he smiled and brushed past her.

X

As soon as he got back to his office, Watson called the local police. He spoke to the same detective as before. He reported the latest evidence pointing the finger at BBS's former chief accountant.

'That doesn't surprise me, sir,' said the voice on the other end of the phone. 'We've been trying to find him since yesterday. We have a warrant now. But when we went to his house, his clothes were gone.'

JFK Airport, New York. André Pielot was heading home. He handed his ticket to the check-in clerk. He had done it so often that he answered her questions as if automated.

'Yes.' He had packed the bag himself.

'No.' There were no electrical goods.

'Non smoking.' He indulged only in what he called 'social smoking'.

'Aisle.' He felt claustrophobic in window seats.

He took back his passport and boarding pass. All very regular. But when he turned away, looking for the departure gate, he was suddenly surprised.

Caroline Sharpe was waving at him.

He stepped back. She was twenty feet away. Had been waiting for him to turn. What was she doing here?

'This is a happy coincidence. Are you flying today?'

'No coincidence. Uli sent me down to see you off. He wanted you to have something, but he had an engagement, a TV interview to do at five o'clock.'

'What is it?' he asked, then stopped himself. 'No, let's get away from the check-in. I'll buy you a drink.'

She smiled. 'Fine.'

They settled on white wine, Californian because the bar had no

French. Pielot led her to a table, rearranging his carry-on baggage on the floor as he sat down.

'Tomorrow morning I am in Paris. Then straight on to a flight home.'

'You told us,' she reminded him, 'family wedding, yeah? Back to your roots?'

Pielot blushed. 'I'm sorry. I'm sure I bored you. I don't go home that often. And my niece does not seem old enough to be getting married.'

Caroline Sharpe smiled as if happy for him.

'You said Uli wanted me to have something,' he prompted.

'Oh, yes.' She had been cradling a plastic bag on her lap. She seemed to have forgotten it was there. From it she produced a small wooden ornament the size of a coconut. The wood was carved into the shape of a bulbous warrior head. 'It's not to my taste, I'm afraid,' she said as she handed it over.

'It's lovely. But . . . What is it?'

'Maawian art. He said if you were going to save the island, you should be honoured.'

Pielot took the object and cradled it in both hands, turning it around in front of his face.

'You haven't changed your mind, have you?' she asked anxiously.

'No.'

'And you have all the data we gave you?'

'Packed in my luggage.'

'Good.'

He looked at her in surprise. Suddenly, all that anxiety she displayed had disappeared. Now she was strangely relaxed.

He lifted his glass and toasted the success of the coming conference. 'I'm going to announce this to the UN,' he said.

At ten p.m. – early by his recent standards – Connor hauled himself out of the office, feeling dog-tired, hand bandaged, the downside of the drugs starting to kick in. Outside the building he found his pushbike lying in an enormous puddle of water with two slashed tyres.

He was contemplating the problem, standing alone in a car park in the dark, when he saw her motorcycle coming. A slim figure in black leather, old-fashioned helmet. The bike was a Harley Davidson that looked like it could use some restoration. Its engine misfired as it slid to a stop on the wet tarmac.

'Trouble?' Alexandra's black hair tumbled out of her helmet.

'What are you doing here?' he asked.

'That's not a nice attitude. I came to do you a favour. I saw you had a flat. I thought I'd wait around and give you a lift.'

Connor nodded uncertainly. She held out a red Bellstar for him to put on. 'Well?' she prompted.

'OK,' he said, injecting all his tiredness into the word, 'give me some room.'

As soon as she screeched away, Connor knew what she was up to. The bike may have been old, but it still had too much power when you gunned the throttle, especially with a passenger aboard. Get him on your bike and scare the shit out of him – some sort of revenge. Revenge for what he still wasn't quite sure. The girl was weird.

They were doing eighty by the time they had to brake and stop for the first crossroads. When she dropped the clutch, she managed a misfiring wheelie up the main road. She changed down, racing-style, for the first bend, over-revved the engine on the exit and held a power slide that left black lines on the drier patches of road.

He closed his eyes.

She kept the throttle wide open. He found himself clinging on, arms around her waist, feeling increasingly green. Perhaps he should have told her about his motion sickness, he thought.

Ten minutes later, quite the worse for the experience but still alive, they arrived at the house he shared with three others, a rented semi on the outskirts of Stratford. The bike rattled to a halt in the driveway. He took off the helmet and handed it back. His chin slumped into his chest.

'Are you all right?' she asked, suddenly looking worried herself.

He turned and bent over and wretched the contents of his stomach into the flower-bed. 'Motion sickness,' he explained, wiping his mouth with the back of his hand. 'Had it since I was a kid. It runs in the family.' He shrugged as if trying to dismiss the embarrassment of his weak stomach.

She didn't reply.

He said, 'You did the tyres, didn't you?'

'You did a deal with them,' she spat. 'With that Thomas.'

'Watson didn't kill your father, Alex. If anybody, it was Bob Collins. His fingerprints are all over the virus.' He knew that statement was a risk and, for a moment, he thought the worst was going to happen.

She seemed to arch her body, eyes aflame, preparing to pounce. Then it all fell away. 'You're siding with them,' she mumbled. 'I thought you were my friend.'

'I am your friend.'

'No, you're bloody not. I hate you. You're a sell-out.'

Connor shook his head weakly. He turned and vomited again into the flower-bed. God, that was his lunch of Yorkie bars and Walkers' crisps coming up. How much more could there be in one stomach?

By the time he got his head up, she seemed to have lost her anger. 'Bob Collins,' she repeated, as if in repetition she could find acceptance. 'I used to call him Uncle Bob. He's worked with my father for years.' She bit her lip.

'There's a warrant out on him. There's no doubt he planted the virus. That makes him suspect number one for . . . for your father.'

Her face set and reset itself as if turning through emotions. 'I'd like to kill him,' she said, much more gently than the words suggested. She added, 'I'm sorry about your bike.'

'It's all right.'

'No.' She shook her head. She looked up and held his gaze with hers. 'You knew, didn't you? You knew before you got on the bike what I was going to do. Why did you get on?'

He shrugged. 'It seemed like a good idea at the time. You know, kill or cure for the family weakness.'

She didn't laugh, but neither, he noticed, was she looking at all angry any more. She seemed crushed and suddenly small.

'What is it?' he said.

'I was just thinking . . . I don't have a family.'

'I'm sorry,' he said.

She hesitated. Uncertain. He saw her swallow, then fix the smile back to her face. 'Aren't you going to invite me in?'

'No, I don't think so,' he said. 'It wouldn't be a good idea. I think I've got some more throwing up to do.'

He turned and walked towards the house.

'Connor,' she called after him, and he looked back. 'I haven't been able to face going to the house . . . to clear his things. Would you . . . Would you come with me?'

He considered for a moment; there was a cement mixer churning away inside his stomach. 'Sure,' he said, 'just not right now.'

XI

Connor and Alexandra met after breakfast. She rode them carefully to her father's house, respecting the travel sickness he had displayed so graphically before.

The Buckley family home was a four bedroom detached in a small estate of a dozen executive houses two miles from the nearest village. The principal attraction of the location was a rural view across local farms through which the only access road wound like a snake. The largest of the farms promised traditional methods on a big sign across its entrance, and opened at the weekends for children to pet its animals.

Alexandra unlocked the front door of the house and led him on a brisk tour, giving a brief history of her father's career as it related to the property. Buckley had never moved since he first started BBS. Good times and bad, it made no difference.

'He spent all his time on the company,' Alexandra explained. 'I spent mine with a series of nannies. Then he sent me off to school as soon as I reached ten.'

Connor looked around. The furniture was elegant, but there wasn't much of it. There was evidence of police activity in most of the rooms, the grey leavings of their fingerprint dust.

Ray Buckley's personal effects were confined to a bedroom full of clothes, a bathroom with his toothbrush and half-used tube of tooth-paste, and a small study cluttered with paper and cardboard files, some lying on the desk and some on the floor.

There was no computer in the study. Connor found that hard to understand. When he pointed it out to Alexandra, she simply shrugged.

'Used to be one,' she said. 'In fact, he had a tied line into the BBS network. Cost a fortune when it was first installed.'

Connor looked at the empty BT socket where he assumed the missing

PC had been connected. Perhaps the police had taken it away as evidence. He felt faintly disappointed.

They agreed to split up and set to work: Connor on the papers, Alexandra on the rest of the house. An hour later, when she came back into the study carrying cups of tea, Connor had completed a first-cut scan of all the documents in the room. Most were of no interest whatsoever. The legal papers, bank documents and share certificates were sorted into three separate files.

'My God, you work quickly,' she said.

'I haven't read them all,' he told her, 'but I think you ought to look at these.'

He held up a small handful of papers, no more than five sheets which he had isolated from the rest.

'What are they?' she asked.

'Just read them,' he said.

Eleven a.m., Thursday. Pielot's plane out of Paris was only a seventeen-seater. There obviously wasn't much call for flights to obscure airports in southern France. It didn't surprise him. The TGV, the fast train, was becoming the dominant form of travel within the country's boundaries.

Pielot struggled along the fuselage, crouched double to make it to his seat. Once there, he belted himself in and tried to catch up on his ration of sleep. Air France had been kind enough to seat a woman with a screaming baby across the aisle from him on the flight from New York. Even the soundtrack of the badly cut and terminally boring B-movie had failed to drown the child's wailing. He had got no peace.

He drifted now into thoughts about this afternoon's bride and groom. He was happy, looking forward to the wedding despite the lack of sleep. He closed his eyes and was practically unconscious by the time the pilot taxied out for his take-off run, dozing as the plane accelerated along the runway and lifted into the air.

It was the bang that woke him . . .

He couldn't think how long they'd been in the air. A few seconds? A minute? Ten? He'd been unconscious.

The plane plunged to the left, a sharp spinning fall, screams around him.

The pilot got the plane back upright, but Pielot could feel that they were still falling and the engines were roaring as if at full throttle.

It felt as if they were going very fast and they were still falling? Had a wing fallen off? What?

80

There was a voice on the intercom, talking calmly about an emergency landing. He took up the brace position.

He could still feel and hear the engines. They were going fast. They weren't gliding in; they were powering in. Too fast. Too fast.

He felt the thump as they hit the ground. Then there was a skidding bumping noise. Out of control, and very fast. Too fast. Too fast. He could hear things scraping very loudly along the fuselage underneath him. Then something must have dug into the ground, because all of a sudden, they were flipped into the air. He was thrown against his seatbelt straps, his head banging against the porthole window at his side. A paperback book struck him on the ear with tremendous force. He was soaked by a flying plastic tumbler of something alcoholic.

Then they flipped upright again. He banged his head again. But now they seemed to be sliding, sledge-like. Decelerating. The thunderous scraping finally fading.

He saw a ray of hope. A moment before, he had been convinced he was going to die.

Finally, it felt like they had come to a stop. Pielot looked at the faces of other passengers, people gasping, tears forming.

One . . . two seconds. He thought of the wooden warrior head that he had transferred into check-in luggage at Charles de Gaulle airport.

Then the fuel tanks exploded.

XII

'What did it mean, Connor?'

'What did what mean?'

'You know,' Alexandra said accusingly, 'the papers we found.'

They were sitting by the bank of the River Avon, the bustle of Stratford on a Saturday at their backs. The weather had turned once again and it was scorching hot.

They had been wandering around the various Shakespearean tourist traps for a couple of hours. Now they were eating ice-creams on the grass outside the RSC. They watched the swans, and the ducks, and the timeless flow of the river.

'I guess it means you're even richer than I thought,' he said after some consideration. 'That trust fund of yours is going to pop into maturity next year and you'll own a five-million-dollar piece of Buemann Oil.'

'That's not what I meant.'

'Well, what did you mean?' he said idly.

'I don't know.' Her voice twisted with pain and Connor wished he had steered the subject away. This had been Alexandra at her best up until now. Alex in blue jeans. Alex with her hair down, a skimpy top, Reebok street-fashion on her feet instead of biker's boots. She was beautiful and the way she treated him made him forget his own awkward geekiness, his bad clothes and bad eyes.

'I suppose I meant "why",' she said, carrying the thought. 'Why is there a trust fund for me? Where did the money come from, Connor? Not from my father.'

'No,' he agreed. He remembered the way she'd insisted on going through every statement in her father's records. Connor had helped her work through the small print of the papers until two in the morning, but more than twenty-four hours later, it still seemed to make little sense.

'Are you ever going to recover his climate model?' she asked, as if this was something she was focusing on as a memorial.

'It's not looking good,' he admitted. 'I've found or restored copies of thirteen files that seem to be part of it, but we're short of two key things. There's a controller file, which I think probably included the main data matrix, and an output file. Both appear to be missing.' He hesitated. 'Watson got what I think is the output file back from the SSEO last night. Apparently your father had sent them a copy.'

'So, in this whole jigsaw, you're missing only one?'

'Yes, but it's the most important. It has the base assumptions in it.'

She sighed in a deflated kind of way. 'I never told you I loved my father,' she said, fixing her eye on a particular mid-river swan.

'Did you?'

'Yes, of course.'

'You just found it hard to say?'

'I wanted to deny it. I guess I don't like feelings that compel me. They make me feel like I'm . . . I don't know . . . not free. I hated him as well, I guess. But not as much as I hate the son-of-a-bitch that killed him. I'd like to . . .' She stopped and he wondered if she was waiting for him to say something.

He said nothing; there seemed to be nothing to say.

Eventually she said, 'To hell with this, let's go and get a boat. I fancy a row up the river.'

She jumped up and pulled at his arm, and he didn't resist. He didn't want to resist. He was happy to tag along.

They walked up to one of the boathouses and Alexandra negotiated with the boatman. She spoke at a hundred miles an hour. Before he knew where he was, Connor was rowing furiously, with Alexandra calling, 'Pull, pull,' like a cox in the Boat Race.

She was smiling and laughing. Smiling and laughing . . . so he just kept rowing.

After a while – he didn't know how long or how far they had travelled – they came to a particularly quiet stretch of the river where the trees hung over the water like an arch and where the banks were downy with soft green grass.

She said, 'Let's stop here.' She gave him the smile again.

He steered towards the bank and she jumped ashore from six feet away, yelling like a pirate boarding a merchant ship.

'I just want to lie in that grass,' she announced and promptly flopped into it. 'Come on, Connor, get that shirt off and try and get some rays on your milky body.'

By the time he had secured the boat to the bank, she was staring contentedly at the sky. He stood over her and took his shirt off. She was singing to herself as he lay beside her.

After a while, she raised her head and looked across his body. 'You know, you haven't got a single hair on that chest of yours.' She propped herself on her elbow and continued examining, as if checking the fact.

'So?' he said.

'You want to see mine?'

She grasped her T-shirt at waist level, raising it high enough to expose herself. She rocked her shoulders so her breasts danced.

When she looked at him again, her own exuberance seemed to embarrass her. She pulled the T-shirt smartly back down. 'I just thought you might be interested,' she said curtly.

To his shame, he realized he had stared at her with horror showing in his face. What had she thought? He tried to cover, saying, 'No . . . I mean, yes. I am, but . . .' It was a stumbling, pathetic effort and he knew it. But how could he explain to her that what was wrong was the quality of her beauty? In his mind, it was still impossible for her to be interested in him.

'Look,' she said, 'I'm not high this time, so there's no need for that gentlemanly crap. I want you to. I mean, you've got me. Take anything you want.'

He looked at her. Her face was still no more than a few inches from his chest. He wanted to say something. But what?

He wanted to say yes. Of course, he wanted to say yes. He wanted to say, 'Yes, this is what I have been waiting for.' But all his thoughts fell over themselves and nothing came out of his mouth.

She rolled back, resuming her sky staring, and he thought he'd blown it. All he'd had to say was . . . well, anything. 'Yes,' should have been easy.

Suddenly, she produced something from her jeans' pocket and slapped it across his chest with an arc of her hand.

He looked down. 'What's this?' he said.

She laughed. Laughing at the way the little plastic package seemed to terrify him. 'This was my last resort,' she said. 'I believe you'll find it's cherry flavour.'

When she heard about Pielot, Patty had driven to her mother's for the evening. Tea and sympathy. She was in a bad way.

Her mother had told her everything would work out, but then Patty hadn't told the whole truth – Pielot's part in the final break-up of Patty and Watson, the French connection.

That wasn't the sort of thing Patty could ever tell her mother. Her mother was a Christian fundamentalist with a degree in theology. She had never put the degree into practice – raising Patty and Patty's two sisters had distracted her from a career – but she read and believed every word of the Bible, from the Creation, through Noah and his Ark, all the way to the blazing visionary climax of the Revelation.

Nevertheless, despite having to temper her story, Patty drove back home in the morning, feeling somewhat better, her system flushed by the tears that were better out than in.

She found herself repeating that mantra again: 'Work, work, work.' She chewed over the questions of Buckley's model, its horrifying prediction for the near future, its historical anomaly. She thought about the non-existent rapid fluctuation it had thrown up, marring the model's perfect past.

Whatever this anomaly might have been, the model seemed to get the occurrence of ice ages right and that was a major achievement. Perhaps she shouldn't dismiss it so quickly.

She thought about the first graph she'd seen, Buckley's prediction of a twelve-degree shift in the temperature in the middle of the southern hemisphere. She mused over the bizarre mechanisms for destruction, as if the world was a ball in front of her eyes, as small as the two-foot antique in André Pielot's office. What could start it? What did 'the Earth Goddess collapses' mean? What did 'Natural climatic event triggers shift' refer to?

Her car veered dangerously from lane to lane. She only just missed a lorry. She pulled herself back on to a straight course, pointing herself between the cat's-eyes.

Suddenly. Very suddenly. Patty remembered something.

This was not an entirely new theory! Buckley's model was like something she had read before!

It was beautiful and awesome and worked out in great detail, yes . . . But it wasn't new.

Ten years ago Patty had briefly studied under Professor Pfister, the man Pielot had called a 'grant junky'. For a couple of terms he'd been a visiting professor at the university where she'd done her PhD. However his views may have changed in the interim, back then Pfister had been proposing something he called the 'Quantum Theory of Climatic States'.

She remembered him saying, 'Think about the extinction of the dinosaurs. The received wisdom says an asteroid comes down and pow!' Pfister had that wonderful enthusiasm that goes with academic obsession. 'OK, so your world temperature may take a hike because of all the dust and shit. But . . . and here's my killer fact . . . it doesn't come back. The dust goes away. The effect of the asteroid goes away, but the earth doesn't go back to its old pattern. It took a million years for the dinosaurs to die out in the new climate – we know that. Doesn't that make you think?'

Patty thought about it. It was years since she'd heard that speech, but she thought about it now. She thought about the words Ray Buckley had written on his last graph: '*Natural climatic event triggers shift.*'

The rest of the journey seemed to pass in a daze. She drove down motorways and A roads and local streets until she pulled up at her front door, but she couldn't actually have said how she did it.

She dropped her overnight luggage in the hall and headed immediately for the study. She knew exactly the journal she was looking for, an old issue of *Scientific American*. She found it and took it back into the lounge to read.

In his original thesis P. J. Pfister – at the time, a PhD himself at Princeton – had proposed that the nature of the world did not change, but always possessed a series of possible climatic equilibria. These showed different temperatures and existed with various different global patterns. Although the world might sit happily in one equilibrium for a long time, some event would come along which gave the world such a kick that it got displaced from its current equilibrium state and came down in another.

In effect, the world was like a record stuck in a groove. It goes on playing the same 'spring-summer-autumn-winter' tune until someone bangs the record player hard enough.

Despite Pfister's passion at the time, the theory had faded from academic view as Pfister had failed to provide scientific data to support it. It had been good enough to secure him a professorship on the West Coast, but nothing more.

Patty fingered the brittle pages of the once-glossy journal. Her eyes scanned the date, thirteen years ago. It was almost the exact date on which she had first met Watson Thomas. She curled back into the curve of the sofa. A shudder ran down her back as she allowed herself an errant thought.

This sofa was the one they had bought years ago from Habitat when they had practically nothing between them and the money was a crazy extravagance. She ran her hand across its fabric; threadbare now but that didn't matter. All the imported furniture they'd bought later, on more successful incomes, meant so much less, tainted as it was by a lesser happiness. She closed her eyes, very small and defenceless, as if the armour of adulthood had been suddenly stripped away.

Damn him!

Thirteen years gone. Thirteen years peeled away. She had calculated – a scientist's weakness – 40 per cent of her life turned to rotting memories, the decaying corpse of a marriage.

Nestling now in that sofa, she thought it strange how, at the end of something, you always seem to find yourself reminiscing how it began. That particular memory was imprinted on her brain, and she ran and reran it like the video of a favourite movie.

A college somewhere in the mid-eighties. Her wearing a Smiths T-shirt and jeans a size too tight. Watson Thomas was a bespectacled weirdo to whom a friend had sent her to buy a computer. PCs were new then. Five-and-a-quarter-inch discs. Little black floppies. PCs cost thousands. Watson Thomas made them for half price.

She had come to love that weirdo, coaxed him from flared Levis into Italian suits, from NHS glasses into Acuvue disposable contacts, seen him rich, seen him poor.

It takes a lot to unravel the knots of the past, and while the pain of the recent years may have tugged at them, and while separation may have slashed at the physical ties, he was still there, tangled in her heart.

She had knocked on his door. That's how they'd met.

He was living off-campus with a Mongolian language student and a Scottish mathematician. Their kitchen table was covered in the inner organs of dead hardware.

'I'm a geologist . . . climatologist,' she told him, 'I need one of these PCs for my work.'

'Research?'

'Final-year project. "The History of El Niño." '

'Sounds impressive. But can you pay for it?' he had asked. Business always came first. Some things never change.

And that's how it started, her need to write up a project, 'The History of El Niño'.

She tried to blank his face out. She used terrible images: water shortage, famine, disease. Death on an unimaginable scale.

Thirty seconds later, still wallowing on her Habitat sofa, Patty had a eureka! moment.

'El Niño!' she shouted aloud.

If she was looking for a 'natural event' that might trigger a change, if Ray Buckley had meant anything by the phrase, surely it must be El Niño.

After all, in the random years in which it occurred, El Niño was the largest climatic event in the southern hemisphere.

The phone ringing in a New York office. A woman answered.

'Hello, who's this?'

'They're on to me. I've been trying to get you since yesterday.'

'Hold on. Calm down. I thought I told you not to call here.'

'They're on to me, I tell you.'

'Robbie, calm down.'

'Shit, I should never have got into this.'

Pause.

'You are in it, Robbie. Remember our little deal.'

'Your blackmail?'

'I didn't blackmail you.'

'I never wanted any of this. I never wanted any killing. My God! They think I killed Ray.'

'I killed Ray, Robbie, you know that. I pulled the trigger with my own hand. But you took the money; you're part of the team. Listen to me carefully. Tell me where you are. I'll get back to you.'

'A hotel.'

'Give me the name and number. It's going to be all right.'

XIII

The funeral was too large even for the sizeable French country church in which it was held. Patty sat near the back, feeling alone in her grief, somehow separate from all the mourners around her. Although she had known André Pielot, although she had slept with him on one aborted occasion, she had known nothing of his family. This was a man who had been inside her, and that was the mark he had left on her, and that's what separated her from everyone else. Everyone else here thought of André Pielot with love, and she thought of him with guilt.

Though God knows, she told herself, trying to ease her tension, there might be another dozen women in this church he'd slept with.

As she cast her eyes about, searching for likely women, she found only Ulysses Masoni. It was not easy to miss him. He came complete with a camera-infested entourage and a shifty-looking blonde who someone described to her as the SSEO's PR director.

After the singing and the solemn words in French that Patty struggled to understand, the congregation filed out of the church. Patty was shaking hands with relatives – men and women with an eye, or a mouth, or perhaps a tilted smile she recognized as decidedly Pielot-ish – when she bumped straight into Masoni.

It took her a moment to realize he had sought her out in the crowd.

He said, 'Doctor Drake.'

She said, 'Patty, please.' Nervously she put out her hand. He engulfed it in an enormous grip and pumped it gently. He nodded at her graciously and introduced Caroline Sharpe. Patty's distrust of the woman was instant, but she couldn't exactly have said why.

'I would like for you to come and meet us,' Masoni said. 'In my hotel? After all this?' He swept his arm over the proceedings before them. 'Now is a time of sadness, but we have things to discuss, I think.'

'We do?'

'We do.' He nodded again and pressed a card into her hand. It was from a hotel in the nearby town, half a mile from the one she was staying in. On the back he had written a time and the number of a room. The tone of his voice suggested something clandestine and when she looked up to answer, Masoni and Caroline Sharpe were already disappearing into the crowd.

Half an hour before the appointed time, she was sitting on her hotel bed in her funeral clothes, still staring at the card, wondering what this man wanted of her. The decision to go was last minute. She undressed, showered and redressed herself in a grey trouser suit. There was no time for more than a dash of make-up.

Masoni himself opened the door. He was wearing flannel trousers, open-toed sandals and a cheesecloth shirt unbuttoned at the neck. He reached across, lifted her hand – slight in his enormous palm – and kissed it.

'*Enchanté*,' he breathed.

'Thank you,' she said, realizing as she said it that the phrase made no real sense.

'It is the only French I know,' he told her. His smile, wide enough to indicate joy in most men, seemed to be forced on his lips and the contradiction jarred.

He shepherded her into the room. It was simple but big. She guessed forty, maybe forty-five, pounds a night. Nothing ostentatious about his use of SSEO funds.

She said, 'I thought you only wore suits.'

Masoni smiled a more genuine, easier smile. He even laughed a little. 'Only on television,' he assured her.

'I'm sorry,' she said, 'that was a stupid remark.'

'I can only take so much time in a suit,' he told her.

Caroline Sharpe was sitting on the bed, looking uncomfortable with her own presence.

In the middle of the room, there were two dowdy armchairs positioned either side of a low table. Patty picked one and sat. Meanwhile, Masoni went searching for something in the en-suite bathroom. Patty looked over, but Caroline Sharpe didn't move or offer to strike up a conversation. She seemed to sit there like a chaperone, and Patty began to wonder whether that was actually her function. Perhaps Masoni had thought she wouldn't have turned up if he hadn't offered a chaperone. Given her hesitation in making the decision, he was probably right.

Masoni came back carrying a wooden bowl filled with water, placed it on the low table and sat on the floor next to it. He tipped in a small sachet of powder.

'We've had a bad time,' he said, 'I thought this might help.'

'Is it medicine?' Patty asked, gazing uncertainly into the grainy liquid, and thinking, 'Drugs, narcotics,' suddenly worried about Masoni.

'I have great problems travelling with this,' Masoni said. 'When Customs see it, they wonder what else I've got. Three full-body searches this year. But don't worry, this is *kava*.'

'*Kava?*'

'Some people call it *yaqona*. Not so much medicine, but a good substitute for alcohol if you want to relax. The preparation is everything. It is a rite, a ceremony, both the making and the drinking . . . if you'll bear with me.'

Masoni went back into the bathroom, returning with a second wooden bowl, some wooden cups and a handful of what looked like straw. He dropped the straw into the liquid of the first bowl and used it to begin gathering up the remains of the powder. He poured off the liquid into the second bowl, trapping most of the gathered powder in the straw.

'The traditional way,' Masoni explained. 'You know, when Ray Buckley first came to Maawi, he brought his *sevusevu*, *kava* root, the traditional gift of visitors, so we could make *kava* together, just as we do now. He stayed two months on his first visit, lived among my father's people. When he was ready to leave, my father gifted him land on the island. He built himself a house there, a cabin, a retreat. He came maybe three or four times. He was a convert.'

Masoni reversed his earlier pouring, capturing more of the floating debris in the straw before pouring the murky liquid back into its original wooden bowl. Then he produced a small wooden cup, dipped and handed it to Patty.

'Don't worry if you think it tastes like mud. It's supposed to. Though we like to think it tastes peppery,' he added, speaking now as an islander, proud of what it represented. Patty had noticed that switch once or twice before. He did it so smoothly. It gave him that rounded feel.

With both hands to his own wooden cup, he raised the *kava* to his lips and drank, nodding towards her to indicate she should do the same. She tried to copy. It did taste like mud. Mud with just a hint of pepper. Twenty seconds later, she noticed a numbness on her lips, a sensation not altogether unpleasant. She laughed out loud. What else can you do when your body starts to fade away?

91

Gathering herself, she said, 'You told me there was something we should discuss?'

'Yes,' he agreed, but he said it as if he weren't ready to be pushed on the point, as if he preferred to work to it slowly.

'Well?' she pressed. *Kava* makes you bold, she thought.

He was silent for a moment, then his body jerked suddenly and he said, 'Are you ready to become involved in this?'

'Involved? I am already involved. André sent me the file you gave him. I looked at it and I thought . . .'

'He gave you the file?' Caroline butted in. The fact seemed to spark her into new life. She sounded alarmed.

'Yes, he e-mailed a copy to me,' Patty said.

Masoni looked at Caroline Sharpe.

'I'm sorry,' she said, not seeming sorry at all.

'Look, you don't need to be here,' Patty said awkwardly, deciding to face the issue head on.

Caroline Sharpe shrugged. 'Suits me,' she said. She got off the bed, collected her shoulder bag from the bedside table and left.

'I apologize,' Masoni said as the door slammed. 'I suppose we're all a little too sensitive right now. First Ray, now André. This is a dangerous business.' He hesitated.

'André was killed in an air crash,' Patty said in amazement.

'True enough.'

'An accident. There were eighteen people on that plane including the pilot. I mean . . . are you suggesting?'

'Who would kill eighteen people just to make one man's death look like an accident?' he said, putting words to her question. 'I don't know.'

He put his wooden cup down and pressed both his palms together, fingers extended. He raised them to his face in an odd praying gesture, pursing his lips and hollowing his cheeks.

She gazed at him, at the stillness he was able to bring to his body. Just as the silence seemed to be going on for ever, he said, 'You know he had decided to do it, don't you?'

'Do what?'

'Not so much a choice as an obligation. He was going to stand up and tell them, the whole assembled company of the United Nations, about Buckley's results. They could listen or not – that choice was theirs. I tried to take the results to some of the governments in the southern hemisphere myself, thinking they would be interested, that they would do something. Do you know what they said?'

Patty shook her head vaguely.

'That they were concerned with the environmental issues, but they were dealing with the problem through diplomatic channels and didn't think wild and unsupported speculations helped their efforts. Brazil actually told me they were too indebted to argue with the "Euro-American consensus" – whatever that means.'

Patty was having trouble focusing on the room now. Her thoughts were darting here and there, out of control. She said, 'So what was it you wanted with me?'

Masoni smiled. 'Caroline and I fly to England tomorrow. The only thing that will help us is hard evidence. The results file you have seen is no good without the model that generated it. The scribblings of a madman – that's what they'll say.'

'A murdered madman,' she reminded him.

'Even so . . . We want to put pressure on the new MD at BBS to recover Ray's work, get the whole model back.'

'Can they do that?' she asked, 'André told me it was lost.'

'All they have given us so far is excuses and a few useless files. Nothing that relates to Ray's real work . . . Without the whole model and its data, we have but a shattered picture. So we will try with the new man. I want you to help me.'

'Look, I can't throw the weight of the Agency behind you, if that's what you're after. I don't have that authority,' Patty said.

'No, it was more your personal influence I was hoping for.'

'My personal influence?'

'You know the man, I think. Watson Thomas? I want you to talk to him on our behalf.'

Patty spluttered on the *kava*. It was as though someone had pressed on something deep inside her and her whole body reacted. 'Technically,' she said, breaking through the shock, 'I suppose I'm still married to him.'

' "Still" married?' he repeated as if the concept baffled him.

'We separated . . . over two months ago. It's over.'

'A Western concept.' He looked her in the eye. Then he put both hands to his wooden cup, lifted it and drank from it. 'You still love him.'

She shrugged nervously. 'The ties that bind, you know.'

'Ah, yes,' he said, 'the ties that bind.'

Those four words seemed to hit her like a branding iron. She was for ever the woman who in Masoni's mind was trying to escape 'the ties that bind'.

She bit her lip. When she was calm enough, she said, 'Look, I should tell you, I found some problems with the results file André had. The model has thrown up at least one anomaly in the past, not dissimilar to the prediction it seems to be making now.'

For several seconds he looked at her as if he didn't know this, but then his face changed, and it became clear he did know. 'It may be so, but let's suppose for the moment that the prediction is accurate. I'd like you to think about what would happen.'

She hesitated, feeling as if she was being drawn into something. What was happening? She was no longer sure the *kava* was quite so benign. 'Worst affected, if the thing were strictly correct,' she mused, 'would be the band of countries between 5° and 25° south. They would see the peak of the new temperatures.'

'And that band includes?'

'Brazil, Peru and Bolivia; the major part of Southern Africa; Australia, parts of Indonesia and most of the islands in the South Seas. All of those areas would become uninhabitable. Too hot for vegetation. Too hot for humanity.' Her mind drifted further, caught by the spell. 'I can imagine the chaotic weather conditions associated with such a shift in temperature,' she added. 'Floods. Winds. Floods and winds like we've never seen. But all this is speculation if . . .'

'Population affected?' he prompted, talking over her.

She tried to count the affected numbers in her head. South America including half of Brazil: maybe 100 million. The affected part of Africa: maybe the same, another 100 million. Australia, New Zealand and the South Seas: less, but . . .

'I don't know,' she said, shrugging.

'I suppose you have worked out what "Natural climatic event triggers shift" meant?'

'Well, I . . . I think it could only mean El Niño oscillation. My guess is that, in essence, Ray's theory says that once you get a high enough concentration of carbon dioxide in the air, his shift can be kicked off by a big weather transient like El Niño.'

Masoni raised his hands in an open accepting gesture.

'You still believe this prediction, don't you?' she asked. 'What about the anomalies?'

'Wind and flood,' he said, 'that's what you described, isn't it? Where else do we find wind and flood?'

She looked at him blankly.

He said, 'In the six hundredth year of Noah's life, Doctor Drake . . .'

*

Here is the lasting brand on Patty Drake. Here are the ties that bind her: all that night, through the nightmares of Buckley's prediction, when she should have been seeing biblical wreckage, she saw instead the face of Watson Thomas. Her mind fixed, perhaps trying to protect itself, on memories of a younger Patty in a blue dress, carrying a bottle of supermarket table wine.

The blue-dressed Patty knocking at Watson Thomas' door.

'Hi, I've come for Watson.'

She is faced by a Scottish mathematician in grubby jeans and a Newcastle Brown sweatshirt. 'This wouldn't be by way of a date, would it?' he asks. His face cracks into a smile, Glaswegian teasing.

'Aye, it would,' she says, mocking his accent.

He waves her along the corridor towards Watson's room. She knocks again and pushes her way in.

The room is small and untidy: bed, writing desk, wardrobe, computer station and scattered printout papers everywhere.

Watson Thomas is sitting on the bed. When he looks up, she hardly recognizes him. His long hair has been cut to a short back and sides. He is wearing contacts that make his eyes red.

'Shit,' she says.

'Nice greeting. You don't like it?'

'No . . . not that. I'm just surprised.'

'I have interviews, you know,' he says.

She hadn't liked his hair long. She'd said so once or twice when they'd just been casual friends growing closer. Now they are on the brink of something more, and she feels him recoiling, ever more nervous, like a flower closing. But she knows he's cut his hair for her. She knows the inflammation in his eyes is for her. And perhaps this denied flattery is the greatest flattery of all.

She loves him for it. She wants him to let her love him.

She nods to show she understands the interview motive, a lie to support his lie. She holds up her bottle of party wine.

'Are you coming, then?'

She stares down at his clothes. He has made half an attempt to join in the party spirit, but chinos and trainers make a strange combination, especially if you compare it with her own, the floaty dress, all bare arms and plunging back.

He looks up at her, then stands.

'You look good,' he says awkwardly. It's as much of a reach as he can manage.

'Watson,' she begins.

'Yeah?'

'Is this a date? I mean, are we dating?'

The question seems to horrify him. Emotion seems to horrify him – that terrible truth she would learn later in thirteen years of painful love and togetherness. But here it makes him all the more endearing. He is a young man who in business – in anything to do with the practical world – seems to sail through with consummate control, besting all who stand in his way. And yet his emotion for her seems to overwhelm him. It locks up inside, seeping only through the tear ducts, and in the fallen hair, and the shaking of his hand when he touches her.

Watson is looking right at her now, but not answering the question.

He says, 'Are we going to this party, or not?'

He is echoing her question of a moment before.

She steels herself and stands before him. She smiles, trying to communicate the message. '*Not*,' she says.

Slowly, he leans across and kisses her.

The ties that bind.

'Hello, Robbie.'

'It's you.'

'I said I'd call. Did you doubt me? Listen, we're going to make Masoni take a little fall. We're going to tidy up a few loose ends and write his name on the whole BBS mess.'

'Fine, but can you get me out of here now? Get me on a plane or something.'

'Sure, Robbie, sure. But first we have some new problems. I need you to do a little job that I'm a little too busy to do myself.'

'I've told you before . . . I don't kill people.'

'That isn't the job . . . Not exactly.'

XIV

Lunchtime at Heathrow, the new BBS management were entertaining their biggest remaining client, the South Seas Environmental Organization at a business lunch, before they all jumped on to their individual flights. Pizzas all round. Monty and Watson eating meaty 'deep pan'; Uli Masoni and Caroline Sharpe sharing vegetarian 'thin and crispy'.

'We put considerable trust in Ray Buckley, Mr Thomas,' Caroline Sharpe said testily. 'I think we're entitled to expect results.'

'All customers are entitled to results, I don't deny that.' Watson nodded, exercising his introverted version of salesman's charm. He wasn't comfortable here, but he was doing the professional thing, a trick he performed with admirable competence. He knew this was about to get ugly and he knew just how well he and Monty had prepared.

'What are you going to do about it?' Caroline Sharpe asked. 'We were relying on your work.'

She behaved almost as if she was out to prove how loyal she could be to the cause, Watson thought. 'The data was corrupted, that is a fact,' he said, 'but we have recovered most of the commissioned modules and we are patching them back together.'

'It's the whole model Buckley built himself that we're interested in.'

'I'm afraid that was beyond repair.'

'So you can build it again from scratch,' she pressed.

'Two problems with that,' Watson said. 'First, it's way beyond what you paid for. Second, I'm not sure we know how.'

'Then you're not recovering our work.'

'I'm going to redo all the work you paid for.'

'I see,' she said curtly. Caroline Sharpe sipped at her glass, mineral water with a twist of lime. There was a hardness to her face now. 'This is about the highest-profile job BBS has right now, am I correct?'

Watson nodded. He wondered if she knew just how short of work they were. More importantly, he was sure she didn't know that the police were already sifting through the accounts, looking for the guilty – the guilty within the SSEO. It wasn't a subject he was about to bring up voluntarily, not yet anyway. Timing was everything.

The woman was in full flight now. 'Ray's death and the computer problems have been splashed all over the papers. I guess you realize that if you don't complete what you set out on, the SSEO will have the bulk of the environmental lobby down on your back.'

'We've already seen your people with placards sending us the message,' Watson said.

'Our people? That's public opinion at work.'

'We will finish what you paid us for . . .'

'Worthless! You know that as well as I do. It's only the work Ray did himself that means anything. We need that. Without it, the rest falls apart; there is no model. If the general public, who have been most generous in their support for our cause, get to hear that you are suppressing information . . . You, a company bank-rolled by a Texas oil millionaire with a dubious record on the environment. They tend to get very paranoid about that kind of thing. They'll probably think – oh, I don't know – that Ray discovered something awful and you are helping certain interested parties to hush it up. Parties that killed him . . . You think you've got problems with protestors at your doors. You've seen nothing yet.'

'You seem very happy that there should be something awful,' Watson said, the words slipping out uncensored.

'What's that supposed to mean?'

He was into the subject. He quite liked how smoothly he'd led her into it. 'It would be terribly convenient, fundraising-wise, to have a big catastrophe that may or may not be going to happen.'

'That's scandalous. BBS's conduct in this whole matter, since Ray died, has been scandalous, and I mean to see that it pays for that.'

'Are you threatening us, Miss Sharpe?' Monty interrupted, right on cue. Up to that moment, he had been listening silently, eating the lettuce left over from his side salad as it lay limply on its plate. This was the role he had agreed with Watson: wait until the SSEO got nasty, then pounce.

'I'm trying to help you, Mr Radford,' she said. 'Perhaps you don't understand how much public opinion is roused by this issue. If you scale down your efforts behind the cause, people are not going to feel good about BBS.'

'Is that your advice as a PR consultant?'

Caroline Sharpe scowled and Monty entered into the contest, matching her look for black look across the table.

After about a minute of silence, he reached down to the side of his chair and picked up a brown A4 envelope and dropped it in the middle of the table.

She looked at it.

Masoni leaned forward and asked, 'What is that?'

'Evidence,' Monty said. 'The whole SSEO–BBS relationship was a scam. By our estimation, at least a third of the money raised by the SSEO to fund the research never reached BBS. It was creamed off.'

'What?' shouted Masoni. He stood up.

For a moment Watson thought he was about to lash out violently, but Masoni seemed to think better of it. He sat back down.

'This is slanderous,' Caroline Sharpe said, suddenly refinding her voice.

'No,' Watson told her, 'it would be slanderous, even libellous, if it weren't true.'

Watson looked at Caroline Sharpe. In that moment, he expected to see shock or alarm in her eyes, but he didn't. He expected to see something, a kind of reaction, but nothing happened.

Holding himself together, he said, 'So you see, the ability of your organization to bring pressure on us is, shall we say, very limited. I should think you'll be spending all your time explaining how this happened to your patrons.'

He leaned back, feeling the Monty–Watson double act had worked perfectly. But then he noticed that the woman still hadn't even twitched. Suddenly, like a bullet, it hit him.

She already knows . . .

Underneath Caroline Sharpe's aggressive bravado, she wasn't concerned what the SSEO cause was, and she didn't care if it crashed and burned.

Watson turned to Masoni who was sitting directly opposite him. A moment ago he had been an erect, proud man, a man it was impossible not to respect, fear even.

Now he was crying.

Watson's world collapsed as if it were a balloon someone had stuck a pin through.

This was the moment Watson would remember later, the moment when the change happened. 'Did he?' he asked, like snapping on a light switch.

Caroline Sharpe said, 'Did he what?'

'Did he discover something awful?' Watson was gazing not at her, but at Masoni.

Masoni's face hardly seemed to twitch as the tears rolled down it.

'His results were very important,' she said hesitantly. 'They added something, something big, to the global debate.'

'You mean, I guess, that you could have splashed them all over the news,' Monty said cynically.

Masoni straightened in his seat. 'I want to say something,' he announced, 'I want to tell you about responsibility.' Then he waited, completely still.

As Watson hesitated, unsure what Masoni was waiting for, it was Monty who said, 'Go ahead.'

Masoni leaned into the table so that his face seemed almost its centrepiece. He said, 'In 1800, at the time of your Industrial Revolution, the concentration of carbon dioxide in the atmosphere was less than 280 parts per million. Today, it is 350. Today, we are adding at least two to that figure every year. You know this?' He swivelled his eyes so they stared piercingly at Watson's.

'I guess,' Watson said.

'Have you ever thought what that means? Let us sit here a while,' Masoni said, 'and take long breaths together. Your lungs are pumping seven, maybe ten, litres of air in a minute. Figures. Just figures, Mr Thomas. They mean nothing.'

He held out his right hand, fingers up, the nail of the thumb pointing into the top joint of his little finger so only its tip showed. 'If I sit here a minute with you,' he said, 'your lungs will breathe in this much man-made carbon waste. Do you feel comfortable with that?'

Watson shivered. No gentleness now. Masoni had vicious eyes.

'If we sit here with our grandchildren in fifty years. . . .' Masoni moved his thumbnail down so it pointed to the lower joint. 'Maybe that's OK,' he said, staring at the hand, 'or maybe Ray was right. You get to a point, a level of pollution, and that's it . . . The Goddess Gaia says no more. She flushes you off the Earth . . .'

His voice trailed out and he sat there thinking, his stillness more impressive than any movement. He kept his thumbnail pressed to his finger. At last he said, 'But in this fingertip, in this half a finger, is most of the money in the industrialized world. The production of wealth and the production of waste are one and the same thing. The richest countries on Earth are also the worst polluters.'

Masoni's hand dropped away, so his eyes looked straight into Watson's. 'You don't believe Ray Buckley was killed for some financial scandal, Mr Thomas. I can see that much in your face. Ask me who would kill Ray Buckley? Any one of the world's biggest companies or governments would have their reasons. You see, they are trying to deny one simple fact, one simple undeniable fact ... That the world is becoming overly populous. A fifth of all the members of our species that have ever existed are alive today. And if we continue to be consumers rather than conservers, soon everything will be consumed.'

Watson sat there. After a moment, he said, 'Tell me more about this work you think is lost.'

Masoni smiled, smiled and started his tale. Over coffee, he spilled everything he knew about Ray Buckley's work, the meeting with Pielot, their hopes for the UN summit, what it meant to a small island in the south-western Pacific as the heat and the waters rose.

Masoni painted a picture. Man pollutes the air and the sea. As the carbon dioxide rises, as the seas fill up with poison, the Gaia struggles for control. Suddenly, the exhausted Goddess lets go. The last whiff of poison is light as a feather, but it is a feather on top of an unbearable burden; it is a back-breaker. And the climate of the Earth is thrown into chaos, into catastrophic change.

Two in the morning. Patty awoke with a wrenching jolt. Half-asleep. Where was she? Oh, yes, back at home. She had got in late last night.

She remembered ringing her mother. 'Hello, Mum, what's the date of the biblical Flood?'

'That's a strange greeting,' her mother had said.

'I need to know. You're the theologian in the family '

'If I remember correctly, scholars say the evidence in the bible places it at around 2,300 BC.'

'Way too late. Shit!'

'That's no way to talk . . .' Her mother launched into scolding tones.

The conversation had gone downhill from there. In the end Patty had been glad to get off the phone, and when she'd done so, she'd gone for the brandy.

That was a mistake, a mistake that was now coming back to her.

She clutched at her head remorsefully, then rubbed her eyes, trying to focus. Was she awake because of a disturbance of dreams or was there a noise downstairs which had roused her?

She lay in the darkness for a while, conscious of her breathing, heavy and insistent. It seemed so loud she couldn't tell if there was someone else in the house.

André is dead – that thought came back to her – and Masoni says he was killed. Perhaps you shouldn't have let yourself be alone. It was bound to give anyone nightmares.

She got up and walked across the room the duvet dragging behind like a winter skin from which she was emerging.

It was then that she heard it, the unmistakable rustle of someone downstairs. She felt her heart smack against the inside of her ribs as if she had been given a jolt by a cardiac resuscitation unit. Now everything in her system was pumping at three times its normal speed.

The data. It had to be Buckley's file they were after. There was nothing else of value.

She looked around. How could she defend it? Thoughts hit her like bullets, jerky and uncontrolled. The beginnings of panic. Real fear. What to do. How to stay safe.

She considered calling for help. The house phone was downstairs, as was her mobile – no salvation there. She went to the wardrobe, reaching in the back, looking for something that might be usable as a weapon. She pulled out an old wooden tennis racquet and a hockey stick, souvenirs from her college days as a sportswoman. She dropped the duvet and headed for the stairs. Only when she was already two steps down did she realize how she was dressed, a little baby-doll nightie that Watson had once bought her as a surprise and unwelcome present. At the time she had told him she would never wear it. Sometimes these things change, she thought.

She heard her desktop computer hit the floor in the study, the smash of its screen. She pushed open the study door and saw a blurry figure, holding her portable at head height. The figure struck it against the far wall and recoiled in the hail of plastic fragments.

Patty took two strides across the room, neatly hooking the figure's neck with her hockey stick. She yanked sideways in the style of a former college first-teamer. Then she volleyed the head – Three Counties Doubles Champion – with an overarm smash as the unbalanced figure fell to the ground. It rolled and groaned. As it turned, Patty saw the balaclava framing the face, the black clothes.

Then she saw the gun . . .

Whether the figure hesitated on seeing eight and a half stone of lace-clad woman, Patty would never know. Neither would she know why she swung her racquet rather than freezing. But she did – a backhand that sent the gun spinning across the floor.

The figure kicked out at her, weaponless now, facing hockey stick and tennis racquet. It pushed itself up against the wall, taking another unladylike hockey blow across the left ear. Holding its arm for protection, the figure staggered, then dived headlong for the window, pulling aside the curtains and breaking through the glass in a single inelegant and desperate lunge.

Patty watched in amazement as the figure rolled through her rose-bed and came to rest on the front lawn. It got up and ran.

Patty didn't even know if it was male or female.

She watched it, numb with shock, numb with the sudden safety. She dropped her weapons and fell to her knees, shaking.

XV

The police had come and gone, making self-important noises about the crime, but in truth they held out scant hope of catching the culprit. Now she was alone.

She had stared at the telephone on and off all day. She had even picked up the handset several times. Somehow she couldn't dial the number.

OK, she hadn't exactly promised Masoni that she would, but on the other hand, when he had asked her for help, she hadn't exactly said no either. And all she had to do was pick up the phone and dial his mobile with its network-switching, find-you-anywhere global facility.

'Hi, Watson. It's Patty.'

Count them, that's four words, not one of them with more than two syllables. She thought about college, thirteen years ago, how she'd thrown herself at him. At least that's the way it seemed. That was far bolder than four little words.

She wondered if it was the sheer boldness of the beginning – the joy, the hope, the innocence – that had caused all the problems later on. Maybe when you're swept away by something, you don't stop to think how it's going to work in the long term. You don't get the ground rules right, you don't even realize that there need to be ground rules. Some bombardment of Hollywood movies taught you that, when you fell in love, that was that. Fair enough, it worked for a while, roughly ten years of a thirteen-year togetherness. Then she realized she was stifled by it all. Some time around their ten-year anniversary, she woke up like Rip Van Winkle and found she needed more . . .

She reached for the phone again, but she fell back making excuses. Whatever Pielot had believed, whatever Masoni said, the model had predicted at least one previous quantum shift that had never happened.

Why would Watson want to spend time and money recovering a model that was most probably junk?

Never happened. Never happened. She repeated this truth again and again, shaking her head to the rhythm. There was no evidence it would happen this time.

When she could stand it no more, she dragged her way to the kitchen. She selected a Mutant Ninja Turtle Mug from the kitchen draining board and poured out half a measure of cooking brandy. It tasted harsh from start to finish. She poured out another. And another.

When there was no more in the bottle, she staggered back into the lounge, seeing its comfortable lines through the hazed loose focus of the drink.

There was that bloody threadbare sofa again.

All of a sudden her emotion exploded into action. The only wonder was that it had taken so long to come out like this.

She didn't scream. She didn't make any unnecessary noise, but when she was done, everything had been either overturned or broken or both. An antique coffee table with curving wooden legs had been attacked and left in the centre of the carpet. Two of its legs were snapped off and lay discarded amongst splinters on the upturned top.

Calm again, she picked up the sofa and pushed it until it righted itself. There was a new ladder in the fabric of one of its arms, but otherwise it seemed OK. She sat down and scanned the rest of the once-fancy furniture, now kicking up its dead limbs with rigor mortis. She leaned forward and picked up a table leg. Then she drew herself back, tucking her own legs under her body, with a sad smile of satisfaction at the carnage.

She knew she could clean it up, oh yes, but it would never be like before. No furniture but what they sat on. All those Habitat sofa days, the exquisite intimacies of early love. Patty and Watson. Watson and Patty. The perfect couple.

Late that afternoon Watson Thomas was sitting in the Thinking Sanctury at BBS. He had adopted his predecessor's habit of using it as a refuge for his thoughts. He had many of them now, such a lot to work out.

He had packed the papers he needed for a European trip that began on Sunday morning: four days of touring the capitals of Europe trying to dredge up business for BBS. They needed it badly.

But his thoughts and worries went deeper than that.

In the beginning he had been convinced he had walked in on just

105

another company with financial skeletons in the cupboard. All right, so someone had bumped off the MD and frauds didn't usually lead to that kind of violence, but most of the other evidence had pointed that way for a while. He thought he was right.

Now he was staring at the possibility that it was something in Ray Buckley's climate model that had got him killed. Had someone put a virus in the network to try to destroy the model rather than to cover up financial wrong-doing? He thought about Masoni, about the protestors who had camped outside BBS. To Watson, their kind of commitment suddenly seemed compelling. He had never thought that way before.

The water in the lake rippled in the breeze. Watson stared out at it like a man expecting answers for everything who suddenly discovers just how much more complex life really is.

Just as it seemed he might melt into his own meditation, the telephone rang and Connor Giles' broken voice screamed incomprehensibly.

XVI

Connor had been working on the recovery programme for days. He was frustrated. The virus was gone, but they seemed no closer to recovering the last of the missing files.

Using the supervisor powers Watson had granted him for the network's operating system, Connor had methodically logged off every computer in the building. What he couldn't understand was that there still seemed to be activity in some of the accounting files.

Alexandra was standing behind him when he had let out the first cry of frustration. She turned and looked at the screen over his shoulder.

'What's up?' she said.

'There's some other fucker on it.'

'On what?'

'On the network. There's someone poking around in an obscure accounts directory. How can that be?'

He saw her face go from tension to anger as the realization hit her. 'Collins,' she said, 'Collins.'

'Yes, but how?' Connor asked. The penny hadn't dropped.

'He's in my father's house!' she shouted. She had turned away, heading for the door.

'What are you doing?' he called after her.

'The old tied line. That's what he's using. I'm going to get the bastard.'

'This is a job for the police . . . Alex . . .Alex.' But she was already gone.

Watson had been the first person he thought of calling . . .

Three minutes later Connor was in the passenger seat of Watson's XK8 Convertible, chasing a motorbike that had long since disappeared.

As he drove, Watson dialled 999 on his mobile and informed the police. He didn't notice Connor's face turning greener as he gave Watson directions to the Buckley house.

They covered six miles in five minutes. Then they had to slow to take the rough track of a road through the farm land. They were turning at the T-junction into the small estate of houses which Connor had indicated when a Ford Mondeo swung out on to the road in the opposite direction. Watson didn't register the driver as being Bob Collins until he saw Alexandra Buckley, Harley-mounted, her black curly hair blowing in the wind, wild-eyed in pursuit.

He cursed aloud, dipped the clutch and pulled the handbrake up hard, initiating a tyre-screaming tail slide which he exaggerated by dropping the clutch again and booting the accelerator. The Jaguar did a 180-degree-turn around a keep-left sign as if someone had thrown an anchor and chain from the driver's window.

He heard Connor moan pitifully. He thought it was in response to the danger of the manoeuvre and, for a moment, he considered slowing and waiting for the police. But then he saw Alexandra's bike accelerating up the road and he knew there was no option but to give chase. Later, he would wonder where that decision had come from and why; he didn't feel he was cut out for this 'cops-and-robbers' stuff.

Ahead the Mondeo was taking the first right-hand bend on the golf course road. Close behind, he saw Alexandra leaning over hard as the Harley struggled to find enough grip to continue the pursuit.

The road straightened again and the Mondeo started pulling away from Alexandra, whilst he and Connor – seated within Browns Lane's sleekest engineering – were closing up to her smoking exhaust pipe.

'Never going to catch him on that,' he said, 'it's knackered.'

He heard Connor mumble, 'Thank God.'

He wondered why the young man had suddenly begun invoking the name of the Lord, but he didn't have time to dwell on it. The speedo-needle was creeping over ninety.

Before they reached the next corner, a sharp left that sent the road looping around the top of the traditionally kept farm, Alexandra suddenly turned her bike off the road, leaping over the shallow ditch that separated highway from pasture land and set off grass-tracking towards grazing cattle.

Watson had only a moment to glance sideways at her before Collins' Mondeo braked hard in front of him, trailing blue smoke in its wake. It understeered badly into the corner, biting only at the last moment as its driver wound the steering-lock onto full deflection. The back end of the car swung around and dropped partially into a ditch on the exit of the bend.

Watson thought it might overturn but it didn't. Momentum and vicious wheel-spin at the front dragged it back on to the road. The delay had, however, allowed Watson and his Jaguar to close within thirty yards.

He didn't see the gravel side-road that was the farm's main entrance. Didn't see it until a 1965 Harley Davidson shot out from it. The bike was sliding sideways when Watson first saw it, as if it were being deliberately turned to face the Mondeo.

Collins swerved right and the car rammed into the base of an oak tree. The shock was enough to lift the rear of the car six feet in the air as it pirouetted around the tree and landed back in the road with its mangled bonnet pointing towards Watson's oncoming Jaguar.

Watson hit the brakes. Not to avoid the Mondeo, but Alexandra's body, which had slid on its back into Watson's path.

'Oh, Christ!' he heard Connor wail.

Watson felt the vibration of the ABS hammering through his foot.

Close. Closer. Too close.

The Jaguar stopped six feet from her.

Watson jumped out and ran as far as the car's front bumper. Suddenly he froze. Gazing up the road, he saw Bob Collins' head sticking out beyond the crack-crazed windscreen of the Mondeo, like a face pressed through a cardboard scene in a seaside photograph.

Alexandra was picking herself up off the ground, dusting the back of her leather trousers and examining a ten-inch scrape above the waistline. 'Got the bastard,' she said without looking at the wreckage.

Watson turned back to the Jaguar just in time to see Connor retch and vomit over the polished walnut dashboard of his xк8.

Patty's mother was remarkably sympathetic when she saw the state of the house. She seemed to treat all the damage as if it had been caused by the intruder, ignoring Patty's guilty admissions.

'Thank you. Thank you. Thank you,' Patty said as they finished cleaning up the lounge together.

'I've arranged a glazier for tomorrow . . . to fix the study.'

'Thank you, Mum, but I could've . . .'

'Nonsense, you need to get over this. You need help. Come and talk to me while I make us some tea.'

'We must have had a gallon already.'

'It's always best for times like these.'

Patty was guided into her own kitchen. Her mother started the kettle. 'I was thinking,' she said, 'about your timing problem.'

'My timing problem?' Her mother had an ability to be remarkably opaque at times.

'Yes, dear, I remember you saying that the Great Flood had occurred at an inconvenient moment in history for you. Of course, you didn't quite put it that way on the telephone.' Her mother smiled superciliously, reminding Patty of the words she'd actually used.

'Oh, that,' she said, blushing.

'I know I told you 2,300 BC, but I thought I'd better look it up, since it seemed so important to you.' The kettle started boiling and her mother broke off to prepare the tea pot.

'And?' Patty prompted, feeling a stab of apprehension.

'Well, this isn't what I believe . . . but the secular scholars would now seem to be guessing an earlier date.'

'An earlier date,' Patty repeated, thinking, 'Get to the point', but realizing how impossible it was to speed up her mother when she was imparting information.

Her mother poured the water into the tea pot and stirred. 'George Smith. British Museum, 1872,' she said, 'he's your man. He deciphered the clay tablets at Nineveh.'

'Nineveh?'

'Yes, I believe that's how it's pronounced . . . nin eh ver.'

'Get to the point, mother,' Patty said in exasperation.

'The Epic of Gilgamesh – that's the point. An earlier scripture found among the Assyrians. That had a Great Flood in it too. If I were a secular scholar, which of course I'm not, I would tend to believe that the biblical Flood was somehow an echo of the Mesopotamian one. The Israelites were captive in Babylon around the time that Genesis was written.'

'Where's that?'

'Right at the heart of Mesopotamia.' Her mother shrugged. 'Too much of a coincidence to ignore, I suppose.'

'And does the Epic of Gilgamesh give a date for the Flood?'

'Not exactly. But it gives a list of kings from the Flood onwards. Assuming average life span, their flood was about 5,500 BC.'

Patty breathed out so hard she thought her body might collapse from the lack of air. Seven and a half thousand years ago, a bull's-eye on Buckley's model.

E-mail to: PPP
From: Weather Station Antarctica
  Thanks for your comments. I agree it's too early to get worried, but I think the evidence is that the progression of these indicators is no longer simply linear.
  I hear what you say about the ozone results from the northern

hemisphere and I agree the Arctic figures aren't showing anything like we're getting down here, but I don't think that in itself makes the data suspect. I know there are potential pitfalls in the experimental techniques, but Ozzie Jack knows his stuff.

On a separate subject, there's some real funny weather fronts starting to form in the eastern Pacific. Have you seen any more from the Galapogos? Tell me if you think this is what I think it is.

Yours,

Weatherjunkie.

P.S. We just got the latest baseball tape. Your beloved Twins aren't doing so good, are they?

XVII

When she started looking, all she needed to confirm the theory fell in place. She kicked herself for not looking at the issues this way before.

Most of the information about past climates comes from ice-core data. What that involves is drilling a very long, deep hole into the ice close to one of the poles.

Analysis, very careful analysis that Patty knew had to be painstaking, had taken our knowledge of climate and atmospheric conditions back 250,000 years, through two ice ages and three intervening warm inter-glacials. The ice layers grow like rings in a tree. The deeper you go, the more you are looking into history. The balance between the oxygen 16 and oxygen 18 isotopes in the ice gives you an indication, albeit indirectly, of the temperature when the ice was formed. So, hey presto, you have a recording of the historical climate of the world.

Or do you?

That was the question Patty had asked herself. Is that what you get? Look at the latitude at which the experiments were conducted.

The so-called 'Thule' core was drilled into the ice-sheet near Thule in north-west Greenland between 1963 and 1966. The 'Byrd' core was drilled in west Antarctica in 1968. The Soviets drilled 6,500 feet into the Vostok ice in the early eighties. That was in east Antarctica. Probably the most famous example is GRIP, the Greenland Ice Core Project. Completed in 1992 under the aegis of the European Science Foundation, a 10,000 foot core was drilled in Greenland at a latitude of 72° North.

What you were measuring was the climate as witnessed close to one of the poles. And what Buckley was saying was that it was possible to get huge quantum shifts in the climate within bands around the centre of the Earth, *near or below the equator*, which had hardly any effect anywhere else: Pfister's 'Quantum Theory of Climatic States'.

Patty went to her bookshelves, re-sorted by her mother after the break-in, and started leafing back through journals and anthologies of academic papers. She went through the piles of the better journals, through the less well-respected, back to the crackpot theory publishers who put into print that which the academic establishment refused to accept.

The process took hours.

But there it was: the nagging thought that had been at the back of her mind became manifest. In 1993 a scientist, Lui Xi, had published the results of his work on rock deposits in China. His technique was not new. He measured the rate of deposition versus time using magnetic susceptibility.

The technique works like this: small magnetic bits get deposited and absorbed into the rock. The orientation of their internal magnets tells you about the magnetic field at the time. Because you know about the history of the Earth's magnetic field, you know when the rock was deposited.

Only there was something wrong with Xi's results. After the end of the last ice age, about eight thousand years ago, the rate of deposition went nuts. It went screaming upwards, suggesting that the climate had suddenly become hot and arid, then screaming back down. There was a flip-flop of temperature. Xi had looked at his results and found they didn't correlate with anyone else's. He questioned his own technique, wondered if the layers of rock he was looking at might have been compromised in some way over the years.

But what Patty looked at, what Patty knew was important, was that Xi's results came from the same narrow band of the Earth in which Buckley's model had predicted the quantum shift 7,500 years ago. Also in that band was Mesopotamia.

The date, she thought, was close enough. Close enough to explain the flood described in the Gilgamesh text and its echo in Genesis. Close enough to match the fluctuation in Buckley's results.

So . . . There was no flaw in the model.

Who knows what provided the 'natural climatic event' back then? Perhaps it was God's hand. Perhaps it was God's hand that had done the same job as 20 billion tons of annual carbon emissions and a strange wind called El Niño were about to do now. As far as she could see, the only difference with Buckley's present prediction was that the shift was hitting the southern hemisphere not the northern.

There was no flaw in the model. She found herself repeating that out loud. She found herself drowning in the consequences, in that fax which she had first seen in Pielot's office.

'Is that what you were trying to tell us, Ray?' she asked aloud, as if to a ghost in the room. 'Is this another biblical Flood?'

Mike Plummer came down the moving walkway into the shopping mall. A huge indoor waterfall was spewing water in artistic arcs over a man-made rock formation. This centre-piece was probably chic when it was built, but now there was flaky sediment on the rocks and the pool at the bottom was full of candy bar wrappers. Such is modern America, he thought, with its predilections for consumption and waste. But who are we to argue? We but serve.

He glanced around suspiciously, checking, double-checking.

She was sitting at a café table, a café that would have been outdoors if it hadn't been for the glass roof fifty feet above them. She was surrounded by the lunchtime crowd, shopping-laden punters. Good, he thought, the more public the place, the more they blended into the obscurity of the masses.

He sat down and slapped a newspaper on the desk under her nose. 'Congratulations,' he said. The headline announced, 'Exclusive: Masoni implicated in charity scam.'

She looked at it as if she had already read its contents and was reminding herself. There was a flicker of satisfaction in her glance.

'So I'm off the case?' she asked, leaning back with her coffee in her hand.

'Pretty much. Though your friend Collins left a few loose ends.'

'He did an OK job. So, he's not a professional. He was all I had at short notice.'

'He was supposed to fix the data so it pointed at Masoni. How long do you think this little scam story's going to run if they find the right files at BBS?' Plummer's face twitched. 'I'm not satisfied. There's also this matter of the results file that's kicking around.'

'I sent a doctored one to BBS,' she said. 'The only other copy was in that Patty Drake's house. Robbie Collins dealt with that before his demise. I dealt with all the copies left in the SSEO.'

'Not enough,' Plummer said. 'I want to be 110 per cent sure this thing dies. We should have taken out all the copies of the results file the moment Buckley bought it.'

'Maybe, but the lack of a model made them hollow anyway. I didn't realize the dashing Frenchman was going to be such a prick.'

'Water under the bridge,' Plummer said. He hunched his shoulders and moved a little closer to the table. 'What about BBS?'

'All they've got is corrupted files.'

'They could get them straightened. We hear this Thomas guy still has his troops working on the problem.'

'Fuck, Mike, what do you want me to do? Just come out and say it.'

'I want you to go and finish it.'

'Back to England? Can't you send someone?'

'Call it a technicality. The Brits have already given permission for you to operate over there.'

'Permission?'

'Yeah, you think the President authorized this without them knowing. Hell, no. This is Special Relationship stuff.'

She sighed, but she didn't say anything.

Plummer looked her straight in the eye. 'Are you feeling a little jaded, honey? Too much action?'

'I did your fucking undercover work here, didn't I?'

'Just a little joke.' Plummer held up his hands.

'Fourteen kills in five years, if you want to know,' she hissed in a shouted whisper. 'And that's not counting the plane, OK?'

'OK. But listen, we're trying to keep this real close. Clearance or not, this thing's like an infectious disease, the longer it goes unchecked, the more people who know, the more wastage there's going to have to be. You understand me?'

'Yeah, Mike, loud and clear.'

'I guess there's not more than a dozen people who know . . . and that's a global number. Most of them are so heavily cleared, they know the launch codes to the nukes, if you get my drift.'

'OK, you don't have to elaborate.'

Plummer drew back, satisfied with her assurances. 'OK, then.'

'OK. I'll take care of it myself. Can I have access to the new incendiaries?'

'What you gonna do? Smoke them out?'

'Something like that,' she said.

XVIII

Connor Giles sat at his computer, furrowing his brow. Seven p.m. had passed and he'd been here since six this morning after only three hours' sleep. The usual debris of the day – crisp packets and chocolate-bar wrappers – were scattered around his office, but the only drug he'd been tempted to put in his system was caffeine.

He reached over and found the telephone under a pile of papers and rang several numbers until he got a reply.

'Who's that?' he said, when the last of them finally answered. 'Alex, is that you?'

'Yeah, it's me.' Alexandra's voice came back up the line. 'I'm packing.'

'Packing?'

'I've decided to leave BBS. I've got the bike fixed. I'm just going to take off. After all that's happened . . .'

Connor hesitated. 'I could do with help here,' he said suddenly. 'I've got to a point where I need two pairs of hands.'

'I thought computers were supposed to remove that kind of problem. Aren't you supposed to be good at software? Besides . . .'

'Come on, I need you now. This isn't programming; this is surgery.'

'All right.'

He heard the phone click dead. A few moments later Alexandra appeared in his office, walking with a limp. She was wearing a baggy jumper and distressed jeans. Her hair was loose and she had hardly any make-up on. Even for Alexandra, this was scruffy.

'What're you trying to do?' she asked, looking over his shoulder.

'Hacking,' he said. He fell silent, thinking. His lips moved as he thought through his options.

'I see you haven't fixed your guitar,' Alexandra said.

'No.'

'Why not?'

'That,' said Connor, pointing at the damage, 'was a sacrifice to your father's work. I won't replace it until we've recovered his model. All of it . . . Right now, I could be playing my old school recorder for ever.'

Alexandra hitched herself up on to the desk. 'You liked him, didn't you?' she asked.

'Yeah, I liked him.'

He shrugged his shoulders and tried to look sympathetic, but knew he couldn't help her. He opened his desk drawer and took out a 3.5-inch disk. It came attached to the remains of a chocolate bar. He divided them neatly, smiling when he finally freed them without irreparable damage to either object.

'Want a piece of Yorkie?' he asked. He broke two mangled blocks off the bar.

Alexandra paused for a moment, then reached out and took them. She handled the ration as if it were a challenge. 'I know you think I'm . . .' she began.

'No, I never . . .' he protested.

'Let me finish. Everyone thinks I'm only here because I'm Daddy's girl. Well, I'm not going to be any more.'

He waited for her to look at him, thinking about the afternoon they had spent at the river, and whether that had meant anything lasting. When she finally looked at him, he said, 'I never thought that. Certainly not when you threw that Harley down the road.' He hesitated. 'You shouldn't go. You belong here,' he added.

'Is that right?'

He nodded. 'You're brave and you're smart.'

'What? "Her-father's-daughter" kind of smart?'

'No . . . You're very much your own kind of smart.'

Alexandra laughed suddenly. She tossed her hair back with her hand. 'You're OK, Connor. Fucking weird, but OK.'

Connor smiled and returned to tapping keys at breakneck speed. He typed in a set of commands, then struck the 'Enter' key with an ostentatious flourish. The hard drive whirred and he sat back to wait. 'I could use some sleep,' he said, yawning widely.

'Why don't you give it up and come back tomorrow?' she asked. 'You'll burn yourself out. Take me for a drink or something. Maybe back to my place.'

'Can't do that,' he said, 'it's now or never.'

'What do you mean, now or never?'

'Watson phoned from Germany. He said he's coming back with a new project for me next week.' He felt suddenly embarrassed. 'Another promotion,' he added. 'He suggested I spent my time having a final try at recovering your father's work.'

'*He* suggested that?'

'Yeah . . . He's not the enemy, you know? Hit "Control" and "C" on that machine over there, will you?'

'When?'

'About . . . Now . . . Fuck!'

'Still no good?'

'No, no good, but I've just realized something.' He tapped furiously for a few seconds. The screen produced a menu, the file structure of Ray Buckley's personal directory.

'I can't read any of these files,' he said, 'but we already have copies of them from other places anyway. It's this one . . .' He pointed. 'This holds the key. All the data that controls the model. But I've just noticed something.'

He pushed the 'Print Screen' button and the laser printer in the corner behind them began to respond. She put her hands on his shoulder and leaned over him towards the screen to see what he was about to print.

'Fuck,' she said as she saw what he was pointing to. Her version of the word was more rounded than his; the vowel had a throatier sound.

'I don't know how I missed it before.'

In the distance the sunset over Buckley's Island was like a picture postcard. Blood and purple and the twinkling of light from the glass dome at the top.

As she drove towards it, Patty couldn't really understand why she was doing this. She was carrying the evening paper with its page-four echo of the Masoni scandal in the US. BBS's name was there in the small print. If that was why she was coming here, she still couldn't imagine what she was going to say to Watson.

Perhaps she thought he would help her. More likely, she wanted to warn him, or find out if he had seen the danger for himself. Things were vague in her mind. She was screwed up – the separation, André's death, the break-in, the Flood.

She pulled up at the security gate, next to the stone bridge that linked Buckley's Island. There was no one – not even a protestor – in sight. She leaned out of her car window and pressed the button on the intercom panel next to the barrier. 'Ring for attention when gatehouse unoccupied,' it said.

'I've come to see Watson Thomas,' she told the voice that answered.

'Can't you find security?'

'I don't see anyone.'

Mumbled in the background, Patty heard some comment about reporters.

'He's not in and, anyway, it's after seven, our offices are closed,' the voice said at last.

Patty could see a dozen cars in the car park beyond the barrier, so she knew that 'after hours' wasn't really an issue. Like all the companies Watson had ever been involved in, they didn't seem to know when the working day started or ended.

'This is his wife,' she said testily.

The revelation drew a long silence from the other end of the phone.

'All right . . . I suppose you'd better come up to reception. I'll see for you,' the voice said begrudgingly. The barrier in front of her rose slowly. She drove through. A yellow delivery van followed her before the barrier came down, the driver waving a thank you which Patty just caught in the rear-view mirror.

Three minutes later, someone came down to reception to greet her. But it wasn't Watson; it was Montgomery Radford.

He was wearing a jacket like a bespangled picnic blanket, as short, as fat and as bald as Patty remembered him. He looked troubled, but smiled mechanically.

'Patty,' he said, offering his hand.

She shook it, suddenly feeling cold and hard. Monty had that effect on her. He turned her into a bitch, someone she liked even less than the normal neurotic Patty.

'Where's Watson?' she asked.

'In Germany, I'm afraid. Not that I'm unhappy to see you, but why didn't you tell us you were coming?'

'I need to see him . . .' She stopped herself. 'No, it doesn't matter. I'll . . . er . . . call him when he gets back. Tell him I was here, will you?' She was turning to go, a sudden pathetic panic gripping at her.

'Patty,' Monty said gently. 'You've driven a long way. Why don't you come and have a coffee at least?'

'No, that's all right. I . . .'

'Please . . .'

Trying not to ask herself too many questions, she followed him through the building, up flights of stairs until they reached the glass dome she had seen silhouetted against the sunset a few minutes earlier. The sun was almost gone now. Small flecks of remnant light caught ripples in the water's surface.

119

'Quite a view,' she said, gazing across the lake. Her words were abstracted, random, as she tried to deal with her host, a man who had, up until now, seemed to go out of his way to annoy her.

'Ray Buckley's Thinking Sanctuary,' Monty said. 'Peace and tranquillity.' He poured cups of coffee from a vacuum jug. Placing one on the arm of a chair, he beckoned her to sit down.

'You want anything in it? I could make it Irish,' he offered.

'No, that's OK. I have to drive.'

'So, you came to talk to Watson . . . About time.' He smiled.

'It's not like that. I actually came to talk about work. About Ray Buckley.' She handed over her copy of the newspaper, the Masoni story uppermost. She leaned back, crossing her legs awkwardly. As soon as she'd done it, she realized how defensive the movement must have seemed.

Monty read the column and nodded. 'You knew Buckley?' he asked.

'My boss had the results of his work.'

'That would be Monsieur Pielot.'

She tried to loosen her posture so she wouldn't appear so ill at ease. 'Yes,' she said, not quite managing the trick.

'They're both dead, then.'

Monty stating the obvious – she wondered if it was deliberate. She nodded, biting her lip at the same time. 'You know about this tangle?' She pointed to the paper.

'I know something about the fraud at our end of it.'

'Is it true?'

He smiled. 'As far as I know, it's accurate. I'm telling you, you understand, because I think Watson would tell you. We found false invoices going between the SSEO and BBS. A man called Bob Collins was involved. He's dead.'

'But you don't actually know it was Uli Masoni at the BBS end?'

'That's something that the American authorities have dug up, not us. But I don't have any evidence that suggests it wasn't Masoni.'

'I see,' she said. 'And is that how much effort you've put into it?'

Monty sighed as if he'd heard this line a hundred times. Patty realized he would have had the same kind of grilling from a dozen journalists in the last day. He seemed a vaguely pathetic figure now, stranded like a whale in the armchair across from hers. 'We're just trying to save a company, Patty. There are people employed here,' he pleaded.

'You sound like Watson.' She stared at him.

'Funnily enough, that's not the way Watson sounds on this issue any more. He's for Masoni, if you want to know.'

120

She hesitated a moment. Then she said, 'I've seen the results, Monty. I've done the comparisons. The model works, and . . .'

'The model worked,' he corrected. 'BBS wasn't lying, Patty. And God knows, Watson's had our best people on it. Whatever it might have been, we can't recover Buckley's work. The viruses destroyed it. We have 93 per cent of a model, fourteen files of a fifteen file set. Unfortunately, the last one had all the important information in it.'

'Then they've won . . . Whoever they are.'

He moved as if he was about to reach out to her, but something prevented him.

'Someone broke into my house the other night,' she said. 'I think my life may be in danger. I think we may all be in danger – you, me, Watson, anyone who's had anything to do with that model. Hell, if the model's right, a handful of people is peanuts.' She broke off and shuffled in her chair. 'What I don't understand is, if this thing is real, why would anyone want to suppress it? It makes no sense to me.'

Monty looked out over the water. He pulled his lips back, baring his teeth. 'It sets one thinking,' he said, removing anything personal from the sentence, 'hypothetically, of course – I'm not subscribing to the Buckley myth.' He smiled and drank his coffee slowly. He swallowed and brushed the wetness from his mouth with the back of his hand.

'I think I ought to tell you something,' he said. He turned to look straight at her, the first time he'd looked her full in the face. 'We've never got on, have we, you and I? But I'm going to tell you anyway. He loves you. He still loves you . . .'

'Why are you telling me this? Is this your idea of a joke?'

Monty held his chin with his hand, finger and thumb sliding slowly forward. He said, 'It's our moments of irrationality that define us, Patty. There's no character in logic.'

'What the hell does that mean? Riddles always were your hobby.'

'It means, perhaps if you understood why you've come running to Watson, you'd understand a whole lot about what you really want.'

'You just don't get it, do you?' she said. 'This isn't about Watson.' She felt an anger rising. It was a wave. It was a tidal wave.

She raised herself from the chair, leaned across the coffee table that separated them.

'Don't you understand?' she said, volume increasing towards a shout. 'Doesn't anyone want to listen? Half the world is going to die!' She smashed her clenched fist on to the table, scattering the cups and saucers and the dregs of the coffee. 'We are going to have A GODDAM FLOOD!'

Connor had kissed her and they were leaving.

She had said, 'Not here. We can't do it here. People are around still. God, now I've got you going, I can't get you stopped.' She had pushed his hand away from her breast.

The warmth of her flesh was still in his hand; he had half an erection.

They were walking quickly along the corridor towards the reception area, heading for her newly repaired motorbike and her bed, when the explosion happened.

It wasn't a loud blast, but the shock of it knocked them backwards. A sheet of flame lashed down the corridor like an orange tidal wave.

He tackled her and pushed her through a doorway into an unoccupied office.

The fire alarms kicked in. Everything suddenly turned to chaos.

Monty had appointed an escort to take Patty back to reception, a thin middle-aged woman whom Patty recognized as the uncooperative receptionist as soon as she spoke.

With this escort out front, Patty was on the stairs between the first and second floors when the building seemed to shake violently. Immediately Patty thought she could smell smoke. A second later, the deafening scream of the fire alarm started.

The corridor outside was on fire. Heat and smoke were leaking into the room and flames were licking in through the doorway.

Alexandra rolled over and got up in one movement. She kicked the door shut.

Connor coughed, tried to raise himself into a sitting position. His legs were splayed inelegantly on the floor and they didn't seem to obey his commands and his head felt numb and woozy. 'Fuck,' he said aloud, the word muffled as if by cotton wool in his mouth.

'Get up,' Alexandra shouted and pointed. 'Out of the window. Come on.'

'I can't ... I ... must've hit my head.' He could see the smoke leaking under the door. What is it they say about fires? You don't burn, you just get overcome. He tried once again to rise, but his head hurt, he had lost his glasses and his legs buckled beneath him like a newborn calf.

He saw a blurry Alexandra leap on to the desk by the window, landing astride a 15-inch monitor and the computer base unit it sat on. She leaned down, picked up the monitor and wrenched it up under her chin. The power lead came away, but the monitor was still attached by its input cable.

'What're y'doing?' he tried to ask.

She managed to release four feet of the cable from the tangle behind the computer. Then she threw the monitor forward, pushing with both hands as if fending a medicine ball off her chest. The monitor smashed through the window, falling on the outside until it ran out of lead.

Monitor and base unit dangled now on either side of the windowsill.

'Come on,' she yelled, beckoning him, 'we've got no time.'

'I can't . . . can't move.'

She jumped down, grabbed him under the arms and hauled him to his feet. In his daze, he couldn't work out how she could be so strong. There was blood flowing over the back of her hands. His or hers, he couldn't tell.

'I love you,' she shouted in his ear, 'I'm not about to leave you.' She dragged him across the room, got him up on the desk.

He got the vague impression of the door blackening, flames bursting across the carpet where he had been lying a moment before. She had taken off a boot and was using it to hammer at the broken glass.

'Jump,' she said.

'What?' he asked.

'We're on the ground floor, stupid!'

Patty's escort screamed and ran in the other direction, going back up into the building.

Patty shouted after her, but the woman was in shock and running. The fumes were coming up fast, and there was siren-noise all around.

Patty couldn't figure which direction to go. Down? Not possible. Up, then? How did you get out at the top of a building if you couldn't fly?

Nevertheless the rising heat drove her up the stairwell, following the screaming woman. She could feel her lungs filling up. She could smell that choking plastic smell as acrid fumes rolled towards her on the waves of heat.

She found herself in a corridor on the second floor, no sign of the woman now, nothing she recognized, though this must have been the corridor she had walked along quite casually a few moments before.

Fire exit?

A light-headed thought. There must be a fire exit, another set of stairs. There was a sign at the other end of the corridor, like a dreamscape from a psychedelic movie. She followed, not knowing if it was real. Her eyes were sheeny with water.

Random thoughts from her life flashed before her. That was a bad omen!

An arrow guided her around the building into its farthest corner. She saw another figure moving in the same direction, but she couldn't focus on it. She was falling to her knees, 20 feet short of the door marked 'exit'.

Suddenly, the other figure smashed through the door, breaking the glass seal of its lock.

Patty felt the rush of cool, unpolluted air. The tightness of her nose and lungs released all of a sudden. On simple instinct, she scrambled to her feet.

She was on the balcony of an iron staircase now.

She was outside. She could feel the night air. The other woman, her escort, the figure in the smoke, was leaning over the rail, coughing and retching into the night.

They were counting numbers by the security gate when the first fire engine arrived. Nine, ten, eleven of them. Most were on their feet, except for a young woman attending a male colleague – her boyfriend by the body language – who was propped against a post. She had one arm around him, the other was wrapped loosely in a bloody tourniquet. She was crying and he was woozily pointing to the bleeding of her arm.

In the middle of the group, the company fire marshal was trying to compile a list, but he was an amateur and the job was impossible. After eight o'clock at night, who knew who was actually in the building?

'Check around,' the fire marshal said, terror thinly disguised in his voice, 'anyone else you know of? Is everyone here?'

Patty had emerged on the far side of the building and circled around trying to avoid potholes and the slippery slope of the lake's bank. She was still shepherding her saviour who was somewhat weakened after emptying her stomach into the grass. Patty kept checking the woman's eyes, trying to remember her long outdated first-aid training.

'Who are you?' the fire marshal asked, as they approached, alarmed to see someone not on his list.

'A visitor,' said Patty.

'What's the bloody point of having a visitor's book if no one signs it?' He brandished a leather-bound book.

Patty shrugged.

'Well, I think everybody's out anyway,' he said.

Patty looked around, counting the people. She saw the young man trying to control the bleeding on his girlfriend's arm. Doing it all wrong, she thought. She started towards them, meaning to help.

Then, suddenly, she said, 'Where the hell is Monty?'

She stopped and turned to the building.

The stone skeleton looked black in the night. But within the bone of its walls, the angry light of the flames lashed at the insides of various windows. Several of these had already burst under the pressure and black fumes charred the outside. Another window on the second floor popped as Patty watched. Its shattered glass showered out, caught for a moment like confetti in the triumphant burst of firelight that followed it. New oxygen finding its mark.

'Oh, God,' she muttered to herself. She could feel the heat on her face and she couldn't move.

The surrounding lake caught the glow of fire. Shimmers and haze and the flickered orange image of the burning shell on the water. A picture, she thought, this should be a picture. It shouldn't be real.

Then she saw Montgomery Radford. He was standing in the glass dome of the Thinking Sanctuary at the top of the building, where Patty had been only minutes before. He was only an outline figure in the glow, but it didn't matter; you couldn't mistake Monty's figure.

He moved with a strange inevitability. First to the right, then back to the left. It seemed he was trying to find a way out. Hopelessly, in a glass prison with only one exit. A burning exit.

Patty tasted the fumes once again, knowing this was the taste now in Monty's mouth. Her nose tightened, reliving that poisonous smell.

To the right and back to the left he went. The scream of fire-engine sirens behind.

If they turned off the sound, this could be a picture, she thought again.

To the right and – slower now – back to the left.

A panel of glass exploded from the dome. Then the following fireball lit it up like a beacon on top of a strangely overfed lighthouse. When it faded, the overfed lighthouse keeper was gone.

She stood there, searching the leaping flames, looking for him to reappear. He did not.

At last, she shut her eyes and let her mind do the searching. But it was not Monty's face that came to her, but the half-glimpsed uncertain face of a van driver.

It seemed now that she had seen it before . . . at a funeral and in a room in a French hotel . . .

Caroline Sharpe . . .

XIX

Watson Thomas pulled up at the house he had lived in for seven years. Patty saw him through her window and thought of the guilty moment when she had last looked out at his car.

He switched off the engine and sat by the kerb for a long time before he got out. When he rang the bell, she greeted him with a painful smile.

He came into the lounge and sat on the sofa, his eyes grazing over the changes in the room. 'I came to see if you're all right,' he said as if he were giving some sort of title to his visit.

'You still have it with sugar?' she asked, delivering tea in a Cadbury's Dairy Milk mug.

'Thanks,' he said.

'I put two in.' She smiled, trying to make the best of it. He had called unannounced, and she was embarrassed to be found in sweat pants and an old jumper.

'Thanks,' he said again. He was holding his mug of tea in both hands, looking around for a place to put it down. 'I see you got rid of the coffee table.'

'Yeah.' She searched for a plausible reason without success. She sank into an armchair and curled her legs under her, acutely aware that this was another of those pieces of furniture damaged since their break-up.

At first sight, he had not changed. She could almost see the tension that kept him upright.

'The funeral's next Wednesday,' he said suddenly.

'I'm sorry.'

There was a pause.

'What will you do now?' she asked.

'I thought I could save the company . . . Maybe that was me, but

126

that's what I thought before the fire. Not any more. I guess we'll call in the receiver. With the insurance, there'll be liquid funds.'

'The building's ruined?'

'It looks worse every time I see it. We can't hold the team together while we rebuild and we can't complete what work we had. That's what a firebomb does for you.'

Watson's face was black and drawn and she realized how much more than just a firebomb this was to him. She uncurled her legs and stretched them out over the edge of the seat cushion. 'I never could sit that way without getting pins and needles,' she said.

She was trying to be casual, but the truth was she could no longer identify the feelings, no longer control them. She knew Watson had lost his only friend. She wanted to reach out to him. But that was no longer her right.

'Would you . . .?'

'No,' he said, then laughed because he had answered before she had asked the question.

'I was going to say, would you like to stay for dinner? Nothing special. I've got supermarket lasagne and a bottle of wine.'

He thought about it and then agreed.

Alone in the kitchen – warming the oven, unpeeling the lid from the lasagne package – gave her time to think, to regroup.

It's strange the way you get to the point where, even if you've had so many good times together, you still can't find words.

She had betrayed him, but he had betrayed her with negligence, and their relationship had been struck dumb. Who knows who was really to blame? She knew only that he felt like a dagger in her chest. Perhaps she should admit that meant she still loved him. Is that what it really meant? The time when that might have been enough had passed.

She came back from the kitchen with a bottle of wine, two glasses and a corkscrew. She handed him the bottle and the corkscrew.

'The packet says thirty-five minutes for the lasagne. Is that OK?'

He smiled. 'I've got no factory to go back to,' he said. He started peeling the metal capping off the bottle to reveal the cork.

'Perhaps that's the answer,' she said. 'I should have burnt down your factory years ago.'

She started backwards as soon as she'd said it. What a sick piece of humour! He stared at her for a moment. Then he laughed. Thank God, he laughed.

He uncorked the wine and poured it. She felt better now, more in control. He announced a toast to absent friends. That was nice. Only when she picked up her wine glass for the first sip did she notice how much her hand shook. She had to grab her wrist quickly with her free hand.

He couldn't help but notice. 'It's not easy this, is it?' he said.

She laughed uneasily. 'When I saw you, I nearly slammed the door,' she admitted.

'But you came to see me at BBS.'

'I didn't know what I was going to say then either.'

'And yet you came . . .'

She lifted her drink again, hand still shaking. The smell of the grape and the dry, butter taste of Chablis reached her as she sipped the wine. 'We had some good years. It wasn't all bad. We were great before it all went wrong.'

'You never took responsibility,' he said very slowly, as if it was an effort. She knew he was venturing into ground that hurt him.

'Neither of us did,' she said. 'Do you believe I wrecked it . . . on my own?'

Watson hesitated. He hid his mouth behind his glass. 'No,' he admitted. 'I wanted to think so, but . . . No, it wasn't you.'

'Thank you,' she said. She added, 'You never asked who he was.'

'No, I didn't.'

She gazed at him. It seemed he wasn't going to say anything more, but she kept gazing at him until he said, 'I guess I always knew it was about you and me.'

'It was André,' she said.

She turned away, not wanting to see Watson's face. This part of her past was her own private hell. She didn't want forgiveness. She didn't think she deserved it and she knew it wouldn't feel real. She said, 'I got caught deliberately.'

'What do you mean?'

'I don't know. I guess it means I wanted you to know . . . how unhappy I was.'

'So you wanted to show me that by getting caught?'

'No,' she said, 'I wanted to show you I still existed.'

He was silent for a moment and she resisted looking back at him.

He said, 'I sold WT Gaming to try to put that right, but I guess we were already screwed up by then . . .' His voice trailed off, as if worn through, and this time she did look back. He was still staring into his wine.

It seemed like he would never look up again and she felt like she'd made a great mistake. With nothing better to say, she said, 'I'm glad you came anyway.'

'Patty, I have a real problem with this whole thing,' he said suddenly. 'If you knew the world was heading for disaster, you'd try to stop it, right? I mean, how shortsighted can anyone be?'

Of course, this was *the* question. She had been asking it in her head without quite putting it into these words. She sat silent for a moment, eyes pressed closed, almost as if she was holding something in. But then it started to come out. It started like a dam crumbling, a few words, and then a torrent.

She told him she had seen the results file and how she interpreted its contents. She told him about the flaw in the model that wasn't a flaw, how she thought Pielot had also been killed. She said, 'This thing is so big. It's so *big* I don't know what I'm doing in the middle of it, or if there's a way out. Yet how can we ignore it if we know Buckley was right?'

'But the model's gone,' he said. 'You've got nothing . . . nothing that separates you from the cranks who say the world will end tomorrow, or the next time the numerals in the date add up to 42.'

'Don't you think I know that?' she snapped. Then more calmly, she added, 'I'm not so stupid that I think I can stand up and announce the second coming of Noah's Flood without ending up in a strait-jacket. Or more likely with a bullet through my head.' She stopped. She looked at the floor and then back at Watson. 'So is that it? Do we just leave it at that?'

Watson sighed and she saw his body sink in the chair as if it had suddenly found a pocket of excess gravity. 'What do you think of Uli Masoni?' he asked.

'Impressive' she said.

'Impressive,' he repeated.

He lapsed into silence. She crossed the room and held him. Just held him.

X X

Cash Buemann surveyed the scene on Buckley's island. Only a few twisted beams stood more than a couple of feet off the ground and everything was black and tangled and looked like someone had thrown down a blanket of soot. Sporadically, small plumes of smoke rose from trapped embers, still glowing below the surface.

Cash tipped his trademark baseball cap back and wiped the sweat from his scarred brow. 'It's not going to be easy to pick my 30 per cent out of this.'

Watson Thomas stood a few feet away, comparing Cash's casual T-shirt and jeans to his own business suit. All in all, Cash had the better dress sense here: it was a baking hot day and they were wading knee-deep in the debris.

'I'm sure I've seen a worse mess than this, though I'm sure I can't say quite when,' Cash added, his twanging accent working hard to convey a morsel of hope. 'Maybe the last time I saw a poison oil well go up. Firebomb, you reckon?'

'That's the police line. A sophisticated incendiary as used by up-market terrorist groups.'

'Shit,' he said again, shaking his head. 'Goddam, I wish I'd known what the hell was really going on when Ray was alive.' He picked his way around some battered metalwork that twisted up from the earth like avant-garde sculptures. He walked back towards his car, parked by the security gate – the only structure still standing on Buckley's island. He stooped and leaned on the BMW's bonnet and cast his eyes out over the water.

'How much did you know, Cash?'

The Texan turned his head and looked straight at Watson. 'I was wondering when we were coming to that.'

'I'm sorry,' Watson said instinctively.

'Don't be. I realize the position I'm in is kind of strange. Being chairman of a company trying to prove global warming gives me a little conflict of interest – that's what you British would call it. Everybody figures I'd want to hush up the results if they were bad. And there's all kinds of rumours floating around that they were . . . Very bad indeed, in fact. Isn't that it?'

Watson nodded, unable to think of anything more subtle.

Cash said, 'Monty never trusted me, right? I could tell.' He took off his hat and straightened the few wisps of hair that grew amongst the scar tissue.

'I watched how my daddy did business for twenty-five years, Watson. He was a hard man; some would say a dishonest one. And I learned all his tricks. I practised them and I perfected them.' He looked across at the ruin of the building. '30 per cent of what lies on that ground was mine.'

Cash stopped and half a minute passed before he spoke again.

'You see my face? I'm doing a hundred miles an hour when I hit a puddle I didn't know was there. 'Fore I know it, I've snapped sideways, hit a fence, and I'm rolling over and over and all I can see is bits and God knows what flying off the car. Then I'm hanging upside down in flames. In agony. I'm dangling in a fire, Watson. I think I'm about to die and then . . .

'Burnt lungs and broken ribs and a list of other broken bones I don't care to remember. It kind of gives you a different perspective on life, don't you think? Some passer-by dragged me out and gave me mouth-to-mouth. My heart stopped twice on the way to the hospital.' He looked straight at Watson. 'You think I give a shit about money? In truth, I never had to give a shit about it, but it takes something like that to give you perspective. I've got perspective, Watson. I could win and lose millions and burn down BBS every day for a week – it wouldn't make a hole in my lifestyle.'

Watson felt like backing away, but he stood his ground. He didn't say anything; he just kept staring back at Cash as if he wanted more.

Cash gave it. He said, 'You want to know the reason I invested in BBS all those years ago? Because twenty years ago Ray Buckley showed me the future and it was about computers. Nine months ago he told me his work was showing absolutely no link between carbon emissions and global warming. He said he wasn't sure yet, but he thought the work everyone was doing on sunspots would eventually show that they were the cause of the temperature rise. They were cyclical, he said, so it would all go away pretty fast.'

'He told you that?'

'Yes, he did.'

'Do you think he was telling the truth?'

Cash thought for a moment. 'I don't know any more. I believed he was at the time. But maybe he thought I was going to stop him. He certainly didn't tell me how much company money he was pouring into the model. In hindsight . . . I guess the company was already leaking at the seams by then. Maybe he figured he needed to give me good news. And maybe he figured telling me that kind of result was what I wanted to hear. I just can't say . . . You know, he was brilliant to the end, just not really that sane about it.'

Cash brushed a hand across his cheek and Watson thought he had seen a tear there.

Watson knew then it was the truth. Monty had been wrong.

'I guess we have to wind up the company now,' Cash said, switching back to business.

Watson nodded. 'I've already picked a receiver. We'll go into liquidation voluntarily. We have a better chance of getting your money back that way. I'll resign, of course.'

'That won't be necessary.'

'Receivers don't like ex-MDs hanging around. They cost money and they clutter up the place. It's best this way.'

Cash didn't answer. He was staring into space. He stayed like that and Watson stayed with him. They both stared, both offering silent prayers to whatever they believed in.

After a while their stillness was interrupted by the rattle of a badly silenced engine. In the distance a battered motorbike was coming along the thin road that led to Buckley's Island. Cash turned to look at it.

'Friend of yours?' he asked.

Watson squinted. 'Alexandra Buckley,' he said.

The bike stopped some way off, its rider looking towards them as if considering options. Eventually, they heard the throttle open and the bike wheel-spun its way forward.

Alexandra pulled it up between Watson's Jaguar and Cash's M-series BMW. She got off and manoeuvred it on to its stand and walked over to them, pausing to remove her helmet and admire the custom paint-job on the BMW.

'Nice car,' she said, gesturing towards the car with an arm that was heavily bandaged from wrist to elbow.

'Thank you,' Cash twanged. He seemed faintly embarrassed.

Watson noticed him nervously replace the baseball cap on his head.

With it, his figure seemed to stand more erect and much of his composure and smiling Texan charm returned.

Cash offered his hand. 'We've met. But a long time ago. You probably don't remember; you were yea high at the time,' he told her. 'I hear you've been in the hospital.'

'They let me out this morning. Twenty-five stitches. I lost a lot of blood.' She hesitated as if she had reminded herself of something. 'I guess I was lucky,' she concluded.

Cash said, 'I'm real sorry about your father.'

She shrugged as if shrugging off an unwanted sympathy. 'I know you can't put it back together . . . my father's empire.' She looked out over the island. 'I've come to terms with that. But for some reason, I have to come out to look at it. It's as if I've missed something I should have realized.'

She started walking towards the ruins. Watson expected Cash to say something, but he didn't; he watched her go.

They stood there, the silence relieved only by a whistling of the wind through the twisted piles of metal.

'I feel like I've let them down,' Watson said in a sudden rush. 'I feel like I've let you down, but I've let them down more . . . all the employees that were loyal to Ray.'

Cash was gazing after the girl. He turned slowly to Watson. 'You didn't throw the firebomb through the reception doors, did you?' he asked. The question was dismissive but not unkind. 'You want to know about guilt?' he added. 'One thing I didn't tell you about my car crash . . . I wasn't alone.'

XXI

The light had gone. Cash and Alexandra had gone. Only a clouded moon relieved the blackness of Buckley's Island. And perhaps that was appropriate, he thought. The vast distance between the moon and the vaguely lit objects on the island was of the scale he needed now.

Watson Thomas stood on the limestone bridge, looking out at nothing. How long ago was it that he had stood not far from here and looked up at the island for the first time, wondering at Ray Buckley's creation with its glass folly?

He had thought he was looking at another failing company, another dream soured like milk in the global heat.

Yes, he was used to empires. He was used to saving empires. Watson Thomas could take struggling companies with ideas too big for their own good and turn those ideas into gold. His first software company had made utilities to translate data from one package to the other; its founders believed they could produce a universal computer language, but debts had forced them to sell the company for a pound. His last, WT Gaming, had made high-street megabucks from the fantasies of three bright young programmers he'd inherited when he bought the bankrupt shares from the receiver.

And that was what he thought he had when he took on BBS – another broken business dream to reconstruct.

He was wrong. He hadn't realized then that Ray Buckley's dream was of an altogether different kind, a dream not measurable in pounds or dollars, or by a stock-market rating.

Buckley was a prophet. A bad businessmen, a failing manager, and probably as awful a father as Alexandra claimed, but he was none the less a prophet.

Watson felt as if he had received the Word, not just about the coming or not coming of global disaster, but about his own life. He saw how hollow his own values had become.

'In seven days, I will send rain upon the Earth,' said God to Noah. 'And every living thing I have made I will blot out.'

E-mail to: PPP
From: Weather Station Antarctica
    I agree. This is El Niño, the spirit child, coming home. And the way it's shaping up, it's going to be a big one.
    Batten down your hatches.
    Yours,
    Weatherjunkie.

PART TWO

XXII

Sunset comes all too quickly in the South Seas. The sun bleeds into the west as if through an unseen hole. Its last dregs bruise the sky.

Ulysses Masoni found himself staring at the torches as his father's people lit them, catching the swirling specks of insects against the brief twilight.

The feast was drawing to a close, a grand affair – two hundred guests beneath the sky, the rustle of palm trees over their heads, the gentle swell of the sea. For several hours they had been sitting on baked sand, eating from twenty low wooden tables, while servants danced between them, ferrying plates and bowls to and from the kitchen. His father had even allowed fireworks . . . Fireworks that peppered the sky to greet the return of the prodigal son disgraced in the West.

Uli could not understand why his father insisted on greeting him like this. The waterline was still six feet up the beach. Further now. Probably a couple more feet since last he was home.

He listened to the chanting, growing louder, more insistent. The *bete*, the master of ceremonies, appeared to inspect the pit, four meters of burning wood and white-hot stones. His assistants pulled back the topmost branches along with their insulation of scorched leaves. Everything was ready now.

Uli scanned the scene: islanders in island dress. His own clothes like theirs, *masi* cloth and the bracelets and anklets of dried leaves. It could have been another century. His fall from grace seemed to have propelled him back through the generations, a punishment of regression.

'Uli,' his father called across the hubbub of the dining tables. 'Come, we must talk.'

As he stood up, his father beckoned him away from the feast, taking him beyond the tables into the cover of the surrounding trees.

'But we'll miss the ceremony,' Uli protested weakly.

'No, the speed of their preparations is the speed of the islands. Slow. There is time yet before the boys walk. Drink with me,' his father said, and handed Uli one of two wooden *kava* cups.

Uli's eyes turned to the ground. 'I've let you down, father.'

'Have you? Did you do what they accuse you of?'

'No, of course not.'

'No,' his father repeated, 'of course not. Then how have you let me down? Because people write lies about you?'

Uli looked up. 'Because I failed. I had the truth almost in my hand. Written as if in stone. They could not have denied it. And I let them take it from me. And now . . . Now I both know and cannot stop the future.'

They were a simple people, as his father often repeated. And for all his education, for all his time in the West, Uli looked to his father for tradition. His father was home. He was the South Seas. He hadn't learnt to read or write until he was eleven, after the war and the Japanese had gone. He hadn't learned English until 1963. Yet here he was, the wisest and most compassionate man Uli had ever known.

His father said, 'Sometimes I think of making war on our enemies. Rather like American Indians did when they defended their lands. Only I imagine my army wearing grass skirts. Armed with spears and daubed on their naked chests and faces with war paint, they advance towards the White House.' He paused and closed his eyes as if picturing it. 'We would take the old ones of the tribe. We would walk rather than run. Perhaps the sheer surprise of such an attack would paralyse the guards.'

Uli laughed, detecting his father's humour, detecting also the bitterness it held. What could a people so small in number do against the giant?

'There may be a chink in their training,' Uli allowed. 'Attacks by primitive tribesmen are probably not on their basic course. But they'd stop you. Spears are no match for them.'

'In such a sacrifice, they do not have to be,' his father said. 'Imagine how they would explain it to the great god of television. A dozen or so elderly warriors in full tribal dress are gunned down by an overzealous CIA man with a Smith and Wesson on Pennsylvania Avenue.'

Uli laughed uneasily.

His father smiled. 'It is just an illustration of scale,' he said. 'Once, when we had enemies, we rowed out to meet them in boats. We battled, man to man. We won or lost. They ate us or we ate them. That was less than a century and a half ago. What a Christian hotchpotch those missionaries have made of us since! Dragging us into a new world.

Poisoning our children. Perhaps we should have dealt with them in 1860 and had done with it.' He drew his hand across his throat to illustrate his point, then patted his belly.

'There was in America at that time a chief called Red Cloud, chief of the Sioux Indians,' he continued. 'He said that of all the white men's promises, they kept but one. They promised to take his land and they took it. I see them taking my land now, inch by inch, foot by foot. I see it melting into the sea with their waste. And there is nothing more I can do.'

By the time he led Uli back to the feast, the *bete* had already begun leading the chosen boys to the pit. Uli realized that he had never been one of those – the chosen boys, the walkers who eat no coconut and must not lie with a woman for fear of the worst kind of burns. And he realized that this was a life choice his father had made for him. He had no option but to be what he had become. He still wasn't sure whether that made it easier or harder to bear.

Chanting, the boys walked across, and Uli watched them, thinking of his childhood friends. Although he had sat with them tonight, he had passed away from them long ago and now seemed stranded between the worlds like a soul caught in limbo.

When Connor called and asked to meet, Watson agreed without really asking why.

They chose the next afternoon, after the matinée at the RSC. *Richard the Third* was playing; Connor said he'd promised to go. Watson drove into Stratford and was waiting in the appointed place, a little tea-shop two streets away from the theatre, a good half an hour before the performance finished.

The tea-shop had thick stone walls, low beams and watercolours of the medieval town. Watson amused himself by watching the mesmerized tourists as he waited.

He was surprised when Connor arrived with Alexandra, looking radiant, if a little nervous. Young love, Watson recalled. He had a vague memory of what it felt like. 'I didn't figure you for a Shakespearean,' he said.

'I'm trying to educate her,' Connor explained.

'Are you sure it's not the other way around?'

'A private ladies' college doesn't seem to have done the job to Connor's satisfaction.' Alexandra smiled and hung on his arm.

They sat down and ordered afternoon tea from a waitress in a black and white Victorian uniform. Watson turned his cup the right way up on its saucer and unfolded his napkin. 'You wanted to talk? You said on the phone it was important.'

'I had a visit from the cops,' Connor said as if he regarded this as a certain prelude to arrest. 'They made me go back through the "finding the body" thing.'

Watson nodded solemnly.

'I didn't tell them anything. Anything new,' Connor assured him.

'What's to tell?'

'I've discovered something, but I'm not sure I know what to do with it.'

Connor hesitated. 'I was not going to . . . Well, I thought it was over after . . .'

Watson noticed that Alexandra's hand was on Connor's sleeve for support. The longer Connor took to get to the point, the harder she gripped.

'We got a back-up for the files we recovered, right?'

'Sure, we kept one off-site. Standard procedure. But what good is it?' Watson asked.

'I was thinking about the climate model.'

'Yes, but we never recovered all the files, so the back-up gets us nothing.'

'There was only one missing file,' said Connor. He hesitated. 'In the end, there was only one. I think the results file the SSEO gave us to work with was corrupt, but if we could have got hold of that missing data file, we could have run the model and that would have created a new results file automatically.'

Watson blinked consciously and shook his head. 'You're not making sense, Connor.'

Connor pulled his shoulders straight. 'Here's the crack,' he said. 'In my attempt to un-fuck the files before they got burnt to hell, I printed this.'

He took out a creased sheet of A4 and unfolded it and laid it out on the table. Watson recognized it immediately, the contents of a computer's file directory.

'Ray's?' he asked.

Connor nodded, and Watson noticed how Alexandra's face contorted at the mention of her father.

'But the contents of these files were corrupted, so we can't get at the data even on the back-up tape. Am I right?' Watson couldn't see any point here. It's all very well to know what the name of a file was, but if the virus has corrupted the file itself, where does that leave you? Nowhere.

'We can get copies of all the files we need from the back-up. But see this one?' Connor pointed.

'This "ENSOeffect".' Watson read the file name on the paper. 'That's the missing data file?'

'The key that unlocks the mystery.'

Waston looked from Connor to Alexandra.

Alexandra said, 'Look at the create date, Mr Thomas.'

Watson looked. He counted back, thinking of the date he was appointed managing director. The date on the file was about ten days before. 'This is not like the Bob Collins thing?' he said. 'You're not going to tell me who was in the building at the time and accuse them?'

'No,' said Connor curtly, 'I'm going to tell you Ray Buckley was on the other side of the world when this was created.'

'What?'

'Ray was killed on the first day he came back after his holiday . . . his holiday on Maawi.'

'So it wasn't him that wrote this file?' Watson asked. 'Is that what you're suggesting?'

'Sometimes you're as dumb as I think you are,' Alexandra cut in.

'No,' Connor said, 'I'm suggesting that this work – the ENSOeffect file – wasn't created on the BBS network. All that was ever on the BBS network was a copy.' He paused to let the implication sink in. 'My guess is there's an original still on a computer on Maawi.'

New York. Caroline Sharpe cleaned out her desk and placed the personal items in a cardboard box that had once held packets of dehydrated mash potato at her local store.

'But what am I supposed to do?' asked the blonde receptionist at the SSEO offices.

Caroline tossed her head dismissively. 'Sweetheart, the party's over. You can wait here for the office to be wound up, but I can't guarantee you'll get paid. Face it and find another job, that's my advice.'

She picked up the cardboard box and swept from the office.

The receptionist was blowing her nose on a ragged piece of paper and dribbling watery black mascara tears as Caroline slammed the door.

XXIII

In the morning, after the feast, everyone slept late. When Uli's father woke him, the sun was already high in the sky. They breakfasted together in the open, drinking coconut milk and eating pineapple out of the husks of the fruits.

Chief Masoni di Masoni said, 'Come and walk with me around my island.'

So Uli and his father walked, not around the island, but around the square mile or so into which his father's kingdom had been effectively compressed.

His father was not an unwealthy man. He could have had the conveniences of modern life shipped to the island. Instead he preferred to live in the most traditional of villages. He made it the island's capital. Two hundred dwellings of wood and mud and straw within a fenced compound.

No electricity. No telephone. Not in the chief's village.

But beyond that primitive fence, both these evils existed. A little off to the left, on the slope of a hill that stretched up from the small bay in which the village lay, was the oil-fired power station that the American forces had built after the Second World War. It was almost hidden among the dense coconut trees that made the whole island look like a beautiful but impenetrable forest. Yet it was there all right, sending power through ugly wires to the more liberal villagers that lived and farmed along the coast and into the interior of the island. These villagers wanted to embrace the world.

Ten years before, they had agreed to share the cost of a telephone exchange to bring the miracle of modern communication to the island of Maawi. Now a Japanese-made box sat in a village three miles down the coast. Until Ray Buckley had built his modern holiday home somewhere in the east of Maawi, that telephone exchange held the only silicon chips on the island.

'Progress,' his father said bitterly, as they climbed the slope on the left among the swaying palms. 'There are thirty telephones now on Maawi. Thirty too many. The leaders of these villages come to me. They say I am behind the times. Maybe I am.'

Uli looked at him, detecting a note of concern in his voice.

'Is there really such discontent?'

His father shrugged. 'They would have me lease land to bring hotels, bring in the tourists. They say they want "real" jobs. They think jobs catering for tourists are "real". They say we should have a republic here, a democratic island state.' He turned back towards the sea, looking down the slope into the waves. 'Who am I to deny them what they want?'

'You are the chief.'

'What good is a chief who will not rule for the best interests of his people? Who am I to say they are wrong? As long as they leave me my little village, I will be content.' He stopped. 'Of course, if Ray Buckley is right, this hardly matters anyway.'

Uli's father squatted down under a coconut tree and ran his hand back over his forehead to push back the sweat.

'I have been thinking . . . and it is true, I do not understand the world you have lived in. What do you think happened to him?'

Uli shrugged. 'The power in the West bends the truth. Anyone who threatens to straighten it is removed . . .'

'And that perhaps is why you were removed,' his father said. The wise face wrinkled as if thinking deeply. 'As I have gradually lost the support of the people, I have been considering. I once told you that even Canute could not push back the tide, but if he had ordered it to come in, he would have seemed all-powerful.'

Uli knelt down next to his father. He sensed a cleverness in the words. 'What do you mean?' he said. 'What do you think happened to Ray Buckley?'

His father's back straightened and he closed his eyes. As he breathed slowly in and out, he seemed to be seeing something, a vision replayed on the inside of his lids. 'Suppose that I knew for certain that he was right. Is there any position in the world from which a man has the power to prevent the disaster he forecasts?'

'President of the United States,' Uli replied immediately.

'Really?' his father said. 'Can this man prevent the tide from coming in?' He paused. 'Can he tell his people not to work tomorrow? I cannot tell the people of Maawi to stay outside the modern world. Can this President ask his people to return from it? Kings and presidents . . .

chiefs . . . men of politics, we are all like weathervanes. At first, you think we are pointing the direction and commanding the wind to blow. Only later do you see how we twist ourselves to maintain that illusion.'

Uli looked at his father and his father's eyes opened.

'You look for villains among those threatened by this truth they deny, my son. But those who know the truth are equally helpless, equally threatened. I hold back the world at the borders of this island. And soon, I will not be chief. And a President who responds to the threat of this disaster . . .'

Suddenly Uli saw the point. In all his troubles, the deaths of Buckley and Pielot, he had assumed the villains were made blind by their own interest. He had not considered they might know full well what the consequence would be.

The temporary head of the European Environmental Projects Agency had been in the post for a week when he got Patty's travel request. He faxed it back with a signature without ever asking why she needed to go to the West Coast of America. That was good, because she was damned sure she couldn't have explained it.

P. J. Pfister – she had to see him. She had to ask him about his quantum state theory. Why had he abandoned it? The question had to be asked face to face.

She decided – given the agency's lack of interest – to stretch the travel permission to its limit, so she booked her flight via New York and allowed herself a night's stopover. That gave her a few spare hours to make a trip into the city the following morning.

She took a taxi to the SSEO.

Climbing the stairs, she couldn't help comparing it to the plush offices of the agency in Paris. Someone had daubed misspelled slogans on the door and a painter was busily obliterating the last of the word 'kunt' as Patty passed. So much for Uli Masoni's supposed misuse of funds, she thought. The guy's extravagance didn't even extend to a building with a working lift.

Inside the organization's offices a blonde receptionist was sitting at an empty desk, reading a copy of *Cosmopolitan*.

'Is Uli Masoni still around?' Patty asked.

'He ain't here no more. He legged it. He ain't even in New York. They've been staking him out at his apartment. I guess he knows he can't come back here. Not after . . . well, after what he done.'

'Caroline Sharpe?' Patty said the name, dreading a positive answer.

146

What would she do if the answer was yes? Was Caroline really the face in the van? Could she have imagined it?

The receptionist shook her head. 'She ain't here any more either. You a reporter? We've had lots of reporters. One or two police as well. Not much else these days.'

'I'm with the European Environmental Projects Agency. Patty Drake.'

'Like that André fella. Was here a few weeks back. Dead now,' the receptionist said, as if Pielot had been a personal friend. She perked up as she added, 'Of course, I only saw him the once.'

'Is this place empty now?' Patty asked, looking around at what seemed like a deserted office. The post was piled up on the floor in one corner. It didn't look like it had been touched for weeks.

'There's some fella supposed to be coming out from the Tokyo office to take care of things, but he ain't turned up yet.'

'I see.'

'That Caroline high-tailed it out of here a couple of days ago. Said she weren't coming back. Mean piece of work, she was. Not like Uli. I thought he was a sweetheart. Like I told those reporters, I couldn't believe he did those things they wrote about him.'

Patty looked around in desperation. There were a couple of filing cabinets that seemed to come from a different century and, as far as furniture went, that was about it.

'Feel free to look around,' the receptionist said, glancing idly at her fingernails as she crooked the fingers of one hand to examine them. 'Everyone else has. They keep pulling out the papers every which way and I keep stuffing them back in the drawers after they're gone. Don't do no good.'

Patty went to the first of the filing cabinets and pulled open the top drawer. Inside there was a graphic illustration of the receptionist's filing technique: everything shoved in on top of everything else, and the suspension files unhooked and confined to the bottom of the pile.

'I liked that André fella,' she continued as Patty gazed at the jumble of papers. 'Came in here with a big balloon tied to him. Caroline liked him. I could tell. Slept with him, I reckon.'

'Pardon?' Patty said. She turned suddenly. She had only been half-listening, had only half-heard.

'Just speculation,' the receptionist said. 'I keep my eye open; I pick up things here and there. Office stuff. She looked at him in a way that weren't just casual interest. Of course, there ain't no one here to gossip with, but I can still make my deductions.'

147

'You make deductions?' Patty felt slightly offended, but she checked herself. 'Tell me more,' she said.

'Well, I saw the way she looked at him. And she came in late the next day. Said she'd been to see him off on the plane. Yeah, OK, get real . . . She's yawning like she's been awake all night and smiling like the cat that's got the cream. I can imagine that's how it was with him too, can't you? He was a good-looking man.' She stretched out the word 'good' as if she wanted to get maximum use from it before letting it go.

Unsure what to say, Patty returned to examining the filing cabinet, trying to control a heart that was pounding at twice its normal rate.

'Everything that told anything I reckon's shredded long ago,' the receptionist said.

'Shredded?'

'I ain't so stupid. That Caroline's here one night late, had herself a little confetti-making party with the office shredder.'

'Are you sure?'

'Oh, I'm sure. There used to be a big file in there . . . biggest one.' She pointed at the other filing cabinet. 'All the correspondence going between her and her contact back in that English company. All about invoices and the state of work and who was going to pay who, and when, and how much. I came in two weeks ago, it had gone.'

Patty pushed the filing cabinet drawer and watched it slide heavily shut against the flimsy sheet-metal frame. She bit her lip and swung around.

'Who was her contact at BBS?' she asked.

The receptionist shrugged. 'I never met him. All I know's his name: Bob Collins. She used to call him Robbie . . . Robbie was always calling Caroline, wouldn't talk to anyone else.'

XXIV

The wind had changed. Along the arc of the equator, the warmer waters had moved eastwards.

Normally, the prevailing trade winds pile the sea off Indonesia two feet higher than off Ecuador, but now this difference lessened, reversed even. And along the South American coast, the normal upwelling of cool bottom waters subsided.

In Spanish it is called El Niño, the spirit child.

Its formation is slow and, for a while at least, a calm period descended on Maawi. Hot, bone-dry air hovered without mercy. Uli Masoni sat on the beach in the shadow of a coconut palm, looking out to the horizon. It was hard to maintain the vision of Ray Buckley's work within this unchanging peace, hard to believe that anything so far distant could reach or despoil his home.

Uli had noticed that he could now circle his neck on his shoulders without the characteristic click that had been there for what seemed like years. He had thought it a simple anatomical defect, but it was just the tension of the Western world, now relieved.

As he sat there, he was not scared of what was to come. Fear was something you had when you had some control over the future. And he had none.

His father said, 'Uli, what will you do now?'

Do? What will Uli do now? He didn't want to think about it, didn't want to even get up from where he sat. This was paradise. And he knew that once a man moves from paradise, he must face up to what he knows.

'Uli?' His father was standing above him, waiting for an answer.

'Look at me,' Uli said. 'I sit under a coconut tree and I wear the *masi* skirt of an islander. But I wear also the training shoes that an American company makes in Korea and a T-shirt from the New York Jets.'

'You will go back, then?'

Without looking up, Uli shook his head.

'Stay, then,' his father said.

'Is that what you want?' Uli asked.

Wearily, his father sat down beside him, finding a spot where the waving palms shadowed his head. He crossed his legs and rested his palms on his knees.

'When you were thirteen,' he said at last, 'you made your own brand of gunpowder, mixed it with the charcoal from the fire. Do you remember that?'

'I burned down the house,' Uli said.

His father nodded. 'It exploded. There was everybody running with water buckets to try to save the roof. Dried grasses burn quickly. I asked you where you got this recipe from and you showed me a book of chemistry. You said, "Father, did you not know that these minerals are there for the taking on your island?"'

'I remember it,' Uli said.

'We still use your recipe to make fireworks for our feast days.' His father laughed. 'It was then I knew . . . A hard thing for a father to see. I pondered long on it. I hesitated.'

'My love of chemistry did not last.'

'Maybe, but a man who makes gunpowder out of the earth . . . It was then I could see I would one day have to send you away. We could not school you on the island.' He paused. 'Let us see if we can make your decision for you.'

Uli's father got to his feet and brushed the sand and small pieces of dried twig from his clothes. Uli did the same.

'Where are we going?' he asked.

'I am meeting with Logi and Wattang,' he said. 'I think you should hear what they have to say.'

Wattang and Logi were important men on Maawi. Wattang's family farmed the largest stretch of land to the north of the island. Logi was head of the village that held Uli's father's hated telephone exchange. Their families had been friends for generations, though Wattang and Logi now represented the dissident factions of the island, those who wanted done with the chief's backward ways.

The pair were waiting dutifully for the chief as he and Uli came back to the governmental hut, the State House. Logi's green Suzuki 4×4 was parked two hundred yards away outside the village limits. The Chief wouldn't allow it in, and Uli was surprised even to see it. His father had said that Logi no longer drove the vehicle.

'Loyalty to you, my chief,' Logi began, using the island language in its most formal terms.

His father exchanged bows with his guests and beckoned them inside. Uli trailed along last, embarrassed by his own presence.

Both Logi and Wattang were very much like his father in age and dress and the weathered look of their skin. Uli felt he was looking back into a past he had no right to see first hand. But if his fall into the past had previously felt like a punishment, here it felt like a privilege.

The State House of Maawi was no more than a one-room wood, grass and mud shack, and although it had rugs on the floor, the roof was a simple criss-cross of timbers so that open sky provided light even when the window shutters were closed. A cover was pulled over at night or when the tropical storms threatened. Inside there was a round table large enough to seat maybe a dozen visitors and as many chairs were pushed against the walls.

Uli's father pulled back a single large wooden chair already positioned at the table. He gestured to his guests that they should select themselves suitable seating.

Behind the chief's chair were two ceremonial knives fixed to the wall. They were about a foot in length encircled by a necklace of twine which carried both the symbols of Maawi and various medals presented to the chief and the chief's forefathers by visiting dignitaries. He took down this organic chain and fitted it around his neck, making sure the metal cross once awarded to his great-great-grandfather by Queen Victoria was positioned in the centre of his chest. Then he sat down.

With the chain came a change in his personality.

'Speak,' he commanded, his tone now steeled to the task of leadership. This was Chief Masoni di Masoni addressing his subjects, and Uli found himself surprised by the change of nuance in the language, thrown perhaps because he had become so used to English.

'We have come to talk about certain concerns,' Logi began, looking up from the reverent bow he had accorded the chief.

Uli noticed suddenly that Logi's eyes were milky now, and he seemed to have aged so much more than the last time he had seen him. When was that? Three years ago at his nephew's ceremony. Before Uli's sister and her husband had left the island, an event his father never talked about.

The chief said, 'Indeed. Could this not have waited until the next council of elders?'

'We represent most of the elders,' Wattang said. 'It is their concerns we wish to raise.'

The chief lifted his hand to the level of his chest and tipped it open, palm upward, towards the two visitors. The gesture gave permission to speak.

'It is a question of succession and democracy,' Logi said. 'You know there is a majority among the council of elders who wish to create a federation with the adjacent islands.'

'You wish to cede all power to their so-called republic,' the chief said. 'I have already seen the results on these islands.'

'Prosperity, investment, education for the children, jobs for the men and women, healthcare for the old. We have seen these results as well,' Wattang said.

'Why do you bring this up when we have discussed it so many times? You also want a new generating station. Are you going to bring that up again as well?'

'We import electricity,' Logi said calmly. 'We have a cable running to Waatu bringing power because our station is not sufficient. This is a fact. We have to draw large amounts of power through the cable to meet our needs. As that power draws in, so our wealth draws out. Like breath.'

The chief sighed and said, 'You are a fool, Logi. You don't understand what "needs" are.'

'My loyalty is to you.'

'To hell with your loyalty,' the chief snapped back.

Wattang and Logi looked at one another. Then Logi looked at Uli, then back to the chief. He said, 'Your son is home on the island.'

'Indeed.'

Logi stopped. He seemed unable to get the next sentence out.

Wattang spoke instead. 'We need to understand the succession.'

The chief laughed aloud. 'You hear that, Uli? They need to understand the succession.'

'Since it is clear that you oppose the will of your people, we need to know what you and your son will do so that we may decide on policy. It is important that we understand how the affairs of the island will be administered.'

'At last count, Wattang, our population was 4,396. There is no army and there are no weapons to hold a civil war. All rulers rule by the consent of the governed, but here perhaps more than elsewhere. There is no force of law. Our police force is three. My entire civil service can be found in the huts that surround us. What could possibly be so important about the administration of such a island?'

'The administration is choking the life out of our future.'

'If you are so concerned about your future, then take it.' The chief stood up, his chain of office swinging under the weight of its medals. Suddenly, he grabbed the Victoria Cross, wrenched the entire chain from around his neck and flung it across the table. 'If you want to know what Uli will do when he wears this, then ask him.'

He strode towards the door, leaving Wattang and Logi where they sat. Stopping in the doorway, he said, 'I weep for you. By God, I thought it was only my son who was a victim of their lies.'

He looked towards Uli, his look melting back towards fatherhood now, the harshness of chiefdom dissolving. And there was a question hanging in his gaze.

All at once, Uli understood what his father had said on the beach and why he had wanted Uli to listen to Wattang and Logi and their complaints.

There was no choice here. Whether Buckley was right or wrong, it didn't matter. The Maawi his father had known was already half-gone. The Maawi he had gone to the West to save was already beyond saving.

He understood something else too. Although the chief seemed the same wise man he had been eleven years ago when Uli left the island for college, he had in fact died. He denied what the elders craved only because it was his imprinted nature to do so. And he could not say yes in death to what he had always said no to in life.

Uli didn't know how to answer Wattang, and he didn't know how to answer Logi. Slowly, he turned and followed his father into the ultra-violet heat of midday.

Patty took a hire car from LA airport and headed for the address she'd been given. She drove for what seemed like hours along the coast road before she saw the first sign to the place-name on her scrap of paper.

Pielot had said that Pfister had gone to the beach on his grants. He had. In the light of early evening, she saw the silhouette of Pfister's enormous white house on his private beach, a few million dollars of gothic arches and verandas that overlooked the sea.

The 'grant junky'.

The bell pull in the front porch created a rendition of Beethoven's *Fifth* inside the house. There was a few seconds' delay before Patty was aware of an eye looking at her through the peephole in the front door, then a clanking of chains and the mechanical clunk of locks.

'Yeah, honey . . .'

She was suddenly acutely aware that it was her looks, not his recognition of her, that had opened the door.

Pfister was wearing knee-length shorts and a T-shirt advertising 'Fat Willy's Surf Shack'. He stood woozily in the doorway, leering at her over the top of Ray-bans that had slipped down his sunburnt nose.

After he had examined her from head to foot, unashamedly concentrating on her legs and breasts, he whistled and drawled the word 'cool'.

'Patricia Drake, European Environmental Projects Agency,' Patty said, her voice ice-cold rather than cool.

'Woh,' Pfister exclaimed. He swayed from side to side and ran his hand back through what remained of his bleach-blonde hair. 'Is that some branch of the thought police?'

'You tutored me ten years ago.'

'I did? What did you say your name was?'

'Patty. Patty Drake.'

'Hell, Patty, you've got a great . . .' He stopped himself and stepped back. 'Never mind. I guess you ought to come in.'

He ushered her into the entrance hall – a spacious marbled affair, overlooked on three sides by landings on the first floor and featuring a *Gone with the Wind* staircase rising out of the centre with red velvet carpeting and a massive rounded window at the top. He led her past the staircase and along a short corridor that ended in an arch giving on to the main room of the house.

This room was predominantly white, at least thirty feet by forty in area, with a patio window that opened directly on to the beach. In one corner there was a grand piano, also in white, and a series of white leather sofas spread randomly around what was otherwise empty space except for a glass-topped table in the centre. A four-foot-square map of the world was encased in the glass top of the table, and various black dots and lines were marked in seemingly random positions on the glass. Patty couldn't work out what they were.

'Nice place, isn't it?' he slurred. 'Cost me some, I can tell you.'

'The climate business must pay well,' Patty agreed.

'Top dollar,' he agreed. 'Let me get you a drink, honey. I can't believe I don't remember a babe like you. Have you changed your hair? Plastic surgery? What?'

He was staring straight at her, moving his eyes from side to side of her face as if looking for the scar tissue. 'We got champagne, bourbon, vodka. We got beer if that does it for you. We got something stronger if you care for a smoke, if you know what I mean? I think we're all out of blow.' Pfister wiped the back of his hand under his nose.

'Do you have mineral water?' she asked.

'Sure,' he said with thinly disguised disappointment. 'Take a seat. I'll be back.'

Patty selected the leather sofa that had the best view of the ocean. The sun was rapidly disappearing now, leaving a bloody stain in the sky.

Pfister returned with sparkling mineral water for Patty and something dark for himself that smelt of alcohol when he leaned towards her. He perched himself on the arm of the adjacent sofa, lifting his glass in an unspoken toast.

'So you're with the agency? That's what you said, isn't it? Pielot's mob.'

'Yes. Scientific advisor. He's . . .'

'Yeah, I know he's dead. Those cats pay you well?'

'Well enough.'

'Shame. I could use someone like you.'

Patty shot him a fiery stare. 'You don't know anything about me.'

Pfister stared back at her blankly and for a moment she thought about her situation. No, he was too small and too stoned to be a threat. Hadn't she beaten off an armed intruder with a hockey stick and a tennis racket?

'I came to get some answers,' she stated flatly.

'Ask me no questions, I'll tell you no lies.' Pfister laughed at what he clearly thought was a joke.

'Why did you abandon your quantum theory of climate?'

'Woh, she asks the big one!' Pfister twisted off the sofa's armrest and took two steps across the room, tottering as if he had been physically hit.

'When I saw you ten years ago, you were convinced you were right. Yet at the last New York conference . . .'

'Hey, you were at that? I must be losing my touch. I don't remember you from ten years ago. And I musta missed you at that conference too. Honey, in my prime, I would have picked you out in a crowd across Grand Central Station.'

'I wasn't at the conference,' she admitted.

The admission seemed to unbalance Pfister. He leaned over uneasily and rested one hand back on the armrest. Then he lowered himself on to the polished wooden floor. His struggle to arrange his legs looked like the first stand of a newborn foal seen in reverse. Finally, he fell the last foot and a half, landing in an untidy sitting position with his back against the sofa and his backside on the floor. Part of his drink slopped over the side of his glass and on to his T-shirt.

'Shit!' he cursed. He pushed the sunglasses back up his nose so that his eyes disappeared.

'Are you going to answer my question?'

'No,' he said, 'I'm going to ask you what you think about it. Come on, you gotta have an opinion in that pretty head of yours.'

'For the last year or so, the SSEO has been digging up solid data that shows there will be a massive shift in climate in the southern hemisphere.'

'Is that so?'

'Yes, it is.'

'And how will that occur?'

'I think it's hard to imagine. I try not to dramatize it too much, but I guess it'll be like a biblical Flood.'

'Forty days and forty nights,' Pfister said, as if pleased with himself.

'A lot longer than that. And a lot more lethal,' Patty said.

'So where's their data now?' he asked.

'That's the point. Several people were killed to stop it getting into the public domain with any credibility.'

'This is all very interesting in a kind of fairytale way. But what does this have to do with me?' Pfister sipped his drink in a manner designed to show his indifference.

'It occurred to me that what they were describing might fit quite well with your former theory. A very fast shift in average temperature across part of the globe. But it doesn't keep on going. It finds a new stable state with those new average temperatures. Only by then, there're whole parts of the world that are uninhabitable. It was the similarity that made me think of you.'

'I abandoned my theory, honey. I mean, it was junk.' He extended the last word, finishing with a dismissive wave. 'The whole bullshit thing went in the dustbin.'

'You threw it in the dustbin,' Patty said, 'and then someone gave you an awful lot of money to carry on your work on a new theory.'

'The US government,' Pfister reminded her. 'Are you suggesting I was paid off?'

Patty looked around at the elaborate and expensive features of the house. 'What would give me that idea?'

'If you're suggesting I was paid off,' he repeated, 'I think you need to consider why the US government would want to cover up the fact the world was going to become "uninhabitable", as you put it.'

Patty looked at him from the corner of her eye, a squinting suspicious look. She knew she had his attention now. He was trying to argue his way to a denial, and that never sounded like the truth.

'I said "parts of the world,"' she reminded him. 'About half of the southern hemisphere to be exact. That's not in the United States, is it?'

Pfister launched himself forward. 'If I tutored you, I must have made a fucking terrible job of it,' he said. 'Don't you realize that during a quantum change – even a localized one – you get fucking crazy weather everywhere during the transition. I'm talking billions of dollars in damage. You said, biblical Flood and, baby, you'd be right.'

He was two feet from her face now, raised up on his knees. She gazed at him, the eyes behind the black glass. 'So you still do believe in quantum changes?'

The question stopped him dead. For fully ten seconds he made no movement at all. Then he took off his sunglasses and his mouth cracked into a smile. 'Fuck you,' he said. 'Look, honey, I don't think we've got anything to talk about really, do you? I mean, you don't want to do any stuff with me. Christ, you didn't even take a real drink . . . so sex seems out of the question.'

'OK.' Patty stood up. She was looking down on him. 'Perhaps you're right, we don't have anything to talk about.'

He raised himself by pulling on the sofa's arm. 'It's a real shame,' he said, 'you and I, we could have made such sweet music. You've got those great titties.'

He took a step towards her. She took a pace back, then she came forward suddenly, thrusting her knee into his crutch. He crumpled and fell, landing on the floor on his side with his hands clasped to his injured genitals. His mouth gaped open, but no sound came out.

Patty stopped under the arch on her way to the front door. 'I used to admire you,' she said, 'ten years ago. What happened?'

She drove back towards the airport and checked into a hotel. As soon as she reached the room, she stripped off her clothes and took a long hot shower. She felt dirty. She stayed under the water for the best part of fifteen minutes.

Coming into the bedroom in a towelling bathrobe, she lay down on the bed and stared at the ceiling. She couldn't believe the picture floating in her imagination. She was seeing a cover-up on a scale she had not imagined; she was seeing inhumanity that was simply unimaginable. *The southern hemisphere is not in the United States* – she'd said the words to Pfister and, as she said them, she had realized she might be putting her finger right on the crux.

Did they know? Was it really possible that they knew all along but were so xenophobically uncaring? She felt certain now that someone had done Buckley's work before him . . . Pfister. Only Pfister had accepted money for his silence.

She told herself this was all too fanciful. No proof. No real evidence. She didn't even understand the mechanism. Quantum states and quantum changes were all very well, but nothing survived after Buckley's death to show how they were triggered. Was it El Niño that did it? She felt it must be, but how?

She pored over the room-service menu and ordered a light salad and a half bottle of Chablis. By the time it arrived, she had unpacked her working briefcase, taken out her replacement Toshiba and started her e-mail utility.

She carried a universal phone lead in the zip-up Targus case that the Toshiba came in. She dropped her hand down the back of the bed and found the telephone socket. This was almost a ritual. She did it every day and could have done it with her eyes closed. After a couple of minutes of struggling with the hardware and software settings, she was dialling into her service provider.

She approached the log-in procedure with some trepidation. She was expecting – or more accurately, dreading – a message from the agency. Soon the new head had to realize that she was following a hunch and spending EU money in the process. Soon there would be a searching e-mail asking her to explain herself.

But not today . . . There was only one message on the menu. The sender's ID she recognized as Watson Thomas. She clicked on the message.

Patty, sorry, but I need to ask a climatology-type question and you're the only climatologist I know. We've found a menu of Ray Buckley's files including one titled 'ENSOeffect'. I think this title might mean something to someone skilled in the art. It means nothing to me. Regards,
  Watson

Patty stared at the screen. She remembered those words on the fax that started all this: 'Natural climatic event triggers shift. The Earth Goddess collapses.' She kept staring at the screen. She didn't know for how long.

Quickly, so quickly that it caused her to fumble and take longer than she would have doing it slowly, she logged off the computer and unplugged it and plugged the phone back in. As soon as she had it operational, she dialled the number of Watson's new flat, which he had given her on their last meeting.

It didn't answer. Cursing, she tried his supposed 'find-you-anywhere' mobile number. All she got was a voice mailbox. Damn modern telecoms!

'This is Watson. Talk after the bleep if you need me, I'll get back to you . . .'

'Watson, this is Patty. We've got to talk live. Live, do you understand? I know what ENSO is. My God . . . Look, I'll give you my number. I'm in a hotel in LA. The number is . . . God, let me look for the number. Anyway it's room 311.' She rummaged about in the drawers of the bedside cabinet looking for something that might tell her the hotel's details.

XXV

Watson's call came at 3 a.m.

She said sleepily, 'You sound like you're in the bottom of a tin box.'

He said, 'I'm hands free . . . using the voice modem on my portable.'

'You could never use anything like normal people. What's wrong with a handset?'

He laughed. It sounded like a ghost in a wishing well.

'What time is it?' she asked. 'Is it morning where you are?'

'No, evening.'

'Evening?' she was still only half-awake. 'How far ahead is England? Eight hours, I thought.'

'I'm not in England, Patty. I'm in Melbourne. In the middle of a heat wave. Even air-conditioners can't cope.'

'What are you doing there?' The shock brought her into some kind of focus.

'Trying to get a plane to Maawi. You said you knew what the ENSO effect meant?'

'Yeah, God, Watson yeah . . . ENSO is another name for El Niño . . . El Niño Southern Oscillation.'

'What's that?'

She swallowed. 'It's the natural event that's going to trigger the disaster.'

During the afternoon, when he could check the same fact no more, Connor called up his bootleg copy of *Adventure Updater* and clicked on the 'update' icon.

Eye candy, he called it. Electronic opium for the times when he didn't want to think about real life.

When WT Gaming had first produced *Adventure Updater* it had been a revolutionary concept in computer games. When you got to the end, you had the opportunity of receiving game updates over the Internet. What hooked Connor was that the link between player and the main system was interactive, so there was always the chance some smart-ass kid was going to upload a neat piece of hacking which the main system would proceed to distribute to the four corners of the earth. Needless to say, the child in Connor wanted to be that smart-ass kid.

He spent two hours immersed in the complexities of a South American jungle and the following two hours trying to hack into the game's source code. All in all though, despite his normal passion for computers, this game and its puzzle did little to quiet the thoughts he had of Alexandra that afternoon. He kept coming back to that one fact he had checked a thousand times.

The police questioning had eventually led him to it, a sort of delayed effect. They'd made him go through the blood thing, the gory body story. It had set him thinking, thinking for a couple of days, to tell the truth, before the thoughts clicked into place. He didn't know how he would tell Alexandra what he had discovered. He wished he had never visited her in the hospital after the fire. Perhaps it would have been better not to know.

She showed up just after eight, carrying his favourite pizza and a bottle of supermarket champagne. Quite how she balanced it all on her motorbike, he could not fathom.

'Squeals on wheels,' she announced herself as she took her helmet off. She smiled at him, checking her own image in the hallway mirror: her old 501s and a black sweatshirt. She shook her hair out of the tangles her crash helmet created and unzipped her riding boots, stepping out barefooted into the lounge. 'Are you going to open the champagne?'

'I'll get glasses,' he said unenthusiastically.

He went to the kitchen and came back with plates and cutlery and two filling-station wine glasses, free with ten gallons of four-star. He popped the cork and poured the bubbly.

'What are we celebrating?' he asked.

'What day is it?' she said, taking her glass. 'Tuesday? Here's to Tuesday. Come on, Connor, my darling, why're you so bloody glum?'

'I've got to tell you something,' he said.

Alexandra sat down on the sofa. She curled one leg up under her body, eyes cast down as if that hunched position could save her from whatever it was. Her face had lost its gaiety.

'Are you breaking up with me, Connor? Is that what it's about? What have I done?'

'No. In fact, I-I-I . . .' he stammered, not really knowing where he was going with this answer. 'In fact, I love you.'

She looked up at him, but all she said was, 'Oh,' very quietly.

'It's your father,' Connor continued, moving faster after the 'L' word. 'You see, I don't think he was your father.'

'What? What are you talking about? Don't tell such cruel jokes.' Her eyes flashed into anger. She was going to lash out now, he knew.

'Be calm,' he said.

'Be calm? Why should I be fucking calm? What are you on, Connor Giles? How dare you?'

Taking courage, he moved forward, putting his glass down before attempting to sit next to her. She squirmed away from him, ending semi-fetal at the other end of the sofa.

'Listen,' he said to her averted face: 'Remember when you were in the hospital after the fire. You lost a lot of blood and they wanted to give you a transfusion.'

'Sure, I remember.'

'I sat by your bed . . . and I . . . I read your chart,' he said hesitantly. 'I checked your blood type. It just didn't register at the time. Your father was O, Ordinary type. I learned that from the police.'

'So?'

'You are AB'

'So?' she said again, raising her voice.

'O can't father AB. It's a fact.'

'How do you know this? You're not a doctor.'

Connor pointed across the room to his trusty computer, sitting on the table on the far side. The last thing he had played with may have been *Adventure Updater*, but he had read something far more serious beforehand.

'A law library,' he told her. '*Blood Tests and the Proof of Paternity in Civil Proceedings – 1968*. I printed the pamphlet.'

He hesitated. She was biting her lip. He knew his words were twists of the knife, but he couldn't stop, not until they were all out. 'The science,' he said. 'You have to get the "A" factor in one chromosome, the "B" factor in the other. You couldn't be AB unless your father had at least one of the factors in his blood type.'

For a while, she didn't say anything. Then she said, 'Oh, God.'

He hovered on his end of the sofa, uncertain whether to reach out to her or stay back.

'Hold me,' she said unexpectedly.

A knot dropped from his stomach. He pulled her wet face into his chest and her face disappeared beneath the wild curls of her hair. He felt her gentle sobs vibrating the ribs next to his heart.

'Who, then?' she asked, twisting to look up.

Her hair was plastered to her cheeks. Her make-up had run.

He wanted to tell her he loved her again. Instead he said, 'Remember the trust fund?'

Her expression never changed. He supposed there was a level of shock where, as more is piled on the top, there is no more physical reaction that can result. He saw that kind of numbness in her eyes.

Uli's morning walk took him several miles along the coast. Far enough, in fact, to reach the outskirts of Logi's village.

The buildings here were all tin-roofed and stone- or wooden-walled. Uli's father called them 'cans', after the canned food he'd seen in the hands of American soldiers during his childhood. But Logi's people were proud of their homes and their village. They were trying to be modern. They had electricity; some had telephones. They used the latest fertilizers on their crops of bananas and other exotic fruits. They even used sonar equipment in their fishing boats. Their trading of goods was the only source of international hard currency on the island, all they had to buy fuel and electricity and what few outside supplies reached Maawi.

Uli sat on a wooden bench under a tree in the dust of the main street. First, he faced the ocean. From where he sat, he could just make out the island of Waatu, the furthest outpost of the federation of island states which everyone but his father wanted Maawi to join. Perhaps it was the fact that you could see the modern world from here and not from his father's village that gave these people such a different view of the future. Education, commerce . . . Uli had studied economics when he gave up chemistry; he could write a list of benefits as long and as detailed as anyone might want. Still, it didn't feel right.

He turned his back on the shimmering image of Waatu. He looked into the village, Logi's village. Idly, he tried to estimate the population from the number of buildings he could see. Apart from the main street that ran along the coast from the little fishing bay to the wooden church, there were four streets heading off, and little tributaries to them, all unsurfaced. He thought maybe 600 or 700 people, maybe more. There were a few cars now and motorcycles, things that had been rare the last time he had visited. They still seemed out of place.

In Maawi word of mouth always carried quickly; the expansion and talk of modernization had made little difference. Five minutes after Uli sat down, Logi's 4x4 pulled up. There was a young man driving; Logi sat in the passenger seat.

'This is a rare honour,' Logi said as he got out of the car. 'The chief's son.'

Uli smiled at him. Logi was dressed today in Western style, cotton trousers, a polo shirt, yet his feet were bare. But it wasn't these that attracted Uli's attention; it was the strange unfocused way that Logi looked at him.

Uli gestured and Logi sat down on the bench.

'At last, somewhere I know I am welcome,' Uli said.

Logi nodded an acknowledgement. 'I was hoping that with your return, you might bring some wisdom to your father.' He wiped a bead of sweat from his forehead. 'It's hot today, no? Even for Maawi. You must be baking after those days in that New York fridge.'

'It wasn't so cold. I got used to it.'

Logi sighed. 'Are you looking for something in the village, Uli? Because I'm not sure we have anything to give.'

'I thought you wanted to know about succession. That's what you told my father. He told you to ask me, but you didn't. When the time for succession comes, he'll be gone. I'll be the one. My father's not the man you need to talk to.'

Logi allowed himself a magnanimous nod. 'How long has it been? Eleven years? Eleven years since you went away to school? You know that was the last piece of advice your father ever took from me?'

Uli turned sharply. He hadn't expected this.

Logi nodded. 'He said to me, "I cannot decide this issue. I am too much in love." And I said "You must send him." And even as I said it, I knew our friendship could never be the same. He would always look at me and know that it was I who sent away his son.'

'He never told me this,' Uli said.

Logi looked at the ground, then raised his eyes slowly to Uli's face. Uli saw the cataract clouds that covered his pupils.

'There is talk on the island that you have discovered the end of the world,' Logi said. 'That this is why you have been cast out and come back to us.'

Uli shrugged.

'Of course, they are poorly educated, unvisioned, and they believe such things,' Logi continued. 'But why would they cast you out for that?'

'I don't know what I . . . what we, in the SSEO, discovered,' Uli said.

164

'I suppose it wasn't us who discovered it, only someone working for the SSEO's money.'

'Buckley,' Logi said.

'You met him?'

'Oh, yes. A good man. I understood nothing he said, but I still liked him. What does it mean to have such a vision of the future?'

Uli did not answer.

'Perhaps it's better not to ask the question when we cannot act upon the answer,' Logi said.

'Maawian wisdom?'

'Maawian wisdom,' he agreed.

'What will you do about my father?'

'He is the chief.'

'Loyalty to you, my chief,' Uli said, repeating the words he had heard Logi use so many times.

Logi nodded.

'But no one agrees with him. According to you, he has no support any more.'

'Perhaps not. But perhaps it is not necessary to agree with those who lead us, only to know that they lead. You think you have discovered the end of the world, but there is nothing you can do with the vision. That is not leadership. Perhaps that is why they cast you out.'

'Everything you say starts with "perhaps."'

'A man loses his certainty, Uli. Just as certainly as I am losing my sight. I married a good woman, but we never had children and she died six years ago. Cancer ... Was it cancer from the sky? From that hole you talk about, you campaign about. My eyes, her life – I don't know. I do know she had no treatment here. We could not save her ...'

'I am sorry,' Uli said.

'You feel uncertain about your father. I will tell you, he came to me and said, "Let me sell some land and help you send your wife to the hospital." Your own mother was dead by then, and maybe he thought he could do this for me.'

'But you refused?'

'My wife refused,' Logi said. 'Who would he sell it to? Even a small hotel would be too much. In truth, I think she knew she was saving us both, your father and I.'

'Saving? How?'

'He was my friend and he could not but offer. But as chief, he could not do for me what he would not do for the rest of his people. And I could not have let him. She knew that.'

165

'Even to save her?' The question slipping out before Uli realized quite what he was saying.

Logi's eyes narrowed as if the tightening lids held back pain. ' "Loyalty to you, my chief." Perhaps there are worse things . . .' He smiled. 'When you have worked out what it is you will do, come to me, and I will help you. I believe that in sending you away we did ourselves a great service, but rendered you none. We need your learning on Maawi, Uli. That was my reasoning eleven years ago. It has not changed.'

Without waiting for an answer, Logi got up and walked to his Suzuki 4x4. As he opened the door, he glanced back at Uli. 'A nice car,' he said, 'but I cannot drive it any more and I have to ship in petrol from the next island. One delivery every three months. I am carted around with two 10-gallon cans at my back. Such is progress.' He shrugged and got into the car and his driver started the engine.

Uli watched him until he and the car had disappeared into the dust up the road.

Patty had to go back to see Pfister again. She knew she did. There were still questions. There was still the big question.

The next morning she ate hash browns and bacon and set off up the road she had driven down the night before.

When she arrived at the house, Pfister was nowhere to be found. She used the bell pull, walked around the perimeter several times, peered in at the windows. Nothing.

She was about to give up the hunt when she noticed a distant figure down the beach. The tide was out and, with the water at its furthest point, a scattering of rocks the size of small cars stuck out of the water, at the left hand side.

Pfister was sitting on the rocks in shorts and a T-shirt, his bleached hair blown by the sea breeze.

As Patty walked towards him, he never looked at her. His head was down, resting on his knees. She thought he might be asleep.

'Professor Pfister?' The sound of her voice roused him.

'You?' he said, turning sheepishly. His tone told her immediately that his high of the previous evening had dived into a considerable low. 'You must take to being insulted really well.'

'I've been told that.' She nodded solemnly.

'I suppose I should apologize,' he said, but showed no sign of actually doing so. 'I was . . . stoned, blasted, you know the phrases. Not that you aren't quite lovely.' He paused. 'It's strange what a hangover will do for you, isn't it?'

166

'I came back to ask you again . . .'

'I remember you now, Patty. Ten years ago, you said. God, it seems a hell of a lot further back than that.' He put one hand up and rubbed the right side of his face. 'You used to admire me,' he said, repeating her own words back to her.

Patty stood her ground, six feet from him, watching what was now a neurotic, a pathetic piece of humanity.

'You were right,' he said unexpectedly.

'I was. About what?'

He looked at her. 'Everything, I suppose. What the hell happened to me?'

She moved closer, bent her head towards him. 'The change is coming, isn't it – what Buckley predicted?'

He nodded. 'There is a growing instability.'

'Buckley thought it needed a natural event to trigger it, some sort of transient climatic event. Could that be El Niño?'

Pfister smiled. 'What defends the balance now is weak,' he said. 'Polluted seas, lost forests. The Earth's appetite for carbon waste has suffered a terminal indigestion. If there was a big enough one, El Niño could tip the balance, start the ice-caps melting. Something the size of the '87 El Niño would probably do it if repeated now with the current carbon dioxide levels.'

'They've only moved a little,' Patty protested, unsure if she actually wanted to believe this, now she was suddenly faced with the cold hard truth.

'A little is all it takes. A straw breaks the camel's back. With the shit we're still pumping, the threshold's getting smaller. In a few years it won't take more than a loose whiff of breeze.'

'So is it true they gave you money to keep quiet? Why? Why isn't it out there in the public domain? Why aren't we doing something?'

Pfister hesitated, then he stood up and brushed the sand from his shorts, dusting down his backside with the flats of his hands. 'Come with me,' he said. He walked briskly past her, heading for the house. 'Come,' he repeated, 'I'll show you it all.'

First he took her to the room with the grand piano and the glass-topped table. He pointed at the black dots and lines she had been unable to work out the night before. 'You know what they are?' he asked.

She shook her head.

'Cyclones.'

She counted. 'There are too many of them.'

'Right,' he agreed. He smiled wanly and added, 'This is an El Niño year.'

'What?'

'That's right, Patty. It's been coming a while now. The westward-blowing trades weakened three months ago. You know, the intertropical convergence zone?'

'Of course,' she said, sounding insulted, 'it's where the weather systems of the northern and southern hemisphere meet.'

'Crudely, yes,' Pfister agreed. 'I'll not argue. In the last month it's moved a thousand miles south. I keep in touch with the remote weather stations around the world by e-mail. They all write to PPP, Professor P. Pfister. I already have reports that the carbon dioxide levels have risen by as much as a part per million. That's in a few months. The poor little surface bacteria are not getting their food. Hence, no absorption of all the shit we're throwing in the air.'

Patty stared at him. 'Will it be big enough?'

'To cause the flip . . . who knows? This time, the next time, what's the difference?' He shrugged. 'There's more.'

He led her through the house and up the main staircase, into a room tucked away at the end of a side corridor on the first floor. Some sort of office had been set up inside, but was obviously little used. Junk lay in the corner, files and personal effects in a heap three feet high. There were a couple of filing cabinets and an antique globe of the world, almost identical to the one Pielot had had in his Paris office. The globe itself was slightly bigger and the brass nameplate on the frame below was engraved with the name of a different nineteenth-century seaman.

Pfister rifled through drawers of a desk until he came up with a wad of papers. He read the top one, then handed it to her.

'This room is everything I took out of my college office, back when I did real work,' he said. 'I kept this as a memento. I told them I'd rigged it so it would transmit over the Internet if anything happened to me. There's great things you can do with the Internet these days. I'm not sure they were ever going to kill me, but I had to have an insurance policy.'

Patty scanned the text.

'How thoroughly did you do your sums?' Pfister asked.

'What do you mean?'

'Did you work out what the consequences would be?'

'Kind of.'

'We worked them out very thoroughly. The government of the United

168

States worked them out very carefully too. It is possible to get a massive shift in the equilibrium temperature in the southern hemisphere without the north suffering that much. As I seem to remember saying last night, you get some pretty crazy weather on the transition. The hurricanes, cyclones and typhoons you get with El Niño are only the start of it. But it lasts, say, six months or so. It's no great shakes. At least not in the northern hemisphere. The US coastline has been battered and bruised before. A few insurance companies take a pasting. What's important is our values.'

'Our values?' Patty repeated in horror.

'Read the piece of paper.'

'*The climatic scenario that Professor Pfister proposes is a threat to the future of parts of the world, but knowledge of it is a deeper threat to the political stability of industrial nations in the short and long term. In summary, all the scenario modelling we have carried out suggests that announcing this threat publicly and/or trying to act to stabilize the southern hemisphere's climate would lead to meltdown of the world economy. There is an estimated 85 per cent chance of full-scale nuclear war centred in the European zone if either of these options are followed.'* Patty broke off. 'I can't believe what I'm reading,' she stammered.

'Reads like sci-fi, doesn't it?' Pfister said. 'Believe it. This was the conclusion of the "wise men" the President consulted. We figured you needed an immediate 50 per cent cut in global emissions to have a realistic chance of getting recovery before a good old "spirit child", El Niño, tipped you over the edge. We asked the political strategists and the military men. How the hell was anyone going to agree that? They tried it every which way in their simulators . . . came up with war every time.'

'War?' Patty exclaimed. That didn't seem to make sense.

'Think about it,' Pfister said. 'The President of the United States ringing up all his worldwide buddies and telling them they ought to completely reorganize their countries' way of life starting tomorrow: a) half of them would be hoisted out by their own political parties the moment they tried it; b) it would cause major civil unrest, shortages, famine even, and any other kind of shit that you can think of from the breakdown of a nation's natural order; and c) there's not exactly going to be a consensus between nations about who is responsible for the mess and who's going to have to do what to clean it up.'

'So they decided to do nothing?'

Pfister laughed strangely. 'They decided the planet could limp on with a ruined southern hemisphere. They didn't fancy risking an economic meltdown and a nuclear winter . . .'

'Because a nuclear winter might involve the United States and Europe . . .'

'Well, I think the conclusion they came to was that you can't fuck up the lives of people used to living in luxury. They're the ones with the bombs and they start throwing them at each other when they don't get what they want.'

'How many people?' Patty asked.

Pfister sighed. 'Allowing for the rescue operation and the taking in of refugees – you have to remember that Uncle Sam and the UN will be launching a major humanitarian effort once it's established that the temperature shift is real and not just an inconvenient prediction – allowing for that, they figured about 300 million. What the hell! The world's way over-populated anyway, right? I mean, we're too many rats in a rat cage. This'll just redress the balance.'

Patty closed her eyes. A silence roared in her ears.

'I've lived with my eyes closed too,' he agreed. His voice had suddenly become breathy and strained. 'You know what that's like? Hell, I just keep repeating the same work over and over. Over and over and over. People who used to be friends think I've lost it. I've lost it all right. I've lost it, but not the way they think.'

Patty kept her eyes closed for nearly a minute. When she opened them, there was the paper, the document marked 'Office of the President Only'. It still had the same words upon it. 'Can I take a copy of this?' she asked.

Pfister leaned over slowly and took the paper from her. At first she thought he was going to offer to copy it for her, but instead he screwed it into a ball. 'You don't understand,' he moaned.

It was then she saw the barrel of a gun, pointing directly at her.

A great heave came up through her body as if she was about to vomit, but nothing came. She swallowed, conscious of a new tightening in her chest. A moment before, Pfister had seemed a defeated man, willing to tell her everything, she thought. But the mood swing . . . It was like panic coming over him. The man was not in control, of himself, of the situation, of anything.

'This is going to come out, you know? Buckley's work was not destroyed. He did the last of his work on Maawi. There are copies still there,' she told him, emphasizing the words, trying to make him see, to turn him around again.

Pfister stared at her. The gun shook in his hand.

She said, 'Don't shoot me . . . please don't.'

Pfister seemed to consider this for a moment. Then he waved the gun, signalling her to move back. He circled around the desk so he was between her and the door. She watched his eyes, pure panic.

'Why are you doing this?' she asked. 'You used to be one of the good guys. Come on, we can break this open. I believe the world has a chance to sort its problems out. Don't you think it should have that chance? I believe in humanity. Are you going to let millions die, just because . . .'

'Shut up!' he shouted. 'I didn't ask you to come here. I didn't ask you to get involved. You came back.'

'I came back because someone's got to do something.'

'Shut up,' he repeated. 'I don't wanta shoot you.'

He was backing towards the door. She felt completely paralysed. She tried to think rationally. Perhaps her best option was to go for him now, while he was as confused as she was. But she couldn't move.

He was ten feet from her, stepping through the doorway, gun still towards her. Ten feet represented maybe a second. Would he pull the trigger? The man had lost everything anyway; he was hollow, she saw that now, scooped out with fear and shame.

While she hesitated, he had continued backing away. She heard the door shut and the click of the lock as he turned the key. Her opportunity had gone.

Watson Thomas went from hotel to airport and back to hotel. All planes were cancelled. He felt like a butterfly caught inside its cocoon, unable to break out. Now he had decided to do the one instinctive, most untight-arsed thing he'd ever committed himself to, he was desperate to start it, to be the butterfly, to be free . . . to actually take to the air. He was shaking with the desire.

'Dust storm coming mate,' the very Australian BA representative at the airport had told him. 'Nothing can take off or land. We had one of these here in the eighties, last time we had a big El Niño. It was a beaut, you wouldn't believe it. If this's anything like, my God, it's one of the wonders of the world, makes you feel like it's doomsday.'

'An El Niño?'

That name meant so much more to Watson today than it had done yesterday.

'I've got to get . . .' he started, then realized how impossible it was to explain his position.

He reclaimed his hotel room three hours after he'd vacated it. With it came a view over the city. At two in the afternoon he saw the blackness rising in the far distance, like the gathering of the worst thunderstorm he'd ever seen. The wind increased; he heard it rushing through the complaining railings as he sat on the hotel-room balcony watching the blackness approach.

A cold front in the weather pushing in under the furnace heat of previous days had dug up a few thousand acres of the outback like an ethereal spade. Now it was carrying it, ready to turn over a gigantic sod in the heart of the city.

Watson looked up as the blackness came closer and closer.

At two fifteen the sun was gone, gone as if Melbourne were in an eclipse. Red dust started to pepper the balcony where he sat and he retreated inside, watching it fall from the other side of the glass. He wondered whether this was the beginning of Buckley's shift. What had Patty said?

That a big enough El Niño would set off an irreversible climate change in the southern hemisphere. Floods. The flushing Flood of Genesis revisited. That sounded like the end of the world. At least, it sounded like the end of this part of the world.

And what else had she said?

When he told her he was going to Maawi, she said, 'Take care . . .'

Take care. There was a warmth to it. And although she had been thousands of miles away, invisible through the network of telecommunications, the bandwidth of her voice clipped by its journey, he had heard her warmth. He had felt her. He had seen her as if she was standing in front of him. A vision. Patty as she had been when she loved him. Perhaps that was something that had simply been covered over and never entirely lost. Perhaps the wind that picked up these millions of tons of dust had also uncovered that buried love.

The cloud passed over in less than an hour and a half. Two or three inches of red-black dust lay everywhere on the city like a perfectly contoured blanket.

Washington DC. They smuggled themselves into the White House through a back entrance known to a few presidential mistresses and a small group of special agents.

Caroline Sharpe and Mike Plummer fell into the latter category. They were shepherded into a side office to await the President. The room was sparse: a wooden desk, two visitor's chairs on one side, a leather desk chair on the other. There were no decorations on the wall and no windows.

'Don't be nervous,' Plummer said.

'I'm not.'

'You're playing with your hair.'

'It's a new style. I'm not used to it.'

Indeed, Caroline was no longer the shoulder-length blonde who had handled PR for the SSEO. She was no longer the smart-suited insider who had fabricated the financial records to implicate Ulysses Masoni. In the week since leaving New York, she had cut her hair almost to a crew cut and dyed herself back to her natural brunette. She had also retaken her real name, and her title: Special Agent Margaret Callaway.

Plummer looked at her hair from all sides. 'Part of your campaign?' he asked.

'I do not want to do undercover work again,' she said. 'I've done it for two years. I hated it.'

'Not enough action for you?'

'You want me to make a formal request, Sir?' She underlined the last word with a vocal flourish.

'OK,' he said, 'but it sure looks like there's going to be action left in this one. I guess you're keen to see it through.'

She hesitated. 'I guess.'

'You're not certain?'

'Shit,' she said. 'Aren't you disturbed by what we've done here?'

Plummer shook his head. When he spoke he took on the tone of a wise counsellor. 'Listen, Margie, we're about to meet the President. We just serve. He takes the decisions.'

'Yeah, but we never . . .' She stopped herself. 'Forget it, you know I'll do my duty, Mike.'

He nodded in satisfaction. '*Fourteen kills in five years*, right? A few more now, I guess. You can count your plane load and your fat accountant.'

'Pielot had to look like an accident. You said so yourself.'

'Fair enough . . .' Plummer shrugged.

The conversation was interrupted by the entry of a tall, dark-suited man.

Plummer turned. 'Mr President,' he said.

The President nodded a brief acknowledgement. 'Good to see you, Mike.'

'This is my right hand, Margie Callaway.'

'Miss Callaway.' The same nod and the offer of a handshake. 'I hear our problem may still go a little shit-faced.'

'Let's say, the operation's not complete,' Plummer said.

'Put it that way if you like.' The President looked straight at Margie

Callaway. 'I saw you a couple of times on the television supporting that man. He was an impressive speaker.'

'He believed in what he was saying, Mr President.'

'Sure, and he could be right. No absolute proof, of course. And he had no answers to the problem, but he did have his finger right on it.' The President shook his head. For a moment the weight of office seemed to crush his shoulders. He crossed the room, put the desk between himself and his visitors, and sat down. 'You called this meeting at short notice, so talk to me, Mike,' he said. 'What do we do now?'

'Pfister called up in a flap this morning. Said some woman called Patty Drake from the European Environmental Projects Agency was on to the truth. He was garbled, not making much sense. He says he's locked her in a room in his house. We should have clipped that man long ago. I knew he would be a loose end.'

The President nodded gravely.

'Anyway. That's not the problem now. I've sent a squad down there.' Plummer looked at his watch. 'Ought to be there any time. It's a simple hit; they don't know the details. However, it's clear we have a situation. The long and short of it is we now believe we didn't get all the copies of Buckley's work.'

The President cursed.

'We believe Buckley had a holiday home on Maawi,' Plummer continued. 'Margie here confirms that. We believe he kept copies of the computer files there.'

'So, these are in the hands of the SSEO?'

'Sir, the SSEO no longer exists,' Margaret Callaway cut in.

'They're probably sitting on a computer and no one on the island knows,' Plummer said.

'So who does know?'

'Definitely this Patty Drake. As I say, no problem there. But, we believe, also a guy named Watson Thomas, the former MD of BBS. We think he was the one who made the discovery,' Plummer explained.

'They are inconveniently married,' Margaret Callaway added.

'I see. What do you recommend, Mike?'

'We have to go there, Mr President, and get those files. We have to wipe them at all costs.'

The President pondered for a moment. That same weight of office pressed him down in the chair. Slowly, reluctantly, he nodded.

'At all costs,' he said. 'How do we cover it?'

'We keep this as it is: Office of the President Only.'

'Meaning your team, Mike?'

'I suggest half a dozen specialists . . .'

'Go on,' the President urged.

'Callaway here will lead . . .'

Margaret Callaway straightened at hearing her own name.

'We'll pick out five others. One of those missions – the kind where the sanction for your actions gets lost or forgotten if anything goes wrong . . .'

'Mike,' the Pesident interrupted, 'I want you to lead the mission personally. This is too important.' He turned to Callaway. 'No disrespect.'

'None taken, sir.'

'I really . . .' Plummer began, but gave up.

The President said. 'You have to lead, Mike. By all means include Margaret here in your team. I have every confidence in her.'

Callaway thought about this for a moment, leaning against the bare wall. 'Thank you,' she said.

Plummer nodded uncertainly.

'I appreciate this,' the President added.

'Just our jobs,' Plummer said.

The President stood up as if indicating the end of the meeting. Mike Plummer moved to shake his hand and Margaret Callaway followed.

As they were leaving, the President said, 'I want you to know, if I was certain about any of this stuff, I'd act on it. But I can't act on it while it's just dangerous speculation. So I . . . we . . . we have to kill it.'

They both turned to look at him. His voice was weak, and unpolitically empty.

XXVI

Patty sat huddled on the floor under the desk. Very small, as if she wanted to melt away. She had forgotten her watch and lost track of the speed of time. How long had she been locked up?

She told herself to get control. Get control. Get control. She needed to assess her options rationally.

Staring at the door, she saw it was a rather ornate wooden design, eight recessed panels chamfered into the main thickness of the door with fretwork ornamentation. The panels were arranged two wide and four high so they covered half of the door's total area. The door must be thinner in these panelled areas, she reasoned, wondering whether it might be possible to break through. But the panels were hardly flimsy. Like the rest of the house, with its wood and marble trimmings, it was built to last.

She got up and walked to the door and banged on one of the panels.

'Professor, let me out of here, for Christ's sake,' she cried forlornly. The 'thunk' told her just how thick the door was. She hit it again and again, right hand and left, feeling the pain racing back through her knuckles.

'Shut up!' she heard Pfister yell after the third repetition. She heard his footsteps shuffling in the corridor. He was on the other side of the door now. 'Shut up!'

'Why are you doing this?'

'Don't you see? I have no choice,' his muffled voice came back.

She thought she heard a kind of twisted emotion despite the attenuation. Pfister had lost his balance. Lost it long ago.

She leaned her cheek against a panel

'You did have one,' she said. 'You did have a choice.'

A pause. She heard movement.

'I'm not responsible,' he moaned.

Although he still sounded muffled, she could tell he was closer now, pushing his own cheek close to the door, she guessed.

'What are you going to do with me?' she asked, exaggerating the plea in her voice.

'I didn't want to,' he said.

'What are you going to do with me?' she asked again, insistent.

'I can't go against the government. No one can.'

'Their grants . . .'

'No one can,' he repeated.

She heard his body slump against the door and the noise of his weight sliding down. She moved her own face down the door and she could hear him weeping, his cheek not two inches from her own.

'Professor?'

Nothing.

She pulled back and looked around desperately. She saw the pile of personal effects lying in the corner. There were three piles of bundled documents, a fishing rod, numerous mementoes of academic conferences consisting mainly of wall plaques and paperweights, a poster featuring the Minnesota Twins, and a battered baseball bat signed three times with indecipherable autographs.

Patty picked up the baseball bat and felt its weight. It would do the job if only she could get him to open the door.

'Professor,' she called again.

Still no reply, but pressing herself to the door, she could hear his breathing. He was still there below the door handle.

She remembered his last few phrases: 'I didn't want to' and 'I can't go against the government.' She realised her folly. She had let out what she knew and he would have told them. Putting Watson in danger – she had put Watson in danger when she was trying to save herself. 'Fuck,' she said to herself.

Pfister might not have the guts to shoot anyone, but he was part of an enormous conspiracy, big enough to make millions of lives look expendable. What chance did she and Watson have? What value?

Images of what had happened to Buckley and Pielot and Monty Radford flashed back to her.

She looked around. She had to get out. It was desperate. Everything compressed into a short space of time.

She looked around again. The globe of the world sat in its castored frame by the desk. What had André Pielot said about his?

It weighed two hundred kilos. That was getting on for five hundred pounds.

This one was bigger. She ran to it and tried to move it.

The floor was polished wood. Thank God! She would never have moved it on carpet.

She manoeuvred it into a position where it had the longest run-up to the door. She had just enough space to get behind and push.

As she was about to lean into it, she realized this wasn't going to do. The weight was enough, but she couldn't get it going all that fast and, hitting the door flat on, it was not going to knock it over as she had hoped.

She thought about the weaker panels. And the baseball bat.

The bat fitted snugly into the frame when she tried it. The butt nestled against the back of the brass nameplate on one side and its length passed under the globe and rested on the iron support bar on the other side. A foot or so of bat stuck out front like a miniature battering ram. She felt pleased. Five hundred pounds thrusting through the length of the bat – that had to give her a chance.

She went over to the door.

'Professor?'

He didn't reply and she couldn't hear his sobbing now. But, on the other hand, she hadn't heard him move or get up either. She imagined his posture, checking that the height of her makeshift battering ram matched that of the panel a foot below the door handle, roughly the place she expected his head to be.

Buckley, Pielot and Monty Radford. There was no choice. She was going to die if she stayed in here. One desperate effort to get out was better than none.

She positioned her heels against the wall to get the best push off. Then she embraced the sphere of the world, counted to three in her head and heaved.

The globe moved and she moved forward with it, trying to make sure it kept accelerating.

Six feet from the door, she had it up to walking pace.

Not fast enough . . .

She heaved until she felt the muscles down the back of her leg starting to tear. Then she fell flat on her face. Her forehead hit wood.

She heard the crash and raised her head. The globe had already hit the door and was toppling back towards her . . . falling on top of her.

She rolled to her right.

Just in time.

The porcelain sphere smashed on the floor. Pieces span. Broken countries and continents in turmoil. Fragments like broken glass went skidding across the boards.

She felt a pain in her hand. She saw a piece of porcelain about an inch in diameter embedded in the crook between her forefinger and thumb. She was bleeding, but otherwise – and by the narrowest of margins – she had escaped injury.

Slowly, she picked herself up, heart still pounding. She picked out the piece of porcelain from her hand. It came out covered in blood – part of the African continent – and she reached in her pocket for a handkerchief to bind the wound. It wasn't that bad. Not life-threatening, she told herself. She turned back to her more pressing problem.

Before it had toppled over, the globe – or more specifically, the globe's makeshift battering ram – had punched a hole in the door's panel, splitting apart the surrounding wood. She bent down and peered through the hole.

There was no sign of Pfister.

Shit, where was he? Had she hit him?

'Professor?' she called out.

Nothing. He wasn't there.

She expected to hear him running towards the door. Wherever he'd been in the house, he couldn't have missed the crash and the shattering of the porcelain globe.

She peered again through the hole.

Still nothing. No sign or sound of Pfister.

She examined the splintered panel around the hole. On impact, the baseball bat had broken roughly in half, but she found she could use what remained of the business end to batter away more of the damaged wood from around the hole in the door. Soon it was big enough to get her arm through.

She reached around . . .

Her first bit of luck. Pfister had left the key in the lock.

She opened the door and went out into the hallway, still half-expecting to find the professor brandishing his gun. God knows what she would do then. But there was nothing else to be done. She had to get out of the house and get out now.

She was hurrying. Running. And binding her wound more tightly as she went.

The light from the enormous round window hit her as she came on to the landing overlooking the ground floor. She crossed to the top of the velveted staircase, the window now at her back.

Then she saw him.

He had tied a rope to the banister that bordered the first floor landing. Looped it around his neck . . .

And jumped.

P. J. Pfister was swinging gently at the end of the rope, three feet off the ground.

XXVII

Watson's life had always been offices and airports and hotels. Reading the stamps in his passport, he seemed well-travelled, but that was an illusion. He had been around the world without travelling, visiting in a workaholic daze. He sat on an aeroplane and it delivered him to a hotel and an office that looked exactly like the hotel and office in the place he'd just left. That wasn't travelling; it was merely waiting around while someone made minor adjustments to the scenery.

But this time it was different. This was the South Seas. This was somewhere quite without the homogenizing influences that blended everywhere else into a single global city.

He could smell and taste blossom on the air when he emerged from his small plane in Waatu. Instead of an airport, there was a rickety jetty and a motor launch, a 12-foot wooden boat with bench seats down the sides and no paint on what was visible of the hull.

He reached in his pocket, took out his mobile phone and switched it on. It couldn't find a signal. So much for 'find-me-anywhere' technology, he thought. It hadn't reached into the beauty of the South Seas. Air pollution, yes, but not the airwaves.

Smiling, he put the phone away and walked across to the motor launch, looking around as he went. He saw coconut palms and strange grasses. Above his head, the sky was a blue that seemed beyond the purity of primary colour.

'Terminal?' he said to the wizened man who sat at the tiller of the launch fiddling with something in the outboard motor.

The man was about five foot eight and well-muscled except for his belly, which stuck out as if borrowed from some other body and added a good three or four stones to his weight. He wore only ragged shorts and his skin was a deep shade of brown that only those who live in the sun achieve.

'You English?' the man asked.

Watson nodded. 'Where is the terminal here?' he continued.

'I take you all to terminal,' the man said, 'over the water on island. This just the atoll.'

Watson hefted his belongings – one suitcase, one suiter and a notebook computer – down into the motor launch.

'Only flat land here,' the man said, 'Waatu stick up like a finger. You see.'

The man started the engine and revved it up and the other handful of passengers from the small plane ambled slowly across and got into the launch.

When they finally got going and the launch pulled beyond the grove of coconut trees, the island of Waatu eased into sight.

The sea between launch and island was blue, the sand on the beach white, and the land so dense with waving trees that it seemed covered in tufted green wool. Its beauty assaulted his senses and, for a moment – no, for longer than a moment, for a minute and more – Watson drank from the cup of nature and forgot.

'See there,' the man said, snapping Watson back from his daydream. The man was pointing to the horizon far out to sea, where the blue of the sky ended in puffy trails of cloud. 'You pick a bad time.'

Watson raised his eyebrows. When the man didn't continue, he wondered if raising the eyebrows was one of those gestures that had no meaning, or even a different meaning, in the South Seas.

'Why is it a bad time?' Watson asked, discarding the use of body language.

'Storms coming,' the man said. 'One. Maybe two days. Very bad.'

Watson hesitated. He realized this man might be one of the few English-speakers on Waatu. There might not be that many chances to ask. 'I have to get to Maawi,' Watson told the man. 'Do you know how I do it?'

The man smiled. 'There be two, maybe three, fisherman might take you for money, you know?'

'OK. Where will I find them?'

'Here and there. If they are at home, not fishing.'

Watson felt a dread that created a sudden sag in his facial muscles. He could be stuck on Waatu, seeing Maawi on the horizon but unable to get there.

'No worry,' the man said, 'I take. You wait now. This evening we go. When I finish. One more plane to meet now.'

The trip from landing strip to Waatu island lasted fifteen minutes. As they neared the island, Watson could see the beach and the line of buildings growing larger and more detailed. They seemed to be mostly family dwellings, some with small boats pulled up on the beach next to them. There was one building like a concession stand with a single open side selling all sorts of strange products, a mixture of local crafts and imported canned food and drinks.

Watson looked back towards the atoll on which the plane had landed. Now they were far enough from it, he could see the long thin strip of its land, surrounded by blotched patches and bands of blue sea that indicated the various depths and states of the coral. Other smaller atolls stretched to the right and left of it, but the one for the landing strip had clearly been chosen because it was the longest and straightest. All the atolls together seemed to form a string of beads around the main island.

'We go over lagoon here,' the man said, indicating the waters between island and its rocky necklace. 'Only channel go out to sea.' He pointed between two of the atolls. 'The Japanese . . .' He shook his head. 'Too dumb to find it.' Still shaking his head, he added. 'We had a good war. Good protection.'

When they reached Waatu, the launch veered away to the right of the beach and tied up at a jetty not unlike the one they'd left on the atoll, and all the passengers disembarked, walking along weathered planks over the last few feet of sea at the shoreline.

'Wait,' the man said to Watson. He pointed to a shelter, a wooden roofed structure with a back wall and open front.

'No customs?' Watson asked, amazed that this ten-foot square shack could be all there was to greet the incoming traveller.

'Me customs,' the man said, stepping back into the motor launch after helping his passengers. 'You want show me your passport?' He laughed and pulled in his mooring rope. The motor growled, then settled and started chugging the launch back out to sea.

Watson considered walking up towards the buildings he'd seen further up the beach, but it was hot and he wanted to be in the shade. He walked instead towards the shelter, laughing when he noticed there was a Coke machine nestled in the back wall – 'Drink Coca-Cola' written on backlit plastic.

He dragged some money out of his pocket, strange coins he'd received at the currency exchange when they had finally reopened Melbourne Airport. Calculating the value of his change, he chinked the right money into the slot. The machine burbled for a moment, before a bottle clunked to the bottom. He picked it out and uncapped it on the crude opener welded to the front of the machine. Then he sat down with his back to the wall and sipped and then gulped the cool brown liquid. He hadn't realized how thirsty he'd become.

He had thought that a Lacoste shirt and trousers and Camel shoes would be perfect for the South Sea heat, but now even the fine cotton was wet and sticking to his skin. He wriggled with discomfort.

It seemed he had hopelessly underestimated. One of many things he seemed to have misjudged lately.

After a while, his eyes began to feel heavy. They fell shut involuntarily and he slept.

He woke with a start. His contact lenses had gone dry in his eyes and he rubbed at them furiously until they watered and gave him some kind of relief. He couldn't work out how long he'd been asleep. He glanced vaguely at his watch, but he'd been through so many time zones recently he couldn't remember how it was set and the position of the hands meant nothing to him.

There was a soft rumble in his ears. The motor launch was approaching. Against an afternoon sun falling towards evening, he saw its dark silhouette.

There was the boatman just as he'd promised.

And another figure standing at the bow ... T-shirt and Bermuda shorts. Hair trailing back like a comet's tail.

He ran forward and stopped on the jetty, half-expecting the vision to pop like a balloon as he moved towards it.

They flew to Houston and hired a motorbike. Alexandra bought a map and threw her leg across the bike and said, 'Come on then, stud, let's go.'

Connor said, 'Are you sure you want to do this?'

She took two or three seconds to say yes. 'Just don't throw up down my back,' she added. Then she kicked the bike off its stand and pressed the starter. He didn't ask again.

She rode with a wildness that had him struggling to hold on to his airline lunch. The faster she went the worse he felt, but he didn't think this was a good moment to complain.

It was getting dark by the time they found Cash Buemann's ranch. A gateman questioned them when they tried to enter the drive.

'Call up the house and tell them it's two people from BBS,' Connor advised him.

'No, tell Cash Buemann it's Ray Buckley's daughter,' Alexandra corrected.

'You-all're lucky the man's in,' the gateman said, waving them through a minute later. 'Just ride on up there to the house. Park that pony somewheres on the left of the drive. Don't scratch the caddies.'

Alexandra throttled up and declutched. The bike roared down the drive with Connor clinging on.

Vaguely visible to either side were the dark forms of cattle grazing behind three-bar fencing. Then the house itself appeared.

Its château-styling was picked out by ten kilowatts of lighting that spread out across the aqua-blue swimming pools and caught the walls of the matching outbuildings. Everything about it seemed huge.

Connor saw Cash Buemann standing at the main entrance of the house, beckoning them. Alexandra stopped the bike some twenty yards short of the door and they both got off and removed their crash helmets. She manoeuvred the bike on to its stand on the left of the tarmac drive as they had been instructed. There was a hard-surfaced lay-by backing up to the cattle fencing for the purpose. Alongside their hired Honda were a Rolls, a Ferrari and two classic Cadillacs.

'I didn't expect to see you again so soon,' Cash called.

Connor assumed this was directed mainly at Alexandra, but the Texan opened his arms, hands spread in a generous greeting that seemed to encompass both of them.

'I didn't expect to be here,' Alexandra said. She planted her feet on the driveway as if making a stand.

Cash was wearing his Buemann Oil cap, which Connor thought strange. But then, in the very few press photos Connor had ever seen of Cash, there was always that trademark hat.

Connor was considering why this might be when Alexandra blurted, 'Are you my father?'

Connor stared at her in horror. How could she simply come out with this? But then, he thought, how else do you ask it?

Cash's eyes went from one to the other, Alexandra and then Connor. His cheery voice dropped. 'I think you'd better come in.'

He retreated as much as led them, taking them through the house to a room with high arched ceilings, polished wooden floors and early nineteenth-century European furniture. The walls were covered in oil paintings.

'Tea, coffee, or something stronger?' he asked, pointing out the servant now standing ready to take their order. 'I have an English butler so we know how to make tea here. Best you can get in Texas, so I'm told.'

For the moment he seemed to have recovered his usual energetic manner, even if it had taken on a forced quality.

Alexandra asked for vodka. Connor ordered tea and scanned his eyes around the various canvases, amazed as he counted two by Eugène Delacroix and what looked like an early Renoir.

Were they real or reproduction, he asked himself. But then, why have fake when you've got money hanging around like wastepaper and you're living so far from anywhere – a Xanadu plonked in the Texas desert – that you've only got your house to spend it on?

The time passed nervously until the drinks were delivered and the butler had gone. Alexandra plopped herself into an armchair in the centre of the room, and Cash perched himself on the armrest of an antique chair some distance away.

'You asked me a question,' he said. 'You want to repeat it now?'

'Are you my father?'

'What makes you think I am?'

Alexandra looked at Connor. Did she expect him to explain the evidence? He didn't want to do that. Connor nodded towards Cash. That was where she should get her answers.

'I know Ray Buckley wasn't,' Alexandra said, taking the hint, 'and I know you've been putting money into my trust fund.'

'I see.' Cash twisted himself around, sliding off the arm into the seat of the chair. He looked at his hands. 'Yeah,' he muttered, 'I guess I am.' He raised his eyes, gazing at her with longing. Connor couldn't imagine what it was the man felt. How could he? He didn't even know the history.

'How did your mother die?' Cash asked abruptly.

'In childbirth . . . my birth,' Alexandra said.

Cash shook his head and took off his baseball cap. 'Try, in a car crash with me,' he said.

To Connor, Cash's scars spoke far more eloquently than his words, but Alexandra's face contorted with anger. She didn't seem to know where to aim herself. 'You bastard!' she said and bit hard into her lip.

'We were coming back from a launch party in London,' Cash continued, his voice steady but strained, 'Ray was announcing BBS's first commercial product. She was eight months pregnant. Ray said would I drive her back home because she was tired.' Cash looked at Alexandra but she didn't look back. 'We'd been having an affair on and off for a couple of years, but it had become difficult . . . I guess, since she got pregnant.'

Alexandra's head hung down into her chest and the tears dripped into her lap as she shook her head from side to side.

'Driving too fast. I was . . . We were . . . just happy to have an excuse to be together.' He hesitated as if waiting for her emotion to catch up.

186

Slowly she raised herself to ask a question. 'Those are the scars?'

Cash nodded. 'The car burst into flames. She was thrown clear. Not wearing a seat belt. She died a few hours later in hospital, after you were . . .' His voice trailed off and he gulped for air. 'Anna,' he said, not connecting any other word to it.

When there had been silence for half a minute and it was clear Alexandra couldn't speak, Connor said, 'And the trust fund?'

'Yes, I paid to put in the Buemann Oil shares.'

'Did my father ever know?' Alexandra blubbed, with just enough control to get the question out.

Cash shook his head. 'He could never have brought himself to believe it. He thought the trust fund was just me exorcising my guilt. I suppose, in a way, it was. But not in the way he thought . . . I loved her.'

XXVIII

When Patty saw him, he was standing on the jetty in front of a wooden shelter, waving his arms, a Coca-Cola machine blinking through its red plastic fascia behind him.

She stepped off the launch and smiled. Without thinking, she opened her arms and he clasped her to him.

He said, 'I don't know what I'm doing here, Patty.'

She held on to him, or rather, allowed herself to be held and pacified him by resting her hands on his upper arm and shoulder.

'When you said you were in Melbourne, I . . .' Her voice choked up. She mumbled, 'You don't realize how lucky I was to get out of California. Pfister . . . I mean . . . I . . .'

He leaned back far enough to bring her face into focus. She let him brush the wayward hair from her eyes with a fingertip.

Patty had thought she knew who Watson Thomas was. When he didn't come home, when he left her for days and her mind got warped, she thought she knew. But she had forgotten the soul that created those dreams. She had forgotten the best parts of those thirteen years. Not the acts themselves perhaps, but she had forgotten the intimacies of their time together – how it felt. She had forgotten that she knew a Watson Thomas who lived beyond and independent of his actions.

His embrace seemed to overcome everything, even the isolating fear of the last few weeks. And she felt the water running from her eyes.

'You go Maawi, we start pronto,' the man in the launch was saying.

He must have repeated the same sentence two or three times. It took them a long, long time to hear him.

XXIX

Margaret Callaway looked around at the four men who accompanied her. Hard men. Order-takers. Doers. Men who had grown up on farms and in small towns where the army and then the special security forces seemed like a career.

They would do the job. Uncle Sam's dirty work. Euro-American whitewash.

Mike Plummer entered the room with a curt, 'Listen up, people.' He spread out a map of Maawi on the table and huddled over it, pushing a coffee cup aside to guard against spillage. The ship they were on was lurching through waves, unusually high for the South Seas.

'We scramble at 06:00,' he said. 'We've got a CH137 transport for personnel and the gear. We'll take one Jeep.'

Plummer nodded to Callaway, indicating that she should take over.

'We haven't had the benefit of usual reconnaissance,' she said. 'We know Masoni's village is here.' She pointed. 'So we'll take the chopper on to this beach.'

'I've agreed that Callaway will lead any negotiations with the natives,' Plummer said. 'She knows Masoni.'

'We'll make this our base, work out a route to Buckley's hideaway from there,' Callaway continued pointing out landmarks on the map.

'How we gonna do that?' one of the men asked.

Callaway glared at him. 'I'm going to take Masoni, or one of his island savages. I'm going to stick my gun in his mouth and I'm going to say, "Tell me where Buckley had his place."'

Callaway's eyes narrowed. She was talking herself into the mission. 'I'll waste them all one by one until I find someone who knows, if I have to. But I won't have to. Masoni knows me. He knows, by now, it was me . . . me who fucked with his little set-up.'

She had frozen into a stone-cold look. It was the way she'd been

189

trained. She could create emotions by mere concentration. Among the men she'd killed were dictators, gorilla leaders and opponents of democracy. Their faces never troubled her, but she had chilled herself to the bone to remove the surprised look of a man who had foreseen the future. And still it kept coming back.

They were sitting at a table out of doors. Patty had just finished her lecture on the consequences of Buckley's results.

Uli Masoni paled visibly as the story unwound and sunk into his understanding. Finally, he got up from the ground and paced in the firelight. It was full dark by now.

'How can this be?' his father, the chief, asked. 'It is not that we doubt the chance for disaster. But how can it not affect all?' He swept his arms out in a circular motion to indicate the world.

'I don't know,' she said. 'I only know that similar things have happened in the past.'

'Long ago?'

'Long ago. Thousands of years.' She looked at Uli. '*In the six hundredth year of Noah's life*,' she quoted back to him. Uli smiled thinly. A shared memory, but never a happy one.

'And El Niño comes to bring this thing now?' the chief continued.

'Now? We don't know whether it's now. We only know it's soon. The stabilizing forces in the Earth's climate are being weakened by pollution.'

'Can it be reversed?' Uli cut in. 'I mean, if the world just stopped polluting itself.'

Patty twisted her expression to try to cover her doubt. 'Pfister said we needed an immediate 50 per cent cut in emissions.'

'We also need the proof,' Watson said. 'We need the proof in our hands.'

'How can this be?' the chief repeated. This time it seemed to be a plea to the gods.

Uli came back to the table and sat down. He looked across at Patty. 'I have a simple understanding. The sun is closest to the equator, hits it straight on, so . . .'

'So it should be hottest,' Patty agreed, 'in normal circumstances. But, in truth, one of the major factors is always the flow of sea currents. Pollution helps warming and starts a melting of the ice-caps. Floating icebergs, changes in the wind, these can permanently and very suddenly alter that flow – the thermohaline flow.'

'And the change is started by El Niño?' Uli asked, looking for confirmation.

'It's the biggest kick that the balance of the climate in the southern hemisphere ever receives.'

'We are in an El Niño year now,' the chief said. He looked upwards into the night sky. 'We are about to see its first storms.'

'I know,' Patty said, trying to disguise the shudder in her voice. 'But I said an El Niño, not this El Niño. It may not be big enough to tip the balance.'

'How will we know that?' Masoni asked.

'Only if it passes and calm comes back,' Patty told him.

'Wait and see?'

She nodded.

'Even if it is not,' said the chief, 'who knows how we will ever draw back from the brink?' He rose to his feet as if to bring their meeting to a close. He put his hand to his chin and looked from Patty to Watson and then to his son. 'Tomorrow Uli will go with you to Ray Buckley's cabin.'

Uli said something to his father in the local language. His father answered and a few short words were exchanged. Uli turned to Watson and Patty.

'What is it?' Watson asked.

'My father says I am to go and fetch Logi's vehicle for the journey.'

'Is that a problem?'

'No, the land my father gifted Ray Buckley is hidden in the interior. It is a long and difficult way, even on a small island and even in Logi's four-wheel-drive.'

'Get sleep now,' the chief interrupted, 'you have a long day tomorrow.'

'We will go to Logi's village at sunrise.' Uli agreed.

'They have phone lines there?' Patty asked.

Uli smiled. 'Oh, yes. There they have phone lines.'

'I'd like to log in and catch up on the weather.'

'But you don't know how severe El Niño has to get?' Watson said.

'No,' she admitted, 'I'd just like to . . . to know how bad it is. And how bad this storm is going to be.'

'Uli,' the chief said, 'give our guests your hut. You can come with me.'

Uli shot a glance at Watson and Patty. Watson caught the full force of its unease. He looked at Patty, who smiled.

'But . . .' Uli began.

'They will want to share,' his father said. He looked at his son, but said no more. The look implied that Uli should know exactly what he was talking about.

XXX

The next day Alexandra rode the ranch with her newfound father. Maybe she thought she owed him something: a chance at being in her life.

Meanwhile, Connor plugged his portable computer into the telephone system and tinkered. He hated horses, so he stayed behind. He called up *Adventure Updater* and clicked on the 'update' icon. Soon he was wading through thick undergrowth, chasing a thirty-foot space monster, armed only with a five-inch ray-gun and a magic pitchfork.

The idea was good, but its execution poor. Soon after starting, he abandoned the game. Compared to *Adventure Updater's* last effort, the trek through a South American jungle, this new scenario was rubbish. The graphics looked like they hadn't been debugged properly. There were inconsistencies in the controls and menus. Whoever had taken over WT Gaming was milking it and not returning the investment.

That made Connor angry in a strange way. Not because it was Watson's old company; it simply offended his sense of what computer software was supposed to do for the world. It was supposed to get better, to evolve into better things. It was supposed to make the world better.

He wanted to break into their website and leave a rude message. 'Don't pay for this, it's crap.' He'd like to flash that on to the screen of everyone who logged on to the update website. He spent most of the next three hours working on it.

Cash and Alexandra came back at noon. As he came out to greet them, Connor could see them smiling at one another, the relaxed body language with which they sat their horses.

He felt a twinge of jealousy which he hadn't expected. The situation was bizarre and his emotions were getting tied up and he didn't know how to deal with any of this. Alexandra got off her horse and came

192

over to Connor and kissed him. For the first time, her kiss didn't make him feel better.

'Want to dip in Cash's pool before lunch?' she asked. 'I'm hot and sticky.'

He shook his head, trying not to look sulky.

'OK. I'm going anyway. Do you mind?' she said.

He knew he had the chance to say yes, but then he'd have to justify it and he couldn't do that. She handed him the reins and walked towards the house. He was left holding the horse.

Cash was watching him, still mounted, the Texan noting Connor's nervousness around the animal with amusement. Cash tipped the cowboy hat that had replaced the normal baseball cap for the purposes of riding. 'Quite a filly,' he remarked.

Connor turned his head to watch Alexandra's rear disappearing through the front door.

'I meant the horse,' Cash said. He cocked his leg and swung himself to the ground. 'But she's a piece of work too. Come on, let me help you. You don't look so comfortable as you do at a keyboard, partner.'

Connor tried to push the horse by shouldering it in the side. The horse took a step but refused to go any further. 'I don't know what to do with the things. They're bloody big. Much higher than they look on telly.'

Cash took the reins and put them with those of his own horse. Connor was grateful to be relieved of the duty.

'Do you love her?' Cash asked suddenly. 'True-love-and-marriage kind of love? Are you her Mr Right, Connor? It's none of my business, OK. But, come on, I see it in your face.' He raised his voice and shouted, 'Bobby, take these horses, will you?'

A youth of about twenty in jeans and a cheesecloth shirt ran from the stables and took the reins. Cash spun around on his heel and started towards the house.

'She don't talk about anything else but you, you know? You're a strange looking son-of-a-bitch, but who am I to talk?' He put his hand on Connor's shoulder and patted it lightly. 'Shit, I've had a daughter for less than twenty-four hours. How should I know how to act? I suppose I ain't allowed to ask them kind of questions these days.'

'I don't know the answer,' Connor blurted.

'Well, that's an answer in itself,' Cash said, seemingly pleased by it. 'Let's go with that one for now.'

He smiled. Three seconds later, when the penny dropped, Connor smiled as well. They walked a few paces, Cash's arm still resting across Connor's shoulder.

'Cash, can I ask you something?'

'Shoot.'

'You were insider trading off Ray Buckley, weren't you?'

Cash pulled back his arm. 'Wo-ah.' he said. 'That's a mighty big statement.'

'Weren't you?'

'So what if I was?' He walked on a few more paces with Connor lingering behind. Cash looked back at him. 'You're a smart one, aren't you? I guess that's why she goes for you.'

'Monty Radford said never trust yourself in a Buemann company. There's always something going on.'

'He said that? I guess he was a smart old buzzard.'

'More like a hippo,' Connor suggested. 'A very smart old hippo.'

Cash smiled crookedly. 'Yeah,' he said, 'for what it's worth, we had a scheme going, Ray and I. But that was ten, fifteen years ago when he needed the money. He'd hack into the finances of the companies he was doing work for, tell me whether to buy or sell their shares. We are none of us angels, son. And don't go getting the idea that Ray was either. He did good things. Maybe he did a fine thing towards the end.'

'Did you make a lot of money?'

'Nope.' The Texan shook his head. 'It was a lot of money to Ray, maybe. And he thought he was paying me back for what I was doing for Alex, building her trust and all. He kept saying I shouldn't blame myself for Anna. The more he said it, the worse it was for me. I nearly told him a couple of times.'

'Why didn't you?'

'Who would it've helped? I'm not ashamed that I loved her. I really think what I did was the best job I could make of it, considering the circumstances.'

Connor looked at him. 'I won't tell Alex,' he said. 'About the insider trading.'

Cash nodded. 'Appreciate it. Let's go and see how our girl works out in the water . . .'

They were on the last half-mile of their walk the next morning when they saw the helicopter.

Patty was struggling to keep up. Uli was out front, dressed in grey calf-length trousers and a white vest. She and Watson, sporting almost conventional Western holiday casuals – the T-shirt, the shorts – stumbled behind as the islander moved with ease on the uneven path. Patty couldn't quite understand this. They were wearing computer-designed trainers and Uli was barefoot yet seemed to get the better purchase on the ground. The strange island man who had come to the West seemed all the stranger now he was back home – a hybrid who stood so oddly in both worlds.

They were passing the outskirts of Logi's village when the noise of beating rotor blades reached them on the breeze, making them look up.

There was the black shape against the dawn sky, moving from brooding cloud to brooding cloud.

'Oh, God,' she said, 'not yet, please . . . I was right. Pfister told someone before he . . .' Her voice trailed off as if the force of the image had knocked the breath from her lungs.

'The establishment cometh,' Watson announced. Turning to Patty, he said, 'It's not your fault.'

She searched fruitlessly for a smile. He was trying to be nice, but it simply twisted the knife in her guts. Why had she ever told Pfister?

'They are going towards my father's village,' Uli said. 'We have time to get to Logi.'

He raised his pace and Patty almost ran after him. Watson trailed at the back. He was carrying his portable computer in a bag strapped over his shoulder; it banged about and he tried to control it and run at the same time.

'Come on,' Uli urged.' Come on.'

Logi's house was the only substantial stone building in a row of huts. It was separated from the others by an overgrown garden. The patchwork lawn full of weeds was some ten feet square and a line for hanging washing stretched across it from the stone wall of Logi's house to the wooden wall of the next hut.

Uli stopped outside a front door that seemed painted to match an entirely different location. He didn't knock; he shouted.

When the old man emerged, he was wrapping a cloth around his middle that stretched down below his knees. 'What is this?' he said. He moved his head from side to side, not seeming to find their faces with his eyes. Patty had an uncle who developed cataracts in his sixties. She recognized Logi's condition immediately.

'Greetings,' said Uli, speaking English for the benefit of his companions. 'Logi, we need your car.'

'And I could do with using your phone,' Patty added.

The old man looked confused for a moment. His lips quivered as if he was about to mumble his misunderstanding. 'All right,' he said at last. He fixed his eyes in Uli's direction. 'If you say you need it, you need it. Let me find my keys. I have a phone in my back room.'

They went into the house which was lit by bare electric bulbs hanging from the ceiling. Western luxuries, thirty years out of date, were positioned like prized furniture: a Dansette record player in a wooden case, an inflatable armchair from the weirdest part of the sixties, an old bookcase of battered paperbacks, and a chrome pop-up toaster sitting on a plastic dining table.

In the back room, clearly the bedroom, Patty found much the same sense of style, but on the bedside table there was a modern Panasonic handset, plugged into what looked like a standard international telephone socket.

'Can we unplug this?' Patty asked, squatting in front of the bedside table.

Logi nodded, still looking uncertain.

'Don't worry,' Uli said.

'Was that a helicopter I heard?' Logi asked. 'Then, there is trouble, no?'

'There is trouble,' Uli agreed.

Watson took over the hardware duties. He plugged in the modem from his portable and switched on. In a few seconds he had his Internet account up and running.

'What do you want? The weather?' he asked Patty.

'You've got mail,' she told him, peering over his shoulder at the blinking icon in the corner of the screen.

'Why do you want the weather?' Logi asked.

Uli said, 'There's a storm coming, a big one, and we need to drive into the interior of the island.'

'Where to?'

'Ray Buckley's cabin.'

'That's a long way from anything. Hard driving.'

'That's why we need your 4x4.'

'Did your father tell you to ask?' Logi said, suddenly switching languages away from English.

Uli nodded. 'You told me you would help me when I knew what I wanted to do.'

'Very well,' Logi agreed.

Patty found an Internet page with the weather map for the area. 'This doesn't look good,' she said, pointing. 'That's a typhoon forming. See the circulating system of winds, the closed isobars. It's heading this way.'

'There hasn't been a typhoon on these islands for forty years,' Logi said.

'Well, there's one heading this way now. It could take any path; it could turn off before it gets here, but we ought to go, see if we can get to Buckley's before it hits.'

'What should we do?' Logi asked. 'About the typhoon?'

'Warn people to get ready,' Patty said.

'We have nothing to get ready.'

'It could still miss, but if it comes this way . . .'

'We have nothing to get ready,' Logi repeated.

'I don't believe this,' Watson interrupted suddenly. He was paging through his e-mail queue and reading a message from Connor Giles.

Have broken through security of your old Adventure Updater. How about that? It's crap now anyway. Am in Texas with Alex, staying with Cash Buemann. Just thought you might like to know.

Connor.

The writer had managed to embed a hidden control character so that his name flashed on the screen at the bottom of the message.

'Every bit the smart punk,' Watson said. 'Still, it's going some to break the security on *Adventure Updater*.'

'Your little baby.' Patty smiled. 'We need to go.'

Watson hesitated.

'Didn't you hear me?' she pressed.

'We need a way of getting the stuff off the island,' he said, thinking aloud. 'The file, or files. Assuming they're there.'

'So?'

'If we could get them to a phone . . . Then we can e-mail anything we find out of here. I'm thinking of the helicopters,' he said gravely. 'I reckon it's not going to be so easy . . . I mean, to get off the island with a bunch of data files tucked under our arms.' He stopped and his mouth cracked into a smile. 'Don't you think modern telecommunications are wonderful sometimes?'

The helicopter swung in over Chief Masoni di Masoni's village. The chief came out and watched its descent. How do you defend your empire against the modern world? Blowpipe weapons and darts? Fishing nets? Perhaps to remain in the purity and weakness of tradition is a folly.

The chief nodded then went back into his State House.

It was not a long wait. Margaret Callaway came in with a semi-automatic rifle nestled in the crook of her elbow, its barrel pointing into the air, poised so it could swing into action at any moment. A large black man similarly dressed in army fatigues and carrying the same kind of weapon stood at her shoulder.

'We're looking for Masoni.'

'Then, you have found him.'

'Not you. Ulysses Masoni, the guy that ran the SSEO. We know he's on the island. We know he has visitors with him.'

'Visitors?' the chief questioned.

Callaway lowered the barrel of her gun.

'This is a rude entrance into a place where you are a guest,' the chief told her.

Callaway's teeth gritted together. 'I don't have time,' she said in a spit. 'I want answers.'

'Then you had better ask a question.'

The chief stood his ground. He parried Callaway's interrogation for several minutes. Unused to someone so unphased by the appearance of weaponry, she became increasingly agitated, her finger twitching around the gun. Still he remained calm.

'All I fucking want is Masoni and his fucking pals,' she said at last. 'And I want to know where Ray Buckley had his place on the island. If you don't tell me in the next ten seconds, I'm going to splatter you all over the inside of this fucking hut.'

'That seems reasonably clear,' the chief agreed. He walked to the large wooden chair on the far side of the table and sat down, his posture regal and straight as he looked back at his interrogator. 'A good position in which to die,' he said.

Before Callaway could decide her next move, there was a rattle of gunfire from outside.

'Plummer! I asked that bastard to wait in the chopper,' she cursed. She stared at the chief for a moment, then swung around in exasperation. 'Keep him covered, lieutenant,' she said, and went out of the hut, swinging her gun back on to her shoulder.

When she came back, the anger in her face had subsided. Something like shock had replaced it.

'They left at dawn for the next village,' she told her companion. 'They were going to pick up a car and drive into the interior. We'll need the Jeep as well as the chopper. Come on.'

'What about him?' He gestured to the chief with the barrel of his gun.

'Leave him.' She glared at the prisoner.

The chief said, 'There was a time when we used to deal with our enemies, before they came with guns and helicopters.'

Callaway and the lieutenant went out, leaving the chief as they had found him, alone in his hut. He sat in his chair, composing himself, then he got up and went to the door.

Across the compound from his hut, he could see a handful of his people gathering nervously. At the centre of their gathering, a shape was lying on the floor.

It was, or had been, the shape of a child.

The child's father knelt in the dust next to the body.

When the chief came to him, the man looked up. He said, 'I had to tell them . . . I have other children.'

The chief nodded. Put his hand on the man's shoulder. 'I understand,' he said.

E-mail to: Connor Giles
From: Watson T

Connor. Have reached Maawi, but am in serious situation. Have already seen the army helicopters flying in. Will try to get Ray's missing file off the island via mail to you. Speed is everything. Can you stand by? Trust you will know what to do with it.

Watson.

P.S. Possession will put you in danger. Distribute wisely for the best impact you can manage. Would suggest politicians, but don't know that any authority can be trusted.

XXXI

An hour and a half into the journey. Patty in the front seat next to Uli Masoni; Watson in the rear.

Watson felt increasingly trapped. All he had seen for the last twenty minutes was a forest of trees on either side of the dust track, climbing uphill all the way. They seemed to be going nowhere, making no progress along an endless brown – perhaps slightly orange – channel cut through the jungle of vegetation. Nature had allowed this nine-foot slot to remain virtually intact, though here and there the odd branch grew out into the path, causing scrapes down the sides of the car.

Watson was sure this latest line of trees was the same as the line they had run along five minutes ago. They were travelling at a crawl, six or seven miles an hour as they bumped over the worst of the soft uneven surface. This forced lack of urgency ate at him.

'You forget what it is to have tarmac,' he remarked nervously.

'I think we're almost at the summit,' Uli told him.

Patty was staring out of the window. 'The wind's getting up,' she warned 'It's all cirrus now.'

'Cirrus?' Watson asked.

'A type of cloud. We'll get rain. That's usual. There're often waves of it hundreds of miles in front of the main cyclone. It's coming this way, I think there's no doubt.'

Uli turned. 'You're really worried about this?'

'Have you ever been in a cyclone or a typhoon?'

'No.'

'Believe me, on an island like this, it could be devastating.' She hesitated. 'All part of the joy of El Niño,' she said heavily.

'I see.' The threat seemed to crush Uli's mood. His head dropped as he tried to drive on.

'Look,' Watson said, 'let's focus on our mission here.' He was trying to bring his business training to bear – concentrate on what you can affect; ignore the rest. It seemed a bit feeble now. He stammered, 'I mean, if this El Niño's the one . . . But I'm trying not to consider that. I'm saying to myself, it's the next one we have to worry about . . . the next one . . . the world has time.'

'The world has time,' Uli repeated lifelessly.

Patty turned to Watson and smiled. He felt a sudden stab of pride. Reinforcement. He wanted to kiss her, kiss her again as he had done in the night. Over and over. Making up for what they'd lost.

He smiled back at her, then leaned forward and put his hand on Uli's shoulder. 'You once told me about responsibility,' he reminded him. He didn't think he had to say any more.

They reached the summit very suddenly. The trees fell away and they climbed for another hundred yards or so and then they were there.

Cupped before them was a valley of black rock, the centre of a long-dormant volcano. They were, in effect, perched on one of its lips. Watson could see the other side a couple of miles away and, in the three-hundred-foot deep hollow of its valley, lines of lava flow and a few outcrops of small bushes and greenery. These grew in those areas where a thin soil had formed over the thousands of years since the last activity.

'Wow,' said Watson.

Uli stopped the 4x4 and got out and climbed on to a chest-high black boulder at the side of the track. He was high enough now to look back over the descending acres of trees to the coast. The two villages – the chief's and Logi's – were clearly visible along the shoreline.

'Do you see helicopters? Any activity?' Uli asked.

Watson, who had climbed up beside him, strained his eyes.

'It's beautiful,' he said. For a moment he was distracted: the flowing carpet of green, the blues of the sea, the air, the scent . . .

Peace . . .

'Come on,' Patty yelled from below, 'there's no time for this.'

Watson turned and started back down. As Uli followed, offering a hand to help him, there was a huge flash of light from near the coast. A couple of seconds later, a rumble like thunder reached them.

'Shit, what was that?' she exclaimed.

Uli span around and stared. Watson jumped back on to the boulder.

It was obvious now that something large was burning, something that lay on the hillside between the two villages. Plumes of black smoke were rising amid a raging fire.

'What's that?' Watson asked.

Without taking his eyes off it, Uli said, 'The island's power station.'

Patty had climbed up unaided. She dusted her hands against the sides of her shorts. 'Shit,' she said again. 'Just like BBS . . .'

'They've figured it out,' Watson said. 'We need to be able to power Buckley's computer. And we need electricity to run the telephone system.'

'I don't have a good feeling about this any more,' Patty announced. 'Does this mean we have to get the whole computer off this island?'

She grabbed at Watson's arm. He pulled her to him and felt her tremble in his embrace.

'Back to Plan A,' he said. He looked to Uli.

The islander's dark eyes had a life of their own. They revealed various emotions as their owner stared at the burning wreck on his island. Fear, grief, anger – like garments tried in a fitting room and then rejected for their lack of size. How could anything fit this?

At last he turned and spoke. 'Like you, I am not ready to quit,' he said. He tried on a smile, insecurely fixed.

'What the hell is there to smile about?' Patty asked, her voice betraying more fear than anger.

'Logi told me that Ray had a generator of his own. Maybe they've cut off the phone system, but at least we should be able to switch on the computer.'

Watson grinned. He released his grip on Patty and opened his arm to gesture towards their vehicle. 'Then, as the man said, let's go.'

They crossed the black hollow of volcanic rock as fast as they could. Uli said it was the only part of the journey where they would be exposed. What he meant, Watson thought, was that it was the only part where they would be easy to spot from a helicopter. Elsewhere, the trees that grew around and above the track protected them. You would need to fly right over the top to see a green car. Even then, you might miss it.

Soon, they were over the volcano's lip at the other edge and descending a track much the same as the one they had climbed on the other side. The potholes were half the size of their wheels, so that they plunged almost axle-deep every time they hit one and they dared not drive at anything more than walking pace.

'Isn't there a better road?' Patty asked. 'Around the volcano, perhaps.'

'There's no other road, let alone a better one.'

'How do people move about on this island?'

'Most live on the coast. We use boats. But Buckley wanted to be alone.'

'He was weird . . .' she started to say, but Uli cut across her.

'Helicopter,' he shouted suddenly. He pulled the car into the side of the road and stopped under the thickest tree he could find.

Sure enough, a few moments later, Watson heard and saw the black form of a helicopter pass overhead.

'Who on the island knows the location of Buckley's cabin?' Watson asked 'Should we assume that they know?' He was pointing into the sky.

'I would guess a good number know the location, but probably only three of them speak any decent English. And one of them is right here.'

'Who are the other two?'

'My father . . . and Logi.'

The wind was still rising when the Jeep came back to the chief's village around noon. It kicked up waves of dust as it sped along the soft track at the head of the compound and turned down towards the coast, into the heart of the village.

The village itself was almost deserted. The chief had sent the women, children and young men into the countryside. All who remained were men in their forties and fifties, citizens ready to stone the Americans and take the consequence.

The chief had ordered them not to, at least for now. If there was sense to this stand against the modern world and all its temptations then, he knew, it was to maintain an island tribe undisturbed, uncorrupted, but most of all alive. They could not fight the invader, not directly. This felt like cowardice. It brought him shame when he remembered his fighting forefathers, a shame that veined through him and turned his blood sour.

The Jeep approached. In it were Callaway, her black lieutenant and Logi.

The chief was surprised to see Logi. Why had they selected the nearly blind leader of the next village as their hostage?

'In the hut,' ordered Callaway, showing the chief, then Logi, the point of her gun, and gesturing towards the State House.

The chief spoke calming words to the dozen or so people who were gathering around the Jeep. They stepped back, allowing Callaway and Logi through the crowd. Then the chief followed where the gun barrel pointed.

In the State House the chief returned to his chair, adopting the same defiant erectness that had angered Callaway before. Logi sat on the floor. Callaway hovered in the doorway, then came over and shoved the table out of the way, forcing it into the corner, so there was no longer a barrier between herself and the chief.

'We have a problem, McEvoy and I,' she said, indicating the lieutenant who formed the silent half of the double act. 'You're going to help us.'

The chief looked at her accusingly. Something about the look seemed to penetrate her cold stare, to break her concentration for a moment.

'The kid was Plummer's doing, not mine. I . . .' She stopped herself, as if uncertain what to say next. Of course, there was nothing she could say.

The chief smiled ruefully.

'Your son has taken off into the interior. For Buckley's cabin . . .'

'I cannot help you. I do not know where that is,' the chief said.

'Your friend here disagrees.' She jerked her head towards Logi.

'I had to tell her this,' Logi said quickly in the island language.

'Shut up,' Callaway shouted.

'That's all right,' the chief said to Logi.

'If you don't stop talking that cannibal language, I'm going to blow both your fucking heads off.'

The chief said in English, 'Did you ever think how limited your threats may be? You think we value the life you would allow us?'

'Shut up! Shut up! Shut up!' Callaway lost control for a moment. She came over and smashed the chief across the cheek with the butt of her semi-automatic. He fell on to the floor, holding his hand to a deep gash below one eye.

'I'm going to start shooting people,' she said, straddling the chief's fallen body.

'We are all here ready to die,' he told her. 'We live in a world that no one cares for. This world. This island. We will die for it . . . rather than live another way.' He turned to Logi. Switching languages, he asked him, 'Are you ready to die?'

Logi said, 'At your command.'

'I told you to shut that crap.' She pressed the barrel of her gun against the chief's forehead. 'Now, I want to know exactly where Buckley's cabin is. I already know you gifted him the land, so you must know where the fucking thing is.'

'This is an island of very dense forest,' the chief said. 'Small, yes, but the tracks inland are poor and you could get lost for days.'

'That's not what I asked you.' She pressed down harder.

'I own so much of the island. It's hard to remember. Most of it I never visit.'

Callaway gritted her teeth, ready to fire. The chief closed his eyes and began to chant. Five, six times – the same word.

'This is hopeless,' Callaway said. She stood back and kicked the chief in his side. 'Don't you savages care for anything? What I need is a hostage whose life's worth a damn.'

She stepped away and put her head through the doorway. She shouted orders to the lieutenant who had remained outside.

Logi scuttled across the floor to kneel over the chief. He put his hand out, trying to feel his way. 'My friend, are you all right?' he asked.

The chief took the groping hand. He gripped it and raised his head from the floor. His cheek was caked with blood, already congealing in the confined heat. 'A flesh wound,' he said.

'They destroyed our power station,' Logi told him, 'and they tore all the wires from the telephone exchange and smashed it. Who are these people?'

The chief grimaced and gritted his teeth against the pain as he touched his wound. 'They are the Christian missionaries we should have eaten when first they came.'

XXXII

The rain arrived suddenly. The dense trees at the side of the track were already bending to the strength of the wind, but with the rain, the winds intensified. In less than two minutes the bombardment of water was as great as anything Patty had ever seen in her career as a climatologist.

She knew this was not the typhoon itself, not yet. This was the hot and humid band of air that precedes the main storm. Hot and humid equals serious. Being inside the car was like being inside a drum. Somewhere outside was the cymbal percussion created by a million gallons of water slushing down through the palms, leaves and branches of surrounding trees.

The Suzuki 4x4 started to struggle in some places on the track as it turned to a quagmire of orangy brown mud. The land sloped downwards in this part of the island as it did generally from its volcanic middle to the coast. Gullies at the side of the track ran with water, which soon burst over their sides and on to the track itself. Within a couple of minutes, the Suzuki was bogged down at a standstill, axles pressed into the mud.

'I'll go and see what I can do,' Uli offered, preparing to get out. The windscreen wipers were having no effect and no one could actually see what he was about to get out into.

'How much further?' Patty asked.

'Not far, another mile, maybe less.'

'Can we walk?'

'Swim, more like,' Watson cut in from behind.

Uli pushed open the door. Visibility was still less than ten feet in the onslaught and the noise was deafening as the percussion overtook the drumming. He shut the door as if abandoning a hopeless experiment.

'Nothing's going to move in this,' he said. 'We'll just have to wait.'

They sat for two hours, waiting impatiently. Patty felt her own unease, and the unease of the two men, but she figured everyone was losing time in this weather, their pursuers as much as they were. It made no difference, she told herself. It didn't make her feel any better. She was wondering not about their pursuers, but whether this storm was the beginning of Buckley's shift, the revisiting of the biblical Flood. Forty days and forty nights?

But instead the rain stopped, its easing and its final demise marked by the fading drumbeats on the roof. At the same time the accompanying wind seemed to take a breather.

When Uli opened the door a second time, there was relative calm. True, a knee-high mud river ran down the track and the waterfall noises were still evident as water poured off the windblown trees, but you could see what you were doing and where you were going.

Uli looked back at his passengers, raising his eyebrows in a question.

'OK, we're going to have to walk,' Watson said, answering the eyebrows. 'Or perhaps wade. Either way, now the rain's eased, they'll have that helicopter back in the air. Our time is short.'

'Has the typhoon missed?' Uli asked.

'I don't think so,' Patty told him. 'I don't think we've seen the storm yet.'

'That wasn't it?'

'I told you, there're always belts of rain wrapped around the storm like ribbons on a maypole. They hit first. The main typhoon, the cyclone, is probably a few hundred miles behind. I can't say we're in the clear until late tomorrow.'

Uli nodded in disappointment. 'Come on, then,' he said, and jumped down into the water. It was running quite hard, a river in flood, and he struggled to hold his balance against the wind and the water blowing into his face from the trees.

Patty and Watson took off their shoes and socks and stepped down into the torrent rather more gingerly than their guide. Watson shortened the carrying strap of his computer before hoisting it on to his shoulder and made sure the main body dangled safely above the water level.

After the first few hundred yards, the track sloped up slightly and the water level subsided to ankle height and they began to walk at a reasonable speed. The noise of swaying, overburdened trees followed them and Patty kept glancing upwards, nervously anticipating the appearance of that helicopter.

Buckley's cabin was exactly as the chief had described it the night before. It was made from piled logs, sitting on a footprint roughly 30 feet by 15. A little to the right was a smaller hut which Patty guessed was an outside toilet, and to the left of the cabin was a clearing, obviously intended as a garden of sorts. The stump of a large tree looked like it had been used as a table and next to that were the remains of a seaside deckchair, an object entirely out of its usual time and place.

The front door was open when Uli tried it. They stopped, all three of them, inside its threshold and gazed, dripping wet, at the surroundings.

In the living area were a bed, a table and chair, a wardrobe and a bookcase. A sink without taps and a small Calor gas cooker were crammed in one corner, while a bamboo writing desk fronted by a second chair was in another. A single naked light bulb dangled on a flex from the ceiling and there were two large shuttered windows without glass. The only items that seemed unusual in this hermit existence were the paperbacks that filled the shelves – mainly a series of Penguin Classics – and a tower-cased personal computer wrapped in a plastic dust-cover that sat on the writing desk.

'It's a strange place from which to save the world,' Patty said.

Watson found and tried the light switch. It did nothing.

'Just checking,' he said. 'You never know your luck.'

'What do we do now?' Patty asked.

'We look for something useful,' Watson said, unconvincingly. 'A back-up tape with "This is everything you need" marked on it would help. Failing that, we need to rustle up some electricity. Otherwise we have to figure out how we are going to get the base unit of this computer back to civilization.' He hesitated. Then he added, 'With a bunch of killers on our tail.'

Uli pulled back one of the shutters to give them better light. 'I'll go and look for the generator, see if I can get it started,' he said.

He went outside while Patty and Watson searched the cabin. They quickly uncovered half a dozen floppy disks and a tape drive without any tapes. Buckley's surviving paperwork was confined to a few cryptic but indecipherable doodles on scrap paper.

Watson placed the notebook computer he had carried so carefully along their paddling journey on the bamboo desk and booted it up on battery power. He started fitting the floppy disks one by one.

After a few minutes Uli reappeared at the cabin door. Patty could guess from his face what he was about to say.

'I found the generator but there's no fuel.'

Almost the exact words. Patty's heart sank; fear rising now its shackles were off.

'I thought you told us Logi kept spare petrol in the Suzuki,' Watson said.

'Yes, but it's a diesel generator.'

Cash Buemann's everyday car was a black limousine with cow horns at the front. Connor felt embarrassed getting into it, but Alexandra held his hand and told him it would be OK.

They were going to Houston to meet Cash's private plane. Cash wanted to make one stop en route, he said, someone who needed a visit.

When they reached the city, they drove into its heart, into its skyscraper centre, buildings erect like fingers gesturing up to the gods of weather.

This was all very nice and the journey was comfortable enough, with the luxuries of CD high fidelity and in-car cocktail bar, but Connor couldn't see where it was leading, or how it had any relevance to the story he had told Cash over dinner the night before.

'Don't worry,' Cash said, 'I know what I'm doing now. This is my territory.'

Their destination, as it turned out, was the office of Senator Paul Radleigh on the fortieth floor of one of the swankiest modern monstrosities in town, with so much air-conditioning it needed its own power station.

'I wanta see Paul,' Cash drawled to the male receptionist in the office lobby.

'Do you have an appointment?'

Cash took off his baseball cap. 'Boy, do you not know who the fuck I am?'

'Yessir.' The receptionist slid down slightly in his seat as if seeking the protection of the desk that stood between them.

'Is he in the building?' Cash demanded.

'Yessir.'

'Then push your intercom and ask him. I don't need no damned appointment.'

Less than a minute later Cash, Alexandra and Connor were standing face to face with the US senator.

The senator looked puzzled at first. He had no clue who Alexandra and Connor might be, and, although everyone knew Cash Buemann, Radleigh had clearly never seen him in this kind of mood.

'This is an unexpected pleasure. Please, please sit down, won't you?'

Radleigh made flustered attempts at hospitality. He ushered his guests towards a ring of comfortable-looking leather chairs.

Alexander and Connor sat down, but Cash remained standing, shifting menacingly from foot to foot. 'I've come for some straight answers,' he opened.

'Sure. Always, Cash. You know you've always been a contributor to my campaign. What's good for Texas oil and cattle is good for Texas. That's always been the way. It's the way I've done it.'

'We'll see about that. I've got a whisper I don't like,' Cash told him.

Radleigh's face contorted, his voice choked when he spoke. 'I can assure . . .' He got no further.

'I heard you tried to put the pressure on a man called André Pielot last time you was in Paris. That don't sound like nothing in the interests of Texas, Paul. It don't sound like nothing in the interests of nobody, 'specially considering that same Monsieur Pielot met a strange and unexplained death shortly after.'

'For Christ's sake, Cash, he died in a plane crash. Where's all this coming from? Sit down, won't you?' Radleigh sat himself down in one of the spare chairs as if encouraging his guest to do the same. He smiled at Alexandra and Connor nervously. Connor stared back at him.

Cash took a step towards his prey, halting more or less in the middle of the circle of chairs, making no move to pick one. 'How much money has my family put into your career, Paul?'

'Now, you know I've served you well. I served your daddy too.'

Invoking Cash's father was not a smart comment, Connor thought. He noticed how Radleigh's face had grown redder ever since they arrived. He was positively pumping blood to the cheeks now, probably not thinking with his normal political precision.

'Who killed André Pielot, Paul?' Cash said, firing the question as he took another step forward.

'Cash, I . . .'

'Who killed Ray Buckley?'

Another step.

'Were you involved in that too?'

'Cash, please,' the man pleaded.

Cash moved so he was standing over the man. Connor thought he might hit him.

But he didn't. He didn't have to. Radleigh looked up like a cowering child. He said, 'This one came down from the President's office, Cash. He phoned me himself . . . personally. I swear, I never betrayed you.'

Cash looked at him and shook his head. 'I have done some things I regret in my life,' he said, 'but how did I ever get a reputation that made you think this crap would be OK with me?'

The rains had started again and the night that followed was wild: wind followed rain followed wind. They battened the shutters as best they could. Even so, the cabin creaked as if the wind would rip it from its foundations.

There had been nothing to eat but an unrecognizable fruit Uli had picked from trees surrounding the cabin before the worst of the rain, so they all turned in hungry, praying for the cabin's integrity.

Patty lay awake, wrapped in an American Express towel and a blanket they had found in the wardrobe. Uli and Watson had insisted on giving her the bed, but it didn't help her attempts to sleep. She was tired and aching, but that didn't help either. She was cold despite the makeshift bedclothes. And scared. She wasn't ashamed of it. She was most likely going to die.

She thought about her companions. One she had loved for thirteen years, through his worst times. And now here he was, out of character, magnificently reaching for something . . . reaching for what? Was it for her?

The other she had seen as a saint, a messiah. Now halo-less, in simple clothes, and stripped of his crowd-pleasing oratory, stripped down, in fact, to a vest and trousers and a scrambling role with the rest of them. The prey of powerful men with weapons at their command who would keep this secret, keep it until it was too late to do anything.

She tried to focus her mind on that reality: even if she didn't die trying to get this computer off the island, half the world was going to die in the fatal climate it predicted.

Her head should have been full up with that thought, but instead she felt empty. Had the change in the world already started? Was it already irreversible?

In the early hours of the morning she finally fell asleep, exhaustion getting the better of her inner turmoil.

When she awoke, there was frantic activity in the cabin around her. Watson's own portable computer was next to Buckley's, which was in pieces on the floor. He was working away at its insides using a dinner knife and a ballpoint pen refill. He had stripped the wiring to the computer's printer and strands of thin insulating wire were laid out on the table as if prepared for some exotic breakfast cookery.

'What are you doing?' she asked sleepily.

Watson sat back from his notebook computer with a sigh. 'I tried every single floppy disk Buckley had here. There's nothing worth a damn,' he said.

'Then we have to take the PC base unit and get out of here? I mean, I know it's going to be a struggle, carrying it on foot, but what choice do we have? The first thing they'll find is this cabin and . . .'

'Then, I suddenly realized,' he said, stopping her in mid-sentence. He held up the hard disk of Buckley's machine triumphantly in one hand. 'I can't get the computer to work without a 240-volt supply, but I can get the hard drive to operate if I can get twelve volts to it.'

'What good does that do? Don't we need the whole computer to work?'

'The hard disk's the memory. I used to be a hardware man, remember. I used to sell computers. The microprocessor is important, but everything that the computer knows is in this hard drive. Connor Giles reminded me of that when I went to BBS. All his crashing around trying to remove viruses. He ripped the heart out of it and smashed it on the floor.' Watson's voice rose in pitch as he arranged his trophy on the table and hefted his own machine up to sit next to it. 'All I need to do is a heart transplant.'

'Where's Uli?' Patty pushed her hand back through her hair, still not with it.

Watson turned towards the door. 'Getting me a twelve-volt supply,' he said. 'This notebook only has ten.'

Patty heard the roar of an engine and went to the window, clasping the American Express livery around her body. She saw the blue-grey of the sky, the floods of water receding. Uli was bumping towards the cabin in the Suzuki 4x4, mud splattered down its sides as if it had taken an elephant bath.

He pulled up with the engine running. 'I've seen them,' he said, getting out. 'The helicopter's up there again. It's only a matter of time.'

'Bring that thing closer,' Watson commanded, 'I haven't got that much wire.'

'What are you on about?' Patty asked with emphasis. She wrinkled her eyes as if she thought she might be dreaming.

'I need the battery, but we've got no tools to get it out.'

'I can't get it closer,' Uli said.

'Let me try.' Watson strode towards the vehicle. 'Go and put some clothes on, Patty. Or, at least, stand back.'

Watson levered himself up into the driving seat, revved the engine and practised running the vehicle forward and back over a distance of twenty yards or so. When he was ready, he gunned the engine up to full revs, dropped the clutch and spun the wheels. The car slithered left and right before attaining any speed. It went sideways as it passed Patty and Uli, who were by now standing in the small clearing to the right of the cabin. Watson got it straightened out and running at about ten miles an hour before it bulldozed through the front door of the cabin. The wooden wall splintered, sending fragments in all directions and the roof of the cabin dropped on to the roof of the Suzuki. The vehicle itself ploughed to a halt next to the table on which Watson had gathered his equipment.

'Bullseye,' he shouted, jumping into the middle of what had been the cabin.

'What the hell?' Patty shouted. 'Have you gone mad? This isn't like you.'

'No, it isn't, is it?' he said. 'But I took your inspiration. If you can do it with an antique globe, why not a Suzuki?'

Uli looked at the wrecked cabin and car. 'What is Logi going to say?' he moaned.

'We can't use this car any more anyway,' Watson said. 'Eventually, if they're up there, they're going to spot it.' He popped the safety catch on the bonnet and lifted it, assessing the distance between car battery and computer equipment. 'I reckon that's close enough.'

After five minutes of fiddling with wires, Watson had the power supply he wanted. They had all crowded around his Heath Robinson assembly of parts, Patty trying to dress and look over his shoulder at the same time.

Suddenly Watson's computer showed the opening screen of Windows NT. Then a second later, the screen said, 'Enter Password.'

'Fuck, he's got it protected,' Watson groaned. 'Why would he have it protected when he's miles from anywhere? In the wilderness, for Christ's sake? Sorry, Uli, no offence.'

'None taken.'

Watson typed furiously. He tried various words. Then he tried to circumvent the protection, a few simple tricks to copy the disk anyway. They didn't work.

Patty lost concentration. It was as though she was in a dream. She was remembering how this started. The meeting in Paris, André Pielot, the fax from the SSEO and the single piece of paper from Ray Buckley.

'*The Earth Goddess collapses*,' she said suddenly.

'What?' Both Watson and Uli stared at her.

'The Earth Goddess collapses,' she repeated. 'It was on the paper he sent, the summary of results.'

Uli opened his mouth to speak, but Watson was already typing.

Goddess? No!

Earthgoddess? No!

Earthgoddesscollapses . . .

No immediate response. They didn't get that instant 'Password incorrect' message. Instead, they heard the hard disk kick into action.

A few seconds later, they were staring at it: Buckley's directory, a complete list of all the files of the model. Including that one . . .

'My God,' Patty said, pointing. 'There it is: ENSOeffect.'

Watson double-clicked on the icon. The various files fell into their appointed places. What he got were pages and pages of data, lines of programme, tables of numbers, figures, the odd equation. Right at the end were the graphs Patty had already seen – the results file.

As Watson paged down, browsing what they had, her eyes filled with tears.

'I don't know,' she said. 'I don't know how I should feel about this . . . I don't think I ever believed it.'

'I didn't want to believe it,' Uli said gravely.

Patty clutched at Watson's arm. This was the most magical thing she'd ever seen. And Watson – yes, Watson – had produced it.

'We have to copy this across on to the hard drive in the notebook,' Watson told them, 'and get out of here. We only need this one file. How long will it take us to get back across the island?'

'On foot, a full day, maybe a day and a half.' Uli looked ruefully at the reshaped Suzuki.

'You know we can't take it. It might as well have a target on it. Can you lead us through the forests?'

Uli nodded, but Patty could tell it was a reluctant nod. He didn't doubt his own ability – he had been born here – it was his pair of white followers he had no faith in. 'If you're done, we had better go,' he said.

'The transfer will take a few minutes.' Watson turned from his notebook, leaving it to work on its own.

'I hope you realize we are no closer to getting this off the island,' Uli said. Patty looked at him. For a moment, it seemed his normally controlled nerve was cracking.

Watson smiled with a calm that was almost shocking. 'All I need is a telephone line.'

'You think we can walk right back across the island, sneak in, somehow power up a dead telephone exchange . . .'

'It's in Logi's village, yes?'

'Yes, but don't you see they will have found that? They went to my father's village. Then, the power station. These people are thorough . . . Look at the job they did on the SSEO's accounts. There's going to be no telephone exchange and no electricity to power it even if there is.'

'I realize that.'

'Just as well.' Uli pulled himself up short. For a second, he stood like a statue.

Patty watched him. And watched Watson. She had seen Uli's courage before and didn't doubt it, but here was Watson suddenly out-braving the man she had admired more than any.

Uli cracked into a smile and started nodding his head as if he had suddenly seen the joke.

As they waited for the makeshift hardware to finish, Patty scanned the sky through the window, suddenly remembering the threatening storm that was out there. The cirrus clouds had disappeared. That was not necessarily good. Looking into the distance over the trees, she could see a wall of cumulo-nimbus forming. She thought she could detect divergent paths between the middle and high clouds – classical.

'Shit,' she said, cutting in over Uli's good humour.

Both men looked at her.

'It may be a long time since I did Meteorology 101, but that looks like the typhoon formation to me. It's almost upon us.'

She shook her head.

Uli looked up through a fissure in the roof created by the Suzuki's entrance. 'If it takes us even a day to cross the island . . .' He allowed his voice to trail off and shrugged his shoulders.

'Look, let's get on with it, OK?' Watson said.

Patty found herself edging sideways to stand more closely at Watson's shoulder.

She felt now rather like a fearless surfer who steps in front of a giant wave and finds herself a passenger. Too late for fear.

Uli pursed his lips and nodded.

The notebook which had been whirring softly as it transferred files suddenly bleeped three times.

'Is that the file transfer finished?' Patty asked.

Watson turned back to the machine in alarm. 'No, the file transfer's already finished,' he said, 'that's the low battery warning.'

When the rains ended, Callaway and Plummer had taken off in the helicopter, leaving only Lieutenant McEvoy and one other soldier at the chief's village. Logi and Chief Masoni were held prisoner in the State House with the two soldiers taking turns to keep watch.

There was no opposition. There was hardly likely to be insurrection when the most lethal weapon the villagers could raise was a small knife used for gutting fish.

The day grew hotter. Steam rose from the ground as the rains of the previous night evaporated out of the sand. McEvoy sat in the shade of the wooden hut's overhanging roof, watching its door. He was feeling sleepy, the after-effects of travel and action now cutting in as the situation was calm. He had received several radio messages from Callaway and Plummer – update reports. They had found nothing, but they were continuing to scan the island; it was only a matter of time.

The prisoners had been quiet for hours. As the senior officer, he had sent his companion to patrol the fence-line of the village.

Slowly at first. McEvoy started to hear a conversation, growing louder. Voices were raised.

Logi shouted in English, 'You have caused this. You, with your isolationist policy.'

The chief replied in a language McEvoy did not know.

Logi countered, 'You betrayed me. You and your son have betrayed us all. I hope they kill him.'

There was the noise of scuffling, furniture banging about. McEvoy got up, swinging his rifle into a position of readiness. He pushed open the door.

The big table and the chief's chair had been turned on their sides and McEvoy could see the chief's body draped over the overturned chair, an arm sticking in the air where it propped against the backrest. There was an ornately decorated knife sticking into his chest.

McEvoy released the safety catch of his weapon and stepped forward.

Logi appeared from nowhere. At least it seemed that way. Actually, he had come from the shadows behind the table, arms above his head, milked eyes pointed, ready to pounce.

McEvoy saw him when he was still ten feet away. Ten feet gave him enough time. He squeezed the trigger and a hail of bullets fired from his rifle into the old warrior's chest.

The body, carried forward by its momentum, crashed on to McEvoy and knocked him over backwards, both of them falling against the door frame. McEvoy untangled himself from what were now bloody remains. He pushed them aside and stood up.

'Jesus Fucking Christ,' he said.

His companion had run across the village compound, through a crowd of villagers summoned by the noise. 'McEvoy, are you all right?'

'Fucking suicide squad here,' he said. He kicked at Logi's body. 'This

216

'un stabbed the chief, then tried a run at me. Crazy sunnavabitch! Keep those damn people back, will you?'

The arriving soldier peered around the inside of the State House. After cursing a couple of times, he realized the villagers were starting to seep past him, gazing at the fallen men. He turned his rifle sideways on so he could use it as a barrier, pushing back the most intrusive of them.

'All right,' he said. 'Shit, get back, you bastards.'

'Get 'em outa here,' McEvoy ordered.

The soldier shepherded them outside, and stood just beyond the doorway staring out at them, sentry-like. Some shouted at him, pointing fingers to accompany words he couldn't understand. He thrust out with the rifle, hitting it against chests to try to quiet the hecklers.

Meanwhile McEvoy thought about cleaning up. He kicked again at Logi's fallen body. The man was dead all right. You didn't take that many bullets in the chest from close range and live. He stepped over and went to the chief. A ceremonial knife was in the chest up to the hilt and the chief showed no vital signs. There wasn't a lot of blood, though.

McEvoy leaned over to see if there was a pulse.

As he did so, the chief's propped-up arm suddenly swung across the back of McEvoy's neck. It pulled his face down, smothering him with a crushing strength.

The chief's other hand had a knife, the twin of the ceremonial pair, produced from beneath him. It arced around and struck into McEvoy's back between two of his ribs. The first thrust punctured one lung. A second, equally accurate, punctured the other and the soldier fell silently dead on the floor, like a ruined balloon.

The chief sat up and removed the knife from his own chest. It had been broken off with only an inch of blade remaining, a trick Logi had invented to make the illusion real. The wound it left was nothing more than superficial. The chief looked at the blood as if it were merely another medal. Then he picked up McEvoy's weapon and stepped towards the door.

A crowd of twenty or more were still shouting at the other soldier and he continued to thrust randomly at them with his weapon as the chief approached from behind.

The chief looked at the semi-automatic rifle he had taken. He ran his hand along the barrel and it was hot. He changed his grip, holding it like a spear in readiness to charge. Then he brought it up to the back of the soldier's head, aiming it upwards at roughly forty-five degrees into the base of the skull. The soldier was still concerned with the jostling crowd.

217

The chief squeezed the trigger.

Bloody debris showered the islanders and the soldier slumped forward, landing amongst them. They stood back screaming.

The chief yelled, 'Bellajang.' The island word for war.

They packed up the notebook computer. Despite its low battery, it now contained Buckley's missing file. Watson disconnected the leads he'd made and bundled them into the notebook's case.

'We might need these wires again,' he said shrugging. He had no idea why. But then he had no idea what they were going to do next. How the hell were they going to get off this island?

Uli shut the bonnet of the Suzuki. 'Are you sure we have to leave this?' he said.

Watson nodded. 'You think you can avoid a helicopter?'

Patty answered with a shake of her head and looked at Uli.

'All right. I understand,' he said. 'I suppose I have always understood. But if we have to leave this car, let's at least try to even the odds a little.' He smiled and reached in his pocket and pulled out a small plastic bag. He opened it. There were three cardboard cylinders the size of torch batteries, each with a touch-paper fuse. 'Fireworks,' he said, 'left over from my homecoming dinner.' He pointed to the car. 'Logi's spare cans of petrol are still in the boot.'

A few minutes later, privately, the chief walked back to where his friend had fallen.

Logi was dead, so the chief spoke his friend's words for him.

'Loyalty to you, my chief,' he said.

'Did you have to do it that way?' the chief asked him in this one-sided conversation. 'Did you have to make him shoot you?'

'Loyalty to you, my chief' Logi said again.

XXXIII

Watson had experienced a mechanical click in his head. He didn't know what it was, but he supposed that when your own death becomes so inevitable, there must be some mechanism to tell your brain that fear is no longer an effective tool. The click seemed to switch the fear off.

They were watching from the trees when the helicopter finally circled down over Buckley's cabin. Patty had hold of his arm, and Uli was crouching in the shadow of an adjacent tree. They had got away from the cabin just in time – 'just' being a very small margin.

'Wait here,' said Uli.

'What are you going to do?'

'Computers are yours,' he said, 'this is mine.'

Watson saw him scamper away into the trees, crouched low, looking like some Indian scout from a cowboy movie . . . only the outfit and war paint were different.

The helicopter hung uncertainly in the air for several minutes. It took most of that time for Watson to realise that there was not enough space between the trees for it to land. Slowly, a rope ladder descended from its underbelly. On the end of it was a soldier in full battle dress. He swung to the ground in the small clearing to the right hand side.

The soldier walked behind the cabin and came out on the other side. He went all the way around twice, then got out his field walkie-talkie and spoke into it.

There would be some strange questions and answers going back and forth, Watson thought. It's not every day you come across a Suzuki 4x4 planted through the wall of a wooden cabin in the middle of nowhere.

'Avant-garde art,' Watson whispered to Patty. 'He doesn't know what to make of it.'

'Shut up,' she hissed back.

'They're 200 yards away, Patty. And there's a helicopter.' He extended a forefinger into the sky, but he took her point and shuffled himself more closely behind the tree.

The soldier approached the cabin, feeling his way down the side of the Suzuki and disappeared inside. Watson caught a glimpse of Uli near the cabin, fifteen yards to the left of it, still in the trees.

A few seconds later, when the fuel tanks blew, Watson could feel the heat wave. It was like a miniature version of the power-station explosion, viewed from closer range. As he darted his head out from behind the tree, Watson saw the car and cabin lifted bodily from the ground. They fell back into a black-red fireball on the spot where the explosion had started.

Wooden splinters caught in the turbulent air of the helicopter's rotor. They blew about like snowflakes caught on a drifting wind. It was more than a minute before they subsided, leaving the remains of the cabin and the gutted car to burn unaccompanied in the stillness.

Watson looked up and saw the helicopter climbing, banking away, retreating from the scene in defeat.

But as he did so, he also saw the storm, the promised typhoon. Clouds moving in from the horizon as if a film were being run on fast forward. Patty was right. The real danger was only just beginning.

XXXIV

A mature storm – typhoon, cyclone or hurricane – may export more than 3,000,000,000 tons of air in a single hour. Patty had told them this so they could be ready.

Typhoons swallow things without digesting them. They swirl them around like a Nordic god swinging his mighty hammer. Torn-up trees and buildings, the bodies of domestic animals – when propelled at 70 or 80 miles per hour, these objects become potentially lethal.

Uli said he knew somewhere they could shelter, but it was miles away and the journey took most of the day, trying to keep off the track so the helicopter wouldn't spot them. Inexorably, the wind rose and the clouds filled the horizon like a gathering fist. Hour upon hour, it got worse.

When the low clouds began to shoot a few hundred feet above their heads, Patty screamed at Uli that they needed to find cover. 'Now,' she said. 'We need it, now.'

The stinging spray of water was already hitting her face and the trees were beginning to bend.

She remembered her equations: 50 miles per hour takes leaves and small branches off trees – yes, leaves were already in the wind now; 70–80mph topples shallow-rooted trees, snaps weaker trees, blows down thin walls. From what she could see, squinting her eyes, the trunks of trees were bending almost at ninety degrees, but so far they were still holding. It wouldn't be long, though.

At 85mph, lifting roofs and snapping trees are general. Beyond that, anything still standing is as likely to be taken down by the debris as by the wind itself. Pressures as high as 1,000 pounds per square yard – that's four fat men jumping on a tea-tray – knock down everything in sight.

'Come on . . .' Her voice desperate, shouting over the noise of the strengthening gale. The air was hard to breathe now, filled with vapour moving so fast.

The time seemed to flow by slowly, as sticky as she felt walking in the mud against the wind. She held on to Watson, who held on to Uli.

The pressure of air seemed to confine them to their own bubble. As far as she could reach was as far as she could see, and she panicked when her grip slipped on Watson's sleeve. She grasped for him, but he wasn't there.

He turned when he felt her grip slide away. They were climbing up a slope which he assumed were the remains of the road. To one side was a fast-running mud river whose depth was a mystery. It had once been the narrow ditch that ran down the side of the road, but it had widened and deepened in the flood.

Patty's right foot slipped away into the ditch and she span around and pitched head-first into the flow of mud.

He heard her scream . . .

It seemed to take him an age to make a decision, but in reality it could only have been a second. He unhooked the strap of his computer case from his shoulder and tossed it in Uli's direction. He didn't know what chance he gave Uli to catch it, because before it reached him, Watson had thrown himself into the flow.

The stream was moving at better than walking pace and the first thing he felt were the rocks that were being carried along in the ooze. He couldn't see Patty any more. The sheeting rain blinded him.

He called out . . .

'Patty . . . Patty . . . Patty.'

Nothing.

He screamed it so loud he felt his lungs would burst. The rocks hit him in the back and his face nearly went under, but he kept on screaming.

He ran into her, rather than found her. She had one hand groping desperately at the branch of a tree that had fallen across the mud stream. She was about to lose strength and lose hold.

He cradled one arm around her back and reached up to the tree with his other. With all his strength he managed to wedge himself in the flow so that his body shielded hers from the worst of the torrent.

Then he shouted out for Uli.

It took their rescuer several minutes to shin across the top of the tree. Watson saw his nut-brown face and white-tooth smile peering down at him through the pouring water.

Somehow Watson scooped his arm under Patty and drove her upwards. She grabbed Uli behind the neck and he helped her climb up over the top of him. As soon as she was safe on the path, he came back for Watson.

Just as Uli reached down, Watson felt a tremendous blow on the right shoulder. The pain and shock dislodged him. The next thing he saw was the tree trunk. And the speed at which his head was travelling towards it.

Plummer ordered the helicopter pilot to land back at the coast. They could all see the storm coming. The pilot circled and put his aircraft down on the edge of the chief's village. Plummer went out to scout around. The whole compound was deserted, except for the bodies: McEvoy, his companion, and Logi.

When he came back, Plummer had Callaway and the pilot set up their satellite communications in the doorway of one of the empty huts – three suitcase-sized boxes that opened to reveal a small dish. They pointed the dish out through the door, keeping the rest of the equipment inside.

'Get me the secure line to Washington,' he said.

Callaway completed the assembly and started making the necessary checks. It was like some bizarre Meccano set.

The helicopter pilot said, 'Sir, I'm not sure it's going to be safe on the ground there.' He was looking up at the rushing clouds and gesturing towards his helicopter.

At that moment, Callaway said, 'I've got the line.'

Plummer took the handset she offered and gave whoever was on the other end a series of codes. The next words he said were, 'Hello, Mr President.' Then he ushered everybody else outside.

Callaway wandered in the direction of the State House, at times bracing herself against the wind and at others trying to prevent it propelling her forward as it swirled and grew in strength. She noticed how branches in the surrounding trees were beginning to look decidedly insecure.

Suddenly, one tree, a particularly old coconut palm that had seen better days, simply lifted out of the ground before her eyes. It dragged across the compound as if transported by the sweep of a large and unseen hand. After accelerating for thirty yards, it smashed into a hut, not far from where she stood. The hut keeled over to one side and collapsed into a pile of timbers.

She might have stayed there gaping for who knows how long, but now the air was full of debris, branches and leaves were flying off other trees, and the wind seemed to have redoubled itself as if making a special effort.

She fled towards the State House, crashing through the door and falling over Logi's body, landing eye to eye with McEvoy's lifeless face.

She screamed automatically, but the scream was lost in the rumble and clatter of the rising wind. 'Fuck,' she said to herself as she sat up and looked around.

This was the most substantial building in the village compound, but the way the wind was blowing in through the windows, she had no confidence that even this would survive.

She went to the windows and forced the shutters closed. These were thick panels of a dark wood, but it wasn't their weight that made them difficult to shut; it was the wind pushing back, seeking entrance.

The rain was pouring down and the slatted uncovered roof let the water fall into the building. It started making pinky puddles out of the various pools of blood around the fallen men.

She was grateful, but not for the water. She realized the building's lack of a real roof significantly reduced its chance of being lifted and blown away.

She stepped back over the bodies, intending to signal to her companions that here was a safe – or at least the safest – place to shelter. She tried to open the door which, unnoticed in the noise, had slammed behind her. Since it hinged outwards, it was almost impossible to push it open against the wind. She put her shoulder to it.

Through the first crack of the opening door, she saw their enormous helicopter rocking violently on its landing wheels as if the gusts had struck up a resonance in its suspension. Plummer was running towards her, carrying part of the satellite system. The pilot was nowhere to be seen. She forced the door further open and tried to call out. The rush of air was now deafening and her voice had no chance of carrying the twenty yards or so. As she watched, two more huts collapsed behind Plummer and she got the impression the wind had turned around specifically to get him.

She saw the rotors of the helicopter twitch into life, its engine firing up. The pilot was trying to move it off.

Meanwhile, the wind had found a loose plank in a nearby building and used it as a reed. A piercing scream chased across the compound. She covered her ears.

Then she saw Plummer fall and saw him blown along for ten or fifteen yards before he could regain his feet.

Then the helicopter fell over . . .

As the pilot had been trying to take off, the rotors chopping into the merciless wind, a fatal gust had caught the aircraft. It fell over exactly as if it were toy: a Sikorsky CH137, a helicopter capable of picking up a tank.

But then, the entire scene seemed like a miniature, a badly-filmed model awaiting a B-movie giant's foot. Plastic helicopter. Plastic figures. Plastic scenery.

One blade of the rotor struck the ground and the whole blade broke off the main axle above the fuselage.

Callaway couldn't remember how heavy those rotor blades were. Pretty heavy, she reckoned. But this one bounced and whipped like a vaulter's pole escaping the jump pit. End over end it went, spinning in the wind. On the second bounce the blade turned sideways and sliced Mike Plummer's body clean in half at the waist. He fell into two pieces.

The helicopter and his fallen figure still looked like toys.

XXXV

She was leaning over him when he awoke, touching his cheek with her hand. 'Are you all right?' Her voice was tremulous.

Watson wondered if he was alive. He wondered if Patty was real. He blinked to confirm the facts.

'Is the computer OK?' he asked.

Then he saw Uli smiling, holding the case by its strap. 'You're an obsessive, my friend,' Uli said.

Thank God . . .

'I think I've done my shoulder,' Watson said.

Uli leaned over and prodded at it. The patient winced in pain.

'I think it must be broken,' Uli said.

'Where are we?'

'A little cave I remember from my childhood.'

'How did . . .?'

'He carried you,' Patty said.

'I need some air.' Watson tried to get up. His head span, but he made it to his feet with his injured arm drooping at his side. He tried to hold it up with the good hand.

He found the mouth of the cave and turned his gaze upwards to the sky. There was no rain and little wind.

'You slept well,' Patty told him. 'It's nearly morning.'

To his ill-focused eyes, the sky looked like a bruise on the seventh day, yellows and purples, every shade of brown and red and grey. The sun was struggling to rise behind the kaleidoscope of cloud.

Watson thought he saw movement in the wreckage of fallen trees some way off.

He was about to dive back into the cave when he saw the face.

Chief Masoni di Masoni was using a stick to aid his passage. The old chief looked grave and tired. His clothes were soaked.

'You were outside in the storm?' Watson asked in amazement as he approached.

'An old chief's strength . . . perhaps his guile.'

Patty threw her arms around the chief. Uli looked as if he wanted to do the same.

The chief's eyes searched from Patty to Watson to his son. 'Two of the soldiers are dead,' he said. 'I killed them.'

'Three,' corrected Uli.

'Three?'

'We also killed one.'

'Bellajang,' said the chief.

'What about the storm?' Patty asked.

'My count was before the storm,' the chief said, 'but Logi also is dead. I think many of my people are dead.'

Uli's head dropped. He bit his lip and looked away. His father put a hand on his shoulder.

'A great sadness,' the chief said, 'Logi died with loyalty.'

Watson stirred. He was feeling up towards the top of his bad arm, his forehead furrowed with pain from the movement. He was starting to sweat.

'What is the problem?' the chief asked.

'A broken shoulder,' Patty said.

'And you have not tended it, my son,' the chief scolded Uli. His son was still staring at the ground. Loss had taken him for a moment.

'Let's go inside and I will look at it,' the chief said.

'How did you find us?' Patty asked.

The chief was shepherding Watson back through the mouth of the cave and urging him to sit on the floor. 'Did Uli not tell you? In all the times he ran away as a child, we always found him here.' He looked down at Watson. 'Now this might hurt,' he said.

Patty noticed Watson cowing slightly. He seemed to sink into the rock. Like her, he was used to trained medical staff, but where were those comforts now? On this island, in this situation, you took what you could get.

'Dislocated,' the chief pronounced matter-of-factly, 'not broken. I can put it back.'

She turned away as the chief took Watson's arm. She was biting into the fleshy part of her hand when she heard the scream. Opening her eyes, she saw Watson with a tear on his cheek, his face white.

'Better?' the chief asked him, as if he thought he might have performed a miracle.

Watson considered the question, moved the arm gingerly, then nodded. 'A little,' he agreed.

'Uli, get your head up. We need warriors now,' his father ordered. To Watson, he said, 'Do you have the information?'

'Yes,' Watson said, 'it's in the machine, but I have no way of getting it off the island.'

Patty said, 'You know, the Americans will keep coming and coming. Just because we've killed the first wave . . .'

'Ah.' The chief mulled the word around his mouth. 'This has always been the problem of the *Indian*.' He stressed the word. Then, rolling his eyes, he quoted, ' "We had a small country. Their country was large. We were contented to let things remain . . . They were not." '

'Who said that?' Patty asked.

'A man called Tooyalaket,' the chief told her. 'He was chief of the Nez Percés when the white men robbed the Indians of their lands.'

The chief suddenly seemed to have taken charge. 'What do you need to get your information off the island?' he asked. 'A boat?'

'No, we'd be sitting ducks,' Watson said. He was feeling his arm, his face tentative if a little brighter.

'What, then?' the chief pressed, as if he could grant any wish once he understood it.

'A telephone.'

'They destroyed the power station and the telephone exchange in Logi's village,' the chief said.

'Yes.'

'Yes,' he continued. 'According to Logi, those telephones were the thirty lines that tied this island to the real world.'

Watson nodded. Patty, Watson and Uli looked at the chief. The chief had paused.

'Of course,' he said at last, 'Logi was wrong. There were thirty-one.'

XXXVI

The thirty-first telephone line on the island of Maawi had been attached to the old electric cable that came across from Waatu under the sea into the power station.

'It was used for the operator of the power station to talk to his friend,' the chief explained.

'His friend?' Patty asked.

'The operator on Waatu.'

'How do you know this?' Uli asked.

The chief looked insulted by the question. Uli tried to explain himself. 'But you never approved of technology when it came. You took no interest.'

'Not approve – yes, I did not approve. But this is not the same as taking no interest. In your time, you have disapproved loudly of pollution. But you have taken great interest in it also, have you not?'

As they spoke, Watson was struggling to his feet, pushing himself off the wall with his good arm. 'We must go now' he said.

Everyone looked at him.

'Now' he repeated. His firmness seemed to energize him. 'Now this storm has passed, they'll have an army on the way. You know that. We must go now.'

'Wait a minute,' said Patty, 'this is crazy. The power station has been burned to the ground.'

'We have to dig up the cable,' Watson said. He looked at the chief. 'I take it the cable was not buried deeply?'

'No,' the chief agreed.

'Six inches? What?'

'A little deeper than that,' the chief admitted.

'But we can dig it up,' Uli said. It was the first time he'd joined their

229

conversation since he heard about Logi. His face was hard, determined, the eyes fixed.

His father said, 'A warrior's face now.'

'A warrior's face now.' Uli nodded.

'Can we be certain that there will be someone at the other end?' Watson asked. 'I mean, I'm assuming they . . . the operators on Waatu . . . will think the power station has gone down in the storms. They may have their own damage to contend with. Are we sure there's going to be someone there?'

'Nothing is certain. I believe you said that,' the chief told him. He smiled and gestured towards the cave's entrance. 'We go,' he said, 'the sun is coming up, but it will be evening before we reach the village. The best time. Poor light for the enemy. And little time to recover from the storm.'

'This is all very well,' Patty cut in. 'Suppose you can connect the modem, have you forgotten there's hardly any battery power left in the machine?'

'I think we'll have enough as long as we don't waste it,' Watson said. He was amazed how much confidence his voice conveyed. Far more than he felt inside.

Callaway scouted for survivors. She had to wade in water up to her waist through most of the village compound. There wasn't a hut still standing apart from the State House.

She found the helicopter pilot on a small patch of raised ground 300 yards from where she had last seen him. One leg was jointed where there shouldn't have been a joint and it lay motionless in his trouser leg with the bone sticking through a bloodied tear.

'Shit,' she said, as she leaned over him. He was still breathing. His body was shaking. His face was dirty and wet with sweat and tinted strangely blue. All the signs of shock. Probably internal injuries, she thought.

'Quite a flight,' he mumbled.

'Are you all right?' She cursed herself for the stupid question. Everyone asks that when it's obvious the person questioned is far from all right.

'Are the reinforcements here yet? Plummer called for back-up.' He said it so quietly, she could hardly hear.

'Back-up?' she repeated.

'Six Apaches. AH-64s'

'Attack helicopters!'

'P-P-President's orders. Napalm the whole fucking island if you have to – that's what Plummer said. I'm f-f-fucked here, aren't I?'

Callaway cradled the man's head and he groaned.

'I got outta the 'copter. But then the wind got me. Hit a couple of t-t-trees. I've got busted ribs . . . a gut full of 'em. F-f-fuck . . .' He groaned again. 'I can't stand this.'

Callaway unzipped the man's flying-suit and half his insides seemed to fall to one side. There was extensive bruising, a purple torso. She wrenched her own head back, repelled, and avoiding the truth.

Slowly, she unhooked the pistol from her belt, handed it to him and walked away.

She wished she had a cigarette to smoke while she waited.

The four of them – Patty, Watson, Uli and his father – began their journey. The grey spiralling column of the typhoon was heading towards the west, whilst to the east light smeared like red blood across the sky as the morning sun burned through the residual cloud. The dense forests lay on their sides as if pushed down like rootless dominoes, one toppling another. Their ripped-off limbs had been scattered, so many and so far it was impossible to tell which branch belonged to which fallen trunk. Here and there a few remaining coconut trees leaned over at violent angles, their palms like tattered flags hanging from a mast, holding on forlornly. Below them the ground had turned into deep mud and pools of grey-brown water. New streams ran here and there, black with trawled-up debris and floating wood.

'It looks like a battlefield,' Patty said.

She looked towards the two horizons. In one direction was the sea; in the other, the rising slope of the volcano. But in either direction, the same scale of destruction.

True, as you looked further, there were one or two clumps of trees, miraculously untouched, protected by the random mercy of the turbulent winds. These were oases in a wilderness, so small and far distant they seemed like mirages. 'God, I can't believe it,' she said.

Uli's eyes crumpled shut when he followed her gaze.

His father said, 'My island. Oh, my island.' And he spoke what sounded like a prayer in the Maawian language.

They all stood reverently to listen.

When he was done, they started walking. Uli led, with Watson and Patty behind and the chief at the rear, following head bowed as if he were being dragged unwillingly through the devastated landscape.

As they walked, their feet sank into the wetness of the ground and here and there they had to climb over fallen trees that blocked the path. They had driven along this track two days before, but it was unrecognizable now.

They reached the crest of the volcano and crossed its mouth in little over an hour. Appearing before them were the remains of the track to the chief's and to Logi's villages.

The chief came to the head of their group and looked down. There was no sign of the villages; where they had been was now a dirty sea. The broad fist of hillside that had once separated the two villages had become a long slender finger jutting into the lagoon. The rise in the level brought by the storm had taken water inland by a good half mile.

'I am looking at this from afar and in this strange light,' the chief said. 'I could not stand it otherwise.'

His cheeks were wet and he did not linger more than a few seconds.

Ten miles and four hours later, they started to come upon survivors. Survivors and non-survivors.

Villagers from the two coastal settlements had run inland. They had no shelter from the storm – inadequate as that might have been anyway – and in the island's interior they were showered by the debris ripped up in the wind.

A man lay in the track in front of them. With the wet dirt splashed across him, he seemed at one with the island. He lay between two fallen trees and the arrangement of his bent limbs and their branches made it clear they had been carried away by the same force. The man's arm, curved above his head, pointed the direction the wind had gone, as if he had been leaving a clue for those who might find him and wonder.

Close by, a woman sat on the stump of another tree, broken off a couple of feet from the ground, the trunk held to the base by the moist bark and outer meat of one side which had bent rather than snapping cleanly. She was cradling a baby in her arms, offering it a plump brown breast.

As the others stopped, the chief walked towards her, calling her name and she replied in the island language. He asked her a couple of questions and she answered, gesturing feverishly into the forest of fallen trees behind her.

'What is she saying?' Patty asked.

Uli cocked his head to listen to the woman, translating for them as the woman spoke. 'She says there was a group of them, a dozen adults, some children. They got split up in the storm. She has seen the body of one other man. And two wounded. Somewhere back in the trees.'

The chief nodded when the woman had finished her story. He came back towards the others. 'I must stay here,' he said. 'There are people needing attention. Medical help. I must stay and do what I can.'

'Stay?' Watson repeated as if he didn't understand the concept.

'My people. My island. Besides we are half-way and I am already too old and tired to go on. I am slowing you down. Uli will lead you.' He looked at his son, then back at Watson. 'You two go. It is best.'

'What about me?' Patty cut in. 'You don't think I . . .'

The chief looked at her, then gazed into the forest where the woman had pointed. Patty knew what he was saying, or rather what he was implying, but she found it impossible to grasp or accept. They had come this far, after all. She turned to Watson. 'What about your arm? I . . .' She suddenly knew she was about to say something about love, but at the last moment she realized it had no meaning here. She let out the breath she had prepared without another word upon it.

'It's really for the best.' Uli tried to fill the gap.

Patty smiled a thin smile, still hovering. Uncertain. She might be a trained first-aider, but . . . Well, it wasn't exactly a hypocratic oath. And weren't there bigger issues here?

The chief's gaze had moved out to the horizon. 'Look,' he said, 'do you see what I see?'

Patty followed him. The storm still dominated the horizon in the direction he indicated, but now its colours swirled like a kaleidoscope. 'My God,' she said.

'What?' Watson asked, hearing her alarm.

'It's hooked,' she said.

'What does that mean?'

'It's coming back this way.'

Watson stared in disbelief at the storm, trying to see the features that Patty and the chief were glued to. 'How is that possible?' he said.

'It happens,' she told him, without taking her eyes from the horizon. She grimaced and turned. 'These things move east to west. Eventually they turn back. Not usually quite this sharply, it's true.'

'So you see,' the chief interrupted, 'now it is time that matters. They must go with speed.'

Uli took Watson by the arm, ready to guide him. The chief spoke to his son – island language. He took out the ceremonial knife that was stuck in the waist of his tattered trousers. He unsheathed the blade for a moment, then slid it back home and handed Uli both knife and sheath.

'Will the storm come back over the same path?' Watson asked, turning to Patty. 'I mean, could it miss us?'

She shrugged helplessly. She didn't know. She felt completely out of answers.

The chief said, 'The Earth Goddess has spoken. And now she will speak again.' He looked at Patty as Uli and Watson prepared to leave. 'You like mathematics, I think,' he said. 'They have a better chance without you . . . And that is all.'

Cash Buemann's entourage had picked up five journalists and a TV camera crew on the way to the South Seas. The scandal story spreading on the back of Radleigh's confession to network television had helped. The headlines were already causing earthquakes in Washington offices.

The typhoon delayed the entourage on Waatu for a day. But Waatu was lucky. Its damage was relatively minor. The winds had blown things about somewhat, but that was the sum of the disruption.

Cash tried to hire the boatman from the airport launch, but he wouldn't set to sea in the conditions, even after the storm had passed over the first time.

'Sea too rough,' the boatman said, 'come back tomorrow.'

Undaunted, Cash tried to buy the whole boat.

'Sea like this. It no go,' the boatman said. 'Nature has strength over money.'

XXXVII

It was approaching evening and the wind was already rising fast by the time Uli and Watson reached that finger of land stretching between the former locations of the two villages. No more than a hundred yards wide at its broadest, it looked like a man-made causeway. In a sense, Watson thought, perhaps it was. But it led nowhere.

On either side he could see debris in the water, sloshing in the lagoon, its usual calm blues now ominous and angry. He guessed one or two of the larger objects were bodies, but he couldn't tell. As the columns of black cloud had come closer, the descending sun had disappeared behind them and there was hardly enough light to make an identification.

Uli kept shouting, 'Come on. Come on.' He was leaping over fallen tree trunks, picking a path through those miraculously still standing.

Watson followed, running to keep up, the notebook computer that held their hope – their mission – slapping against his thigh as he manoeuvred.

They came upon the army Jeep, turned on its side. There were no passengers and it was far from any of the island's roads.

'Must have been picked up and dumped in the storm,' Uli said, pausing for a breather.

'How far to go?' Watson asked, dropping to his haunches. He was worrying about his heart and lungs, wondering whether this pace was safe for a chief executive unused to physical exercise. He tried to imagine Monty in the same position. But Monty was dead.

After a very few seconds Uli was ready to go again. Before Watson could protest, his guide was disappearing into the distance. He had to get up and run.

Two hundred yards from the end of this storm-created causeway, they finally reached the old power station. Several clumps of coconut trees had survived in the immediate vicinity, so it wasn't easy to spot until they got very close.

The fire they had witnessed from the volcano's summit had ruined the buildings and the equipment in the surrounding compound, but as ruins, they seemed peculiar, distinguished from the rest of the ruined island by their black charring.

The central building was windowless and skeletal. The compound where the generator and its associated transformers and switchgear had been was now a mass of twisted metal, the spikes of its surrounding safety fence curled back upon themselves as if some mighty god had unpeeled them.

'Where's this cable?' Watson asked, stopping in front of the skeleton, leaning over with his hands on his knees to catch his breath.

'As far as I remember, it must have run almost directly along the line of this hill into the sea.' Uli opened gestured with a flat palm. 'A hillside used to be there,' he said, 'and the cable had to go through the two atolls.' He waved towards the tips of the two atolls, a mile distant – what was left of them, bobbing above the new water-line.

They walked beyond the power station towards the sea. There was the trace of a gully in the wet ground, as if someone had once dug and refilled a trench, but never allowed for the subsidence that comes with settling.

'Is that an illusion?' Watson said.

Uli shrugged. 'It's the best clue we've got.'

Watson watched as the big man got on to his hands and knees in the middle of the small depression in the ground and began to burrow into the soft wet earth with his bare hands and ceremonial knife.

He had met Ulysses Masoni in a restaurant over a business lunch. Attired in a Western suit and Armani tie, he had been one of the most elegant men Watson had ever seen. He remembered Uli's speech – Uli, who was now digging in the earth like an animal.

Watson went and found a broken-off branch and started poking down into the hole Uli was creating. After a minute, a foot or so down, he felt something hard.

'I've found it. It's there,' he said. 'Keep digging.'

Uli's frantic scrabbling uncovered a black plastic pipe, five inches in diameter.

'What's that?' Watson asked, alarmed that they might have dug up the wrong thing, a sewage pipe perhaps.

Uli plunged the ceremonial knife into the pipe. 'Feeder duct,' he said. working quickly with the knife. 'Inside, I hope.'

In a few seconds, he had cut a hole large enough to expose the inside. To begin with, a lot of water ran out, but then they could both see a large red cable.

'That's the power cable,' Uli said. He put two fingers into the hole and worked them around. 'Let's see if I can find the other.'

In a couple of seconds he cried out in triumph. He hacked a bigger hole into the plastic duct so he could get all his fingers inside. After some struggling and painful straining, Watson saw a black cable about a half-inch in diameter hooked out on Uli's thumb. Watson bent down, turned so he could use his good arm and hooked his own fingers under the cable to help. They pulled until a loop of it was clear of the duct.

Uli looked at Watson and smiled. 'Shall I cut it?'

'Sure, let's see what we've got.'

As he said it, Watson felt a sinking dread. In all this wetness, might he yet be standing over a dry well? Suppose this cable was no longer connected. Suppose there was no one in the power station at the other end. Even supposing all that worked in their favour, could he even connect the thing without the usual convenience of plugs and sockets? What standard did they work to here? Pulse dialling? Tone dialling? What?

He wiped his muddy hands against his shorts, but they were already so wet and soiled that the wiping made hardly any difference. He took the notebook computer out of its case, opened it and uncoiled the modem cable from the side pocket. He plugged one end into the appropriate socket on the notebook and reached out to borrow Uli's knife.

With the two cables cut, they examined the ends, counting the wires within each, hoping to find a common colour code.

'All the colours of the rainbow,' Uli said.

'Nearly,' Watson agreed.

'Can you do this?'

'I used to build computers,' Watson said, trying to dredge up the last reserves of self-confidence. He took up the knife and started work, baring the ends of the insulation on the individual wires.

'Here goes nothing. I'm switching this on,' he said at last, hitting the power button.

'Go on, then,' Uli agreed.

'I already have,' Watson said, deflating.

'What do you mean?' Uli asked.

Watson shook his head. 'I mean, the batteries are dead.'

*

237

The people of the island had left their homes, or rather their huts, with what they could carry and nothing more. Patty found herself binding wounds with rags torn from the casualty's own best clothing.

The wind had used the group of islanders like balls in a pinball machine, bouncing them off trees for points. There were any number of broken limbs, cuts, bruises. There were fatalities. Somehow she didn't blanch at these.

She wondered what it was that had decided that she should be here, tending the injured. She wondered why Watson was here at all, why he was running to try to get a computer file off the island, risking his life.

She thought about what she had said to Pfister. 'I believe in humanity.'

She realized it was something to do with values.

XXXVIII

'I'm not going to be beaten.' Watson said it again: 'I'm not going to be beaten.'

'But we can't get the machine on,' Uli protested.

'I don't care. I'm not going to be beaten.' Watson closed his eyes and tried to think.

He opened them a moment later. Something had disturbed him. His companion was gazing out over the lagoon.

'Helicopters,' Uli said in a charged breath. 'Helicopters.'

Six black dots were running in front of the storm; the one out in front was much closer than the others.

Watson shouted, 'I'm not going to be fucking beaten. They didn't die for nothing . . . None of them. Not Buckley. Not Pielot. Not Monty.'

He gathered up the notebook computer in his arms, disconnecting it as he did so. 'Take me back to the Jeep,' he commanded.

They ran back along the promontory to where the army Jeep was lying on its side. Watson put his foot through one headlight glass and began unscrewing the bulb.

'What are you . . .?' Uli tried to ask, but couldn't get the question out. The first of the helicopters roared over their heads.

'Did he see us?'

'I don't think so. He wasn't very steady in the wind,' Uli said, gazing after it. He turned back to Watson, who was now holding the headlight bulb. 'What are we doing?'

'Find the battery on the Jeep,' Watson instructed. 'I'm going to use this as a resistor. I'm going to try to jump some power into the notebook batteries.'

'But that's twelve volts driving straight into ten.'

'That's why I need the resistor.'

'You'll cook them for sure.'

239

'I'm all out of other ideas, Uli. Now find the damn battery in this Jeep while I rig up some more wires.'

Watson removed the batteries from his notebook. He wired them through the headlight bulb with the leads he'd insisted on taking when they had finished in Buckley's cabin. In minutes he was sitting holding two bare wires over the twelve-volt starter battery in the Jeep, the cells from the notebook resting on the top of his leg.

'It would have been simpler if we'd charged this up before we torched the Suzuki,' Watson admitted.

'How're you going to know when it's charged?' Uli asked.

'I'm just going to wait till my leg burns,' Watson said. 'I figure that'll be enough.'

The terminals sparked as he pressed the bare wires on to them. A few seconds later, he brushed the notebook batteries off his thigh and rubbed what was now a particularly sore patch of skin.

'OK, let's run,' he said. 'We can't have long before they spot us.'

Back at the power station, Watson reconnected the computer. This time, when he pressed the power button, he heard the familiar whirring of a hard disk executing a boot routine.

'Hallelujah.'

While he waited for the screen to show, Watson looked up and towards the horizon. In his excitement, the last few minutes had passed quickly and he hadn't noticed what was happening to the weather. He was surprised to find how strong the wind had become. The storm was returning, just like Patty had said. And there were five enlarged dots, buzzing towards him, big enough now to see the bubble of their cockpits. They swayed a little from side to side in the air, caught by the winds of the storm they were trying to race.

'Not far out,' Uli confirmed.

'OK,' Watson said. 'I need you now. I don't speak the language. This has got a voice modem, but you're going to need to get close in all this noise to talk to the man at the other end. Tell him we need a line to the outside world.'

Watson pulled himself back from the computer, moving himself around so he provided a windbreak for his colleague. The strength of the gusts had lifted an order of magnitude and a whistling noise started, a plaintive howling from the ghosts of toppled trees.

Uli leaned down within six inches of the screen and craned to hear any noise from its tiny speaker. 'I hear a dial tone,' he said, 'at least I think that's what it is. Start dialling.'

'OK, but this is a guess. I don't know what number to dial,' Watson told him, operating the keyboard over Uli's shoulder, 'I'll try zero. Tell me if you hear ringing.'

He started hitting keys again. He was still working furiously at the keyboard, when Uli suddenly said, 'Hello,' and started speaking in his own language. It took Watson several seconds to register the voice on the other end.

After a short exchange, Uli scrabbled to his feet, taking up his knife as if he were a workmen gathering his tools at the end of a job.

'He says he can – ' Uli struggled for a word – ' "patch" you to the main exchange.'

A helicopter passed over. Neither of them looked up.

'That's great,' Watson said when its thunder faded. He reached for the notebook and set the modem programme into action.

It ran for several minutes before the machine began to bleep.

Watson moaned. 'We didn't get enough juice in. Just pray, OK?' He tried to will the machine to work faster, as if its speed could be improved by audience participation.

The noise of helicopters got louder and another of them thundered over head. A streak of bullets splattered into the wet ground ten yards to their left.

'Shit!' cried Watson.

'That guy was nearly falling out of the sky,' Uli said. 'Keep working.'

'We're being shot at!'

'Yes, but we're not being hit. Keep at it!'

'We can leave this to run and leg it,' Watson said.

Another line of bullets hit the ground even further away than the first. He looked up to see the helicopter lurching through the air as it tried to hold its low-level pass in some sort of straight line against the wind.

When Watson turned back, he saw Uli staring in horror . . .

But he wasn't staring at helicopters.

'Gentlemen, I think you should move back from the computer.'

Watson followed the stare to its target. He saw all the details of the gun's barrel before he reached the woman.

'Caroline!' Uli said.

'Not quite,' she replied, a cruel little curl to her lips. She was struggling to stand in the wind, but the pistol seemed to have a will of its own, its aim staying straight against all the odds. 'Actually, my name is Margaret Callaway. Would you like to know my rank?'

Watson looked at Uli. He saw the way his eyes passed up and down the woman he had once regarded as his second-in-command, his friend, his confidante. Dirty army fatigues now. A different name. A different hair colour. A gun.

'I don't believe you're going to do this.' Uli said. He had to shout to make himself heard. 'I don't believe you had nothing invested in the SSEO. You believed in it.'

He was edging sideways, putting himself between the gun and Watson. More precisely, perhaps, between the gun and the computer that contained Buckley's work.

'Stand aside,' she said.

Watson glanced at the computer. A few seconds. They needed a few more seconds. A few more seconds of time and a few more seconds of battery.

She fired while Watson was still looking at the notebook. The shot sounded strange against the howl of the wind. For a moment, it seemed that Uli had somehow avoided the bullet, or avoided the effect of it. Perhaps it had been blown off course . . .

But there was a hole in his back where the bullet had exited. A red patch was growing in his mud-stained vest.

He didn't fall. He seemed to melt. Slowly. In super slow motion. Legs first, so his body dropped down to its knees on the very spot he had stood a moment earlier.

The woman took a stride to her right. She brushed her hair back against the blast of wind. Then she took aim at the notebook and emptied half a dozen shots into its body.

Just before its screen died, whether from battery fatigue or lead poisoning, Watson saw its last message: 'File transmit complete.'

She turned the gun barrel towards him and he heard it click. No shot, just an empty click . . .

As he looked up towards her in surprise, he saw the ceremonial knife appear in her chest. It wasn't until she had collapsed that he realized who had thrown it.

Uli fell back face down on the floor as Watson ran to him.

He turned Uli's torso with his good hand. The eyes were rolled sideways. There seemed to be no life at all.

He said, 'Uli, the file went. It went.'

Watson saw the lips quiver, the face take on a faint smile.

'Thank you . . .'

I X L

Watson dragged himself into the burnt-out building just as the world seemed to go into eclipse. A minute earlier, he had been able to pick out the column of the swirling storm, but now it was upon him and everything was black as night.

The rain fell, or rather, it came at him from all angles, propelled on the velocity of wind, so that it felt like looking eyes-open into the head of a high-pressure sprinkler. The roofless skeleton was little shelter against that, though it did keep him from the worst of the wind.

What was it now? A hundred miles an hour? A hundred and fifty? Two hundred?

He heard debris striking the outside of the building. He felt the vortices of air, trying to lift him from where he sat.

But they weren't quite strong enough, and he sat huddled in a corner and clasped his knees with his good arm and closed his eyes and hugged himself.

What kind of a man was Ray Buckley? he wondered. What kind of a man was Ulysses Masoni? Or André Pielot? All of them, he supposed, had seen the peril they were walking into and they had walked into it anyway. Now, he, Watson Thomas, had delivered their message.

The Paradise Hotel, Waatu. Third floor, room 306.

Connor watched the cloud formation through the patio window in amazement. The speed and scale of the storm was awesome and he was guiltily glad it was off in the distance, missing them.

He looked down. The pool boys had removed everything that could move from the perimeter of the hotel's swimming pool, right down to the iron-framed recliners and the five-foot saplings in ornamental pots. Even so there was a bin-full of rubbish blowing about in the wind.

'Come back here,' Alexandra called from the bed, 'the storm will blow out. We can get to Maawi in the morning.'

'What's left of it,' he said turning from the window. Alexandra was propped up on the pillow, arm stretched out towards him, one naked breast resting on top of the other as she lay on her side, making a lopsided cleavage.

He shrugged.

She laughed. 'Mr Floppy not ready to play? I could try and do something about that.' She pouted her lips towards him.

'Being caught in a storm with you is hard work,' he said.

'Are you complaining?'

'No, but I'm counting, and I know what is and isn't possible.'

'Go play with your little computer again. I know you're dying to. God, this must be the third time in the last two hours.' Her face struck an expression of mock disappointment. Then she said, 'You can have ten minutes, no more.'

He went over to where the luggage had been left – two small shoulder bags and the Targus case of a Dell notebook that had been missing from the BBS asset register at the time of the fire. Connor opened the case and placed the Dell on the writing desk. He unplugged the phone and plugged the Dell's modem into the empty socket. This was well-practised now; it took less than a minute.

When the computer booted and dropped into the 'mail find' programme, the first thing he saw was the e-mail from Watson. From the menu, he read the details of the attached file.

The numbers matched. The creation date and file size were the same as he had read on the menu at BBS. This was the 'ENSOeffect' file.

His heart nearly stopped.

X L

The storm blew past in the night and, despite the remaining heave of the sea, Cash's entourage was able to set off at dawn. The boatman put up only a token protest. The offer of ready money was enough.

In the last mile before reaching Maawi, the launch was buzzed several times by helicopters. One swooped low over them. An Apache, one of the journalists with military knowledge had said.

The helicopter looked down on them, as if counting the contents: a Texan oilman, his daughter and her boyfriend, a posse from the media. *What the hell are they doing here*? It hovered uncertainly, then passed on.

The launch was hardly made for these choppy waters and even the weather-ignorant contingent were beginning to realize the scale of chances they were taking.

'Don't worry,' Cash said. It wasn't convincing.

By the time they finally made dry – or rather wettish – land, they had ankle-high water sloshing through the lower decks.

Partly for this reason, their landing site was chosen entirely at random and, once ashore, they had no idea in which direction to go. The boatman shook his head when asked. The reshaped island was confusing. Where were the villages?

They started to walk south and had just found the remains of the Sikorsky washing about on the shoreline when their buzzing helicopter returned. It spiralled down and landed fifty yards from their position. Two armed soldiers emerged from below its slowing rotors.

'Are you guys crazy, coming here?' the leading soldier barked. The wind, still quite strong, forced him to use all the power in his voice to make himself heard. 'This here area is off-limits to civilians.'

Cash stepped to the front of the group. He took off his baseball cap. 'On the orders of who?'

'This is a disaster zone,' the soldier said with slightly less confidence.

'We are guests of Chief Masoni. I believe he still represents the rightful government here.'

'I don't know about that, sir.'

'Well, maybe you'd like to go back into your little craft and get on your little radio, and ask if the government of the United States has suddenly ceased to recognize the legal government of a sovereign state.' Cash gestured back to the helicopter.

The soldier looked at him blankly.

'A state recognized by the United Nations, I should add,' Alexandra said, moving to her father's elbow.

'When you talk to your commanding officer,' Cash added, 'tell him I've got representatives here from the London *Times*, the *Washington Post*, *Das Bilt* and several other major international news agencies who would like to know the score.'

'Are you part of the early relief force?' Connor asked, trying to sound like one of the journalists Cash was describing. 'Do you know how much aid the United States and Europe will be sending?'

More confusion.

'Don't you think you ought to be calling for backup, for Christ's sake,' the journalist from the *Washington Post* added. He turned to a colleague who was carrying a video camera, complete with boom microphone. 'Hey, Charlie, get your crew up here and interview this guy. He's the first one in to bring relief. A goddam hero. What's your name, son?'

Before the soldier could answer, Connor Giles shouted, 'Look!'

They all turned to look in the direction he was pointing.

Watson Thomas was leading a small group of islanders. Patty was clinging to his arm as if holding on to the most important thing in the world. On the other side of Watson was an old but impressive nut-brown man in the traditional clothing of the Maawian people: the chief.

'It's good to see you.' Watson said. 'What took you so long?'

Cash stepped to the front of the new arrivals. He stared at this apparition before him, and his lopsided mouth fell open.

'Watson Thomas, I presume,' he said. 'It is you under that mud, isn't it?'

Watson's eyes darted to Connor.

'I got the message,' Connor said quickly. 'I plugged it in with the other files. We have ourselves a complete model.'

'And?'

'And now every kid who downloads from the website of *Adventure Updater* gets a free copy of Ray Buckley's work.'

Watson laughed. He didn't know where that desire came from, but it was unavoidable. 'A little unconventional in terms of spreading news.' he said.

'Oh, I sent it to the TV stations and news agencies as well, but I figured you can't trust them,' Connor said. He turned to his fellow travellers. 'No offence, guys, but too many people have already been silenced.'

Cash looked at Watson. 'I brought this little party over,' he said, gesturing towards the group of media reporters. 'I'm trying to be a new man. I hope it ain't too late.'

Chief Masoni di Masoni raised his hand to his head and pulled off his ceremonial head-dress.

'I welcome you,' he said, extending his arm to indicate the entire party was included in the greeting. 'You will come and take the *kava*?'

'*Kava*?' Cash repeated. He turned his scarred head and scanned the far away sky. 'Shouldn't there be a rainbow or something? You know, God's covenant?'

'That comes only when we are safe from the rains for good,' the chief told him. He looked out over the ruined land. 'Safe,' he said, as if the word had long since lost its meaning.

EPILOGUE

E-mail to: PPP

From: Weather Station Antarctica

Hey, Prof, we haven't heard from you in I don't know how long. Are you all right up there?

I know we've been quiet ourselves. The old 'spirit child' had us worried for a while. It was almost like this time it wasn't going to let go its grip.

But hey, we can see now the conditions are on the turn, so all is well with the world. It'll be interesting to see when we get the results what this one's done to the carbon dioxide levels. Ozzie Jack says he thinks it had an effect on the ozone layer too. I told him that was a load of horse-shit.

Are you planning on going to the Tokyo thing again? I am. It's the only chance I get to let my hair down (what's left of it these days). We could pick up a few geishas, visit your favourite karaoke bar. I love that fish that you eat raw, fresh and clean out of the ocean.

Yours, Weatherjunkie.

P.S. I just heard we got ourselves a new President back home. What gives? Why are all the news bulletins being so coy about the reasons the old one resigned? Still, I guess the truth will come out in the end. It damned near always does.